Always
True To
Heart!! :)
~Marisa Gol—

# THE REAL TRUTH

## ABOUT *Love*

. . . . . . . . . . . . . . . . . .

## MARISA GOLDSTEIN

**BALBOA**
PRESS
A DIVISION OF HAY HOUSE

Balboa Press books may be ordered through booksellers or by contacting:

Balboa Press
A Division of Hay House
1663 Liberty Drive
Bloomington, IN 47403
www.balboapress.com
1-(877) 407-4847

Because of the dynamic nature of the Internet, any web addresses or links contained in this book may have changed since publication and may no longer be valid. The views expressed in this work are solely those of the author and do not necessarily reflect the views of the publisher, and the publisher hereby disclaims any responsibility for them.

The author of this book does not dispense medical advice or prescribe the use of any technique as a form of treatment for physical, emotional, or medical problems without the advice of a physician, either directly or indirectly. The intent of the author is only to offer information of a general nature to help you in your quest for emotional and spiritual well-being. In the event you use any of the information in this book for yourself, which is your constitutional right, the author and the publisher assume no responsibility for your actions.

Any people depicted in stock imagery provided by Thinkstock are models, and such images are being used for illustrative purposes only. Certain stock imagery © Thinkstock.

Printed in the United States of America

ISBN: 978-1-4525-7033-4 (sc)
ISBN: 978-1-4525-7035-8 (hc)
ISBN: 978-1-4525-7034-1 (e)

Library of Congress Control Number: 2013904414

Balboa Press rev. date: 02/17/14

*This book is dedicated to the memory of my unconditionally loving grandma, Ruth.*

# Introduction

HELLO, MY NAME IS WILLOW Mazer. You know me. Well, not personally, but part of me believes that as you read this story, you will realize just how much I remind you of yourself, your sister, your best friend, or perhaps the random stranger you just met on the airplane or at the coffee shop. My story started off this way: Here I was, your average thirty- year- old, on my way to visit my grandparents in Florida, minding my business, and looking to escape a little for a few reasons. One, I had just come out of another disappointing relationship that didn't quite go my way and I needed a distraction. Two, my beautiful and unconditionally loving grandmother was dying of Alzheimer's, and I wanted to spend some time with her. I thought if I decided to make this trip, perhaps I could be reminded once again how love really works. And three, well, let's just say I was sort of in a transition period, not quite sure what I wanted to do for the rest of my life, but that was all about to change. Telling you about the number of people I met during my journey who were influential would be an understatement. Let's see, first there was the handsome stranger I met en route,: second, the wonderful published poet who became sort of a mentor,: then there was the loving janitor at my grandmother's nursing home,: and so many others who helped to remind me of the real truth about love. I also learned a very important word during this story that changed my whole life and perspective on *God*. Yeah, I said, God, but don't go running away thinking this is one of those preachy stories about a girl who found God by making all of these drastic changes. No, no, I learned the truth about God and love through one simple word *Agape*, which in Greek means "unconditional love". Of course there were amazing signs and feelings of divine comfort that let me know I was never alone, and that the universe was guiding me all along. You'll like this story, because there is a place in your heart that will soften and remember what your life is really all about.

# Chapter 1

I WAITED ANXIOUSLY TO GET on the plane, tapping my red-polished toes on the ground. I always hated waiting to get on a plane, and even more so now since terror threats were heightened to new levels. I was on my way to see my grandparents. I felt it was time to reconnect and hope for the best. For the last few years my grandma had been suffering with Alzheimer's, but I didn't dare use that word around my grandpa, he liked to refer to it as advanced dementia. Anyway, I was on my way. My grandma, to this day, had always been the most loving, God-given human spirit to touch my life and that of many others with the unconditional love we all dream about and want to believe in. My grandpa, along with my father, has also been one of the most loving men I have ever known, but a depressed soul. He always told me if it were not for my grandma bringing meaning to his life, he would have been forever lost and lonely. Well, now, ever since she had deteriorated mentally, so had his happiness.

I looked to my left and noticed a handsome, maybe late twentyish male, with strong arms and tough hands. He reminded me a little of my ex-boyfriend from college, but with lighter features. He was checking me out, or so I wanted to think. I was a little undone today, in sweatpants and barely any makeup, but didn't really care. Who was I looking to impress anyway, the old men at the nursing home? Oops! I also forgot to mention, no one could ever use the words "nursing home" in front of Grandpa - he preferred to use the word "facility."

I heard the flight attendant call, "Zones one to six may now board." Finally, I could get on. Well, what do you know - Handsome Stranger was sitting a row in front of me to the left. I hate, and I repeat, I *hate* to ever check bags on a flight, so I always overstuff my handy wheelie carry-on to the max, which usually weighs more than I do. I knew that I was going to struggle to lift my bag, and

1

thought to myself, *okay, if Handsome Stranger offers to help lift my bag above my seat, maybe there is potential here.* I proceeded to pop open the overhead, and before I even attempted to lift, he generously, and with an adorable smile said, "Would you like some help?" I smiled and said, "Thank you so much. I appreciate it." I sat down in my aisle seat - of course, the aisle, just in case I had to go to the bathroom a few dozen times, which I always seem to do, and I don't want to have to bother the other people in my row during flight time. Cute guy subtly turned around to check on me. Again, I smiled and offered him a piece of gum for the flight, and he said, "No thanks," but smiled anyway. I took a deep breath and contemplated what to read. I had two choices: one was a book about happiness and the other was my latest guilty pleasure magazine full of Miley Cyrus's love life and Charlie Sheen's bad behaviors. I had to admit, I was a little bit embarrassed to read either in front of Handsome Stranger. Maybe not the happiness book, because no one really needed to know I was forever on a journey in search of the true meaning of it! If cute guy saw it, he might have thought I was a depressed, needy chick, which I am *not*! Anyway, I didn't want to show my gossip magazine either, because I hated to admit that I *love* to indulge in the juice of celebrity lives. As much as I like to make a joke of what's going on in their worlds, I secretly wish I could have as much fun as it looks like they're always having, whether it's dancing on top of a bar or going shopping with their designer handbags and shoes (which cost more than my monthly rent). Dammit, why hadn't I just bought a copy of *USA Today* or *Newsweek*? So, which one? Okay, happiness book it was, but quickly. I opened it so no one could actually see the title. We took off after a few minutes, and again I took a deep breath. I was tired. Lately, I had not been sleeping well, and my emotional levels were depleted as I was still mourning my last love. We'll get into that later; I'm too exhausted to share my thoughts on him right now.

The flight was actually quicker than I expected it would be, and we were landing before I knew it. Handsome Stranger offered to take my bag down, and I said, "Thank you," and let him. He walked ahead of me, and I got a little nervous wondering if he would be waiting to have an official conversation with me at the end of the ramp. I walked off the plane with my ridiculously heavy wheelie, and he was, in fact, standing there. Shit, what did he want? I mean, yes, I was flattered, but I wasn't in the mood to converse and didn't feel much like flirting. I told myself to chill out and just smile and be myself. Yes, even now at thirty, I still have to tell myself that sometimes. *Okay, here we go.* He smiled and said, "Is this home?"

I replied, "No, I'm here to see my grandparents, and you?"

"No, not home. My grandma is having an eightieth birthday party, so I came to do the family thing." *How sweet,* I thought, *he flew all the way to see his grandma.* He was getting a few extra points.

We slowly strolled down toward the baggage claim area, making small talk, and in the back of my mind I was wondering, between my airplane hair and now my airplane breath, college sweats, etc. *Is this guy still thinking I'm cute?* Also, is he going to ask me for my digits? I wasn't sure I wanted to give them up as I had just come out of a long- term relationship.

I noticed that he stood at a nice height, and within our chatting I could also tell that there was definitely something comforting about him. I liked the simplicity of his look. He had genuine eyes, again, strong hands, and I liked the way he was dressed in what looked like his favorite jeans, a comfy T- shirt, and work boots. Hmmm, I wondered what this guy did for a living. He was carrying a FedEx carry-on bag. Did he work for them? I asked, "So, do you work for FedEx?" "Yeah, part –time. I am the guy who helps load and unload the packages on and off the planes at the airport."

I said, "That's pretty cool."

He smiled, "I love being by airplanes. What can I say? It's the little kid in me."

I liked his answer. I giggled and changed the subject. Then I asked where his grandma lives. "Oh, she lives in Running Hunter, in Boynton."

Oh, my God! I smiled and said, "Wow what a coincidence, my great aunt also lives there."

He naturally said, "Small world." In my mind, I was thinking, *oh* is this a sign?

I forgot to mention that every night before bed, I get down on one knee, like every other little star gazed girl, and pray to God for whatever I feel I need. Would you believe me if I told you that last night when I got down to pray, I said, "God, please let me get to Florida safely tomorrow, and if there is anyone important you think I should meet on the airplane, I am all ears, eyes, nose, and whatever else you want me to use, just know I am paying attention."

The truth is, even though I have caught myself at times saying, "Oh, what a coincidence!" I have actually believed in just the opposite. There is no such thing. And, the people you meet at random times, either on an airplane, at Starbuck's, walking through a park, and ladies, even sometimes at a bar, you are meant to meet. These people can bring something to your table, you just have to know when to listen and pay attention to what is being shared. They are not just potential lovers, they could be somebody in a career you are thinking about, or also going through a similar situation in their life that you can commiserate with, you get my point! So guess what? I am for sure now, paying attention.

We finally arrived at the baggage claim area. Now came the awkward part. I obviously didn't need to wait for my bag, but he did. I was wondering, is stranger going to pull out a cheesy one-liner that I am sure I have heard before? I didn't even wait one more second for it to feel weird, so I threw out my hand, and said, "Thank you so much for helping me with my bag, I realize I didn't catch your name."

He smiled, shook my hand back, and said, "Will, and you?"

"Willow."

"Neat name," he said, but we obviously both giggled for the root of his name is mixed in mine. So now I was really thinking, *hm-m-m*, another sign? Will and Willow - how cute! Or, some may think ew-w-w how annoying would it be if you were married? Family members, calling out either one of your names, and you both have to yell, "Yeah?" "Oh sorry, honey, not you, I was looking for your husband, or your wife."

Some of you might be wondering how I got my name. According to my father, while my mom was still pregnant with me, the two of them went away on a weekend trip to the Berkshires. He told me the story that on a beautiful sunny day in the mountains, while my mom needed to take a nap, he decided to take a walk to the nearby lake. He said when he arrived there, it was like the lake was meant just for him, and there was not a soul around, which he thought was strange, it being a weekend. He saw this single deep brown wooden chair sitting right below a beautiful swinging willow tree. He decided to take a seat and try to meditate in nature for a little while. He told me at that point he and my mom had come up with a few names they loved, but nothing stuck with them just yet. However, he knew that whatever name they were going to choose, it had to be something closely related to nature. He said he closed his eyes and felt one of the branches from this willow tree "gently tickle his cheek" when the wind blew. It was right then and there at that moment that he thought, "Willow! That's it! So every time I look at my little girl, I will be reminded of the sweetness I feel in nature." He also loved the symbolism reflected in the flexibility and freedom of the trees every time they moved. He came back from his walk, woke up Mom from her nap, and they agreed. Willow it would be.

Back to the present. I looked at Will and said, "Okay, so again, it was nice to meet you, who knows you might just be on my plane ride home. Anyway, have a nice time with your family."

He looked disappointed, and said, "That's it? How about you take a risk and have a drink with me sometime?"

Instead of saying, "Sounds great, I will give you my digits," no, no, my immediate response was, "You're so sweet and I am flattered, but I just came out of a four year relationship - not a good time." Can you blame me? I hadn't been on a date in four years.

He said, "Relax, I'm not asking to meet your grandparents, it's just a drink, not a walk down the aisle."

I realized he was right, of course, and then responded, "You're right, I'm sorry, but I'm telling you now, I'm a spontaneous girl, if I call you, you're either in or you're out".

He said, "Like I said, it's just a drink."

I decided to put his phone number in my cell phone and not give him my number. This was just in case I changed my mind and decided to never call him. He looked somewhat disappointed that I didn't reciprocate with mine, but you never know these days. I had been borderline stalked before, and would not take that chance. I gave him one last smile and my special "Willow Wink" just to keep his attention.

As I pivoted, I could see through the reflection of the glass that he was checking out my butt. Uchch, I just remembered I had not been to the gym in over a month. But I then realized that if this guy was looking for a date with me dressed the way I was, bed head and all, he could probably care less about the few extra pounds on my tooshie. I took a deep breath, smiled and reminded myself that your thirties aren't about having the tightest ass or the perkiest boobs. Although I am proud to say, they are still pretty firm. However, they are about being more accepting of who you are at your core. At least that's what all my self-help teachers are preaching these days. I am slowly starting to believe it. Okay, on my way to Gram and Gramp's.

# Chapter 2

THE TAXI DROPPED ME OFF at the facility around noon. As I walked through the front entrance, I had a lump in my throat and a churning in my belly knowing the depressing hallways I was about to walk through. As I tried to hold my breath from the smell of urine and bad cafeteria peas and carrots, I walked extra fast to get to my grandma's room. When I got to the door, I noticed that it was closed. I gently opened it and saw my grandpa's tired eyes look up at me from his *New York Times,* and my grandma sleeping with her mouth open. Grandpa gave me the "s-h-h-h" with his index finger. We decided to step outside to not disturb her. I hugged him hello.

"Hi, Gramps, how are you?"

He smiled a pushed smile, but said, "Okay, how was your trip down?"

"Okay, I met a handsome stranger on the plane."

"Oh-h-h," he gave me a half smile.

"Nice guy, but you know me, I'm not even remotely ready to think about going on a date, because I still feel like I'm mourning Tom."

"Okay, Willow, I won't push the subject, but hasn't it been at least three months since you have broken up? All I am saying is, don't wait too long, for I would hate my granddaughter to miss an opportunity with a 'who knows' stranger on an airplane." He gave me a wink. I must have gotten that wink from him.

"Okay, Grandpa, I will let you know. How is Grandma doing?"

"Not good, my love, and this place is not good - lousy all around, food, most of the staff, and comfort." I was pretty sure my grandfather was still having reservations about putting my grandma here, but it was too hard for him to take care of her all by himself. Between trying to feed her, lift her, and bath her, it became too much to bear.

Either way, I have to say, I was blown away by the loyalty exemplified by my grandpa all that time. He epitomized what every woman hopes her husband will turn out to be - through sickness and health, thick and thin, you name it! Sometimes, I found myself contemplating which was the harder pill to swallow, my grandma not being able to do a thing by herself, or really recognize me? Or could it possibly be watching the lonely pain my grandfather was in, from losing his one true love? Either way, it was depressing and I needed to get some air.

I coerced my grandpa to come outside with me. He told the nurse that he'd be running out for a few minutes, and kissed my grandma's head and said to her, "I will be right back, Lu." Lu is short for "Luciana." My grandma was what we like to call a pizza bagel. She is half Italian and half Jewish, a delicious mixture. My grandpa's name is Lex. I always thought it was kind of cute that their names sounded cool as a couple, Lu and Lex. It rolled naturally off your tongue whenever you said it.

Grandpa Lex and I took a walk around the courtyard, which was smaller than my living room. As soon as we started walking I noticed a beautiful butterfly circling around my head. I finally felt my anxiety level begin to lower.

I stopped and looked at my grandpa and said, "Grandpa, I know this has been really hard, but as a family we will get through this, I promise. I'm here right now for a few days, so whatever I can do to help, please let me know."

"Thanks, my love, what you can do is, actually, please go to Wal-Mart or Target, and get Grandma some new nightgowns, but make sure you get the ones that snap in the front - the *front*, not the back, the front." One more time Grandpa, cause I didn't hear you the third time. Always, always, he repeats a request, for he never fully trusts that I will get the right thing.

I smiled at him and said, "Okay, Gramp, I got it, the nightgowns that snap in the back," and gave him my Willow Wink, to lighten up the mood.

He smiled back and said, "Okay, Grandma shouldn't be without me by her side for too long; let's go back in."

After about an hour of just sitting and catching up, I told him I was going to run out to the store and get Grandma her nightgowns and some stuff for myself for the weekend. I could only imagine that my grandpa hadn't gone food shopping in God knew how long. I guarantee his fridge was empty, with the exception of one prune juice, one container of skim milk, rubbery fat-free cheese, and possibly one old mustard jar. I was also thinking his cabinets only have stale pretzels and cans of soup older than I. Did I mention how skinny he looked? I decided to go to the store and pick up something to make him for dinner that night. He needed some home cooking. He was spoiled their entire marriage. My grandma's Italian roots performed very well at dinner each night. However, over the last five years, she could no longer cook. I always told myself Grandpa may not have been able to cook much, but nobody on this planet could have loved anyone as much as he loved my grandma. Cooking skills were understandably excused, and even when he tried to cook, or I should say *toast* something, he always put his love into it. I remember when I was a little girl visiting them, he would toast my bagel, add just the right amount of butter and cut it into fours – 'ya know, cute little sections for my little fingers to be able to grasp. How could you not love this man?

On the way to the store, I remembered that my aunt Ellen, who lives at Running Hunter, is the biggest yenta there. *Yenta* is a Jewish expression for a gossiper. The good news was that I did not give "Stranger from Airplane" my aunt's name, which meant he couldn't ask his grandma if she knew her. However, the bad news was that I also did not get his grandma's name, and if I wanted to get the 411 dish on Will's family, I was going to have to ask my aunt if she knew anybody having an eightieth birthday party at her club. This was asking for trouble, digging into my life, which she always managed to do. I was supposed to have dinner with her one night while I was here, but I was thinking instead of going there I would invite her over for dinner at my grandpa's so I could avoid accidentally running into Will. I decided to call her on the way, to see if she wanted to come tonight.

"Hi, El, it's Willow, your favorite niece. I'm here now in Florida and I'm cooking a homemade dinner for Grandpa tonight, do you want to come over?"

"Hi Doll, I would love to, but I am meeting the ladies for a late bridge game, can we do it tomorrow?"

"Sure, can you come over at about 7:00pm? Grandpa doesn't like to leave Grandma until she is put to bed, so this would give us about a half an hour to catch up alone before he gets home."

"Sounds great Doll, see 'ya then." I realized when I hung up, that I probably should have run this by my grandpa first, because he and my aunt have not always gotten along well. This is my grandma's younger sister. She's the complete opposite of my grandpa. She is a social butterfly involved with her bridge, golf, shuffleboard, men, vodka and tonics, lots of vodka and tonics, gossiping. Or, as my grandpa likes to say, "Willow, you know how I feel about her putting too much of her own two cents into how she thinks Grandma should be handled. She opens up that big obnoxious and critical mouth of hers. I will not tolerate it at this point in your grandma's life." I would figure out a way to gently tell him that she'd be joining us tomorrow. There is nothing that some homemade baked ziti with garlic bread and Caesar salad can't cushion. Mmm, I was already getting hungry.

After dinner, Grandpa looked at me with a big grin and said, "Willow, my dear, I have not had such good homemade cooking made with love, since your grandma cooked me her last meal. I have forgotten just how great real food can be. So, thank you darling, I am stuffed, and now I have to excuse myself to go to the bathroom." I still didn't bring up Aunt El coming over tomorrow, so as he walked toward the bathroom holding his belly, I yelled, "You're welcome, Grandpa, and by the way, I invited Aunt El over tomorrow night for some more good eats."

He turned around and looked at me and said, "Willow, at least let me relieve myself first please, which now may take a little longer than I thought, and then we can talk about this."

I didn't answer and started cleaning up the dishes - my least favorite part.

After about ten minutes, Grandpa returned, and as full as I was, I put out some cannolis for desert and poured him his evening coffee, with milk, never any sugar. He looked at me and as always with the question, "Willow, honey, you did not put any sugar in Grandpa's coffee, right?"

"Oh no, Grandpa, I put extra sugar in this time, just the way you like it!" I followed with my Willow Wink.

Grandpa looked at me and asked, "So what time is this thorn in my ass coming over tomorrow?"

"She is going to come a little early so she and I can catch up while you are still with Grandma. It's not a big deal. I'll make something easy. I promise we will not talk about Grandma. I will keep the conversation light over dinner. We'll talk about the men she is dating, the cards she is playing, and the Running Hunter gossip, okay Gramps?"

"Okay, Willow, but you know I don't have the energy anymore to be criticized about how I take care of your grandmother. Nobody loves and cares for your grandma like I do." He always said that part extra loud, as if I didn't already know.

"I know," I replied, "and you're right, nobody takes care of Grandma like you do. Alright Gramp, I'm tired from the flight today, I am going to get into bed. See 'ya in the morning."

As I was walking toward the guest room, he hollered, "Goodnight, love, and sweet dreams about a stranger on an airplane."

I yelled back, "Very cute, Gramp, goodnight."

I slept surprisingly well that night for the first time in a few weeks. I woke up early and decided to take a walk around my grandpa's complex. I thought about taking my iPod but then decided, eh, I would rather just be with silence in nature this morning. As soon as I walked outside, I saw the most luscious red cardinal I have ever seen in my life. He was just sitting on this little broken branch outside Grandpa's condo. He looked at me, tilted his gentle head, and flew off. *Strange*, I thought, you usually don't see many cardinals in Florida. Call me bizarre, but I felt some sort of connection when our eyes met. *Hm-m-m.* When I am in nature my senses definitely open up.

I took a deep breath, smiled, and started my fast walking around his complex. As I moved and shook off old residue, I had to admit, my ex-boyfriend crept into my head. I know I said I would save it for later, but now might be a good time to start. I met Tom a little over four years ago at a bar (of all places). I know what they say about meeting anyone substantial around dirty dive bars. However, when I met him, I felt a very strong connection right out of the gate.

At some point, through the wisecracks, sarcastic cat and mouse chase, Miller Lites and cigarettes, I found myself standing one on one right in front of him, and as loud as that bar was, I could only see and hear *him*. He had a certain comfortable openness that allowed me to speak of things I wasn't able to talk about before without fear of judgment.

Whoosh-h-h. Fast forward! Before I get carried away with this romantic introduction to an evening, the bottom line is, in the end, all the things I thought would be reciprocated in the partnership, just kinda stopped. I mean I get it couples inevitably grow apart. But if you must know the real truth, I think Tom and I ended because he did not believe in unconditional love – the kind that I have always yearned for. This isn't because I'm a hopeless and unrealistic romantic either. At least I don't think so. It's okay, though, I am starting to realize that moving forward, whoever the next man may be, whether it's Stranger from an airplane, or the next "who knows guy", he will hopefully love me for me, and believe without a doubt in unconditional love. The good news is my relationship with Tom did not end on a bitter note, just a disappointing one.

As I came back from my walk, I picked up my grandpa's *New York Times* from the driveway and started thinking about my grandma and the reality that she really was getting worse. Part of me was aching, but another part of me was beginning to make peace because I knew that her time was around the corner, and I thought that she was okay with it.

I walked into the house and made some coffee for Grandpa so it would be ready when he arose, then I decided to go over and see Grandma a little early. That way we could have some alone time. I showered up, and left Grandpa a note that I would meet him over there whenever he woke up. I took the extra car (it had been collecting dust in the driveway for over a year), and pulled up to the facility with a little numbness, and a little sadness. Deep breaths, Willow, deep breaths.

When I got into her room, she was already sitting in her chair, dressed and watching cartoons. Part of me felt offended for her. I knew she could no longer speak, but come on, *cartoons?* Please show my grandma a little more respect, nurse! I went over to kiss her forehead and smile at her, then she looked up at me, and even though she couldn't say anything, I felt like she somehow knew it was really me.

I took her hand, and said, "Good morning, Gram, it's me Willow. You look so pretty this morning! Come on, Grandma, we gotta get you some fresh air before the smell of this place takes over."

I unlocked the wheel chair, and brought her outside to the mini courtyard.

I decided to sit in the shade on a bench, and pulled her up next to me. "Okay, Gram, let's just sit and breathe this air in. We can watch the birds, butterflies, and whatever else wants to hang out with us this morning. I will tell you about my life, and you don't have to say anything, just listen to your granddaughter. That's all I need, Gram."

This was what we always did growing up. She would patiently hear me talk about what was happening in my dramas, from breakups with boyfriends to career changes, always insistent that he, or this job, was the one. As I sat with her I was having flashbacks of late nights hanging out with her in her mumu and slippers in her kitchen. I would always seem to be bawling my eyes into a big bowl of leftover spaghetti followed by chocolate gelato. Yep, Grandma sure loved to feed me when I was sad. It was sort of her way of soothing me. I loved her for that, except it had become a bad habit throughout my life into many late nights, when it was just me and my leftover pizza followed by a row of Oreos.

If she could speak now she would say, "Willow, please my love, don't take everything so seriously - enjoy it for what it is. So intense, my Willow, so intense. Lighten up my love and eat some more spaghetti."

So I decided to tell her about my mourning Tom and the ending of that relationship. I then followed with the Stranger from the Airplane story. For the first time that day, I saw her smile. Wow, I was wondering, could she possibly understand, a little bit of what I'm saying? Or could she just be reacting to my smile, as I was telling this story? Either way, I was happy to see what I felt could be a slight connection. I'll take it. Then, once again saw the most radiant red cardinal land on the tree next to us. "*Look*, Gram, how beautiful, and see - he even matches my red toe nails!" This time, I did see her smile. She always loved it when I showed her my manis and pedis. I was goose bumpy, but sad because Grandpa missed this moment. I made a mental note to be sure to tell him what she saw and how she smiled. He has a hard time believing how much she was really understanding these days, what she was picking up. However, I then remembered how much my grandma had always loved birds, especially red cardinals. She even had a little collection of them on her dresser. *Hm-m-m.*

After a while, I took Grandma inside and wanted to play her some music. Aside from Grandpa, my grandma had always loved music more than anything. She used to tell me that whenever she and my grandpa would argue, she would always put some music on. It would make them laugh and they would end up dancing right then and there, and soon make up. Anyway, I ran down to the activities room to ask the nurse's aide if I could borrow her CD player.

I had bought Grandma some of her favorite CDs before I came, which included Barbara Streisand, Neil Diamond, and Celine Dion. I also bought her a single, one of her favorite songs of all time, "Earth Angel" by the Penguins. I think I get my passion for music from her. I always believed music had a unique power to capture moments in our minds and hearts that could not always be explained. It's just something you feel inside. I wanted to give Grandma a moment to reminisce about a time when music felt loving just for her. I had started on this whole alternative therapeutic kick, so let's see what happens.

*Hm-m-m,* what to play, what to play? I decided to put "The Way We Were" on, by Streisand. That was Grandma's favorite movie of all time. She always thought the chemistry between Robert Redford and Babs was fantastic. I had to agree. As I started to play the music, she looked at me and I smiled, "Gram, listen, it's one of your favorites, remember how handsome the character of Hubbell was?" She did smile and actually pointed her finger at me and moved it back and forth like it was her way of dancing. Again, I was thinking - where is Grandpa?

After about a half of an hour of shuffling around music, I said, "Okay Grandma, I am now going to play your favorite song, I have saved the best for last." I popped in "Earth Angel," and just as I hit play, who should walk in but Grandpa. No coincidence, this was the song he dedicated to her for their whole life. He stopped and looked at me with wide eyes and said, "Willow, where did you get this?"

"Hey, Grandpa, I bought them for Grandma, I know how much she loves music, so I pulled together a few of her favorites and wanted to play them for her. They say music can be miraculous and Grandpa, I think it is. She has smiled at me a few times, and she occasionally sways her index finger to the music. This must mean she is retaining something."

He looked surprised, "Really?"

"Really, Gramp, watch this." I turned up the song a little, and I looked at Grandma and said, "Gram, look who is here, it's your boyfriend and he has come to sing you your song." I looked at him and gave him the Willow Wink, and gave him a look to start singing along with the music.

He began, and before you knew it, from her wheelchair, she reached out her hand to my grandpa. She didn't say anything, but it didn't matter, this was her way. I looked at him and nodded my head with a smile. He started to fill up, but kept singing the song, right until the end. When the song came to a close, he leaned down, kissed Gram on her forehead and said, "Oh, Luc, I am the luckiest man on the planet to have found my earth angel in you." He looked at me and winked back and mouthed, "Thank you." I smiled.

I decided by late afternoon that I needed some time for myself and told Grandpa I was going to go home, take a swim, and get dinner prepped for Aunt Ellen. I kissed Grandma goodbye, and reassured Grandpa as I was walking out that I promised to only pour

Aunt El's first drink very lightly, so she didn't get diarrhea of the mouth during dinner. He looked up at me and said, "Yes, Willow, and please do not let her get too drunk."

"Gramp, I promise, I have it under control."

The doorbell rang at exactly seven o'clock. I opened the door, "Hello darlin, how's my niece?" She leaned forward and kissed my cheek. After all of these years, no matter how much I tried to not get her hot pink lipstick on my cheek, it always happened. I was also still trying to figure out how to get rid of the smell of her toxic floral perfume that stuck to my clothing. Uch-chc-h-h-h-h.

"I'm doing just fine El, how are you?"

"I am fabulous doll. I met a fantastic gentleman about 6 weeks ago, and look what he got me already?" She pointed to a hunky, chunky, gaudy looking necklace that only women of her bridge group could appreciate.

I smiled politely and said, "Oh-h-h how nice and sparkly!"

"Mmm-hmm, honey, and let me tell you, his taste in fine dining is even better. He took me out for a lovely steak dinner followed by dancing. I think this guy could really be the one, Willow."

Not that I have room to talk, but how many times have I heard this one before? Believe it or not, my Aunt Ellen has never been married, only been engaged three times. Every time she was about to walk down the aisle, she always seemed to chicken out, protesting they were not good enough for her anyway.

The last one was my favorite - his name was Morris. They lived together for eighteen years, so I guess you could say they were pretty much married. He passed away five years ago and left her a substantial amount of money, which she was living on. "El, it's been only a few weeks."

"I know, doll, but there is something about this one. I am telling 'ya, his name is Harold by the way." I saw her starting to open the cabinet, looking to make herself a vodka and tonic. I prepared for this, so she wouldn't make it too strong. "Hey, El, look I already made one for you."

"A girl after my own heart, thanks." She waved me to sit next to her. "So tell me Willow, what is cooking in your male department?" Here we go.

"Well, you know Tom and I broke up a few months ago. I am still grieving him. However, interestingly enough, would you believe me if I told you that I met a handsome stranger on my flight down here, whose grandma lives in your complex?"

She opened up her eyes wide and said, "Get out of here! Tell me, tell me who his grandma is! You know I know everybody important at Running Hunter."

"Well El, that's the thing, I didn't get her name, so I don't know. The only thing I am sure of is that she is having an eightieth birthday party this weekend, which he came to celebrate with her. But, Aunt El, I am begging you, please DO NOT get carried away in trying to figure this one out. If you are going to get sneaky, which I know you're going to do anyway, will you at least try to be discreet about it?"

She waved her hand in my face, "Willow, leave it up to your auntie to get the scoop, and you have my word on not being too snoopy about it." *Yeah right*, I thought, she's going to do what she does best.

"I'm serious, El, do not do anything that could embarrass me."

She took another sip of her drink, lifted her brow and said, "Willow, my dear, I promise. So tell me how do you think your grandpa is doing with all of what is happening to Grandma, and I mean *really* doing?" OY, although part of me was thinking she might actually really be genuine in asking. Just in case, I decided to pour myself a glass of some heavy red wine.

"Um-m-m, I think he is really struggling, but I think that even though I know you two don't see eye to eye on everything concerning her, he is doing the best he can to take care of her."

She leaned back on the coach, "Willow, I know your grandpa loves your grandma more than life itself. I am just frustrated because he is so controlling in what he thinks is best for her. I mean doesn't her sister get any say in this at all?"

"Aunt El," I pleaded, "Let's not get too deep into this tonight. Grandpa will be home in the next few minutes, and I want us to try to enjoy dinner. I know you are frustrated, just know that she is in good hands."

She lifted her drink up and tapped it to my wine glass and said, "Okay, doll, I will let it go for Grandma Lu's sake tonight."

I was relieved. However, I was hoping that once Grandpa walked in, the vodka hadn't taken precedence over her big mouth. I heard the garage door opening.

Grandpa walked in the through the kitchen, hung up his hat, smiled at me, barely looked at Aunt El, and said, "Hello, ladies, let me freshen up, okay?"

As he walked by, Aunt Ellen looked at him and sarcastically said, "What, no kiss for your favorite sister in law?" I shot her a look with big eyes. As he walked to the bathroom, he pretended not to hear her. "Oh, so now, he is going deaf too?"

"Aunt Ellen, please let's have a half decent meal, and cut the man some slack will 'ya? He is exhausted and my grandma probably didn't each much. He always gets frustrated when she doesn't eat much. Now come help me lay out dinner."

Dinner was a bit awkward - full of weird silent moments and a lot of face making. It is funny to think that no matter what age you are, you can still take on childish behavior, a roll of the eyes here, and middle finger gesture there, you catch my drift.

After dessert, Aunt El told me that she had a late night hot date with her new man Harold, so she would get going. As she put on her coat, Grandpa couldn't seem to help himself and said, "I would lighten up that perfume you have on El, Harry what's-his-name might gag if he gets too close."

Now she was annoyed, and protested back, "You know what, I was trying to be civil on my sister's behalf, but I knew you couldn't resist pressing a button or two. And by the way, his name is Harold, not Harry." I was a little surprised because it's usually the other way around.

He stood up and said, "Oh, lighten up El, I am entitled to crack a few jokes here and there, too."

I gave him the *come on, Grandpa* Willow look, and said, "Alright Aunt El, let's get going, it's getting late and we don't want to keep Mr. Future Hubby waiting."

Grandpa yelled back, "What, future *what?*"

I shouted back, "Grandpa, enough."

I walked Aunt Ellen to the door and she kissed me on the cheek. I was again overwhelmed by the smell of her obnoxious perfume, and thought I might vomit my pasta right back up. "Okay, El, I will talk to you before I leave. And remember, do not, I repeat *do not* be too yenta-ish in getting the scoop."

"Willow, I said I promise. Goodnight, darling, I am off to have my nightcap with my Harold. Tell your grandpa, if anyone needs lightening up, he should take a look in the mirror. I think he's jealous, Willow, that I am out and about having fun while my sister is somewhere else." She might be right, but I didn't have the energy to get into it with her.

"Aunt El, let's talk about it another time, okay?"

"Okay, doll, you're right; I am sorry."

I walked back in and looked at my grandpa with my hands in the air. He looked at me and said, "What did I do?"

"Gramp, you're kidding me right? 'What did I do?' What was that about and why did you feel it was necessary to squeeze one in?"

"Willow, honey, I am sorry, I couldn't help it, I was in a bad

debating what it was I really wanted to do. After I moved out of Tom's house, I decided to move back in with my parents until I figured things out. For the last eight years or so, I had been selling clothing for a big corporation. I quit my job about four months ago and had been struggling with what to do. Yeah, ask me how my self-esteem is doing right about now? I was both unemployed and living with my parents, temporarily, at the same time.

Well, technically I was doing my poetry on the side and waitressing here and there which kept me somewhat busy. However, I knew it was time to start switching into serious mode! What to do? What to do? To tell you the truth, sometimes, I wished I could just pack myself up, move to Tuscany, write books, draw, and drink wine all day - sort of like Diane Lane in the movie "*Under the Tuscan Sun.*" I was smiling now as I just had another vision of my grandma saying, "Willow, my little dreamer, always a dreamer." I would have to figure this out soon, for according to my therapist, too much time on my hands, was not a good thing for an over-thinker like me. Deep breaths, Willow, deep breaths.

As I got myself dressed and showered, I realized that today just might be the last day that I saw my grandmother alive. I found it hard to swallow that thought, and again took a deep breath. I walked out into the kitchen and Grandpa was finally up making his coffee.

"Morning, Gramp, how did you sleep?"

"Not great, my love," he lamented, "I had a dream about your grandma that woke me out of a dead sleep and could not fall back for a while."

"Sorry to hear that, want to talk about it?"

"Willow, I want to talk about a lot, I just can't seem to do it right now," he sighed. "It's too hard for me. I am trying to figure this all out and how I will be able to deal with this inevitable pain that your grandma is slipping further and further away."

I saw that his hand was shaking while he poured his coffee into his favorite New York Yankees mug. I put my hand on top of his and said, "Gramp, I know, you don't have to say a word, just know that you are and will always be loved by Grandma, even though she can't say the words out loud. I know she feels this in her heart."

"Thank you, darling, you are just like her in a lot of ways, you know that, right?"

"Yes, Gramp, I know it. Now how would my grandpa like a delicious Willow omelet before I go see Grandma?"

Finally a smile, "Sounds great, could you add some buttered wheat toast on the side?"

"Coming right up."

After breakfast, I told Grandpa that I would meet him over there.

On my way to Grandma, my cell phone rang and it was Aunt Ellen, I knew it. "Hi El, let me guess, you already got the scoop?"

"I did, doll, and the party was last night here at Running Hunter," she reported. "I heard it was a big bash. It turns out his grandma has played golf a few times with my girlfriend, Shirley. Her name is Salma. She is a very nice lady, married to a real looker who I have seen playing golf a few times. They live in one of the nicest homes here at the complex. I think his grandpa was in the banking business, so they are very comfortable if you know what I mean, jellybean."

"Aunt El, I don't care about their money, I just want to know if they're a nice family."

"Willow, doll, they are nice. So listen, I was thinking you should stop by today before you go home tonight and we could subtly have a drink at the bar, and maybe we could accidentally run into Will's grandma, and maybe even him."

"Aunt El, sorry that won't be able to happen. I'm going to hang with Grandma for the most of the day, and have an early dinner with Grandpa before I go. But, thanks for asking. Look, Aunt El, truth be told, I am not remotely ready to even think about other men. When

I am ready to call Will, I will. Do me a favor, don't try to push fate any further than I am ready to have it pushed. Capish, Aunt El?"

"Okay, Willow, I got it, just don't wait too long. You wouldn't want this nice Jewish boy, from a nice Jewish family, to be snagged by some other girl, who we know could never be like my favorite niece."

"Got it, Aunt El, and love you for it, but I will keep you posted. And, I promise, you will be the first one I decide to call if I do call him."

"That is a promise I will hold you to. Have a safe trip back, darling, and love 'ya." "Love 'ya, too."

I pulled up to Grandma's assisted living facility. I went into the room, and she was still sleeping. I quietly went in and sat beside her bed and just looked at her resting peacefully.

I decided to pull out my favorite little quote book that I always keep in my purse. I like to randomly turn to a page that I am hoping will have an extra special meaning for me that day. Let's see, oh, a good one. I like to read them out loud so that I will remember them better. Today's quote: "Even through all of your pain, I can promise you three things: the sky will always return to blue; the birds will continue to fly; and God's love for you will never change." I liked it, and needed to hear it.

Grandma's eyes opened. Did she hear me? Maybe. She looked right at me, and I swear I thought I saw a faint smile like the one I saw yesterday. I smiled back, "Good morning, Grandma. I'm sorry if I woke you up with my morning meditative quote. What's a good word today from my Grandma?" She always used to say that to me on the phone, "So, Willow, my love, tell Grandma what's a good word? I only want to hear the good stuff first." I smiled again thinking about her positive energies.

She looked me in the eyes, and did not take her eyes off of mine. I almost felt like this was her way of trying to connect with me, even though she couldn't speak. I took her hand and placed it in mine. It was nice and warm, just like I always remembered it to be. My hands are always cold, so it felt extra comforting. She actually squeezed it a little. Again, this must have been her way of letting me know she felt my presence. "Yes, Gram, it's me, Willow, I am here with you." I thought music was miraculous, but the power of human touch can be extraordinary, too, because I did actually see her smile this time. My eyes filled up a little. I was overwhelmed with emotion, yet comforted by being able to be present in her company.

I didn't do anything for about ten minutes but rest my head on her shoulder and hold her hand. I liked to think she was passing her loving energy into my hand, so when she leaves this Earth, she will be leaving me with what was truly mine to have. Gram Lu always knew I had times of struggling with anxiety and sadness in and out of my life, and would do her best to try and help pull me out of it.

Again, I heard her speaking in my head, "Willow, my love, please don't be so sad - sadness weakens and dims the light on your spirit. It is meant to be radiant like the sun. That is the truth, my dear Willow, please believe it! There is nothing else you need to do in this life, but trust your own inner spirit and that beautiful smile of yours. You are beautiful, my Willow, just as you are. Don't be afraid to show the real you, ever."

Boy, did I miss those talks! Then I had another flashback of Grandma Lu telling me that her middle name is Ruth, which if you add the letter T in front of it, spells the word TRUTH. She told me that her mother did that on purpose to always remind her that her middle name is a reassurance if she is ever in doubt as to what the real truth is. Her mother said that she was wonderful just as she was, and to never feel like she had to change for anyone. Also, she could instill this in her children and grandchildren some day. I had to admit, I was starting to appreciate more and more the history behind my family's names, on both sides!

I sat up and looked at her and said, "Okay, my dear Gram, Miss Luciana Truth, I mean Ruth, I mean Truth, let's get you dressed so I can take you outside for some of Mother Nature's good loving!" I gave her my Willow Wink. She did smile back - she must have had a moment of clarity and love.

I called the nurse in and asked her to please dress my grandma in something yellow or orange, anything bright. I stepped out for a few minutes and decided to call my sister Carla, who was back home in Philadelphia, where I originally lived. The phone rang. She picked up and said, "I was waiting to hear from you. How is Gram? More importantly, how is Grandpa holding up?"

I sighed and said, "I know, I am sorry I haven't called you back, I have been sort of sitting on this, not knowing how to tell you just how sad it's all gotten. Carla, Grandma cannot do anything on her own anymore. She can't eat, speak, or go to the bathroom. She is wearing diapers, as you already know. However, I am happy to share with you that there have been a few times over the last few days that I did feel a connection with her, and saw her smile a little. Truth, I hate to say it, but my intuition tells me that her time is coming sooner than I think we expected."

"Oy, Willow, so are you saying I should come out there to say my goodbyes ASAP?"

"Yes, Carla, I think it may be time. I know you're tied up with the kids, but try to make plans sooner rather than later if you can. As for Grandpa, I don't have to remind you just how sad he has become. It's hard to watch him. Part of me is afraid to leave tonight. One, because it could be the last time I see Grandma, and two, I'm afraid to leave Grandpa alone."

Carla sighed, "I hear 'ya, Sis. So why don't you stay a couple of extra days? It's not like you have a job to come back to or any major responsibility right now."

"Ouch, thanks for reminding me, Carla," I shot back.

"Willow, don't overanalyze my comment. I just meant that you do have the most flexibility in the family right now, so hang out for a few more days."

"You're right, "I said, "I know, I was thinking about that myself. I'll look into it later. Let's change the subject. How are my delicious nephews?"

She responded, "They're great, everything is fine. I'm more worried about Grandpa right now. Maybe I can get Mom and Dad to help out Marcus (her husband) with the kids for a few days and fly out to be with you and grandpa, what do you think?

"Carla, didn't you just tell me that I have the most flexibility and should stay? You are tied up with the kids. It's okay; I will take care of things."

"Willow, you know my intuition is just as strong as yours, and I'm feeling an overwhelming need to come out ASAP. So, let me just look into flights as well. What could be more important than my saying goodbye to my grandmother before it's too late?"

I said, "Okay, by all means. I am sure Grandpa would love the extra company. Call Mom and Dad and see what you can manage, and I will figure out my stuff too. Call me in a few hours."

We hung up, and I was thinking that as much as I hated to admit it, she was right. I didn't have a big time job to get back to, and I was not quite ready to hop back on the plane home. A few extra days, to clear my head and be with my grandparents was the right thing to do. Carla was right, something in my gut told me to stay because Grandma might not be around much longer.

We aren't twins, but throughout our lives we have had that "twin psychic power thing" you may have seen on the Montel Williams or Maury Povich show. Our whole life we have always sensed when something was not right with the other, or if something bad was about to happen.

I will never forget, once when I was in college, I had one of the worst nights ever with an ex-boyfriend of mine who got a little rough verbally with me, which shook me up with anxiety and God knows what else. I was full of fear. I remembered running back to my dorm at two in the morning, and as I was walking in the door, my phone was ringing. I was thinking it was my creepy ex, begging me to come back, but no, it was my sister, Carla. "Willow, are you alright? Something just woke me out of a dead sleep, and I had this sinking gut feeling you were in trouble. I had to call and make sure you were okay." We had a lot of those growing up, which I was always thankful for in times of need.

Speaking of family, I had barely spoken to my parents in the last few days, too. I may have been avoiding it a little. I thought that maybe I should call them now and let them know what was really happening. I'm not sure how I felt about telling my mother that her mother was slipping away. I had sort of danced around how bad it had become. My mother picked up the phone, and I could tell by her tone she was not in a good mood. "Morning, Mom, it's Willow."

"Morning, Willow, how is Grandma today?"

"She's hanging in there, Mom. She smiled at me a few times, but something tells me we are coming to a close. Carla is about to call you and Dad to see if there is any chance you could help out with the kids for two days, she wants to see Grandma ASAP. Also, I think I'm going to change my flight and hang out for a few more days."

"What are you saying, Willow? That it's going to happen tomorrow?'

I sensed that annoyed, stressed out tone, but took a deep breath, "No, Mom, not necessarily. I am just saying that something tells me that I need to stick around for a few days, and Carla wants to be with Grandpa and me. Can you and Dad pull through for us?"

She snapped a little and said, "What do you mean can we pull through? Of course we will do what we have to for our family, let me talk to your father and we will try and make it work. I am thinking I want to come out too, now."

I knew her snapping was guilt coming out that she was not there and I was, and she probably felt like she should have been. I had learned not to say those things even though I knew what was going on, so I responded with, "Thanks, Mom, I really want to hang for a little more with Grandma and Grandpa. As far as you and Dad coming out, that is up to you, I know how super busy you both are, Carla and I can handle it, so don't worry."

"I am not worried about you two handling it," she responded, "I am just aching to have one more goodbye with my mother. I will figure it out with your father. Okay, on a lighter note, so, Willow, what is this I hear from your Auntie Ellen about a cute stranger you met on the airplane? How come she called to tell me and not you?"

"Mom, I didn't tell you because I really didn't think it was a big deal I thought there were more important things to chat about than my meeting men." Truth was, I hadn't told my mom because I knew how much she had been dying for me to meet a nice Jewish boy for the last thirty years and I was not ready for her to push me into calling him.

"Willow, you are crazy not to call him, I hear his grandparents are very nice. I won't push this one, but don't wait too long, something tells your mother that this could be a special one. Besides, Willow, you are the one who is always convincing me about the power of signs and no coincidences in life, so my dear, to me this is a sign."

"Mom, are you sure this has nothing to do with the fact that he comes from this ideal Jewish family that you would love me to build my white picket fence with?"

"Oh, Willow," she sighed, "Lighten up. I know you think you've got my dreams for you all figured out. Maybe I really just want you to be happy, I mean *really* happy someday!"

"Alright, Mom, let's get into this later, I want to take Grandma out for some fresh air. Tell Dad I love him, and call me when you guys know if you can watch the boys for a few days."

"Willow, we will take care of it, just take care of my father will 'ya, and see if you can talk to him, you know what I mean by talk to him, you are the only one, Willow, who can really get through to him."

"I know, Mom, it's not easy, but I will try."

"Willow, that's all I can ask of my girl."

We hung up, and again I took a deep breath. Mom does that to me from time to time. We have had our share of differences growing up, for sure, so I sometimes have to breathe through some of my old resentments. I realized as I took these deep breaths that now is the most important time for this family to come together. We need each other, and that is what Grandma would want more than anything. I walked back into the room to take Grandma for a stroll.

As I pushed my grandmother around the complex, I began to feel some sort of tingling up and down my arms and legs. It was my intuition speaking to my body. I sensed that my grandmother was going to pass in the next few days. Part of me thought it was my negative thoughts, but something more powerful told me I could have been right about her impending death. One way or the other, I try to think positively. Thank God I was there with her. I gently pushed Grandma around and around the complex contemplating how to prepare for this. I felt like I was in sort of a walking meditative trance, not speaking a word, just reflecting.

Before I knew it, once again a red cardinal flew by Grandma and me, landing on the tree to our left, which startled me right out of my trance. *All right*, I was thinking, this was too weird, this had to mean something more than what I was used to seeing.

I had not been able to get access to a computer since I have been here. My grandparents didn't even own a typewriter. I didn't want to have to worry about emails on this trip or to get caught up with

31

the Internet. However, I felt compelled to look up the meaning of these cardinals. Maybe one of the nice ladies at the front desk would let me use their computer for a few minutes if I told them I needed to check out changing my flight to help my grandparents. Well, part of it was true.

I wheeled Grandma back into her room and asked the nurse to stay with her for ten minutes. I walked up to the front desk and gently smiled at the big bosomed nurse and told her that I was in a situation with my grandparents. I asked if there was any way I might be able to use her computer for a few minutes. She told me that she normally does not do this, but because she and some of the other nurses have soft hearts for my grandpa and his devotion to my grandmother, she would let me use it, if I was quick.

I responded, "Thank you so much, I promise to be quick." I went online and decided to change my flights for a few days from now. Then, I went to the Google box, and typed in a query about the meaning of red cardinals and spirituality. My eyes began to enlarge as I read that cardinals can be a way for angels to show you that your loved ones will be in good protective hands when their time has come. I also saw a bunch of stories people had written saying that once their family members had passed, they continue seeing red cardinals in various places, whether it was outside their windows, when they would take walks, or the bird would fly past their cars. All the writers of the stories said how much comfort they had knowing their loved ones were safe. I tried to tell myself *at least I know she will be in good hands*. I decided to not share this with anyone in my family - I was not sure they would believe me, anyway. With the exception of my grandmother and sometimes Carla, my family has not always been so open to what happens in life that cannot always be explained.

I was proud of myself as I decided to not even check my email, and I closed out and logged off the computer.

Grandpa showed up not too much later, and I told him that I was going to stay for a few extra days and that Carla was hoping to join us. Normally he might question why, but he surrendered to the idea.

After a few hours, I got the call from Carla that she was arriving the next morning and could I pick her up at the airport? I was glad she was going to come. She was close to my grandparents, but not as close as I was. I felt sad that my grandma hadn't had a chance to meet either of her grandsons. When she was diagnosed a few years ago, she and Grandpa gave up flying altogether. My sister, who is nervous about flying to begin with, wouldn't want to take the boys out while they are so young. I knew that if my grandma was better, and she could speak, she would tell you that spending her last remaining time with her great-grand sons would have been her wish. I decided to let Grandpa have some alone time with her. I told him I wanted to run a few errands, but would come back to pick him up and take him out for dinner that night.

He looked at me and said, "Willow, my love, I don't need to go out for dinner, let's bring in."

"Grandpa, your granddaughter has not been on a date in months. Can you please do me the honor of at least having a hot meal with me, and maybe a little drink to loosen up? Come on, Gramp, when was the last time you were out anyway? Grandma won't mind. If she could speak right now, she would say, 'Honey, please go do something other than watch me all day, I am okay, trust me, now go be with your granddaughter, and don't forget to bring me home some dessert!'"

He smiled and said, "Okay, but only because I love 'ya so!"

After a few errands, I drove back to the facility to say goodnight to Grandma and pick up Grandpa for dinner. As I got ready to walk into Grandma's room, I saw the door slightly cracked open and I heard my grandpa humming to her and saw him gently rubbing her head. I decided not to go in, and let him have his moment with her. I was silently moved by this gesture. Again, I daydreamed about the possibility of having a man to love me like this someday. What could be more tender and true than a man who is not afraid to show his loving and comforting nature to his lady, and not just during the toughest times in her life? That is who my grandpa is. After a minute or two, I walked over to Grandma, kissed her on the forehead and told her I would be taking her boyfriend on a hot date tonight, but we would be sure to bring her some dessert for tomorrow.

"Grandpa, I'll wait in the lobby for you."

As I walked down the smelly halls, I saw an older African American man mopping the floors, dancing around with his headphones on as he cleaned up somebody's mess on the floor. He looked so happy.

I was curious, so I smiled at him and asked, "What 'ya listening to this evening?" He pulled off one phone, and with cute crooked teeth, smiled back and said, "One of my favorite songs, darling, 'Three Little Birds' by Bob Marley. You know it?" I giggled, and of course, was now paying attention because this was for sure a sign - it's one of my favorite songs.

"Do I know it?" I begin to sing the lyrics back, "I rise up this morning, smiled at the rising sun, three little birds, each by my doorstep, singing sweet songs to a melody pure and true, saying this is my message to you!"

He raised his eyebrow with amazement and naturally said, "Well then, darlin', don't worry about a thing, because every little thing is going to be alright!"

I felt a joy in my belly and said, "What is your name, sir?"

He said, "Well, my name is Lucas, honey, Lucas Brown which means 'light' but you can call me Luke. And you?"

"My name is Willow. I'm not sure what it means, other than its relationship to my father's love of nature."

"Oh-h-h-h, Willow, what a beautiful and unique name, but I'm not surprised, because I can tell just by looking at you that you are both!"

I started to blush a little. I put out my hand to shake his and said, "Luke, it is a pleasure to meet you."

He smiled and said, "Say, you wouldn't be the granddaughter of the lovely Luciana?" I nodded. He said, "I knew it, you have her eyes. She may not speak much but her eyes say a lot to me. You know they are the windows of the soul, and I see nothing but love in them. So, I know her condition is tough to see, but Willow, darling, trust everything will be okay, no matter what!"

I felt immediately comforted, smiled, and said, "Thank you for the message, Luke, and for making my day!"

"Willow, the pleasure is all mine, and I hope to see you again soon, and don't forget, like Bob says, that every little thing is gonna be alright!" He winked at me, and of course, I Willow Winked him back. As I walked down the rest of the hall, I couldn't help but continue to smile. I was reminded of how much I love the connections we mysteriously make with other humans sometimes, where we get to share and comfort each other at just the right moments! What do they call it - serendipity? Angels in disguise? I like to think its God with a funny sense of humor!

I picked up Grandpa and drove us to this little Italian place around the corner from his house. When we arrived, the hostess sat us down to a basket of intoxicatingly drippy, buttered garlic rolls and cheap red table wine. I looked across the table at my grandfather and said, "So, Gramp, what will it be tonight?"

"Willow, honey, I appreciate you trying to make an effort to get me out, but I am really not hungry and I'm quite tired."

"Grandpa, I know you are, but listen, no matter what, it's important, even in the worst times of our lives that we still try to stop and smell the roses. That after a morning shower, which we know always happens in Florida, the sun will come out again." I picked up the drippy garlic roll, took a bite, smiled, and said, "Or even enjoy this hot, scrumptious, buttered delight, possibly followed by a piece of chocolate cake! So you know what, Grandpa, this is what we are going to do this evening: no more depressing stuff, let's just enjoy each other's company right here and now. You don't need to feel guilty that Grandma isn't here with us tonight!"

I pushed the basket toward him and his glass of wine, and said, "Live a little, will 'ya?"

He smiled, "Okay, my love, you win. You sound just like your grandma more and more each day!"

I say, "I will take that as the best compliment any day, thanks, Gramps!"

"Alright Willow, what do you say, we toast to still being able to see the beauty in the small things! I like this toast."

We actually had a very pleasant dinner, and I was surprised to see that he ate a little more than usual. He told me he wanted to bring Grandma a piece of angel food cake. He said it's her favorite. "I want to bring my angel, a piece of angel, okay, Willow?"

"Of course, Grandpa!"

As we were getting ready to leave the table, I saw him take the pink rosebud, next to the salt and pepper shakers, out of its little innocent vase. He gently wrapped it in his napkin. "Willow, I know we said good night already, but do you mind if I drop off her dessert and lay this sweet little rose next to her bed? This way, when she wakes up tomorrow, she will know I was there!"

What could I say? "Grandpa, a girl could never say no to a man with a heart like yours! Of course I will take you!"

# Chapter 4

I woke up, made Grandpa his coffee, and got myself ready to pick up my sister at the airport. I felt a little uneasy this morning; I was glad Carla was coming - I needed a little distraction from all the heaviness of the last few days. I thought that I was sensing that Grandma was ready to join her other loved ones. I never really knew my great-grandparents, but I know she was super close with them. When Grandma was able to speak and understand our conversations, we definitely had a good one-on-one talk about the whole life after death situation. She was always a believer, like me, that it exists.

I remember one late night, sitting together, she told me that when it is her time, she would be happy to join her mama and papa in heaven, or whatever you want to call the afterlife. She said that no matter what, she trusted that it was a place full of nothing but love and peace, and she promised to watch over me, and to always let me know she was there if I needed her. All I would have to do is call for her, and she would give a sign in her own way! I took a deep breath. Oh, my God, I just realized since the red cardinal had always been one of her favorite birds, would this be her sign? Ah-ha! This was God's way of giving me a heads up, it must be, especially since I just read online that this was what cardinals could mean. I decided to possibly let my sister in on this one for now. I had no one else to really share it with who wouldn't think I was a little nutty either.

I got myself dressed, left Grandpa a note that I would pick up Carla and meet him at the facility. I grabbed the keys and got in the car, turned on the radio and I felt filled with nothing but love as my other favorite song was on the radio. I smiled when I heard, "I see trees of green, red roses too, I see them bloom for me and you, and I think to myself, What a Wonderful World." Ever since I was a little girl, no matter what the situation that was going on in my life, this song always made me smile. I felt good - this would help me set the tone for my day!

I pulled up to the arrivals area and saw Carla and her big Jackie-O sunglasses waving at me. She hopped in the car, and before I could even get a word in, she said, "I have to tell you something sort of bizarre that I have noticed over the last few days, and I need to tell you now!" My gut was thinking *cardinal?* But I decided to keep my mouth shut and just listen.

"So," she starts, "yeah, yeah, my flight was great. Listen, so I was taking the boys for a walk two days ago, and this beautiful red cardinal kept sort of flying around, dancing from tree to tree with the boys and me. Now, you are probably thinking, 'that's what birds do, Carla,' but here's the thing, yesterday morning when I woke up and went for my quiet run at the crack of dawn, which I always do, you know it's my time for me, my little red friend was sitting on the tree next to our house. Wait, I'm not finished! This morning, I ended up taking a taxi to the airport. I went to kiss the boys goodbye, I got in the taxi, and one flew across the street as we were pulling out of the driveway. So you know, Willow, I don't totally believe in signs, however, something in my gut tells me... I'm not sure what, but something. I know you were always into this stuff. What do you think, Willow? What?" she demanded

"Okay, Carla, take a deep breath. Can I speak now? First, let me say that I am so glad that you are here, and secondly, don't get all freaked out, but I, too, have had the same experience with a red cardinal in my own way over the last few days. I think I know what it means. You know how Grandma has always been into nature, specifically birds and butterflies, especially birds, especially red birds? Well, I think this means that it is a sign that Grandma's time is coming, and whoever above is letting us know that she will be fine and protected, and more importantly, this will be her way of letting us know she is okay when she goes. So how are my cutie nephews anyway?"

She sat all upright looked at me and said, "Willow, wait what? Can we not change the subject for a second?"

"Carla, listen, we knew this time was going to come, let's just try and look at this as something to take comfort in, not be afraid of, and nobody on this earth has ever wanted us to know the truth about love more than Grandma Lu, so let's look at this as a sign of love! Let us have this, you and I just for us. We don't have to tell anybody about it right now, besides no one would probably believe us anyway."

She took a deep breath, too, and said, "Okay, this time, I will try and look at it that way, but this is a hard one for me you know that. All I can say, is I am glad to be here to say my final goodbyes."

"Carla," I warned, "don't say anything to Grandpa right now, he is fragile and scared, we will tell him when the time is right."

"Willow, I know, you don't have to tell me, I know my grandpa a little more than you think I do. Change of subject - so have you had the balls to call what's his name from the airplane yet?"

"Oy, Carla, no, not yet, I'm pre-occupied with what is happening here, I don't have time to think about men right now! So to answer your question, "NO I have not called him yet, but yes, I have toyed with the idea, perhaps when I get back into town!"

She nodded her head, "Oh Willow, it might not be such a bad distraction to meet a stranger for a drink! You should call him, maybe he's still here in Florida. *Oh-h-h-h*, you should totally call him and see if he wants to meet you tonight! I'm here now, Grandpa is not alone, why don't you call him?"

"Whoa, Carla, slow down! I am not ready yet. As I mentioned to Mom and Aunt El, and Gramps, and now you, I will call when I feel ready!" I exclaimed.

"Okay, Okay, but don't wait too long, you never know when you might be missing an opportunity!"

"Carla, all I care about right now is saying goodbye to my grandma. Capish?"

She rolled her eyes, and said, "I heard 'ya, sis. So, speaking of Aunt El, I would like to see her even if it's for five hot minutes full of stories of her latest man!"

I smiled, "Yeah, I saw her a few days ago. She thinks she's going to marry this one, just like the last two. Call her and invite her over for a visit later today, just remember that Grandpa can't be in her company for too long -'ya know the whole water/ vinegar combo is not going to work, so if she comes, take a walk with her or something, so she's not in Grandpa's space."

"Okay, I will call her," she decided. "Doesn't she live where the guy from the airplane's grandma lives?"

"Yep, and I begged her not to get nosey with the grandma. But knowing her, since we have last spoken, she probably got some more scoop! Apparently his grandparents are living in the ritzier part of the complex. As if I gave a shit about money. That would be lovely, but you and I both know, Carla, that money is the last thing on earth I would ever look for when trying to find my mate! I'm much more interested in how much his heart is capable of giving, not how much his bank account, or family's bank account, is worth."

She smiled, "My sister, Willow, the poet, the endless romantic novelist, the teacher of love's lessons!"

"Go ahead. Laugh it up Carla, but you know that when it all comes down to it, the man who will win my heart, is the one who will look into my eyes and say, 'Willow, there is nothing you can do that will make me love you any less, I love you for you!'

She raised her brow, "I got it, and so this fantasy man will say what Tom wasn't able to say?" I gave her the look of *you had to bring it up, huh?*

"Carla, I wouldn't say that, and I am not sure if I'm ready to fully talk about the ending of our relationship, which you and I both know was over way before we actually said it was. However, the bottom line is that I loved Tom but somewhere deep within my soul, I knew that I could never build a life with someone who didn't believe in the kind of 'loving no matter what' unconditional love we all want.

"Now, I am not saying, he didn't have it buried somewhere deep within himself, but how long should I have waited to know if it ever may come to life again? Four years was long enough. My only wish for him is that he will be able to let go of his anger. The good news is that it did not end ugly. He and I did walk away respectfully, knowing that it couldn't work. I am gently starting to forgive him for hurting me. More importantly, I am starting to learn about forgiveness on lots of levels. Though, I have to admit, there are some days I know I will miss looking into those intoxicating blue eyes of his."

She looked at me and smiled, "Wow, Sis, it sounds like you're getting some good clarity on this. I'm glad you've opened up to me a little, and just so you know, whoever the next man may be, he'll have something just as powerful, if not more powerful, than those baby blues, I promise!" I smiled back, not wanting to say any more, knowing she was right.

We walked into the facility, and I saw Carla covering her mouth and nose, and making that face. I looked over at her and said, "Get used to it. There is nothing like the smell of urine, split pea soup, and bleach all mixed into one yummy scent to make your day!"

She swallows, "Uchch, that is just wrong!"

"Well, Carla, I should warn you, you are unfortunately going to start to see a lot of things that just feel wrong here at the facility. Many of the people who live here do not have anybody, I mean *nobody* besides the nurse's aides to keep them company, or to talk to. I hate to say it, but the care here in general is not so great either. But, we don't have to get into how much the health care industry is a wreck! All I know is Grandma Lu is so lucky to have a family, especially a husband like Grandpa to see her through her final days. I'm heartbroken at how many people here are left to die alone."

She nods her head in disbelief and said, "Alright, let me get my mind set on Grandma - do you think she will remember me?"

"Carla, honestly I don't know, but it doesn't matter anyway. All that matters is that you do what you can when you walk through that door to make her smile and make her feel loved. I had a few moments where I felt the connection. So, to answer your question again, my heart is saying yes in her own way, she will remember you."

We walked in, Grandpa looked up from his *NY Times* and smiled, "Lu, look who is here, it's your other angel Carla." Carla walked over and kissed Grandma on the forehead, "Hey, Gram, it's me Carla, your other favorite granddaughter from Hollywood!" She put her big Jackie O's on to play the part.

Grandma was looking at her curiously, not smiling, just checking her out. Grandma always liked to say that in curious situations, when I would ask her, 'What are you looking at?' she'd respond, 'I'm checkin' things out, Willow, you know I always like to scope things out!' I must have gotten my curious and analyzing nature from her.

I smiled at Grandma Lu and said, "Gram, I know you're checkin' her out, it's okay Gram, it's Carla, she came all the way from up north to see you!" I looked at Carla, "I have an idea. Let's sing something she will remember together, like we did as little girls with her. Music always seems to spark something in her. How about 'You are my Sunshine'?" So we start together, "You are my sunshine, my only sunshine, you make me happy when skies are gray, you'll never know dear how much I love you, please don't take my sunshine away." Grandma finally smiled.

Carla looked at Grandma Lu and said, "Gram it's me, and guess what, I brought pictures of your great grandsons to show you. I sing this exact song to them every night before bed. It helps them fall asleep better! You taught me that, Gram." My great grandfather used to sing it to my grandmother as a little girl. She has passed on to my mother, and now to Carla and me.

Carla pulled out her pictures of my nephews. "See, this is Jack, and this is Max. Aren't they beautiful?" Grandpa looked at me and nodded his head. At this point, I knew what the nodding meant - it meant that he wished she could speak and understand more. I looked at him, and gave him the head tilt towards the door and said, "Grandpa, let's go get some fresh air and give Carla and Grandma some alone time." He agreed and we walked outside into the courtyard and sat on the bench.

Grandpa leaned back and put his weathered hands above his head. "Willow, darling, I am so grateful you girls are here with me. The truth is, I'm not sure I could be going through this without you. I know time is running out and I am trying, Willow, I am, to prepare myself, it's just tough," he lamented.

"Grandpa, I wouldn't be anywhere else in the world then here with you and Grandma right now."

He made a big sigh, and said, "You know, Willow, I am not sure if I ever told you this, but if it were not for your grandma I would be a miserable, old man. When I hear you sing songs such as 'You are my Sunshine,' I tear up, because we certainly didn't sing songs like that in my house as a kid. I am not sure if you knew this, but I grew up in a sad household, very different from your Grandma Lu's. My father, your other great- grandfather, never smiled and never could tell me he loved me. As for my mother, your great-grandmother, she hid a lot in her books and whisky."

I raised my brow, surprised.

He nodded. "That's right, you heard me right, whisky. When you hear the word whisky, you think of mostly men, not Mom though; she was made of iron on some level. At least that is what I thought growing up. My father would sometimes be verbally abusive to us, or even worse, cold, and not say a word when he was depressed, so you would tip toe on eggshells, never really knowing what kind of mood he would be in. When that would happen, I remember your great-grandmother, my mother, would always walk out of the room and go in the study. She would grab the whisky and sit down to read her Hemingway novels or something else heavy. I remember she also always wore black and her skin had a very milky complexion. She hated the sun. No wonder she was so depressed. Anyway," he stopped and shook his head, "sorry, I didn't realize I was getting carried away on my depressing childhood. Let's not go there.

"However, the reason I brought this up was that I am so grateful to have found a woman who could teach me a little more about love, and more importantly loved me for me. I wasn't sure that I would ever find someone who would care how sad my story was. Also, Grandma Lu's mom, your other great-grandmother accepted me right away. She made me feel like family. I loved that Grandma Lu's family helped to redefine what a real family should feel like, full of nothing but unconditional love!"

I was wondering if his ears were burning, thinking about the conversation I just had with Carla. All I could do was look into his sweet, sad eyes and say, "Grandpa, I understand more than you think. Who doesn't want someone to love them for them, no matter what!"

He grabbed my hand, kissed it and said, "Willow, my love, any man would be the luckiest man in the world to have you as his partner! I hope you find somebody just as special as I found in your grandma."

"Me, too, Gramps, me, too!" I leaned back with him on the bench, neither one of us saying anything, and we just sat in silence.

I realized in this moment that no matter what age you happen to be, that we all have the same yearning for love. When we're robbed of it as children, it becomes extra hard to find it. And, when we do find it, it's almost as if we find ways to push it away, because we don't feel we deserve it. I am not talking about the desperate one-night stands or hook-ups for the sake of a warm body next to you just to fill the voids. I am talking about the potential real love that walks into your life that you manage to push away, because deep down you are afraid you are not good enough for that love. *Hm-m-m* interesting thought. I was wondering also why Will just popped in my head. Could he possibly just be one of those men that could show me what it means to love unconditionally?

As we were getting ready to get up to walk in, a radiant red cardinal flew past us and landed on the bush to Grandpa's right hand side. He looked at me and said, "Hey! What do 'ya know, its Grandma's favorite bird! I'll have to tell her we saw one. I still think she can hear me, you know? Even though she may not be able to answer me back, Willow, I feel it my heart."

I smiled at him and said, "Then, Grandpa, you should continue to believe that, for your heart always knows."

He smiled and said, "Come on, love, let's go check on the ladies."

I nodded, and contemplated when Grandma would be leaving us. I wasn't feeling as afraid.

We spent a few hours with Grandma. Later in the afternoon, I noticed that she seemed a little more lethargic than usual. I also noticed that she never ate her breakfast and she barely ate any of her lunch. No appetite and tired, *hm-m-m*. I read once that at the ending of Alzheimer's, patients stop eating. However, I know Grandpa said there were days where she didn't eat much, anyway.

Grandpa looked at me and said, "Girls, why don't you go out, just the two of you, for dinner tonight. I would like some alone time with your grandma. I feel like just hanging with her. Better yet, you should call your Aunt Ellen, Carla, she is probably dying to see you and tell you al-l-l-l about her latest sugar daddy."

Carla smiled and I rolled my eyes. "Grandpa, are you sure you want to be alone?"

"Tonight ladies, yes, I am not sure why, but something tells me she needs a little extra TLC from me, besides her head feels a little warmer than normal, she might have a temperature. Willow, can you grab nurse Delicia, she is my favorite one, and the only nurse I really trust here. I want her to take Grandma's temperature."

"No problem, Gramps."

I went searching down the hall for Nurse Delicia. I know it sounds like 'delish. 'It's kind of ironic, because that was always one of Grandma Lu's favorite words. Delicious! Everything in life she always described as *delicious,* and not just with food. When Carla and I were little girls, she would always say, "Come snuggle, my delicious girls, with your grandma in bed." Gosh, I miss that! Carla and I talk about my nephews in the same way now.

I find nurse Delish and asked her to take Grandma's temp. - 102 degrees. I looked at Grandpa who was patting his bald head with his hankie. He sweats quickly when he's nervous. Nurse Delicia told us she was going to give her some liquid Tylenol, and suggested we put her in bed. She told us that Dr. Cohen had left for the night, but she promised to check on her all night to make sure she was okay. The hard part about all of this was, because Grandma couldn't talk, you always ended up trying to guess what was going on.

Grandpa looked at Carla and me and said, "Better yet, why don't you go get me a change of clothes and my toothbrush before you go out to dinner. I am staying the night. Girls, don't give me a hard time about this, I know she will probably be fine, but I won't sleep a wink at home, so just in case." Under any other circumstances we would have told him he was being ridiculous, but we gave him a break, and did exactly as he asked.

Carla and I ran home and picked up Grandpa's things. We decided to call Aunt El, she was thrilled to know that Carla was here now, too. She told us to meet her at seven o'clock at this yummy authentic Spanish café called Tina's Tapas. She promised that they had the best Sangria, fun mixed drinks, and incredible homemade empanadas. That sounded just about perfect, since we needed a little lightening up.

When we got back into the car, I asked Carla if she thought we should be leaving Grandpa alone, and if one of us should stay with Grandma tonight instead. She half giggled at me and sarcastically said, "Willow, do you honestly think Grandpa is going to allow one of us to stay with her, and him not stay, too? It's pointless, besides where do you want to sleep - on the comfortable cold floor?"

"Good point, I just feel badly."

"Willow, stop with the guilt runs, will 'ya already? The fact that you are here right now and doing everything you can is enough. Besides, now you're making me feel guilty, and I don't have the energy for that. I already feel guilty enough that I'm not with the boys right now.

I said, "Carla, I am sure they are fine. Let's have some sangria and mojitos and try and not think about everything. Even if it's for an hour, let's give ourselves a break. You're right, let's leave the guilt at the door. Besides, after Aunt El goes on and on about her new man, you will want to get mucho buzzed."

We picked up a sandwich for Grandpa from his favorite deli to have for dinner, and dropped off his clothes. He promised us that he was fine, and would call if he needed us. We headed to the restaurant. As we walked up, I heard this incredible flamenco guitar coming from inside the restaurant. To the left I saw Aunt El, waving her hand "over here, over here!" But to my right, I looked up on stage and saw this extraordinarily handsome man with dark hair, olive skin, and blue eyes making love to his guitar on stage. He made eye contact with me and smiled, with, of course, the most amazing smile. Oh, my God, my heart was pounding. I was transfixed between his smile and talent. I was nervous, but I smiled back and walked toward the table. I purposely let Carla sit in the inside, just in case I wanted to check out Mystery Guitar Man a few more times. We ordered a few drinks with extra lime. After we went through the whole situation with Grandma's update, I heard Aunt Ellen telling Carla the story about her new man, Harold, while also pointing out a new pair of earrings he bought her since I last saw her. Nice, if you like hoops that weigh more than tires.

I started humming that song in my head - "Do your ears hang low, do they wobble...." After a few minutes, I was able to tune them out, for Mystery Guitar Man had just started playing what now sounded like a sexier version of a Carlos Santana song that I love called 'Samba Pa Ti'. I loved watching him playing that guitar, eyes closed, feeling his passion through every note.

Out of nowhere, I heard, "Willow, Willow, did you hear me?" Aunt Ellen snaps her cheesy pink fingernails in my face, "Willow honey, did you hear me?"

"Sorry, Aunt El, I was distracted by the guitar and that handsome guy on stage."

Aunt El lifted her brow and said, "Oh really, you don't say. That is Bernardo. He's here a few nights a week. My fellow and I come here once a week for a delish meal, and to sometimes dance a little. I know there is no dance floor, but get a few of these cocktails in us, and we don't care. We let down what hair of ours is left and cut loose. Bernardo never cares, he just keeps on playing. I am pretty sure he is single if you're interested. However, the ladies love him. I see women flirting with him all of the time. Anyway, if I remember correctly, he is originally from a small town outside of Barcelona."

"He came here to help his cousin with a business in construction. Unfortunately, it did not pay him very well, and he was unhappy doing it. He said he really wanted to pursue his passion in music and hopefully open up his own nightclub sometime soon. I think that is what he is trying to do now, and this is for extra money. He sounds sexy doesn't he?" she asked.

"Aunt El, leave it up to you to get the dish on everyone. Yes, he is attractive, but no thank you, I am not interested, just intrigued by his music, and maybe his eyes."

She smiled, "Willow, darling, I don't suppose you have called Will from the airplane?" "No, Aunt El, not yet. I told you, when I am ready, I will."

She added, "Well, to be honest, Willow, I actually met his grandmother today at the club. I was walking out from lunch with my golf girls and she was walking in. Very nice lady, pretty, and very slim, I think she may have had a little work done on her face! Anyway, our mutual friend introduced us. Turns out her grandson left this morning."

I look at her, annoyed, "Ellen, I asked you not to subtly get yourself…"

She interrupted me, "Willow, I did not say anything to embarrass you, I promise. All we did was giggle that the two of you met, and we hope you decide to call him. That's it, darling, no pressure, no nothing."

I heard the music stop in the background. This sexy Spanish accent came on the microphone and said, "I am going to take a short break, but will be back soon." Aunt El who cannot help herself as usual, starts waving her hands at Bernardo as he is walking off stage, "Yoo-hoo, Bernardo, over here honey! Come meet my nieces."

Oh, my God. I was mortified and wanted to crawl under the table. I kicked Carla's foot and she gave me the shrug and look of 'like, what else would you expect from Aunt El?' As Bernardo walked toward us, I took a deep breath looked at Carla, pointed right to my teeth, and silently asked her *do I have anything in them?* It was the *quick, tell me* look. She shook her head *no* and smiled. He walked up to the table - oh, my God, he was drop dead gorgeous, even better looking close up.

Aunt El said, "I would like you to meet my beautiful nieces? This is Carla and this is Willow. Ladies, this is Bernardo."

I reached my hand out, and he kissed the top of Carla's and then mine. I was blushing, but also thinking right away, *slickster! Don Juan!* How many chiquitas have lain in this man's bed?

He smiles, "Ladies, it is pleasure to meet you both." We were both blushing, and said, "You, too."

I smiled and said, "Your playing is amazing. Who taught you how to play a guitar like that?"

He smiled back, "You are so kind, thank you. My father, actually, and my grandfather. I grew up in a little village where most of the community had a passion for music. So for my whole life, I was always surrounded by it. You should hear my mama sing, too. I feel blessed to have this gift in my genes. So gracious."

I started to turn down the judgment dial and thought, Don Juan or not, this is a man who takes pride in his work and family - I liked that! I saw what looked like the owner waving at him to come over. Bernardo nodded and pointed his index finger, giving him the *one second* look.

He said, "So, how long are you ladies in town for?"

Carla answered, "We're not sure. Unfortunately, we're not here for pleasure. Our grandmother, Aunt Ellen's sister, is very sick, and we're not sure how long she has."

He put his head down and said, "I am so sorry to hear that. I know, for myself, aside from my mama, there has been no greater love than the one from my grandma. Ladies, I will say a prayer for you." Either this guy is really good, or truly genuine. I chose to think maybe a little of both.

He said, "I apologize, but my boss is waving me over. It was a pleasure meeting you." He smiled and looked me in the eyes and said,

"I hope to see you again very soon." He walked away, and I checked out his butt. Not bad.

Aunt El said, "Did you see that?"

I replied, "See what?"

"Did you see the way he looked at you?" she asked.

"Aunt El, what are you talking about?"

"Willow, he gave you those sultry *I want to get to know you more* eyes."

I then rolled mine and said, "Oy, give it a rest Aunt El, will 'ya? And, as far as Will, I told you what is meant to be, will be."

She looked at Carla, and said, "Do you think we will ever be able to crack this nut's shell for the possibility of new love?"

Aunt El waved her hand and said, "At this point, how about just a date? Willow, when was the last time you were kissed by a passionate man? I mean really kissed like you felt like you were floating in the air?"

*Hm-m-m*, I realized I couldn't really remember and thought that on some level she was right - it would be so nice just to be kissed.

Carla looked at Aunt El and said, "You got me. I don't know. But Willow, I have to agree with Aunt El, he was checking you out."

I modestly shrugged my shoulders and said, "El, I appreciate your looking out for me, but let's talk about something else."

Through the rest of dinner, I found myself looking back up to the stage a few times, and making eye contact with Bernardo each time. I was wondering if he was undressing me with his eyes, like I was doing to him with mine. I am such a goofball, but a goofball who would love to make out with a hot guitarist who speaks with a sexy accent. Doesn't every girl secretly want a night with a guy like this? Anyway, after a few more drinks, I realized I was feeling definitely buzzed and exhausted. I saw Aunt El go up to pay the check and talk to the owner. *Then* I saw her walk up to the stage and slip Bernardo a little piece of paper. I was now freaking out wondering, if she was giving him my phone number. I saw him smile and nod, and she kissed him on the cheek. He waved to Carla and me as we were walking toward the door. I was buzzed, so of course I gave him the Willow Wink.

Aunt El said, "Okay, ladies are you ready to go?"

I looked at her, steaming, "Aunt El, I swear to God if you just gave him my number...." She interrupted me, "Willow, relax, I just gave him my honey's phone number. Harold said Bernardo should call him anytime, if he ever has any questions about starting a new business. I am trying to help the guy out Willow, not set you up like you always think I am trying to do."

I was suspicious, but sarcastically said, "Oh, sorry, but it wouldn't be the first time El."

I handed Carla the keys and she looked at me and said, "You don't really believe her do you?"

I smiled, "What do you think?"

We kissed Aunt El goodbye. As we were pulling out of the parking lot, a car pulled in front of us with a bumper sticker that said, "Life is too short, not to have fun." I smiled to myself - possibly a sign that I needed to make out with a hot Spanish lover? Or, call a nice genuine mystery man from an airplane? Either way, I knew it was time to start thinking about dating again - at least going out on a date.

I had trouble sleeping through the night because my mind was really on whether or not my grandma was okay, and I was worried that my grandpa barely slept on that lazy chair thingamajig. I looked over at the clock, 5:37 a.m., uch-ch are you serious? I knew I was not going to be able to fall back asleep, so I got up quietly, decided to make some coffee for Carla, and put my shoes on for a brief walk. I came out of the bedroom and saw that Carla had already beaten me to it. I looked over at her head buried in the *New York Times*.

She looked up at me with big circles under her eyes. "Carla, you are up already, I thought for sure you would sleep in a little?"

"Willow, I could barely sleep last night, I was too worried about Grandma, and of course Grandpa's mental state, and ate too much bean dip on top of it. Do I have to get into specifics?"

I nodded, "Me, too, me, too. Hey, what do you say we go for a little walk, and maybe it will help to clear out our heads a little? Didn't Grandma always say that? 'Girls, whenever you are in dismay or stressed about something, you need to be in fresh air to clear the clutter out of your mind. Mother Nature knows her girls better than you think, so get outside!'"

Carla smiled. "You're right. Let me go brush this old sangria, now coffee breath, out of my mouth, and we'll go."

We started walking and Carla asked me, "So, what do you think Grandpa will do when she is gone? Stupid question. What do you think we should do with Grandpa when she is gone? I mean, you know no matter what, we are not going to want him to be alone. Do you know if Mom and Dad plan on moving him back to be closer to us?"

I shrugged, "I'm pretty sure that Dad has already looked into a place for him to stay, sort of like an assisted living/community type situation for adults where he can do stuff and be social. This is somewhat ridiculous because you know as well as I do that he never likes to be social with anyone besides Grandma, which he can no longer do! He has a few co-workers he still talks to, but no real meaningful buddy relationships. I try so hard not to ever get frustrated about that. But, truth be told Carla, it bothers me. How do you not want to be social with anybody, ever? I get it if you are depressed or in a shitty mood, but he doesn't even watch a baseball game with anybody but himself. How boring is that, nobody to even high-five after a good play."

"I'm sorry if I'm sounding harsh. But, I am telling you this now,

Carla, when Grandma goes, which could be any day now, besides us, who is Grandpa going to lean on or get a break from his pain? You can't lock yourself all freaking day and night in your lonely apartment with a *New York Times* and a shitty cup of instant coffee to fill your day or take away your pain!"

Carla looks over at me and said, "I couldn't agree more, but the man is eighty-five years old, this is who he is, he ain't changing anytime soon, as frustrating as that may be." I nodded as well.

We walked for about twenty minutes, and as we are getting ready to walk inside, don't you know, there it was, sitting on the telephone wire above, making a bird call of some sort.

Carla looked at me, "Oh, looks like we have a little friend coming to say *good morning* to us, or is he saying *today is the day, ladies?*"

I smiled and sarcastically said, "You don't know that Carla. Come let's go shower and head over there."

We walked into the room and found Grandpa passed out on the chair, which he had now somehow placed right next to her bed. Grandma Lu was sleeping as well. I gave Carla the sh-h-h-h finger and told her to go find the doctor so he could tell us himself what was really happening. I waited outside the room and saw Carla coming back down the hall with Dr. Cohen. He smiled that smile at me to let me know, without saying it, prognosis was not great.

"Good morning, you must be Willow."

"Yes, good morning, Doctor, how are you? Thank you for coming down, so what is the scoop, Doc, and please we are grown-ups, and we're here to help Grandpa, please tell us the truth and nothing but the whole truth."

"Well, ladies," he replied, "I'm sorry to tell you, but we ran some blood work very early this morning and her breathing has become heavier, neither are what we hoped might be just a minor setback. At the end of this, as you probably already know, she is ready to go. I don't know when, it could be tonight or tomorrow. She has stopped eating and she will continue to want to keep sleeping. I am sorry, ladies. The best you can do now is try to plan accordingly. Your grandpa is a saint, you know," he added.

We nodded at him - of course we knew.

He smiled, "In all of my years of practicing, I have never, and I mean never, seen so much devotion as that man has. God Bless Him!"

"Thank you, Doctor, for your words and your honesty. Does he know yet?"

"No, I was going to tell him about a half an hour ago, but I didn't want to wake him up. He looks so peaceful lying next to your grandma. I figured I could do it with the two of you and him."

I felt my stomach drop and officially might have wanted to vomit my breakfast up, but instead I looked the doctor right in the eyes and said, "I think that's a good idea, I mean for Carla and me to be with you."

He agreed and told us to wake up my grandpa, give him a few minutes and then he would come back to tell us. I looked at Carla, took a deep breath, and said, "Are you ready to do this, 'cause you know, there is really know easy way of doing this."

She nodded, "Willow, I can't imagine, even if it's been in his own silent way, that he hasn't somehow prepared for this."

I nodded as well, "Okay, let's get him up."

We walked into the room and I went over to Grandpa gently placed my hand on his shoulder, and said, "Hey, Gramp, we're here. Wake up."

He looked up and smiled at me and I said, "How are you this morning? What's a good word?"

He yawned and said, "Not a good word. I was pretty much up all night just looking at her. I think she is ready."

Carla and I looked at each other, shocked that he had even been able to say it. Part of me already felt relieved that this might not be as hard as I thought - because he felt it himself.

I silently nodded with him and said, "Actually, Gramp, we just spoke to Dr. Cohen who is going to come down in a few minutes and explain everything to us."

He looked me in the eye and said, "Willow, my love, its okay. I also spent half the night telling your grandma how much I loved her, and if she is ready to go, I am setting her free. I don't want her to suffer anymore."

Again, I was shocked, but somehow knew that he already knew. Carla walked over and grabbed Grandpa's hand, "Grandpa, we are here, and we love you, and we will do this together."

He kissed her hand, "I am so lucky to have both of you!"

I heard a knock at the door and Dr. Cohen walked in. "How are you doing this morning, Lex?" Grandpa half smiled at him. Dr. Cohen put his hand on Grandma's forehead and looked up at her monitor. Then he looked at Grandpa and said, "Lex, your wife is deteriorating a little faster than we expected. As you know, she has stopped eating and her blood work is showing a decrease in her cell counts. The best we can do now is try to make her comfortable. I am so sorry, Lex, I know how hard this must be for you."

Grandpa put his hand up as a stop sign as if to say *Doc you don't need to say another word.* He looked at Dr. Cohen, "Doc, you have been great through all of this, I can't thank you enough. I know it's time, I made my official peace last night."

Doc looked at me and Carla, smiled and nodded, "Ladies, you have a special grandfather who is stronger than you think." He winked at my grandpa and said, "Lex, I will give the nurses a heads up. I am here all day, and I will be on call tonight if you need anything."

Grandpa said, "Thanks, Doc, I know."

Dr. Cohen replied, "Okay, I will leave you all alone to have your time together and to make plans."

He walked out and I looked at Grandpa, "Are you okay?"

He nodded, "Girls, do me a favor, give me a few minutes to wake up. Go call your mother and father and give them a heads up as to what is happening, and I will meet you back here in a little bit, okay?"

"Okay, Gramp, whatever you need, we are here."

Carla and I took a walk outside into the courtyard where she called her husband, and I made the call home to Mom and Dad.

My mom answered, "Willow, how are you? I was up half the night not able to sleep, feeling like something was going on with Grandma, but not sure."

"Mom, it's not good, you and Dad should make plans to fly out of here ASAP. Grandma is sick and has totally stopped eating, and Dr. Cohen confirmed that this is it, so it could be tonight, tomorrow, but time is limited. You don't have to worry about the kids, as you know Marcus made the choice to stay with them. Carla's on the phone with him now, and is telling him to stay home while we do this together, the four of us, meaning you, me, Carla, and Dad." There was a long pause. "Mom, are you there?'

I heard her starting to choke up a little, "Yes, Willow, your father and I will get the first flight out of here today and we'll see you tonight. I'm just hoping my mother will hold on until I get there to say goodbye."

"Mom, my heart tells me yes, and Grandma always told me I could trust that."

"Willow, thank you so much for being there. I'll call when we know the details of our flights. Before I get off the phone with you, how is my father handling this?"

"Mom, you would be surprised, but he's okay. He told us he was up half the night saying his goodbyes, and he's ready to let her go.

So, don't worry. Something tells me I was meant to be here with Grandpa, so you don't have to thank me. As sad as it is, it also feels right."

We hung up, I looked over at Carla and she said, "I took care of it, and no - because I know you were going to ask me - no, I don't want the boys to fly out right now. I will explain it to them someday. Marcus understands this, too."

I smiled back, "I hear 'ya, Sis. With luck, Mom and Dad will be here early this evening."

I told Carla that I needed to take a step outside and to go back in the room to be with Grandpa. I felt anxiety rush me a little more than I wanted, so for a change, air was what I needed. As I was walking down the hall, I heard whistling coming from one of the rooms, and then I heard someone humming what sounded like a Billy Joel tune. Just to confirm, I peaked in and found that it was Lucas, the loving custodian, cleaning up another accident from the floor. He had his back turned from me, so all I could see was his headphones and his skinny head.

Then out of nowhere I heard, *"I love you just the way you are.................."*. I smiled again - how perfect that this man had reminded me once again, that this was something I needed to practice. He must have heard me.

He turned around, and with the brightest crooked tooth smile said, "Well, well, Miss Willow, say it ain't so, you caught me singing my song. This has always been one of my favorite songs to my lovely wife, Lorraine. We have been married for forty years. Don't be trying to estimate how old I am, either. I take pride in my work, and I will retire soon enough."

I smiled back and put my hand up, "I would never ask how old you are, you have too young of a heart and voice of gold to think of anything else." I thought I saw him blush a little.

He took off his earphones, "So, Miss Willow, how is your grandma doing today?"

"Well, Luke, not so good. We unfortunately just got the news from the doctor that it is time. She has stopped eating, and there's really no response at all when we try to engage her. But please don't feel sad for us. We are actually more at peace than I thought we would be. Aside from my grandpa not having her love by his side anymore, the only other thing I'm a little sad about is that my grandma won't be here to remind me of all the things I should know to help me through this next big phase in my life. Luke, she has been the one person I have always felt I could run to with a non-judgmental and unconditional ear to help me out. Sorry, did I just over-share with you?" I asked.

He smiled and said, "There is no such thing, darling, as over-sharing with me. It sounds like your grandma and I have a lot in common. Would you be open to a little advice from a silly, skinny, messed-up-toothed old man like me?"

"Luke, I couldn't think of any one more perfect, by all means share, and just so you know, I don't see your messed up teeth when you smile - I just see you and your heart."

"Okay, sweet Willow, here is what I can tell you. Your grandma was and will always be a part of your life, even if she is not physically there to speak to you, she will be in spirit, if you know what I mean. She will watch over you and make sure you are protected."

I smiled, "I believe that, Luke, I do."

He nodded back, "Good darling, then we are off to a good start. But, here is the best part, when you are in doubt of what to do in the future, all you need to do is think of your grandma or pretend your grandma is there to give you the advice you already know is now in your heart! Have you ever heard of the word *agape*?"

Awhatta? I looked at him, perplexed.

He saw the expression on my face, "Willow, sweetheart, something tells me that whatever it is you are about to go through in this next phase, you should take a peek into its meaning. My wife and I have stood by this word all throughout our marriage. I actually think it is what has kept us together for all of these years. Okay, I know, I know, you want me to tell you what it means. The word is Greek for *unconditional love*. But, Willow honey, this is not just meant for relationships with others. This is a term that you should understand in relation to yourself and the kind of love God has for you. So, Willow needs to learn to love Willow, too, you understand?" He looked me right in the eyes and nodded.

I put my hand on my chin and rubbed it, "Luke, you are a special man among men. Your wife is a lucky lady. I appreciate your sharing that word and its meaning, and will look into it more. I'm guessing, by your song to your wife, that you have mastered this agape for yourself, loving someone no matter what!"

He took his rubber gloves off and reached for my hand. Normally, this would have grossed me out, since he had just been wiping up God knows what off the floor, but I didn't care. I let my hand gently rest in his. He squeezed it a little and said to me, "Willow, this may take time, but some day you will understand why all of this happened the way that it did, and no matter what direction you decide to go in, don't ever let anyone get in the way of Willow needing to be Willow. Be yourself, be who you are, and life will show you what it is really about, not what you actually thought it was."

I teared up a little and thought to myself, *my God, I've never had anyone make me feel quite as safe with this notion.* "Luke, I can't thank you enough for your kind words. They have come at a perfect time, and I needed to hear them, and feel them in my heart, and I do."

He smiled, "Willow, trust that. You know that feeling you have right now in your heart? Your grandma and *you know who upstairs,* (he looked up and pointed his finger above), live there always. So there is nothing to ever really worry about okay, honey, you understand?"

"Luke, I know I just met 'ya, but I gotta hug 'ya."

He didn't even pause. He grabbed me tight and whispered, "It's all going to be okay, Willow, I promise."

As I got ready to walk out the door, Luke said, "And don't forget - Agape."

I turned around, "Thanks, Luke. Agape, got it!" After a deep breath, I looked up and smiled. I am convinced God must have brought me an angel, and I said, "Thank you God."

I popped a piece of bubble gum into my mouth. Oh yeah, did I forget to mention my love of bubble gum? I chew it to remind me I am still and will always be a kid at heart. As I was popping my bubbles away, I saw nurse Delish on my way back to the room. She stopped me in the hallway and said, "Willow, right?"

"Yes, Delicia, right? Love your name by the way!"

She responded, "Thanks! When I was younger, kids would always make fun of me, but now I've sort of learned to love it.

She leaned toward me and said, "I just want you to know, that I heard the news about your grandmother, and I am going to make sure she is very comfortable. She may have not spoken a lot, but she has a heart of gold. I do not know everything there is to know exactly about this disease. However, I have seen many patients who suffer from it over the years, and you can always sense the ones who had a lot of love in their hearts, and than the ones who somehow hardened their hearts, and you felt sad for them. Your grandma had the sense of nothing but love. I just wanted you to know that, although something tells me that you are a lot like her, you already know this yourself."

I teared up, "Thank you, Delicia, for those kind words, and I am working on this. I do believe I'm a lot like Grandma, but I'm hoping to find a lot more of her in me as I grow up!"

She put her hand on my shoulder, "You will, Willow, just give it time. Come on let's go check on your grandma. By the way, your Grandpa Lex, does he ever smile?"

"That's all he did when Grandma Lu was at her best," I answered, "She brought lots of light and love to him. He smiles, you just have to know him underneath that sad sourpuss." I Willow Winked her.

She winked back and said, "I know he does, I am just teasing. I see how much love that man has for her. I am envious - I wish my husband loved me in that way."

"Don't we all on some level?" I replied.

"Mm-hmm, say it ain't so, child!"

As we were walking back into the room, my cell phone rang, and I told Delish I would meet her back in the room. I didn't recognize the number, but for whatever reason I decided to pick it up. "Hello?"

"Is this not the beautiful Willow?"

Oh shit, it's Bernardo. I should have known better than to trust my aunt. I nervously played stupid and said, "Yes, it is, who is this?" As if I didn't know already - how many men with Spanish accents did I know?

"Well, it's Bernardo. Please don't be upset at your aunt - she said you might get mad at her thinking she was trying to set us up. The truth, Willow, I asked her for your number. I was afraid if I asked you myself, you would shoot me down."

I was shocked. Most men wait at least until the third date to have the courage to tell 'ya that one. I half laughed, "Bernardo, its okay, really its okay. I like your honesty."

He giggled on the other end, "If that is the case, what do you say? You let me take you out for a drink tonight?"

"Bernardo, thank you for the offer. Unfortunately, my parents are on their way into town - we got word this morning that my grandmother has had a setback and may not make it past the next twenty-four to forty-eight hours, so I'm not sure how long I will be in town and what is happening. The timing is not great. So, I am not saying never, I am just not saying okay to the next few nights."

"Willow, I am so sorry. If there is anything I can do, please let me know. I completely understand, but may I ask one request of you before you leave town?"

"And what would that be Bernardo?"

"I ask that even if it's only for one hour, you will meet me somewhere. Willow, when I saw you last night something in those beautiful eyes of yours told me this woman needs to smile again. So, even if it's only for an hour, will you give me that chance?" God, this guy is good.

"Bernardo, you are charming. I will call you, when I can. I now have your phone number in my phone, so I will find you before it's time for me to go home."

"That's all I ask, Willow. God bless you and your family, call me soon."

We hung up, and I smiled, how does this guy know, or sense, my sadness? Oh, yeah, he's a musician; all of us artists have that radar for sensitive souls. We innately want to reach out to one another on other levels besides the bedroom. That is at least what I was trying to tell myself, so I could try to not judge this guy just to be a player. If nothing else, I had just gotten a little ego boost.

We spent the next few hours sort of sitting quietly watching Grandma rest. What else could we do? I decided to ask Grandpa if he was thinking at all about what he wanted to do for the big picture, as far as staying in Florida or coming back to Philly with us.

He shook his head and said, "Willow, I am not sure I can give you a complete answer right now, but I am thinking that I would like to move closer to you all within the next few months or so. Let me get my house in order and have some alone time and I will make my way up. I hope that is a good enough answer. But for now, I just want to sit here with my angel's remaining time, and love her like there is no tomorrow - because there may be no tomorrow."

I saw him tearing. "Gramp, it's okay, whatever you decide. I just don't want you to be alone too much. Believe me, I know about wanting to be alone, and it's not always the best choice, especially at a time like this." My cell phone rang, it was my mom telling us that they just landed, and would be there within the hour. She had already called Aunt Ellen to pick them up and take them to the nursing home, so we didn't have to leave Grandpa. My grandpa said he needed to stretch his legs for a little, but did not want to leave my grandma - not even for a second. But, I suggested that at least he let Carla walk him to the cafeteria for a cup of coffee, and I would sit with Grandma and promise to not let her out of my sight. He somehow agreed. I secretly needed for him and Carla to leave, as I wanted to say my goodbye in my own way, just in case there was not time later when Mom and Dad came.

As they left the room, I decided to kick my flip-flops off and gently sit at the edge of her bed in my Indian-style fashion. I placed one hand over the sheets onto her frail foot. I looked at her. She was so quiet and still. I wasn't sure what to say, so I figured I would just talk.

"Well, Gram, what can I say? This is never an easy thing to digest. I just want you to know that I love you. I love you with all of my heart. I am so grateful to have had a grandma who could show me the kind of love every human yearns for in his or her life. You know, Gram, that feeling of delicious laughter, and fun, and unconditional love dripping with all of Grandma Lu's goodies. I like that. Boy, Gram, we had fun didn't we? You sure knew how to brighten my days. All of my silly crying over silly boys. There was nothing your late night laughter and feedings couldn't fix. I will miss it all. My wish for you is that you go to a place where you get to be you again, 'ya know before your dementia sort of took control. But, Gram, I don't care what scientists or any other researchers out there say, I believe that there are moments such as these, when a dying person who has so much love to share, can somehow hear me or feel my presence. I have stood by this all along. Regardless, I know in my heart that you will watch over all of us to make sure we are okay. Grandma Lu, Grandma Lu, I hope that you can make sure that Grandpa is especially okay! Let's not let him slip into the funk of all depressions. Give him your own signs in your own ways when you can, to let him know you are still with him, even if he doesn't believe in it. Just know I will do my best to be here for him, too. I'll try to remind him of all your goodness when he may be expressing feeling blue. What else? I can tell you that I am not sure where I'm heading with my future on a lot of levels - job, living, men, you name it. But, I at least hope whatever I decide to do moving forward, I can stay more true to myself and have a little more compassion along this journey. Thank you for teaching me that as well."

"And yes, Grandma, I will remember as you always say, 'Each day is a new found day!' Where did you come up with this stuff anyway? Who taught you, Gram? I wonder that sometimes. On another note, I hope you won't mind, but sometimes when you are gone, I am going to want to talk to you anyway. So, I am hoping you will lend that gentle ear of yours when I am calling. I already know the answer to that. Just want to give you a heads up! How about you show me a red cardinal or some other awesome beauty of nature. You always loved that bird! Something tells me red cardinals, for sure, are what I know I will see. What else, what else did you always love? Oh yeah, how about a dragonfly? They are uniquely beautiful just like you! How could I forget? I just had a flashback of playing in your garden once as a little girl and being afraid of one that was flapping around. And I remember you saying, 'Willow honey that is not a flying monster. That, my love, is a flying angel. They are good luck, sweetness, and they fly around you to remind you of your loving light. They will not bite you, I promise!' Grams, you always had a way of helping me to not be afraid. I love you so much for that too."

"Okay, just so you know, Mom and Dad and your sister, Ellen, will be here very shortly. Try to hang on till at least later tonight so they can all say their goodbyes.

"Grandma, let me say one last thing. I will try to honor you every day in every way. I can do this just by remembering the importance of smiling. I will smile at everyone with no judgments, like you always said. And, let me tell you one more time today - I love you with all of my heart, and when you are ready to go, go Grandma. Go to where your heart can continue to shine and you can share all of your incredible wisdom in heaven, or wherever else you may choose to go or to be in your next life. But, whatever you choose, stay an angel at heart!"

I felt myself tearing up and for a second I thought I might be imagining it, but I actually felt my grandma's foot move a little back and forth.

I sat up more and said, "Gram, I knew it, you can hear me, can't 'ya? Thank you so much for listening." I got so overwhelmed with that feeling of love that I knew I couldn't have been imagining it, because her foot moved again.

I looked up above and said, "Thank you, God, for letting me have this. Just let her hang on, if possible, so Mom can say goodbye, too."

My mom and dad arrived shortly after my talk with Grandma. Aunt Ellen stopped in for a few minutes to say hello and hug her sister, and decided to let my mom have some private time. I watched my mother looking at Grandma. She did not say a word - she just walked over to Grandma Lu, placed her hand on her forehead, kissed it, and asked if we would all step outside to allow her some alone time with her mother.

My father and I decided to stroll out to the courtyard. He waved me to come sit next to him on the bench.

"So, how is my Willow doing? We haven't really talked a lot since you've been here. How are you holding up with all of this?"

"I'm hanging in there. I think I already sort of made my peace, but I'm more worried about how Grandpa will handle this. He told me he will not be ready to move out nearer to us for a little while."

"Willow, I will take care of Grandpa's next steps, don't worry about it. I am actually more interested in what you are going to be doing."

I was sort of queasy thinking, *oh, my God, is my father really going to be asking me about my future plans right now of all time?* So, I couldn't help but be a little snappish and said, "Dad, are you seriously going to ask me about my future right now? Can you give me a little time to mourn Grandma, who hasn't even passed yet?"

"Willow, slow down, that is not why I said that. I was actually thinking that maybe you wanted to stay with Grandpa for a little bit, keep him company for a few weeks. He is definitely not going to want to come home with us, and he should not be alone. You are one of the few family members who can usually keep him in check. What do you think?" he asked.

"I'm not sure, Dad. I will have to sleep on that one, but I'll certainly stay for a few days. Let me think about it, okay?"

"Of course, Willow."

A few hours went by with us taking turns just sitting with Grandma, and smiling, and reminiscing about all of our fun times growing up with her. My grandpa was very silent through most of the conversations, but smiled from time to time. Eventually, we all ran out of things to say and became exhausted.

I looked at my watch and wondered if Carla and I should spend the night. My mom insisted that she and my dad were going to stay with my grandfather at the facility. She promised to call me if anything happened, no matter what time of the night it was. Carla and I went over and kissed Grandma goodnight, and said we loved her and would be back first thing in the morning. As we walked out of the room, I looked back one more time at my grandma's soft face. Her eyes were closed and she looked very peaceful to me. Part of me wondered if she was already in transition.

Carla and I got into the car. She turned her head and said, "I think this is it. I think we just said our last goodbye."

I nodded and said, "I think you're right and I am actually okay with it. I had a special moment with Grandma today. I think she heard me when I said my goodbyes to her because she gently moved her foot, which I was holding."

She smiled, "Maybe, Sis, maybe."

The phone rang at 4:32 a.m. I picked it up, but I already knew what the call was about.

"Hello?" I answered tentatively.

"Willow, sweetie, she is gone," my mom said. "She passed about twenty minutes ago." I heard her burst into tears.

"Mom, you okay?"

"Yeah, honey, just sad. She went very peacefully but I am sad, this is my mother, my sweet and loving mother."

"Do you want us to come over?" I asked.

"No, honey, your father and I are wrapping things up now, and I want to allow your grandfather a little more time alone with her before they, well, 'ya know. So, I will call you soon and let you know what the plan is when we know."

"Okay, Mom. Tell Grandpa I love him."

"Will do, and tell your sister what is going on."

"I will, Mom." I hung up, closed my eyes, and decided to get on my knees before I woke up Carla.

"Dear God, please, please make sure my sweet grandma is protected and taken care of. Please also do not allow my grandfather to fall into the worst depression because of this. Please help my family to get through these next few days. I love you, and tell Grandma how much we all love her, too!"

I walked into the other guest room and gently tapped Carla on the arm. She said, "I'm up already, and I know, I have actually known for a while, intuitively, just wanted to sit with it."

"Okay. Mom says we should hang tight until she calls us with what to do."

Around 6:30 a.m., my mom called and told us to come over. My sister and I got dressed. We were pretty much silent on the car ride over. As we pulled up to the front of the facility, I looked over at Carla and said, "So, what shall we say to Grandpa?"

She sighed, "I don't know, but I think it doesn't really matter - he knows how sorry we are."

"Yeah, I suppose you're right," I answered. "I just feel icky inside for him. You know what, forget it, this time I am not going to plan this out, I am just going to try to let out whatever comes out!"

She nodded. "I agree, and whatever will be, will be, at this point."

We got out of the car and I grabbed Carla's hand, which I can't remember doing since I was little girl when we would cross the street together. We both looked at one another, took a deep breath, and at the exact time said, "Okay, let's do this!"

We walked into Grandma's room and saw that she had already been moved from her bed. I looked over at my grandpa folding some of her clothes, and my mom staring out the window while my father was doing some paperwork for the hospital. The tension was thick and heavy, yet quiet all at the same time. I knocked on the door to raise their attention.

I immediately made my way over to Grandpa and hugged him. He tapped my back as I went in for a big bear hug and said, "It's okay, love, she went peacefully I know that."

"I am so glad, Gramps, that is how I always pictured it."

Carla joined us for a group hug. My mom turned her attention toward us and kissed us *hello*. I looked up at her and asked, "So, what are the next steps?"

She sighed, "We will have a service for her in two days. But for now, your father and I were up the entire night with Grandpa, and we need to get some rest. I say we get some bagels, go back to the house, and try and get some rest for now. We'll take Grandpa home. Why don't you girls pick up the bagels and meet us over there? Also, do me a favor. Invite your Aunt Ellen to come, too. She's been waiting to hear from me."

My grandfather immediately looked up with a disgusted look on his face and said, "Really, do I have to see her right now?"

My mother looked at him with a serious look on her face and said, "Dad, come on, it's her sister, she wants to be with us."

He rolled his eyes, "Fine, I am too tired to argue."

My mother pulled me aside and said, "Thank you again for being here with Grandpa over the last few days. He needed it, and I think he could use your company for a little more time if possible."

I felt a little surge of anxiety and thought to myself, *no pressure, Willow, to stick around*, but I knew that this was my mother's way of putting it out there so it didn't feel overwhelming to me.

I nodded and said, "Sure mom, where else would I have been? As far as the next few weeks, I told Dad I have to think about it, but I am pretty sure I will stick around."

She smiled. "Sounds good to me."

She gathered her things and took my grandfather and dad home. Carla and I, as promised, picked up bagels and went right back home.

Breakfast was very quiet. Even Aunt Ellen barely said a word. We all sort of stared at each other while we spread our cream cheese and piled tomato slices on top of our bagels. I didn't really have much of an appetite. Also, Aunt Ellen's perfume usually makes me not want to eat to begin with.

I looked over at my grandpa, who was resting his elbows on the table while his hands rested on his head. He was not even making eye contact with any of us. I looked at my mom to look at him. She nodded at me as if she knew already.

She said, "Dad, are you alright?"

"Yeah, love, you know, I think I want to just go to sleep. I am exhausted, nobody take it personally."

"It's okay, Dad, go lie down, we'll talk later." Grandpa went back to his room and shut his door.

He didn't come out until about three in the afternoon. His eyes were swollen and watery. I was lying on the couch trying to write something I wanted to say for the service. Grandpa looked over and smiled at me. "What 'ya doing love?"

"Hi, Gramps. Oh, just writing something sweet that I want to say about Grandma. There are not enough words."

He said, "I second that, there are no words for the greatest woman in the world."

I smiled, "Hey, Grandpa, I just made some fresh coffee - good timing!"

"Thank you, where is your mother?"

"She went out with Aunt Ellen for a walk to get a little air," I replied.

"Oh, okay, and your father and Carla?" he wondered.

"They're both passed out in the guest room."

"Okay, did anybody bring my *New York Times* in yet today?"

"Grandpa, I already have it laid out on the kitchen table for you. Go sit down and I will get your coffee ready for you!"

"Thanks Willow, what would I do without you?" I just smiled.

# Chapter 5

LATER THAT EVENING, I FELT heavy and drained in the house and wanted to get out. I told my family that I needed to clear my head and take a little drive. They all knew me well enough to know that this was not that unusual for me - to want to escape a little. Of course, my father said while I am walking out (as if I am still in high school), "Don't come home too late."

"Dad, I am not going on a date, I am going for a drive." I Willow Winked him and he nodded back. Now, I am not sure if my father subconsciously knew, but I somehow ended up deciding to stop by the tapas restaurant my aunt had taken us too, 'ya know, the one where that hot Spanish musician was playing? Okay, okay, I know, but I really felt like I wanted a nightcap to help me sleep. What would one innocent drink hurt? I was in mourning, and I didn't even feel like looking for an excuse anyway.

I walked into the bar area, and what do you know, Bernardo happened to be playing. I saw him look at me, and his face lit up with an incredible smile. I felt my heart pitter-patter. I smiled back and headed right to the bar. I sat next to what looked like a fifty- something older gentleman with an ugly wrinkled Hawaiian shirt saturated in that hippie patchouli smell, dirty fingernails, and sandals that looked like they possibly could have been worn during Woodstock.

He immediately looked me up and down, and with the worst whisky breath I have ever smelled, said, "What's cooking, good looking? Hey, what 'ya drinking? It's on me."

I rolled my eyes and thought to myself *are you freaking kidding me right now?* I was in no mood to deal with this shit! But, being the nice girl I am, instead of being a total bitch, I held my breath (so I didn't smell his) and looked into his desperate eyes and said, "You're sweet, but no thanks!"

"Oh, come on, pretty lady, what's one drink?" The bartender must have known him as a local and said, "Jim, leave the nice woman alone and let her have a drink in peace. What will it be, darling?"

"Hi, yes, can I get a Corona Light with a lime?"

"You got it!"

Smelly drunk Jim looked over at me and said, "Sorry, I didn't mean to bother you, just lonely since my wife left me last year!" *Not now* I am thinking! Normally, I would have indulged in a little of my psych 101 on this guy to help him out.

I was so drained I didn't have the energy, but I looked at him and said, "Sorry. Jim, is it? Hi, I'm Willow," and shook his hand, but quickly turned my back to let him know my handshake was not an invitation. In the meantime, I looked back up on stage and saw Bernardo giving me the look of *do I need to be saved?* I nodded at him with a *don't worry* look, but deep down I was thinking *can you come over here and pretend like you are my boyfriend?*

After about ten minutes or so, I saw Bernardo making his way toward me. I felt a little nervous, but smiled at him. He wedged his way right between drunken Jim and me and the bar. I guess he hit Jim's shoulder in the process, because next thing you know, I heard in slurred words, "Hey, watch it!"

Bernardo looked at me and rolled his eyes. "Sorry Jim, but do you think you could move over and give my lady and me a little space here?" *Hm-m-m*, he had just called me his lady. He must have read my mind. Interesting.

Jim giggled, "Your lady. Sorry, I had no idea - she looked free to me." Then, under his breath I heard Jim whisper to Bernardo, "Nice rack." I saw Bernardo shake his head again and turn toward me.

"Sorry, he is a local one here. We try to keep him in check, when possible."

I smiled, "No problem, but shouldn't we at least go on a few dates first before you refer to me as 'your lady.'" I Willow Winked him.

He started to blush a little. "Sorry, I was only trying to save you from what looks like a man overstepping his boundaries."

"Bernardo, I'm kidding. I know you were. Besides, I should give you a little heads up, I like to be sarcastic and break balls a little. Can you handle that?"

He smiled with a little more ease and said, "I got 'ya, just please try to be a little gentle with my balls, that is!" He winked back! I liked this guy. He can dish it back. He ordered a Captain and Coke and for me, another Corona Light.

We toasted one another and he said, "So, how are you really doing, and what brings you to this bar tonight?"

"Well, for starters, my grandma passed last night, but I am doing better than I thought I would be doing. My family is a little numb right now and quiet, but I think we all sort of expected it was coming, just not as quickly as it did. Grandma is at peace, so I believe I can be at peace, too."

He nodded as if he understood and said, "I am sorry for her passing. I felt the same way when my grandmother passed a few years ago. But please continue..........."

I said, "So, to answer your first question, we will see. This will obviously take some time, but my biggest concern is my grandfather right now. She was his whole life. He didn't believe in love including happiness until he found her. They were your classic love story, every little girl's dream."

He interrupted me and said, "You say that in sort of a *you don't believe it yourself* kind of a way." I gave him the confused look and he said, "Willow, do you not believe in that fairytale kind of love, meaning it's possible?"

I tilted my head to the side and found myself saying, "Bernardo, that is a whole other conversation for another time, but to give you the short version, I believe in unconditional love, 'ya know, the kind of love where you love one another no matter what. However, what I don't believe in is thinking that somebody else in going to fill the void."

"Sometimes, I think Walt Disney might have jaded my thinking, and other little girls' concepts, 'ya know the whole prince coming to save me by finding my lost golden slipper? It's not real. Truth is, Bernardo, I don't want a man to save me, I just want a man to love me for who I am. However, I also know that at the end of the day, if you don't have enough love for yourself then it's going to be very difficult to have anything even remotely resembling yes, the storybook kind of love. Does that make sense?"

Out of nowhere, Luke, the sweet custodian, popped into my head with that word *agape. Hm-m-m.* I suddenly realized that I had gone off on one of my tangents - not meaning to, but couldn't help it. Ladies, you totally get it.

He took a swig of his drink and looked like he was thinking about how to respond. I flirtatiously put my red fingernails over his hand, which I then saw were desperately in need of a new manicure, and said, "Sorry, have I over-shared a little too much! Forgive me, my emotions are a bit off balance tonight."

He placed his other hand on top of mine. I felt a little tingle up my arm. He looked me in the eyes and said, "No such thing, Willow - I mean as over-sharing. This is who you are, just be that."

Again, Luke popped in my head. I think I remembered him saying the same thing! I was also thinking that not only is Bernardo completely gorgeous and plays music, but now he was encouraging me to be myself. Nice change of pace for once. Most of the other men I had dated were always trying to make me into something I wasn't.

Getting back to my hot Spanish friend, I smiled and said, "I like your answer about just being me, and to answer the second part of your question of why I am here? I needed to get some air and a good distraction for a little, how does that sound to you?"

I then realized I was feeling a little vulnerable, so I toughened up and said, "But don't get too cocky thinking you were the answer to this cat's meow, if you know what I mean!" Again, I Willow Winked him.

"Willow, I get it, I don't care why you here, I am just glad you are. His eyes met mine for a little longer of a stare, and I felt my knees get weak.

Bernardo looked at me and said, "I have only a half an hour left of my set, what do you say, I play you some of my sweet music and we talk where it is a little more private. I only live two blocks away."

My first reaction was again, *smooth operator taking advantage of a vulnerable woman.* But I found myself thinking back to what my Aunt Ellen asked me a few days ago, "Willow, when was the last time you were kissed or felt......" I suddenly realized if nothing else, oh, my God, this guy could be exactly what I needed just then, at least for that night! Although I still found myself saying, "Bernardo, it sounds tempting."

He stopped me from talking and put his index finger up to my lips and said, "Willow, I am not going to take advantage of you, I just want to get to know you a little. One innocent drink and one song for you, how does that sound?"

What could I say to that? "Maybe, we'll see after I finish this beer. Now go back up on stage and see if you can really reel me in. Play me something good!"

He smiled, "You got it!"

He took one more swig of his drink, kissed my hand, and said, "Don't go anywhere! I will make it worth your while I promise!" I wasn't even sure what to think now. I looked down at my watch; it was 9:30. This is where part of me wished I was not staying with my grandpa. However, being in my early thirties, and feeling guilty about possibly coming in after midnight somehow just felt wrong. I decided to text message Carla to let her know where I am, and to tell Dad or Gramps that she knows the guy I am with and that everything is okay, not to worry. She didn't even text me back, but instead called me right away.

"Hello?" She giggled, "What are you doing?"

"What do you mean?" I retorted.

"Willow, I am all for the fact that you need to get a little, but just be careful will 'ya? Just 'cause Aunt El thinks this guy is okay doesn't mean I trust him. You are also vulnerable right now."

"Carla, relax, I am just going to hang out with him for one lousy drink, and if we make out it wouldn't be so terrible! But, no way is it going further than that."

In the back of my mind, I was contemplating the possibility if it went further, but do not need to share that part with her.

"Okay Willow, but I want immediate details in the morning."

"Whatever, Carla. You are completely making more of this than you need to. There is nothing that I will need to report back to you!"

She giggled, 'Mmm-hmm, I know you better than you think. We will see."

"Okay, Carla, we'll see." We hung up and I went scrounging in my pocketbook for some breath mints for later, 'ya know, just in case. In the background I heard Bernardo speaking into his microphone, "I would like to dedicate this next song to a very special lady. It's an oldie, but goodie, and no, it's not Spanish."

I felt my face getting flushed while he began playing his guitar. He played the coolest version of "Unforgettable" that I had ever heard. Wow, this guy really had talent! Who could take a classic Nat King Cole song and play it the way he does, with his guitar? I was buzzed at this point and becoming butter in those beautiful hands of his.

As he packed up his equipment, I started to have second thoughts about whether or not I should go. I then asked myself, *what is one make-out session going to hurt?*

I saw him walking toward me smiling, "So, did I pass the test, will you have one nightcap with me at my place?"

I smiled, "How did you know that was one of my all-time favorite songs? It reminds me a lot of my other grandpa, on Dad's side - warm memories as a young girl. How did you create that cool version with your guitar?"

"Willow there are a lot of cool things about this guy that you can know more about, but in privacy, not with guys like Jim the drunk around. So, what do you say, one drink?"

I leaned back with that cute hesitation look and said, "Oh, what the hell, but don't try any tricky stuff. I can smell you smooth talker Betty Crockers from a mile away!"

He giggled, "Where does the Betty Crocker part come from?"

"Bernardo, Betty Crocker the cake lady, don't you get it? Cake is my analogy for sweet." He lifted his eyebrow.

I continued, "Sweet talker, now you get it!"

He gave me the *a-ha* look and said, "Okay, sorry it took me a minute to get it, but growing up we didn't have Betty Crocker cake mix out of box. My mama made everything from scratch!" He winked at me and handed me my purse and said, "Shall we?"

"We shall."

We walked up a narrow set of stairs to a cute little studio apartment. To my right hand side, there was a romantic picture of a man playing a guitar next to woman in what looked to be a café. On top of his mantle, there were a few pictures of his family and a beautiful statue of Jesus. To my left side there was a bookshelf, sort of hiding half of his bed, so I guess there could be some privacy. He walked into his kitchen, grabbed a set of matches out of his drawer, and lit a vanilla candle. I liked the simplicity of this place - not too many electronics or expensive showy items.

Bernardo grabbed two light beers out of his fridge, and waved me over to sit next to him on the couch. I felt like a little shy 7th grader whose new boyfriend of the week might try to make out with her for the first time. This little girl is nervous because she's not sure if the grown-up will remember how to kiss. I sat down, took a swig of my beer, and could barely swallow it - it tasted skunked. I didn't want to hurt his feelings, so I swallowed it anyway, but immediately put it down on his coffee table. He realized they were bad, because he took a swig of his and said, "Uch-ch, my beer is bad! Yours?"

I smiled, "Yeah, sorry, didn't want to say anything."

He grabbed both off the table, and said, "I am sorry, and I guess since I don't have a lot of company too often, and rarely drink outside the bar, they got old. What else would you like? I have wine, or tequila?"

I debated but decided *no way* on the tequila because I never got over a horrible experience when I was in 10th grade where I vomited tequila for a day, and wine would have put me too sleep then, so I smiled and said, "How about some water? I think I'm done drinking!"

"No problem!" He threw me a bottle of water and decided not to drink, either. He came back to the couch, grabbed his guitar, and started playing it lightly with his awesome hands. "So, Senorita Willow, what would you like to hear?"

"How about we give you a break since you just played for hours, and tell me a little more about you. I'm already impressed with your guitar playing, so we don't need to do that." I Willow Winked him.

He put the guitar down, and put his hand on my thigh, and said, "Okay, what would you like to know?"

"How about your passions, besides music, what makes you happy?"

He repeated the question back to me, "What makes me happy? Well, being with my family for one. I miss them so much, I try to visit my mama at least twice a year. I wish she would come here to see me, but she has a fear of flying, and it is a *long* trip!"

I nodded my head, this guy was gaining some points, 'ya know, for the love of his mama. He leaned back, "What else? I love watching sunrises, I like to write, I like women with long dark hair and beautiful smiles like yours." His answer felt a little cheesy to me. But I still blushed, and said, "And how many beautiful, long dark-haired women with smiles like mine have been here?"

He scratched his head and said, "Um-m maybe..." He pretended to count on his fingers, and he looked at me, "Sorry, I lost count..." He winked back at me. "Willow, I am not sure how many movies you have seen where the Spanish man is nothing but a suave lover, or what kind of men you have dated in the past that might paint that picture, but I can assure you, this isn't one of them, comprendez?"

"Bernardo, just playing, comprendez?"

"I just want to reassure you I am not out for some, what is it that you guys here call it, some ass?" I giggled. "So, Willow, what about you? What are you passionate about?"

"Me? Well, I am passionate about my nephews, who I adore more than anything else on this planet." He smiled. I continued, "I'm also passionate about poetry, music, and anything creative. Oh, yeah, and I am especially passionate about vanilla ice cream with colored jimmies on top."

He looked at me oddly, "Jimmies?"

"Sorry, I mean sprinkles. Where I come from, that's what we call them. You know the fun rainbow-colored sugar looking things you put on top?"

He said, "Oh, yeah, I love those. So, poetry, huh? I knew there was a deep side to you! Behind those eyes lies a true poet!"

I smirked, "I don't know how deep, Bernardo, but true. Yes, I know I've always been one who felt a lot more comfortable expressing myself on paper rather than with words."

He smiled and said, "I can see that. But you know the mouth can express itself in other ways, not just by talking." He started to lean in slowly. Now I *did* feel like I was in some romantic movie. I decided to surrender to the fantasy. He grabbed one side of my cheek and gently kissed me. I felt my knees get sort of weak. Had to admit, not a bad kisser, and thinking this was just what the doctor ordered, at least for the night! He stopped and took my hand, stood up, and started walking me to his bedroom. Maybe it was the booze, or feeling sad from the loss of Grandma, but I felt like for once I just didn't feel like over-analyzing - should I, shouldn't I, should I? My feet won, because I followed him in. We sat down on the bed. He laid me down, and pulled off my shoes. I had just realized, shit, I didn't shave my legs that day - the day before, but not that day. I hoped I wasn't stubbly. I soon remembered my ex-boyfriend telling me once, that as much as guys make fun of unwanted hair on any parts of our bodies, when it comes down to it, they could care less in the heat of the moment. I finally relaxed, closed my eyes, and let this man play around a little. Soon enough, I felt him ready to undo the pants. I guess the old me kicked in, because before I knew it, I stopped him.

He sat up, "Is something wrong?"

"No, Bernardo, everything is too right. But I have to tell you, as tempting as it is, I will not be sleeping with you."

"Willow, relax. Who said anything about sleeping with me? How about just letting your hair down a little? Okay!"

He pulled the hair clip out of the top of my hair. I lay back down, closed my eyes and allowed him to play a little more. After about a half an hour, we lay next to one another and held hands - no talking, just holding hands. It felt nice. I had not held a man's hand in a while.

I looked at the clock and realized the time. I sat up, "Oh, my gosh, where did the time go? As much as I would love a round two of playing, I need to get home. I know I am grown woman, however something feels weird for me to be out late while staying at my grandfather's, and also that I lost my grandmother this morning."

He looked at me and didn't say anything. "What, did I over-share again?"

He smiled, "No such thing, remember? No, I am just sad because I am wondering when I can see you again. Are you going to go home after the funeral? Will you possibly be sticking around Florida a little bit?"

"Good question," I thought about it. "I don't know yet. My parents really want me to stick around so my grandpa isn't alone, but I'm not sure. Something tells me I will stay for a little for that exact reason. However, I'm a little hesitant because I feel like I have already been escaping reality long enough."

He put his hand over mine and said, "And what have you been escaping from?"

"I don't know. Getting my life together, figuring out what it is I want to do for the rest of my life. You know big picture stuff. Wow, let me stop here and say this is another conversation for another time. I am exhausted and want to get some sleep. Thanks for a fun time. I'll call you and let you know my plans."

"You promise?" he pled.

"I promise."

"At least let me walk you back to your car."

"That, I would appreciate."

He walked me back to my car, kissed me one more time with memorable passion, and I drove home. As I was on my way, I was hoping that nobody would be up. I was definitely not in the mood to explain where I had been.

As I pulled up to the house, I saw that all the lights were off and felt so relieved. I gently walked into the bedroom, praying not to wake up Carla. I took off my clothes in the bathroom so I wouldn't make extra noise - we had to share a room for the night since my parents were in the other guest room.

As I sneaked into bed, I heard her turn over. She looked at me and said, "So, did you get any?"

I sighed and said, "Sorry, did I wake you?"

"What do you think? You know me, I have such sleeping issues, I've been tossing and turning for hours," she sighed.

"Did Mom and Dad ask you anything?"

"I just told them what you told me to tell them - you are with a trusted friend, and you won't be home late. However, according to this clock it is 1:15 a.m., so please fill a sister in."

"Not much to fill in," I retorted.

"Willow, you've got to be kidding me. You have been out for hours, and you are not going to tell me anything? Come on, I am married now, with kids. I get to live these fun adventures through you! So give me something, would 'ya?"

"Alright, again not a big deal. But, if you must know, we went back to his place, talked a little, he kissed me, and I have to admit, he is a pretty good kisser. Then we went into the bedroom. No, we did NOT have sex, it was tempting, but you know I am not a one night stand kind of girl."

"Well, did he get past second base?" she asked.

"Carla, really, you did not just ask me about rounding the bases, what are we in middle school?"

"No, but I am curious."

"Clearly, again, without getting into details, we rounded a couple of the bases, and dabbled a little, but no home run! Good enough description? Are you satisfied with that?"

"For now," she grudgingly replied. "So, when are you going to see him again?"

"I don't know. I told him that I was unsure of my plans for how long I would be staying, but I promised to call him at some point."

"So are you going to call him?" she continued to press.

"I don't know," I mused. "I mean, yeah, it was fun, but I don't feel like complicating anything else in my life right now."

"Willow, for the love of God, will you just for once let yourself have fun and let loose, without analyzing everything you do, or trying to control every behavior? Let loose!"

"Carla, I appreciate what you're saying, and I get it, I know I need to loosen up a little more, but I will call him when I feel like it. Goodnight for now, I'm tired."

"Goodnight."


I woke up at about nine, which was rare for me. I never usually sleep past seven o'clock. I saw that Carla was already out of bed. I washed up and went out into the kitchen. Everyone was sitting at the table eating breakfast. I felt all sorts of stares at me as I walked over to the stove to make a cup of tea.

My father said, "That was some ride around the corner, Willow."

"Dad, I am not sixteen years old anymore, so if you must know, I stopped by this local Spanish café and had a drink with a nice guitarist named Bernardo, that Aunt El can testify is a total gentleman. Is that a good enough explanation for you?" I snapped.

"Willow, relax, I was just being your curious protective Pappa!"

"Dad, it's all good, just a friend."

My mother took a sip of her coffee, "I have heard that before."

I huffed and looked at her, "What is that supposed to mean?"

"*Willow*, relax just playing - we could use a little humor this morning."

I rolled my eyes, "I suppose. Is Grandpa still sleeping?"

Carla answered, "Yeah, I think he was up most of the night. I came out at some point to get a glass of water and noticed his light was on, so I am thinking he will probably sleep in."

I poured myself a bowl of cereal and sat down. "So, what are we going to do today?"

My mom folded down the paper, "We are going to just be here with Grandpa and prepare for tomorrow's service. Have you thought about what you want to say?" she asked.

"I wrote a little something, but I need to make a few changes. I'll fix it up today."

"Sounds good. I'm also going to go through some of Grandma's things, do you want to do it with me?"

"What kinds of things?"

"You know - clothing, pictures, and jewelry, whatever you girls want to take. As long as I am here in Florida, I want to do what I can. I know Grandpa won't be able to do it himself."

"Okay," I agreed.

We spent most of the afternoon going through Grandma's stuff. Carla kept a few purses and a little jewelry. Me, I found two special things that I believe were meant for me to have. One was a cute little poem Grandma had written about birds. And the second gave me chills when I saw it. When my mom opened up Grandma's jewelry box, lying perfectly on top was a dragonfly necklace. I had a flashback of our conversation before she passed away about my telling her that would be the extra sign she would give to let me know she is with me. This was it. I decided to share the story with Carla and my mother. My mom smiled when I told her and said, "There you go, Willow, your first sign." I was thinking *if she only knew.*

I spent an hour in the backyard writing over and over again what I wanted to say about Grandma. I was worried thinking about tomorrow's service and my grandpa's mindset. He had spent most of the day in bed. I wondered if depression had already begun to set in. I also thought about the possibility of his being open to seeing a grief counselor. However, I quickly came back to reality when I remembered he told me he didn't believe much in shrinks anyway. So freaking old school!

Somehow, I must have fallen asleep on the lounge chair, because I was awakened to my cell phone buzzing with a text message. I looked down at my phone, and hit open. *Thinking of you* - Bernardo. I smiled - I had been hoping to get a little something knowing he was thinking of me. I waited about fifteen minutes, of course, to text back. Don't want him to think I was waiting around or anything. I texted back, *sweet*, with one *X* and one *O*. Just a little hug and kiss, very Willowish. Give 'em just a little, but not too much.

In the meantime, as I was sending this text, a huge FedEx truck was pulling up in front of the house next door to us. I couldn't help but think of Will. I smiled again. Another sign? I wondered how he was doing, but I was not ready to call him. I had to admit to myself that it was kind of nice to have some fun potential with two men. However, I also wondered if I should even bother calling Will now, knowing that I was probably going to be staying here. Why start something? I shook my head at myself and *thought this is ridiculous*. Who cares about men right now? Your grandpa needs you.

I got up and went inside and checked on him. I couldn't believe he was still in bed! I looked down at my watch. It was 4:32 p.m. I saw my mom painting her nails at the kitchen table. "Mom, has anybody checked on Grandpa?"

"Yeah, he came out for a few minutes to get a glass of water, but went right back to bed. I asked him a hundred times if he needs anything, and he said, "No," and said that he wanted to be left alone for the rest of the day.

"Willow, you know I have to let it go for today, and give him his space to be crabby and sad. This is how your grandpa deals with things," she explained.

"I know, I just hate to see him like that."

"We all do, honey. Did you finish what you want to say for Grandma?"

"I did, I think she will be pleased. You know I believe she will be there tomorrow in spirit."

"Yes, Willow, I know how much you believe in this, so maybe," she conceded.

"No, Mom," I was definite, "Not maybe, she will."

I could tell my mom wanted to say more, but didn't want to start a heated debate on whether or not there was life after death. "Okay, Willow, then yes, she will love it and who knows, maybe you will see your dragonfly?"

"Now we're talking, Mom." I Willow Winked her.

# Chapter 6

THE NEXT MORNING WE ALL woke up fairly early to get ready for the service. I made extra coffee knowing that we would all need a little extra pick-me-up. My grandpa was so quiet, and his eyes were super puffy. I looked down at his big black clunky Grandpa shoes and noticed he was wearing two different colored socks. I didn't have the heart to tell him to change them, so I let it go. However, I did smile thinking that if Grandma Lu saw them she would say, "Schmucko, you got two different socks on."

We all hopped in the car, and didn't say a word on the way to the gravesite. As we pulled up, I felt a lump in my throat. I grabbed my grandpa's hand as he got out. I looked him in the eyes, and I squeezed his hand and said, "Gramps, it's going to be okay, I promise, Grandma is going to a good place."

He kissed my forehead and says, "I know love, I know."

We walked over to the big, deep whole with the big, deep shovel. I saw my Aunt Ellen, and a few of my grandma's old friends who flew out for the service, and a couple of local ones, too. The rabbi said what he needed to and then asked if anyone would like to say something. I felt my father's hand on my shoulder and another lump form in my throat. I told myself that I was not going to cry no matter what, and I would get through it.

So, I pulled myself together, and said, "I always told my grandma that I knew the sweetest part of me came from her! My Grandma Lu was one of a kind. Grandma taught me the true meaning of unconditional love and how to be a better person. Her positive attitude toward life was magnetic. Everywhere we would go together, she would always have a light around her. People, even strangers, would naturally gravitate to her. She always had a way of making me, and others, feel good about themselves. I am so grateful for the memories of the times growing up I spent with her and my grandpa. She made all the moments spent with her filled with fun and laughter, and again, her love! But most importantly, moving forward, I am especially grateful to have witnessed the love she gave my grandpa, and Grandpa, the love you gave her - true role models when it comes to devotion and unconditional love. I truly feel I am the luckiest granddaughter on earth to have had my Grandma Lu, and will forever keep her close to my heart and soul. I love you, Grandma!"

I could hear lots of tears around me, especially my grandpa's. I felt him take my hand and squeeze it. Her best friend, Constance, said a few sweet words as well. Constance and she lived next door to one another when they lived in New York. When Constance and her husband decided to move to Florida, Grandma thought it would be a great idea as well! At first, Grandpa Lex was against the idea, but he knew how inseparable the two of them were, and that the long winters in New York really did suck. Besides, being close to her best friend is what made Grandma happy, and that's all Grandpa ever wanted.

As we were walking from the gravesite back to our cars, a large, flappy, buzzy thing started to make circles around our car. I felt my heart melt, and my mom and sister stopped in their tracks when they saw it. I saw my mother put her hand over her mouth, and my sister Carla smiled at me.

My dad looked puzzled and said, "What, ladies, what is it?"

I pointed over to the car. My father gave me the *yeah, so?* look and said, "What am I looking at - the large dragonfly going around and around?"

I looked him right in the eyes. "Yes, Dad, that is exactly what we are looking at. I asked Grandma before she passed away, if she would send me a dragonfly to let me know she is in a good place."

My grandfather looked perplexed, but smiled anyway. My father said, "Hm-m-m, interesting coincidence? Maybe, just maybe."

My mom said, "Thanks, love, sorry if I ever doubted your whole sign thing before, because I believe it now!" I smiled.

We got into the car and our beauty flew away. I debated telling them about the whole red cardinal thing, but Carla beat me to it, on the car ride home. She told them the whole story about our experiences over the last two weeks. Both of my parents were sort of confused, but a little more receptive than before.

My grandpa was completely silent through the whole thing. I finally looked over at him and asked, "So, Gramp, what do you think of all of this?"

"Willow, love, I don't have an answer, and as much as I would love to believe in all of this stuff, it's really hard for me. You know, the last few years I have come to question God, and all sorts of other things, since your grandma went through everything she did. I wondered a lot that if there was a God, then how could he let my beautiful wife go through what she did?"

"Gramp, I understand what you are asking, but I believe that because Grandma Lu was an exceptional woman and lived and exceptional life, that she was okay with it even until the end. You see, Gramp, even though she may have come in and out of her dementia, she always, always, had the same incredible loving and open heart. I also think that she may have actually been better than we thought at times, meaning it was harder for us than her. Anyway, I believe that no matter what, God and Grandma wanted us to remember her beautiful heart and continue to know that she will be loved, and she in turn will continue to love and protect us."

My mother said, "Willow, honey, I think that is a good answer, and Dad, I think your granddaughter is smarter than we think!"

He sat back and crossed his leg, "Ladies, I love you for trying to help me see alternatives, but this will take more than flying insects or birds to make me think otherwise." He was steadfast.

My mother sighed and said, "Fair enough, Dad, fair enough."

# Chapter 7

WE SPENT THE NEXT TWO days taking care of basic things. Carla left early the third morning to head back to be with my nephews. My parents were leaving sometime that same night, and I was a little worried about being alone with Grandpa. I decided to take a walk by the lake not too far from his condo. I wondered what I was going to do here in Florida. Carla had mentioned to me while she was here that I should consider getting a part time job. I felt my belly rumbling and guilt burping itself up through my system, just thinking about it. You see, I sort of always carried this fear that if I did not do what it was I thought God wanted me to do, that I would keep suffering somehow. I knew in the back of this annoying mind that it really is a very fatalistic attitude, but I have always struggled with believing in free will. Don't know why, just have. I remembered briefly after college that I had read this incredible book called _Conversations With God_, by Neale Donald Walsch. It's about a man who went through many struggles in his life. After years of being fed up about what to do with his pain, he one day decided to write God a letter. Would you believe me if I told you that God responded to him, and not just in one book? He has written many more which have validated that God is a loving God no matter what we decide to do. Religion and authoritative figures in our lives have somehow tried to prove otherwise, but God is trying to show us, and tell us, another truth every day. This book helped me through a lot of illusions I had created and helped to reassure me, that we do indeed have free will. I still, sometimes in moments of questioning, seem to come back to it. It has become my spiritual handbook.

As I started to pick up the pace around the lake, I began to think that maybe for once I was exactly where I was supposed to be - spending time to help heal my grandpa's pain and learn more about myself, outside of everyone's judgments back home. Then, out of nowhere, that word Agape popped back into my head! And, for the first time, I thought about unconditional love for myself *not* in relation to another. *Hm-m-m.* This was starting to make a little more sense. God loving me, and me loving myself all at the same time. That would be a nice thought to start holding onto. As I was in deep thought, my text message went off again and I somehow knew it would be Bernardo.

I looked down, *How are you doing?*

I texted back, *Hanging in thanks, how r u?*

He responded, *Okay, but wishing I was looking into those pretty eyes.*

I smiled and texted back, *Cute!*

He then wrote, *So, can I catch a glimpse of them soon?*

For a second, I debated if I should play it cool and make him wait, but then I realized that I don't know anybody around here besides Grandpa and Aunt El. It might be nice spending time with people closer to my age, especially hot Spanish men.

I texted back, *How about tomorrow?*

He responded, *Perfect, how about you come over, I will make you one of Mama's special recipes?*

I texted back, *Sold, just not too spicy, I might want to save these lips for something later!* I know what you are thinking, that I am such a flirt. That's what Carla always liked to tease me about, well actually, she always liked to call me a tease. Hey, the way I see it, a girl gets to play just as much as the boys do.

He texted me back, *Cute and I hope so!*

I replied, *If you're lucky, and what can I bring?*

He texted back, *I will be lucky, and how about a bottle of red and be here by 7:00.*

I answered, *Got it, see 'ya then.*

When I get back to the house, I saw my mom and dad had their bags packed and were ready to go. My mom asked to speak to me, so she pulled me aside outside. We sat on the bench out in the backyard.

She said, "Willow, honey, I know your grandpa can be difficult at times, but try to be as patient with him as possible."

I rolled my eyes, as if I didn't already know this.

"You don't have to roll your eyes at me, I know you know. I am just reminding you in case you might get a little more frustrated than usual. I also know you know how hard it is to get your grandfather to want to do anything, so all you can do is offer to get him out a little, whether it's to the movies, dinner, park, whatever, just try your best!"

I nodded, "Mom, I know how to take care of Grandpa, you don't have to worry."

"Willow, I'm not worried, I just know you will also need time for yourself, so don't feel like you have to baby sit him all day, either. Maybe you'll want to get a part time something to fill that space."

"I know," I replied. "I thought about it, I'm having dinner tomorrow night with Bernardo, and maybe he could get me a part time job at the Spanish restaurant he works at, or knows somebody who can hook me up, or even Aunt El - you know she knows everybody."

My mom smirked, "Bernardo, huh? I guess you won't be calling that nice Jewish guy you met from the airplane anytime soon?"

"Mom, give me a break would 'ya? Besides, now that I'm hanging here for who knows how long, I'm not sure about calling him anytime soon. But again, I will let you know if and when I do."

"In the meantime, let your daughter have a little fun with, yes, Bernardo. I haven't been in the company of a man in a dating fashion besides Tom for over four years. Now is the time for me to have me time. Comprendez?"

She smiled and said, "Yes, Willow, I got it." She knew not to push too much.

My parents left around six o'clock, and I told Grandpa I was running out to get us a pizza for tonight because I didn't feel like cooking. He said he had no appetite, but didn't care what I got as long as his half of the pizza was plain only. Everything he eats is usually PLAIN only, unless I cooked for him and didn't tell him all of the ingredients I used. Grandma Lu always said his appetite was "boring." So, of course I told him I was getting extra anchovies on top just to tease him. He barely cracked a smile, but I knew he knew I was trying to cheer him up.

When I got home I saw that he had opened up a bottle of red wine, which was already half-way done. Grandpa barely drinks, although I knew he probably wanted to numb out a little. I was pleased that he had at least set the table.

"Hi, Gramps, I have our pizza and Caesar salad!"

"Willow, if I even see one of your creepy toppings touching my side of the pie I won't eat it!" He was immovable.

"Gramp, like I told you, I told them not only to put extra anchovies on top, but extra spinach - your other favorite."

He waved me over. "Come, sit down and have a glass of wine with your grandpa tonight!"

"Sounds good, but take it easy, Gramps, you're on some medication that may not mix well with alcohol."

"Oh, Willow, don't worry about me. I am drinking this wine to help me sleep tonight. I have not slept well at all the past two nights," he explained.

"Okay, well, why don't you try a mild sleeping pill instead?"

"Willow, you know me better than that! Alright, let's change the subject. What's this I hear about you meeting up with a hot Spanish guy?"

"Oh, Gramp. No biggie, Aunt El introduced me to him when Carla and I went out for dinner with her a few nights ago." Why did I feel like I had to defend myself?

"Willow, honey, you know better than to ever get involved with someone your Aunt El is trying to set you up with." He winked at me.

"Ha, ha! Everyone needs to chill. He is nice guy, who is here right now, and I could use some male company besides you. No offense, Gramps, not that I don't love being with you, it's just that it's been so long since I hung out with a guy who wasn't Tom." I really did want him to understand.

"Willow, honey, I know. I am just teasing."

"I know gramps and I love ya for it!"

"So, I have a quick question, Grandpa. I was going to have dinner out tomorrow night with Bernardo, would you be okay with that? I mean, I don't want you to be by yourself, but I figured we would spend most of the day together. Knowing you, you will be sick of me by afternoon and could use the break. I'm going to go food shopping again and make sure you have something to eat for dinner, anyway."

"Willow, honey, I want you to do whatever you want to do while you are here. Don't feel like you have to baby sit or check in with me every two seconds. I am just grateful you are here!"

"Okay, just let me know whatever I can do," I replied.

"Thanks, love. For now, toast your Grandpa with one more glass of wine."

We ended up finishing the bottle and watching reruns of "All in The Family" on the couch. It was nice to see my grandpa laugh a little again, even if was to Archie Bunker.

# Chapter 8

I STOPPED AND PICKED UP a nice bottle of Spanish wine upon recommendation from the sales clerk. I was hoping to impress Bernardo with my wine taste. As I pulled up to his apartment, I felt my heart start to beat a little quicker and my hands got clammy. I pulled down the little mirror on the driver's side, did one last check of my teeth, popped peppermint gum in my mouth, fixed my cleavage, adjusted my lip gloss, quickly spritzed some of my vanilla body mist, and out of the car I went.

I walked up the stairs and heard Santana playing in the background. I was trying to remember if, when I was buzzed, I told Bernardo how much I love Santana's music. As I knocked on his door, I smelled incredible aromas coming out from underneath his front door. The music was sort of loud, so I knocked again assuming he didn't hear me. He opened up the door with this incredible smile and beautiful white linen shirt, which showed off his naturally bronzed skin.

"Hola, beautiful, how are you this evening?" He wrapped his hand around my waist and pulled me into him close. He kissed me right on the mouth. He must have been sampling something before I walked in because he tasted like hot peppers, sweet hot peppers, but yummy.

"I'm good, how are you?"

"Bien, now that you are here."

"Bernardo," I swooned, "If the smells coming from outside of this apartment are the foreshadowing to an awesome home-cooked meal, I am psyched."

"You should be, Mama taught me well."

I smiled. I handed him the bottle of wine, a little nervous hoping it was the right pick. I saw him staring at the bottle, smiling.

I said, "Well, did I get a decent one or garbage? Blame the quirky wanna-be wine snob who helped me at the store."

"No, Willow, it's perfect. I love this kind. I have had this many times with family dinners back home."

"Awesome, so let's open it up and let me try it."

He grabbed two wine glasses. "Make yourself comfortable, dinner will be ready in about fifteen minutes."

I sat on the couch, and yelled across, "Do you want some help?"

"No, no, Willow. Tonight is for you. I just want you to relax and enjoy. I know you have probably had a few stressful days. Speaking of which, how is your family doing, especially your grandpa?"

I realized, before I responded, that I had yet to tell Bernardo my full plans for sticking around. I guess part of me didn't want him to think he might have something to do with it, and the other part of me wanted to not give a crap what he thought, and I knew he might be able to hook me up with a part-time job.

I decided to hold off on details. "My family is hanging in, thanks. They all left yesterday. It's just Grandpa and me for now."

He smiled and said, "Oh, yeah, and how long will Willow be sticking around in Florida?"

*Geez,* I was thinking, *so much for putting this conversation off, way to get right into it.* "Um-m-m, Bernardo, that remains to be determined. I'm not sure yet. At least for a couple of weeks."

He lit up, "Really, you mean I might actually get a second, maybe a third date if I am lucky, as you put it?"

"Yeah, if you are lucky, but let's get through the first, and we will see." I Willow Winked him.

"Ouch," he said.

"Bernardo, did I mention that I love Santana?" I changed the subject.

"You might have mentioned it in conversation. Carlos is one of my idols, he always has been. When he plays that guitar, the whole universe is listening. I try and play like him sometimes."

I smiled, "I couldn't agree more, and you imitate him pretty well!"

He lit a candle and placed it on his cute little round table. I took a sip of my wine. "Yum, this wine is good."

"Told 'ya."

He waved me over to come sit down. He brought over what looked like a delicious salad and some hot rolls. He lifted his glass to mine. "Cheers to a relaxing evening in the company of a beautiful soul."

"Bernardo, I like your toast. You, too. So, what are we having this evening?"

"Well, Willow, first we have a delicious salad with chickpeas, sliced almonds, roasted peppers, and Mama's homemade dressing. We will also be having an awesome dish my mother made up - sort of like a paella, but it's baked. It's chicken, mushrooms, sausage, asparagus, and rice, again with a homemade sauce. I also have chickpea potato pancakes."

"Bernardo, this all sounds fantastic." Meanwhile, I was thinking *Oh shit, I hope I don't get the toots, chick peas always seem to do that to me,* and I am also thinking *Did I remember to throw a roll of Tums in my purse?*

Each course was more delicious than the next. I especially loved the chickpea potato pancakes. They reminded me a little of the ones Grandma Lu used to make growing up, but we called them latkas. She always served them with applesauce, too.

I looked over at Bernardo, who downed the last sip of wine from his glass and said to me, "So, what do you think?"

"Doesn't my plate say it all?"

Next thing I knew, I heard one of my favorite Santana slow songs come on. "Oh, Bernardo, this is one of my favorites, sad, but so good."

He reached his hand across the table, stood up, and said, "Shall we?"

"What? Dance right here, right now?"

"Why not, Willow, live a little."

This guy was good. I figured what the heck. I was buzzed enough that even if I tripped on him, I knew he wouldn't let me fall. I stood up, and nuzzled my way into his chest. I could feel the heat coming off him. I was feeling flushed as I felt his cheek subtly pressing up against mine. He smelled really good, too. I know some women think cologne is cheesy, but I have always found it sexy in a way as it heightens my senses, unless, of course he has used the whole bottle. Not Bernardo though, he had just the right amount on.

The song came to an end and he gave me a cute dip. "So, would you like dessert, or do you need a break?"

"I think I am full and need a little break. Let's retire to the couch and digest a little."

"Sounds good, should I open up another bottle of wine?"

"Um-m, why not? You trying to get me drunk, Bernardo?"

"Drunk NO, relaxed enough, yes!"

He leaned back on the coach, kicked off his flip flops, placed his hand on my knee, and said, "So, what else should I know about Willow?"

"Well, what else do you want to know about me?"

"Well, if you could spend one day anywhere in the world where would that be?" he asked.

"That's easy," I answered right away, "Tuscany. I've always been fascinated by the Italian culture, and every time I look at pictures or see videos of the country, I envision myself coming alive on all levels."

He smiled, "Tuscany is beautiful. I was fortunate to have been there when I was in my mid-twenties. An ex- of mine and I went on a romantic getaway for a long weekend."

I made a sarcastic smile, "Oh, really? My turn to ask, since I haven't yet - has Bernardo ever really been in love, and if so, who was she?"

I saw him prop up and flinch a little, "Are you sure you want me to answer that? It could take a little while."

"Um-m-m, yeah I want to know, and you don't have to get into every gory detail, just be real about it."

"Okay, to answer your question, yes, I have been in love twice. The first was my first love, Annabella. I was eighteen; she lived two houses over from me. We grew up in the same neighborhood. We were flirty friends who finally admitted our mutual crushes to one another one night when we drank at a party. We had a good relationship for about two years. It ended when she moved to Brazil to be with her real mother, who got sick. Long distance can be way too hard, especially at that age."

I shook my head as in *yes, I got it!*

"So, that is the story with numero uno, as for numero dos, well this was a complicated one. If we are having an honest talk, I was engaged to her."

My eyes opened a little wider, "Engaged?"

"Yes. Her name was Mya. We met at one of the clubs I was bartending at in Barcelona at the time. She was a model and aspiring actress."

Meanwhile, I was thinking in the back of my mind that she probably looked like Gisele or that hot Victoria Secret model, Adriana. So I came right out and said, "Let me guess, smoking hot!"

He didn't hesitate and said, "Yes, but looks can only take you so far. Anyway, it was a very passionate relationship."

*They probably had lots of sex, I'm sure.* I tried to put my mid-twenties insecure comparing mind aside and listen.

I smiled to myself and let him finish his story.

"Mya and I had a lot of fun, but she did not do a very good job managing her drinking and, yes, drug habit. I tried for a while to support her addictions, but it started to get old for me pretty fast. Besides, cleaning up vomit or holding her hair after rough nights got old quick. I know she had a tough upbringing, and I think I was trying to save her on some levels. You know what is it they say in psychology, that maybe I was trying to be the father figure she never quite had. Who knows? All I know was I could not save her from her pain.

"And the official ending of our relationship was when I found her lying to me about a relationship she had begun with a photographer. I always had a feeling this guy had a thing for her, but I tried to tell myself it was just a cliché, 'ya know, photographer hitting on model? Well, unfortunately I was right. She claimed she never cheated, but I walked in on a photo shoot once where I saw him adjusting her bikini in a way that …"

He paused and I could see him getting upset, like he was reliving the story. I put my hand on top of his.

"Bernardo, you don't have to say another word, I got your point, and I am sorry, and I know the conclusion of this story is that it all came down to trust, right? You couldn't trust the woman you were with, aside from all of the other baggage."

He squeezed my hand, "So, you are right and I called off the engagement. Last I heard she was living with some older sugar daddy producer type. Oh well, odious to that one!" Part of me could tell he was still a little bitter, but I appreciated his honesty.

He leaned back again, "So, what do you say we change the subject?"

"Okay, what would you like to talk about?"

"Actually, I was thinking we have done way too much talking tonight, and it might be time to not talk and for me to …"

He took his one hand and cupped it on my face and kissed me. I let him kiss me passionately, and next thing I knew he picked me up and carried me into the bedroom. He gently lay me down on the bed. One by one, he slipped off each article of clothing. He looked me in my eyes, and said something in Spanish, which at the moment made me wish I had taken that language instead of French in college so I could understand.

I squinted my eyes and said, "What did you say?"

He said, "I said that you are so beautiful and I feel lucky to have met you."

I smiled but didn't say a word, and kissed him. Whether or not this guy was throwing me a line, I didn't care. I wanted to be with him, and for once, I did not want to analyze the consequences of how I would feel afterward, if I slept with him. I am proud to say that I can count on both hands, even less, how many guys I have slept with. I was never your one night stand kind of a girl, and I knew this was going to be out of character for me, but I told myself I was going to give myself permission to let go.

He looked at me, opened his drawer next to his bed, pulled out a condom, and said, "I want to feel all of you and make you smile again, and for you to feel passion again, let me give you that!"

It felt a little "dirty Hallmark" to me, but in the moment, I decided to let go. For an uptight girl, I was happy to share that Bernardo was everything and more. He did not disappoint, and I did have fun!

I lay there for a little while and looked over at the clock and saw that it was after one a.m. I knew Grandpa would be sleeping, but I wanted to get home anyway and just be in my own bed. I saw that Bernardo had fallen asleep. I gently got up put my clothes on. As I put my shoes back on, I must have awakened him up.

He sat up in bed, "Going so soon?"

"Oops, sorry I woke you. I was trying to be quiet."

"Miss Willow you were not going to try to sneak out of here, were you?"

"Bernardo, not without kissing you goodbye first. I had a lot of fun. Dinner was fantastic and dessert was even better, so thank you!" I Willow Winked him on that one.

He placed his hand on top of mine, "You're welcome, even though you never got to actually try my dessert, which means you will have to let me cook for you again."

I smiled, "If you're lucky!"

He pulled me close, kissed me again, and said, "I am lucky to have met you. On another topic - so, I was thinking, do you need a part time job?" He must have been reading my mind. He said, "You know I might be able to see if you could get a part time serving job at Tina's, where I work. I also have a friend though, who runs an awesome breakfast joint, if you would prefer morning hours."

"Bernardo, that is so sweet. Thanks. I am not sure what I want to do, but I was thinking I wanted to get a part-time something, so could you inquire about both places for me? I would appreciate it."

"You got it, bella!"

We kissed goodnight one last time. He walked me down to my car and we said goodnight. On the car ride home I had to remind myself that I had fun and I'm *not* a slut.

I woke up the next morning. I had bizarre dreams about my ex-boyfriend and Mystery Man from the airplane, not together, but notable that I was interacting with them both. Part of me felt badly that I never called the sweet guy from the airplane, but again, back burner for now.

I walked out from the bedroom and saw Grandpa was already up drinking his coffee, and of course, reading his *NY Times*.

He looked up, "So, how was it? Can he really cook a good meal or was he full of burritos - I mean bologna?"

" Ha-ha! Good morning, Grandpa. Yeah, it was incredible."

He smiled at me, "I see, and I also see you are glowing, he must have fed you well!" He winked at me.

"Ee-w-w, Gramp, please. He made me a delish dinner and we talked. That's all." Yeah right!

"Well, Willow, that must have been some conversation that got you home almost two a.m."

"You were up? I thought for sure you were sleeping."

"Willow, love, you know my sleeping is so crappy the last few days.

Besides, I don't care what time you get in as long as you get in. I am not sure how I am going to feel about you sleeping out yet. I know you are a grown woman, but give me a little time." He was having trouble with this one.

"Grandpa, you don't have to worry, okay? Even if it is in the middle of the night, I will come home. I won't leave you alone yet!"

He smiled. "So, did you ask Mr. hot tamale about a part time job?"

"I did, and he is going to see if there is an opening at his place or a serving position at a friend's breakfast joint, which feels a lot more like me anyway!"

"Good. So Willow, I was thinking today we might go out and get me a bike."

I raised my head, "What did you just say? A bike? I have never heard you interested in riding before. You don't really like to do any exercise, sorry to say, but you know I am right."

"I know, I know, Willow, but I was up last night thinking that your grandmother was always trying to get me to do something healthy like ride a bike. Besides, up until a few years ago, she always loved to ride! Her bike is still sitting in the garage. I was thinking maybe you and I could ride around a little. Obviously, I won't be like what's his name Lance something, but I can go slow. I know I am eighty-plus something years old, but I would like to try it. If I was able to use the fitness center ones, I am pretty sure I can use the regular."

"Armstrong, Gramps, Lance Armstrong, and of course you won't go fast, but it will be good to get you in a little shape. Fantastic idea, let's do it! We just want to make sure we find you one that has a comfortable seat for your tooshie. You know they can sometimes be really uncomfortable you know where."

"Gotcha, you don't have to get detailed. I saw an ad for some sales. We can go after breakfast. Speaking of, you wouldn't happen to be in the mood to make your grandpa one of your famous omelets, would 'ya?" he implored.

"You don't even have to ask twice. Coming right up! So, listen, I was also thinking that as long as we're out, that it might be time to invest in a new computer. In this day and age, this is how the whole world works. You would be amazed at how much you can look up. Besides, you can finally finish reading your *New York Times* on line. More importantly, email is how I stay in touch with my friends, so I sort of need one anyway. Dad already told me he would pay for it. I need a new laptop. It's my early birthday present. So, what do you think?"

He sighed, "Willow, I don't need the computer, but for you, love, we will get it. I know I can always cancel what do you call it? Internet something connection when we actually move."

"Thanks, you are the best, Grandpa! I'll call the local cable company to see if they can come over tomorrow and maybe set up".

I was elated to think of the idea of his getting outside and not being completely bottled up in this house, and the possibility of his actually working on a computer.

We found great deals on both a computer and a new bike for Grandpa. You should have seen my grandpa riding around the store testing it out! If Grandma Lu had been here now to see it, she would have cracked up. Although something told me she was watching us from up above, giggling in her own way!

Grandpa said he wanted to go for a bike ride as soon as we got home to really test it out around his complex. We put some extra air in Grandma's tires, and the two of us headed out. I was pretty impressed that he was able to move the way he did. I told him we should go slowly for the first round, not to over-do the first day. He agreed, and we headed back toward home.

I looked down at my watch, it's after three p.m. I was hoping to have heard from Bernardo by now about the potential job, and of course, to tell me he was thinking of me. No sign of either. I knew I could call him, but my rule was, in the beginning, let them call first.

He must have sensed my longing, because at twenty after three, my phone rang. Yes!

"Hello."

"Hello, Willow, it's Bernardo. How are you this afternoon?"

"I'm well, Bernardo. What's cooking with you?"

"Well, I have some good news. I told my friend Robert about you and your experience, and how cute you were. He said he would love to meet you. Any chance you are free tomorrow afternoon to meet with him? This is the friend who runs the breakfast place. It's called Dotty's, named after his grandma, who used to run it before she passed."

Oh-h-h, another sign, perhaps. My father's mother's name was Dotty - well Dorothy, but Dotty for short.

"Bernardo, I appreciate you setting this up, and I like how you threw in the whole how cute I am."

He giggled, "Did I say cute? I mean beautiful."

"Nice, thank you."

"He said to come any time after two o'clock because it dies down then. They are open from seven a.m. until three every day. So, if this is a go, I hope you don't mind getting up early. I should also mention that he doesn't have many shifts free, but could at least give you a couple days a week. I will text you the address so you can Map Quest how to get there" he offered.

"I prefer getting up early, and Bernardo, as I mentioned, I am not picky so whatever he has, I will work with it. This is awesome. Thanks again."

"You're welcome, and you know, you could really thank me by stopping by the restaurant tomorrow night, because I am playing and would love to see your pretty face."

"Mm-hm, we will see."

"Ah, Willow, give me something to look forward to" he pleaded.

"Come on, Bernardo, there always has to be a little mystery, right?"

"Willow, I don't need a mystery, I need to see your smile."

"I'll do my best, Bernardo. I'll call you, regardless."

"Sounds good. Adios, beautiful."

"Bye."

Thank God I had bought a computer and had been able to get someone to come out to hook up the Internet in our house this morning. I saw my grandpa walk by a few times, watching me mess around, with curious eyes.

"Grandpa, you can come play. It's not going to bite you, I promise! Come here, I will show you the *New York Times* website. You'll love it."

He stood over my shoulder in amazement. Next thing I knew, he sat down next to me and started clicking away.

"See? I told you you'd like it." He smiled because he knew I was right.

"Alright, Gramps, I have got to get ready for my meeting with the guy at the breakfast joint. Do you want me to make you something before I go?"

He was completely distracted by the computer, "No, honey. Go ahead, I will make something for myself. Besides, I might be busy playing on this new toy."

# Chapter 9

I PULLED UP TO THE breakfast place and walked in and it immediately reminded me of the place where I was waitressing in Philly. Just the right amount of tables. It smelled like a mixture of chocolate and banana pancakes with French - fried something. My mouth was watering.

I saw a young waitress walking over toward me, hocking away on a piece of bubble gum, with jet black hair pulled into a pony tail, bright red lipstick, and black fingernails. Her nametag said Brenda. I smiled, but she did not.

"You must be Wilma."

"Ah, actually it's Willow."

I went to reach out my hand to shake hers, but she looked at me like I had two heads. Right away, I was thinking *this is a classic misfit girl who is probably still angry with her parents for God knows what, and hates cheerleaders or any type of stereotypical girlie stuff.* I knew this type - they had always tried to bully me when I was younger in school, but because of my genuine nature, I could always make them see me for me, and not assume I was a snobby princess.

This will be a tough nut to crack, but I am on to it. She looked me up and down and said, "Whatever. Wilma, Willow. I'll go get Robert. Wait here."

I saw this nice, tall man behind the grill smile and wave me over. Ah, a friendly face! I walked over.

He introduced himself, "Hi, I'm Devin."

"Hi, Devin, I'm Willow, nice to meet you."

"Nice to meet you - what a lovely name. You gonna work here?" he asked.

"I hope so, although I'm not sure how welcome I might be." I nodded my head over toward where Brenda walked.

He giggled, "Oh, please don't pay her any mind. She's always bitchy, and gets jealous of new waitresses, especially pretty new waitresses. She's probably afraid you will take away her tables or something."

"Well, Devin, I've worked in the industry myself, and I'm not catty like that at all. I'm fair as anyone else."

He flipped a pancake and said, "Like I said, it's all good, Willow. She will warm up eventually."

"Thanks, Devin."

I saw who I was assuming was Robert, walking over toward me. He was a handsome older man with grey hair and a tan, weathered face. He looked as though he might have been a fisherman on a boat most of his life.

He smiled and put out his hand, "You must be Willow. Bernardo has said lots of nice things about you. Here, come sit down and tell me a little about you."

"Well, as I'm sure Bernardo has mentioned, I have been a server on and off for the last few years at a local breakfast place outside Philadelphia. I am super friendly with customers, and I work very fast and as efficiently as possible. I am definitely into making sure customers are happy. Where I worked, we had a lot of locals and we were like family."

He smiled, "Sounds a lot like this place."

I was surprised as I was trying to figure out where the Brenda family part falls into place.

He pulled out a calendar, "So, Willow, as Bernardo probably told you, I don't have a ton of shifts, but my daughter, Eliza, is about to go back to school next week. You will meet her, so I could probably give you three shifts to start, and we will see how it goes. How does that sound?"

"Well, Robert, that sounds fantastic! I really appreciate your giving me a shot."

"Anything for my friend, Bernardo. He's a great guy, hell of a guitar player, too."

I smiled, "Tell me about it!"

"So, Willow, I'd like you to come into tomorrow for a few hours to shadow my daughter and get a feel for how we run things around here." I nodded. "So why don't you come by after the rush, which will be about ten a.m. and you can train a little? Do you have any questions for me? As for dress code, just wear jeans and any plain-colored top, and of course, make sure you wear your hair pulled back.

"I'm sure you were also curious about pay. You make $3.50 an hour and anything else - your tips are yours to have. Since you don't know how long you are going to be here, I will probably pay you under the table. I hope you're okay with that."

"I'm completely fine with that, and thanks again."

We shook hands. As I was walking out I saw Devin waving toward me.

"Bye, Willow, see 'ya soon right?"

"Yes, Devin, tomorrow as a matter of fact. I'm going to be training with his daughter, Eliza."

"Cool," he said, "see 'ya then."

As I left, I could feel Brenda's eyes piercing through the back of my head.

On my way home, I decided to pick up stuff for my grandpa and me to have for dinner. I also knew in the back of my mind that I definitely wanted to stop by and see Bernardo to say hello for a little bit. I pulled into the grocery store parking lot and noticed that a car parked next to me said 'AGAPE' on the license plate. I smiled and said *okay, God, I am paying attention.* I immediately thought of Lucas and that word. What are the chances I was seeing it on a plate? Unconditional love.

I picked up my groceries, and for some reason felt compelled to stop by the facility where Grandma Lu had been to say a quick hello to Lucas, and tell him what I had seen. I wasn't even sure he was working, but figured I would give it a shot. I pulled in, and the feeling in my stomach dropped a little as I'd not been back, nor intended to go back, since Grandma had passed. I walked in and went up and down the halls looking for him. I saw a man standing with his back toward me, plugging in some sort of monitor in a room. It looked like the back of Lucas's head.

"Lucas, is that you?"

"Hey, darling, what are you doing here?"

"Luke, believe it or not, I came to see you. I had to share something with you that I thought you would appreciate."

"Well, I am thrilled you are here! What is it, darling?"

"Luke, I just went to the grocery store to pick up some stuff for grandpa and me. Would you believe me if I told you the car parked next to mine had a license plate that said 'AGAPE'?"

He leaned his head to the side and gave his staple cute, crooked-toothed smile, "Well, Miss Willow, I would say yes, indeed I do believe it, and I do believe it was meant for you to see. You are being given a message, sweetheart, that you need to start thinking more about. When my wife first introduced me to that word, I started to get signs that I was meant to see it, too. One time, I was waiting by the bus stop, and there was an advertisement for a new book written about it, just sitting on the bench. Imagine that, right?" He winked at me.

"I got you, Luke, I just wanted to share."

"Glad you did, honey, so how are you and your family doing?" he asked.

"We are actually doing fairly well. My parents and sister left already, and I've decided to stick around for a little with Grandpa.

Not sure how long, but for a while until he's ready to make the move back to Philadelphia where I am from."

"Oh-h-h, glad to hear you are gonna stick around. I hope you will stop by a little more. You know, I love the old folks here, but it is always nice to see a young, pretty face like you once in a while."

"You got it, Luke. I better get back. I have groceries sitting in the car and don't want Grandpa's ice cream to melt on me. He is not a happy camper when that happens."

"Okay, honey. Don't be a stranger, come see me soon!"

"Will do Luke," I promised.


I made a quick dinner for Grandpa and me, and then decided I wanted to stop by and see Bernardo. So, instead of calling or texting him about the job, I would just show up and surprise him. When I pulled into the parking lot it looked surprisingly packed. I walked in and noticed a large table of what looked to be some sort of bachelorette or girls' night out party happening. There must have been about fifteen women, and they were annoyingly loud. Most of them looked like Barbie dolls, with more plastic than I could describe.

I immediately went looking for Bernardo up on stage, but didn't see him. For a second, I thought *oh shit, did he decide not to work for some reason, did he get the night off, shit did I get dressed for nothing?* Then I scanned around the bar and found him talking to some mysterious blonde who was flirtatiously spinning her straw around and around as he was talking to her. My stomach did get a knot, but I decided that before I jumped to conclusions, I would carry my ass right up to the bar to see how he responded. As I was walking toward him, he made eye contact with me and lit up. Good sign.

I saw him say, "Excuse me, will you?"

He met me half way, laid the biggest kiss ever on me, and said, "I was hoping you would show up."

I sarcastically said, "Oh yeah, you looked pretty comfortable to me." I Willow Winked him, as if I was totally cool with the fact he was schmoozing with some Baywatch babe.

"Who, her? She is part of that crew of obnoxious women sitting at that table. I went on my break fifteen minutes ago, and she practically jumped up from her table to come and ask me to have a drink with her. I told her "No, thank you," but she ordered one anyway, and kept talking, and talking, and talking some more. Blah, blah, blah, she wouldn't shut up. So, thank you for saving me."

It sounded like a believable story, but I rolled my eyes at him and said, "Whatever, you are free to flirt. I don't blame her, when I saw you playing for the first time, I was intrigued, I admit it!"

He smiled with those gorgeous teeth, "Um-m, is it possible that Willow might be a little jealous? I don't mind - it's kind of cute on you. Forget the plastic, she is not my type, I like the real thing." He pulled me in again to kiss me.

"So tell me, how did it go today at Dotty's?"

We sat down and he ordered two light beers. I guess ding batty blonde got the hint because she took her drink and her fake boobies back to her table.

"Um-m, it went well. Robert is a really nice guy. I'm training tomorrow with his daughter, Eliza. The only little glitch is that there is this miserable girl there named Brenda who seems like she might give me a hard time – the jealous type who's paranoid I'm going to steal her tables or something."

"Willow, forget the petty high school drama girl and just remember it's a job. Besides, I know a lot of locals come in, and I bet you'll get to know them well. I hear they are great tippers, too."

"You're right, thank you again for setting it up."

"You're welcome," he answered. "How did I get, as you like to say, 'lucky enough' to see you tonight?"

"Um-m, I was feeling spontaneous and wanted to maybe see your handsome face for a few hot minutes. I don't want to be all hung over for my first day, so I am only going to stay for one."

He smirked, "I won't complain, I'm just glad that you decided to show up. I missed you the last two days and have been thinking about the other night a lot."

"Oh, yeah? What about it?"

"Well, what not about *it*, everything about *you*, your eyes, the way your body felt." I started blushing. "Should I continue?"

"No, not now, but please do continue at another time. Say, I was thinking do you like to shoot stick?"

He looked at me funny? "Shoot stick, what is that?"

"Pool, silly."

"Oh-h-h, sorry. In my country, we just call it billiards, or 8-ball, or whatever else. But, yes, to answer your question, I do shoot stick, and fairly well. Why are you asking - for a challenge?"

"Well, I was thinking one night this week it might be fun to kick your ass in a game or two."

"Wow, a girl who shoots stick, that is kind of sexy. Sounds great. There is actually a great dive bar a few blocks from my apartment where I have played with a few of my buddies before."

I smiled, "Sounds great, I love dive bars. The dirtier the better."

He laughed, and I saw him look down at his watch, "Shoot, I am sorry. I already have to go back up, will you stay for a song or two?"

"I will."

He kissed me sensuously for five seconds and went back up on stage. He looked extra hot tonight. I watched him play a few songs and when I finished my beer, I blew Bernardo a kiss goodbye, and left.

When she went to grab the apron, Trisha came back in with a trail of cigarette smell behind her. The odor kind of made me queasy since I had quit a few months ago. She was a little hard-looking, with a Farrah Fawcett seventies hairdo and jet-black roots, long fingernails, lots and lots of gold jewelry, and big boobies. I was thinking if what Eliza told me is true about her dad's crush on her, he must have a hard time concentrating when she is around. Those bazunkas are hard to miss.

I immediately introduced myself to her, "Hi, I'm Willow, the new girl."

"Hello, sugar, nice to meet 'ya, if you have any questions along the way, let me know. You'll like working here, I promise."

"Thanks, I look forward to it."

We spent the next few hours going over the register, writing out orders, and I shadowed her when she was taking orders. She introduced me to a lot of regulars. There was one in particular I felt drawn to, whom she had not yet introduced me. I wasn't sure why, but there was something about his energy that told me I should get to know him. He was an older gentleman, probably in his late fifties. He had this great red hat on that reminded me of one my grandpa had worn a few times, but not in red, my grandpa wouldn't be caught dead in red, but the style was like his. He had on cool glasses and this fun looking red watch. How often do you see a red watch? Interesting.

He was reading a book very intently as he took gentle bites of his rye toast. He seemed very comfortable in his skin, but perhaps the kind of man who also liked to be alone. *Hm-m-m*, maybe a writer, a philosopher?

I know you are probably wondering how I can tell all of this just by looking at him. Well, Grandma Lu always told me I had a special intuitive gift for reading people. I wondered what this guy did for a living.

I waved Eliza over after she placed an order and asked her, "Who is the mystery man with the funky glasses and fun hat and watch?"

"Oh, that's Ed. He is an interesting one. He actually has a hat and watch in every color. One day, I asked him what's up with the hats and watches. He told me that depending on his mood and energy each morning, he decides what color he is going to wear. He also has a fun collection of hats. I believe he's writer or a poet, something I can't remember. He doesn't talk a ton, but if you ask him questions he will answer. I think he is one of those mysterious types. I like him though. Every once in a while, when we talk about my future, he'll throw out some sort of quote or say something that makes perfect sense in the moment."

I smiled. I was excited, he sounds just like the kind of person I could click with. I asked Trisha if she minded if I asked Ed if he needed a refill on his coffee. I told her I was interested in what he was reading and wanted to get to know the customers a little. She said that of course I could, and that he was "a brilliant and eccentric man with a good heart." She told me herself that he always intrigued her. She said he comes in at least five times a week, and if he's not reading something, he's always jotting something down on paper. She knew he was a published poet, and she was always curious about what he was writing on those scraps of random paper he carried. She told me one day, when he went to the bathroom, she couldn't help herself and sneaked over to look at what he had written. She said it was one of the most romantic things she had ever read. Now I was really intrigued.

I walked over to him with the coffee pot and gave him the most welcoming Willow smile I could muster. "Hi, would you like a refill on your coffee?"

He looked me in the eyes with a confident smile and said, "Please, yes. So, I take it you are new?"

"I am. I just temporarily sort of moved here from Philly to take care of my grandpa for a while."

He put down his book while I was trying to look at the title. "That's sweet of you."

"Yeah, well my grandma just passed away, so he needs a little looking after. Besides, I am in what they call a 'transition phase' of life, no need to rush back to reality."

For a second, I realized my need to over-share with a stranger who was probably not interested in me, then remembered Grandma, and even Lucas, saying to me, "No such thing."

He smiled. "So does Miss Transition Phase have a name?"

"Oh, yeah, sorry. It's Willow."

"Willow, what an interesting name. Let me guess - your parents were hippies?"

"No, my father always had a love of nature and felt inspired one day sitting by a lake under a willow tree."

I thought he, of all people, would appreciate my story. He must have, because he smiled. "Cute story. Did you ever hear the song *Willow, Weep For Me*, by Billie Holiday? Also, a willow tree is known to be a spiritual tree full of wisdom." Now I know we were meant to meet because Billie Holiday is one of my favorites!

I smiled and said, "Of course, Billie is one of my favorites, too. As for the wisdom part, I didn't know that, but I like the sound of it, so thanks."

"Well, Willow, my name is Ed, and I can tell already you have a great father. Anyone who is inspired by nature is okay in my book and I can tell you are a creative one - anyone who can appreciate Billie Holiday's melancholy heart has an old soul."

"Thanks, Ed. I was curious - do you mind my asking what you're reading?"

"Oh, this - this is a classic romantic novel which takes place in the early 1900's. It's about a young woman who comes from a wealthy family whom she doesn't quite feel she fits in with. Her family, of course, wants her to marry a man she is not remotely interested in. She's sad because no one cares about what she really wants, only what they want for her. I'm at the part where she just met a handsome man while running into town. He sells newspapers."

I put my hand up to stop him, "Let me guess, she is now going to fall in love with the man from what her family believes to be from the wrong side of the tracks, and they will eventually ride off into the sunset."

He smiled, "Well, something like that, I'll keep you posted. What can I say, I am a sucker for romance. Besides, I should mention, I am a poet."

"Wow, I knew I was drawn to you for a reason. That is awesome. I write poetry, too. I haven't had anything published because I'm just coming out of the closet with it."

"Well, Willow, since you're coming out of the closet with your writing, do you think one day you might have the courage to share a poem or two with me? You know there is no such thing as coincidences, right?"

I smiled, "I know, I do indeed know."

He laughed and said, "I should also mention that I'm also not just your average poet who writes about broken hearts. I also write about spirituality. You know, things related to God, angels, and such." He paused to see my reaction to what he was saying.

I smiled and said, "I get it more than you realize."

I pointed to the guardian angel necklace I was wearing.

He continued, "I can see the angels and your grandma smiling now, they're saying, 'Let's introduce Miss Willow to a published poet so he might be able to give her a few tips on her writing and have the courage to share more.' And something tells me that you're aching to show more of who you really are, and perhaps your poetry will do just that. Does that make any sense?"

"Wow, thanks, it does and I know you're right. I just need to start sharing it more. Okay. I feel like I've taken enough of your time. I appreciate your talking to me. I've enjoyed it immensely. I will bring you one of my poems some day. I'd better get back to my training. It was a pleasure to meet you, Ed. By the way, I love your hat!"

"Willow, the pleasure was all mine, and thanks, this happens to be one of my favorite hats, too. You'll see, I wear lots of different ones, and not just on my head!" He winked at me.

"I hear 'ya, and I like your metaphoric style. Enjoy the rest of your day."

"You, too."

As I walked away I was feeling a little more confident in the sense that I had picked just the right place for my transition. I also loved the idea that he said my grandma and the angels were smiling. This is a man who got it on all levels. I realized that the girls here must have it wrong, for a man who keeps to himself, he sure had a lot to share with me. Maybe he was just misunderstood, or maybe I just might be the gal for him to mentor somehow.

As I was on my way home from work, Bernardo called me. "So how was your first day?"

"Hi, great, the people are so nice and I met this really intriguing older man who is a poet, imagine that."

He laughed, "I told 'ya you would like it. Um-m so this older poet, should I be worried he is going to sweep you off your feet with his romantic tongue?"

"Ha, ha, no. But. I can tell you that I hope he'll be able to give me lots of pointers on how I might be able to get my poetry published or any other insight. Bernardo, I think I mentioned to you before my dream of having my poetry published someday?"

"You did, and I am only teasing. So, what do you say we shoot that game of stick tomorrow night – I'm off."

"Only if you're prepared to get your ass kicked."

"Oh, I like the challenge already. Come over around seven. They have awesome greasy wings at this place. Tell me you like wings, and you are not afraid to get your hands dirty?"

"Bernardo, please, I just told you I love dive bars, and the greasier the food the better, sounds great! I will see 'ya then."

We hung up and I realized, with the exception of Carla, I haven't spoken to any of my close girlfriends in a while - we have been phone tagging since I got here. Besides, I wanted to tell them about Bernardo. I decided to try my friends Melody and Krystal first, hoping I could conference them both in.

"Hello?"

"Mel, it's Willow."

"Ah, Willow, it's so good to hear from you!"

"Wait, Mel, I want to conference Krystal in."

The phone rang, "Hey, Krystal, it's Willow and Melody. I decided it would be much easier to tell you both at once what has been going on instead of my repeating the story."

They both said at the same time, "I'm so sorry about your grandma."

They had each had tried to leave me messages when it happened, but we kept missing each other.

Krystal said, "So, how are you?"

I replied, "I'm actually better than I realized. I decided to stick around for a while - I didn't want my grandpa to be alone. As a matter of fact, I'm on my way home from a little part-time job I got at a cute breakfast place."

Krystal continued, "Willow, wow, so since we have really spoken, you have decided to stay in Florida, gotten a job, anything else we should know?"

I paused, Melody laughed and said, "Oh, my God, Willow, you haven't fallen in love yet or have you?"

Krystal then said, "You have."

They knew me so well.

Melody said, "You have, haven't you? Who is he? We want all the details."

I took a deep breath, "Okay, first of all, I haven't fallen in love. However, I have fallen into like for sure. He is a hot, and I do mean hot, Spanish guitarist I met out one night at dinner with my aunt and Carla. My aunt apparently eats there a lot and knows him. He's a musician, and Krystal, I'm not sure I have ever heard anyone play guitar like that." Krystal's boyfriend is a musician.

I continued, "So, to make a long story short, he asked my aunt for my number and you both know my Aunt El, she probably sneaked it to him. Whatever, but he called me. I blew him off at first and then the day my grandma passed away, I was feeling a little vulnerable so I decided to go out and get some fresh air, and ended up at the bar he was playing. We chatted, flirted, you name it. He invited me over for an awesome homemade meal and ladies, I can't believe I am telling you this, but I slept with him already."

They gasped and both said, "What! And you didn't call us immediately to tell?" Krystal continued, "Willow, you must really like this one, or you must be letting loose on some level, if we never heard from you. The Willow I know would have already called me, obsessing that she did a slutty thing and would want me to reassure her that she is entitled to a little fun - which you are!"

"I know, Krystal, can you believe it? So out of character for me. But, I feel like maybe since I'm unsure how long I am going to be here anyway, that it was a little bit of a free pass for me to have some fun!"

Melody said, "I agree. It will be a good distraction and help you get over Tom."

Krystal added, "Hey, speaking of men, whatever happened to the guy you met on the airplane?"

"Oh, right, Will. Well, he already left Florida, and besides, now that I'm here and clearly distracted by other things, what's the point?"

Melody then said, "Oh, yeah, I got that message, too. So, Willow, I hear what you're saying, but the way you two met, I wonder, besides the Willow I know always likes to put herself in other people's shoes. So, even if you never plan on seeing this mystery man from the airplane, if it were the reverse, wouldn't you want to know what happened to him, why he never decided to call? Willow, just call him and let him know you decided to stay. He sounded really nice from what you said."

Krystal said, "I agree."

I then said, "Ladies, he is really nice, but, well, you're probably right, hopefully if I decide to call, I'll get his voicemail and can just leave a casual message about me ending up staying. Shit, why didn't I just get his email now that I think about it?"

Krystal replied, "Willow, don't overanalyze, and you don't have to do it, just a thought."

"I know, enough about me. So, how are you guys doing? I miss you lots. God what I would give for a ladies night!"

Melody went first, "I'm okay, work is the same, and Wayne is the same. What can I say Willow? Uch-ch everything is freaking the same. I need a change so bad! I wish you and I could do one of our run off road trip weekends."

I said, "Like I said, girls, anything would be great."

Melody said "Oh, shoot, Wayne is calling me on the other line, I gotta run. I'll call you soon." She hung up.

I said, "Krystal, are you still there?"

"Yeah, I'm here."

"So what's cooking with you? How is Davis, work?"

She replied, "Davis is good, just don't see him so much since he's out playing a lot. Work is good. I think my calling as a life coach is finally sinking in."

I said, "Aw-w that is great, I knew you would be awesome at it. You've always had great advice skills."

"Thanks, Willow. So, you should try to come home for a weekend, besides I know how much you probably miss your nephews."

"You're so right Krystal, maybe sometime soon."

I heard her phone beep and she said, "Shoot, that's my work calling. Let me call you back soon, sorry to cut you off, so good to hear from you."

"You too, love 'ya. Bye."

Melody and Krystal are two of my closest friends. The three of us have always been little wildflowers together. They have always completely and unconditionally stood by my side. They are like soul sisters to me. I knew we'd be great friends ever since I met them in the seventh grade.

We all had art class together and were partnered up to paint a large tile to put up on the ceiling of our school. For some reason, we felt inspired to paint a beautiful sun with stars, flowers, and all sorts of mystical things. Our weeks of designing a beautiful masterpiece ended up with lots of chats about boys breaking our little twelve year-old hearts. Even at this age, we liked to discuss our horoscopes together, analyzing and waiting for something magical to always happen. I can't begin to tell you how much we have gone through together. I missed them and thought about maybe going home soon for a weekend so I could see them.

# Chapter 11

MY SECOND DAY OF TRAINING was good. I met a lot of other nice customers. Brenda was also serving and she was not friendly, but not a total bitch either, so I was pleased. I decided to call my Aunt Ellen on my way home from work, since my grandpa had mentioned she called yesterday to speak to me.

"Hello, Willow is that you?"

"It is El, how are you?"

"Okay, darling, how are you holding up? Grandpa told me how happy he is that you are staying - me too!" Say, you want to come over for dinner tonight? They make delicious cheeseburgers by the Golf grill?" she asked.

"Thanks El, I can't. I already have plans. Can I come over on Thursday instead?"

"Sure, doll, and you can invite your grandpa if you would like. So, what kind of plans, you wouldn't be meeting up with Bernardo?" Oy, here we go.

"Yes, Aunt El, I am meeting him. You were right - he is sweet and we are having fun. I'll fill you in when I see you, and thank you for letting Grandpa come if he wants to."

"No problem, I know I am not his favorite person, but now that my sister is gone, I feel like we should try to make somewhat of an effort to get along. So, back to Bernardo, did you smooch yet?" Of course she would ask me that. As if I would share.

"Uch-h, I'm not getting into details like that."

"Just playing, I am glad you are having fun. Alright, come over around six o'clock." For a second I got nervous - what if I run into Will's grandmother? Then I thought, the chances are probably slim, and I'll make something up if that happens.

I met Bernardo at his place and we walked over to the pool joint. When we walked in, I could see the place was a lot like the bar I used to work at after college. I saw the tables were all worn out with ripped felt and some cigarette burns. I could smell hot wings and French fries coming out of the kitchen.

We sat at a little round top table, ordered two beers and an order of wings with blue cheese. I asked for ranch dressing too, with extra carrots and celery. This was so I could sort of feel healthy eating vegetables to mask the grease. As we sat and waited for the food, we decided to play a game or two of pool. I was happy to say that I beat him both times. Every once in a while when I would bend down for a shot or he would bend down for his shot, we would try to flirtatiously distract one another. It worked for me, but not for him.

Our food came and we got messy quickly. Bernardo looked over at me at one point and started to giggle.

"What is so funny?" I asked.

He told me to lean forward and grabbed a napkin and wiped hot sauce off of my cheek.

"Oops, sorry," I said.

He giggled again, "Don't be sorry, it's so cute to see a pretty face with wing juice."

I smiled back. We played a few more rounds after we ate. He only beat me once. We both felt tired and headed back towards his place. I wasn't sure if it was the wings, or the beer, or too many carrots, whatever it was, I could feel those unwanted rumbles in the belly. I was petrified that I could end up having to go to the bathroom, which I refused to do at his place. That is the sort of thing I only ever felt remotely comfortable doing after at least a few months' together, not a few dates. I was wondering how I was going to tell Bernardo that I did not feel well, not running away from him, just wanting to call it an early night.

He must have realized I was not quite right. He grabbed my hand, "Willow are you okay?"

"Um-m, you know what, Bernardo, I am actually feeling really nauseous right now."

"Oh-h-h, do you want to come up and lie down for a little?"

I was thinking *yeah right and clog up your bathroom, no thank you.*

"Thanks for the offer, but you know what, I think I want to just go home and call it an early night. I want to lie in my bed. I'll make it up to you another time, I promise."

"Willow there is nothing to make up, it's okay. I just hope you're not blowing me off 'cause you have some other hot date lined up." He winked at me.

"No, Bernardo, no other hot dates, just a tummy ache." I barely kissed him goodnight, for I could not get into my car fast enough and get home to a bathroom. As I was driving home I started to feel super anxious and was sweating profusely. This then turned into an anxiety attack because I started obsessing that something might be seriously wrong. I managed to get home, barely made it to the toilet, but made it. I got into bed and tried to calm down from the night. I placed some ginger ale next to my bed and a bottle of Pepto. It took me a while, but I did fall asleep.

I woke up early the next day and still felt off. I also spent the majority of the day on the toilet. I wondered if I must have a bug, or ate bad wings. Although I guess Bernardo would have been sick too, which I knew he wasn't because he would have called me, for sure, to tell me! All day I made tea and tried to sleep in bed. I watched soap operas and cheesy movies. I called my dad as I always did when I felt sick. It was the little girl in me who always still liked the reassurance from her daddy that she was going to be okay.

"Dad, hi it's Willow."

"Willow, how are you?"

"Dad I have some sort of weird stomach thing, and I feel more anxious than I normally do. I am all sweaty and just not right, Dad!"

"Willow, honey, it's probably an annoying twenty-four hour stomach flu you might have picked up from your job. Who knows what kind of germs you're around? If you don't feel better by tomorrow, go to a doctor. I am sure Grandpa or your Aunt Ellen knows someone."

"You're right, Dad, thanks. You know I always feel better when I talk to you. If Grandma were here right now, she would be the one I would go to, but we know that is not an option anymore."

He took a deep sigh, "I know, sweetheart, it's okay. You know you can always call me. For now, just drink plenty of liquids, tea, Gatorade, and have some toast when you feel like you can eat."

"Love 'ya, Dad. Tell Mom hi."

"Will do, love. Call me tomorrow and let me know how you are. Love 'ya, too."

"I'll call you," I replied.

We hung up and I decided to finally call Bernardo back. He had left me two messages, but I was in no mood earlier to talk. He picked up right away.

"Hey, Willow, I was worried about you all day. How are you feeling?"

"Still not great, I must have picked something up at work. So, I am just trying to rest." I didn't want to get into the details of how many times I had gotten sick on the toilet. Not the hottest visual for the new guy you are dating.

"Oh, Willow, sorry. I hate stomach-related stuff. Is there anything you need? Do you want me to bring you something?"

"You are so sweet. No thanks, I have my grandpa, and I am just going to try to sleep it off. Thank God I didn't have to work today. I would not have been a happy camper having to serve food. I just hope I feel better tomorrow because I'm supposed to go in, and would hate to have to call out the first week."

"Willow, if you are sick, you are sick. Don't worry about that. Besides, Robert is a cool guy when it comes to that stuff. He is laid back with his staff, except for his daughter. He expects a lot from her."

"I know. She told me he wants her to run his business some day. But, I got the impression she's not interested in that at all."

"I know, he has shared that with me, too. Anyway, you get some rest, and please call me if you need anything. I mean anything."

"Thanks, Bernardo. I'll call you soon, when I feeling more like me."

I somehow made it into work the next day. I wasn't feeling one hundred percent, but I was determined to not call out. I only ended up having to go to the bathroom once, but was able to function. However, I still felt extra tingly and sweaty! I decided to make an appointment with a doctor my Aunt Ellen suggested, who was the daughter of a friend she plays golf with. I was so grateful they could squeeze me in first thing Thursday morning. My grandpa said he wanted to come with me to keep me company. Since my grandma was not around, Grandpa as a stand-in would have to do! Now, I know I'm thirty years old, but every once in a while it's nice to have someone to hang out with you in waiting room and distract you from worrying.

We arrived at the doctor's a few minutes early. The girl who checked me in looked miserable. She had over-bleached highlights and a sour puss on her face which told me she was either really unhappy in her life, hung over, or just woke up on the wrong side of the bed. Either way, I always hated a staff person's grumpy demeanor when you went to doctor's offices. Is it too much to ask to crack a little bit of a smile when people are coming in to be seen? People want to feel comforted when they see doctors.

Grandpa and I sat down and read boring magazines. After about fifteen minutes a big woman called, "Willow, come on back."

She took my blood pressure and said it was low. She asked me to step on the scale, which I had not done since I got to Florida. I had lost five pounds, which I was thinking was related to going to the bathroom a hundred times. The nurse told me to wait for the doctor.

After a few minutes, in walked this tall blonde woman who looked like she knew her stuff!

She put out her hand, "Hi, I'm Dr. Carol Sloan."

"Hi. I'm Willow."

"Willow, cool name, so what can I do for you, Willow? It shows me on your chart that you have had diarrhea and hot flashes for the last few days. Yikes, that must have not been too much fun." I shook my head.

"So, Willow, tell me, just so we can rule out all sorts of stuff, when was the last time you had your period? And are your periods regular or normally off?"

I wondered why she was asking me this, but I answered. "Now that I think about it doc, I have not had a regular period in the last three months."

She then asked, "Is there any chance you could be pregnant?" For a second I panicked thinking Bernardo and I did wear a condom, but there is always that remote chance it was a crappy condom. "Um-m I don't think so, but we can check."

"Okay, how often have you been having these hot flashy feelings and anxiety attacks?"

"Well anxiety is something I have been challenged with for most of my life," I answered, "but as far as the hot flashy feeling, just the past few days. Also, the weird part about the anxiety is sometimes I have been feeling it out of nowhere, like even just watching television or when I was at work, not thinking about anything in particular that would make someone anxious, just feel it though. It's kind of hard to explain, but..."

She stopped me and asked, "Willow, have you been forgetful at all?" Again, wondered why she was asking.

"Um-m-m-m, I did have a few brain farts at work yesterday with customer's food, but not major. So, maybe a little, but if you don't mind me asking, what would my memory have to do with an upset belly or extra anxiety?"

"Well, Willow, sometimes our thyroids can be off and I just want to rule it out, and also our hormone levels can be wacky and cause all sorts of unpleasant responses in our bodies, that is why I also asked about your period. So, do me a favor, go tinkle in this cup and come back. I also want my nurse to draw your blood just to make sure there is nothing we are overlooking."

I gave her a nervous look. She said, "Let's not jump the gun, it could just be a very unpleasant flu bug that your sensitive body is responding too, maybe your electrolytes are off. Willow, it could be anything. I always tell my patients, don't worry until it's time to worry, and even if something comes up, you still don't have to worry because we'll take care of it."

She looked at me with a semi-comforting smile and looked up and pointed. "Willow, I don't normally say this to my patients, although you seem like an open girl."

I smiled, "I am, Doc, I am."

"So, do you believe in something greater?"

I knew exactly what she meant, "I do."

"Then, Willow, you trust that if ever there was something really wrong, you know the real doctor upstairs will take care of things and heal you through anything."

I decided right away that I liked this doctor, and wished she had been around for me as a kid. "I know doc and thanks."

I went to pee in the cup with my heart racing, hoping that I was not pregnant, although my gut already told me I wasn't. I came back in and the nurse drew my blood and told me to wait back in the room for Dr. Sloane. I was super anxious just thinking about what I would do if I were pregnant. Not ready yet.

She flung open the door. "Well, Willow, you can breathe, you're not pregnant. So breathe, I know you are not ready for that yet." Could she read my mind? "I won't have your lab results for a few days, but promise to call you when I do. In the meantime, try to take it easy, drink a ton of fluids, not juice though, it can cause more upset, stick to water and Gatorade. We'll figure out what it going on. Sound good?"

"Sounds good."

I grabbed her card and left with Grandpa. When we got in the car, Grandpa was so sweet - he put his hand on top of mine and said, "Willow, love, I know I am not Grandma, but I hope I am just as much of comfort, as she was."

"Grandpa, you are perfect. Thanks for coming. I liked the doctor, too. They will call me with test results in a few days. I'm just glad to have off from work for the next two days."

"Me too, love, let's go rent a movie or two to watch, sound good?"

"Sounds perfect, Gramps."

We got home and I felt dizzy. I laid down on the couch pulled Grandma's favorite blanket over me. I swear part of me could still smell her on it. Grandpa made us some more tea and we relaxed. I called Aunt Ellen and obviously rescheduled our dinner. There was no chance I was going to eat burgers or fries on this belly. But, I told her since I had off tomorrow, maybe I would stop by to see her so we could catch up.

I woke up the next morning and felt physically a little bit better, still anxious though. Can't explain it, it was just there, that icky feeling. I told Grandpa I was going to run out for some more Gatorade and maybe stop by Aunt Ellen's. I called her on my way back and she was just finishing up her golf match and told me to meet her at the grill for lunch. I was not in the mood to eat yet, but told her I would have some tea while she ate.

I pulled up and was praying that I would not, by chance, run into Will's grandmother. Besides, I had no makeup on and looked like crap with my old manicure, ripped Daisy Duke shorts, and an old hooded sweatshirt. Then again, I was more worried about the fact that I had not contacted Will yet, slept with someone else, and was not sure when I was returning Philly.

I took a deep breath and walked into the grill. It was a classic sight of grandmas and grandpas living the life in Florida. They were all in their golf shirts with visors on their heads. I could hear a lot of gossiping around me. "Did you hear about this one?" "Oh, and I told my grandson...." "Can you believe they served it cold?" You name it, I heard it.

I scanned the room and saw Aunt Ellen in the corner on her cell phone. She saw me and waved me over.

"Hi, doll, I ordered you a cup of chamomile tea with honey just the way you like it."

"Thanks, El."

"How are you feeling? It's not going to make you sick if I eat a burger is it?"

"No, El - don't worry if I feel sick, I will get up. As far as how I am feeling, a little bit better today. However, I have some other unwanted symptoms, a little more anxiety and hot flashes. I don't know. I'm waiting for lab results, so we will see."

"Oy, it sounds like menopause, you'll be fine honey. So, catch me up on other stuff besides your health. How is your new job? My friend Grace has been there and says they have great French toast. And tell me about Bernardo." She winked. I knew she couldn't wait for that one.

"My job is fun, and they do have magnificent French toast, it's a breakfast/ lunch place. I got a couple of shifts a week, so it will do for now. Bernardo - he is fun. Yes, Aunt El, I am having fun. He is not only a hell of a guitar player, but a fantastic cook. He made me dinner one night."

She leaned back, "Sounds good. So did you get that kiss I was talking about?" I couldn't believe she was asking me these questions

- like I am still in middle school. The waitress dropped off her hamburger, extra well done with extra pickles. Who eats their burger like a hockey puck?

"Yes, Aunt El, I got my great kiss. Okay? Satisfied? You know there is no way I am going to give you any more details than that."

"Okay, doll. I'll leave it alone for now, just glad to see you are letting loose a little. How is your grandpa, I guess he couldn't make it?"

"He is surprisingly better than I thought. He bought a bike, believe it or not!"

"Get out of here! I don't think I have ever seen your grandfather even walk to get the mail, I thought he was a lazy bum."

I gave her my *be nice* look. She took a bite of burger, and with a mouth full of food as she always does, said, "Sorry, I am just surprised, happily surprised, he is getting exercise, but surprised. Your grandma would be thrilled. She was always trying to get him to do something."

I said, "I know he is trying. I guess it's his way. I just wish I could at least get him to go somewhere where he could hang out with some men. 'Ya know, talk politics, sports, whatever. He never really did any of that. It was always just Grandma and him or their friends, so I don't know."

"Willow, honey, listen. Your grandfather is who he is. You don't have to do everything for him. He is more independent than you think. Your Grandma Lu would tell you the same if she were here."

"I know, El, thanks for listening. So, how is your man?'

"Oh, 'ya know, I think I might not be so sure about him" she confided.

"What? I thought you said he could be the one."

"I know, but I was kind of disappointed that he wasn't more sympathetic to me losing my sister. I was a little turned off that wasn't more, I don't know consoling, maybe?"

"Really, Aunt El. Well, what could he have said or done that would have made you happy?"

"I don't know - something more than he did. We will see. I told him I needed a little space right now to heal from my loss. I know it's contradictory with what I just said, but that is my excuse for him now. I guess you could say I am testing him a little."

I smiled. Again, no matter what age, sometimes the passive-aggressive nature in us comes out.

"Okay, El, whatever you feel." She waves her hand like *whatever.*

"So, Willow, I don't mean to bring this up to stir the pot, but I was curious. Do you think you will ever contact Will to let him know you are staying here, and before you get all huffy and puffy with your auntie, let me tell you why I am asking. You see, his grandma caught me on the golf course this morning and asked me if I knew if you ever contacted her grandson. I told her I didn't know, I played dumb, Willow, I did, but I felt bad. She told me that he was coming out to see her again in a about a month or so. I didn't want to tell her you decided to stay, not her business, but again…"

I put my hand up to stop her, "Fair enough, I promise to call or shoot him a text this week and let me know I stayed," I promised.

"Okay, love, I just, oh shit."

"Oh shit, what El?"

"Oh my, his grandmother is coming into the café right now, hopefully she is getting take-out. Keep talking to me, we will pretend like I don't see her."

Great, I knew this was going to happen. I tried my best to keep calm. It didn't work. She spotted my aunt and said, "Long time, no see."

She started walking over toward us. She was a striking looking older woman. She had on dark sunglasses and red lipstick. She had a great figure for her age! This must have felt terribly awkward though, for my aunt, since she didn't tell his grandma I stayed. I could tell Aunt El was nervous.

"Hey, Salma, long time, no see."

She looks at me like who is this? I felt bad, so I took the initiative with my bad hair, nails, and all, "Hello, I am Willow, Ellen's niece."

She looked shocked and gave my aunt sort of a weird look, like why didn't she say anything. "You don't say? Well, small world, I am Salma, I'm Will's grandmother, 'ya know, the one you met on the airplane a few weeks ago. Wow, you are still here?"

I was trying to think of something to say that would cushion the fact that I knew she knew that I hadn't called him.

"I'm still here. I'm not sure if my aunt filled you in, but my grandmother, her sister, passed away, and I didn't want to leave my grandfather just yet." I figured I couldn't be too bad of a girl in her eyes, for staying with Grandpa.

"Oh, no. I am sorry - I didn't know that, and I am sorry to hear it. Ellen, I am sorry for your loss."

My aunt waves her hand, "It's okay, but thank you."

Then there was an awkward silence. She fixed her bracelets on her wrist and said, "Willow, it looks like you made quite an impression on my grandson. You should give him a buzz. Of all my grandchildren, he takes care of me the best!"

I turned red, knowing I didn't want to have this conversation and said, "I'm sure he does. You know I have been meaning to call, but since I got so wrapped up with my grandparents, it was hard to focus on anything else, if you know what I mean." I felt guilt rush through my body thinking about Bernardo, but I needed to say something.

She waved her hand, "Oh, Willow, no need to explain. I understand. Well, I am not sure if your aunt has informed you yet, but he is actually coming back out soon to join my husband for a golf tournament. So, maybe if you're still here, you can catch up then?"

I smiled and politely said, "Sounds good." Sounds good? I didn't know how else to respond.

"Okay, ladies, I am off to pick up my lunch to take home for my hubby and me. Willow, it was nice to meet you, and you can call my grandson, I promise he won't bite." She winked at me, kind of reminded me of a Willow Wink.

I smiled back. "It was nice to meet you, too, Salma. And yes, I will call him."

She looked at my aunt, "See 'ya on the golf course, Ellen, sometime this week I'm sure."

"Will do Salma."

She walked off I looked at my aunt and sighed, "Oy, what are the chances?" "Willow you have to know, I swear I had nothing to do with this one. If anything, I was nervous, not sure what to do or say as you can see. Uch-uh, I hope she doesn't talk to her friends about me."

"Why would she gossip to her friends about you?" I asked,

"I don't know, forget it. You're right I am an old lady. Who gives a shit anyway what she says?"

"Exactly, in the meantime, no way of getting around this one now. I am going to have to contact Will somehow. I'm sure she probably called him right away to tell him she just met me."

She smirked, "You got that right. But honey, he does sound nice, just know she is trying to make her grandson happy. That's what we do. We always want the best for you kids. You know, if your Grandma Lu were alive now, she would say the same thing."

"I know, El." We hung out for a little while longer and talked about grandma.

# Chapter 12

I'M HAPPY TO SHARE THAT in the next few days my diarrhea had stopped, but I was still having more anxiety than I wanted. I wondered where on earth was this coming from? Was I nervous about being in Florida and feeling once again unsure of my future? Was I feeling guilty like I was sort of hiding here? I couldn't help but overanalyze what was going on with me for whatever it was, it felt awful. I was hoping the doctor would call me today with the results from the blood work. Regardless, I still managed to get my butt into work.

I was happy to see Ed walk in and sit in my section. Today he was wearing a bright blue hat that said "Your Soul Knows" on it with, of course, a cool blue watch to match. I walk over with a cup of coffee and extra cream, which I now know he likes.

"Good morning, Ed, good to see you."

"Oh, good morning, Willow. How are you today?"

"Hanging in, Ed - just getting over a bug of some sort, feeling a little antsy in the pantsy, but a little better."

He smiled. "'Antsy in the pantsy', I don't think I have heard that expression since my elementary school teacher used to tell me that's what I had. I would never sit still in class."

I laughed, "You know what I mean, I am a little more anxious, than I would like to be!"

He sipped his coffee, "Oh, yes, anxiety is something I'm very familiar with. You know what the greatest cure for that is, right Willow?" For a second I thought he was going to say sex, so I raised my brow.

He smirked, "No Willow, not sex, although it does help, I'm talking about meditating followed by writing. I've written some of my best poetry after I've meditated or surrounded myself with nature."

I was beginning to like this guy more and more. I said, "Well, as far as meditating, I have been practicing it for the last few months and yes, it does help. As for the writing, well, maybe I need to do that more."

He leaned back and said, "Willow, sometimes if there isn't something physical going on, we feel anxious because there's something we are not really looking at, or we aren't saying. Do you understand what I mean?"

I half smiled, "Sort of."

He placed his hands over mine and said, "In other words, I'm saying that true writers usually have some sort of creative, antsy pantsy energy that needs to come out, or there's something they need to express. Sometimes, that running all over the place feeling you are having will not solve itself until you put it down on paper."

I said, "Oh, I got 'ya, sort of like a creative release?"

"Exactly. So, when do I get to see one of your poems? By all means, Willow, please do NOT, not show it to me because you think it isn't good enough and I am going to rip it apart. I respect writer's privacy and have always been gentle with feedback. The only thing I ask of others, who have asked my opinion, is they're real in what they're writing, and most importantly they are writing from their heart. Whether it is light or dark, I tell them to write it all out so you can express what you need to through it."

I was so fascinated by Ed's words of wisdom that I almost forgot that I was working. I saw a couple waving me over for more coffee. I nodded at them, and gave them the *one-second* finger.

"Ed, wow. Thank you for your insight - I feel inspired already."

"Good, Willow. You know, you should actually carry around a little journal and jot down any ideas that may come to you when you feel inspired, like I do." He pointed to his notepad.

"I think I'll do that, Ed, thanks. I would love to continue this conversation, but I have to go refill more cups. Silly me! Ed, what would you like for breakfast today?"

"How about two eggs over easy, side of bacon, extra crispy, rye toast of course, with extra grape jelly" he rattled off with practiced ease.

I smiled, "Grape, hm-m. I would have pegged you for a strawberry kind of guy."

He smiled back, "I like all the flavors, just in the mood for grape today."

"Gotcha. I'll place your order. By the way, love the hat, Ed."

He held the rim and said, "Oh this? It does, you know."

I said, "Know what?"

He smiled, "Your soul, Willow. When in doubt, it does know, even when you think you are lost. That is that wisdom within us that does, *indeed*, know truth."

"I believe that, Ed. I'm just trying to figure out how to get more in touch with it, you know!" I Willow Winked him as I walked to pour others' coffee.

I had to admit, I felt a little special because part of me thought that he probably doesn't give any of the other waitresses as much attention or talk time as he does me. When I walked back toward the grill area, I saw Aaron, Devin's cousin, pouring strawberry syrup into Devin's coffee. So, of course, when he went back to take a sip it would be too sweet! He could be a little prankster!

Trisha walked over to me with cigarette breath and whispered, "Looks like you have made a connection with Ed." The way she said it almost made me wonder if she might have a little bit of a thing for him, like she was jealous.

"Yeah, he is super nice. He said he would try to help give me a few tips on my poetry."

"That's sweet. He is kind of cute isn't he, in a weird kind of way?" I knew it!

I smiled at her, "You like him, don't you?"

She blushed a little. "Well, I don't know if it's 'like', I think I'm just intrigued. The truth, Willow, most of the men I've dated don't have a romantic bone in their bodies. They all seem to hate their mammas, drink a lot, and could give a shit about what I want out of life."

I realized low self-esteem comes in all shapes, ages, and sizes. "On some level, I know what you mean, Trisha. Why don't you try to get to know him a little?"

"Oh, honey, he's way too smart for me. I barely finished high school."

"Trisha, that is part of your problem! You *are* good enough, smart enough. You have to believe otherwise or you will continue to choose men you think - well, I don't have to tell 'ya." She looked a little defensive. Maybe I overstepped my boundaries.

"I'm sorry, Trisha, I didn't mean to offend you."

"No, honey. I'm looking at you all funny because I never thought of it quite like that. Were you a psych major or something?" she asked.

I laughed, "As a matter a fact, I was. Truth is, I have been to a few shrinks myself, so consequently I know patterns when I see them."

She smirked and said, "I hear 'ya, honey. Someday I will find my Prince Charming." I wondered if she had any idea about Robert's affection for her.

I spent the rest of the afternoon hanging and giggling with Devin. He made me feel comfortable, sort of like the older brother I always wished I had. On a side note, I hadn't seen Bernardo in days. Just a few chats in between. Part of me was avoiding him because I was still a little under the weather, and part of me knew I was avoiding him out of fear of getting closer to him. It's no surprise that at this point, I'm trying to work through some commitment issues.

When I was on my way home, my cell phone rang - it was Dr. Sloane.

"Hello, Willow, it's Dr. Sloane."

"How are you, Dr. Sloane?"

"I'm well. How are you feeling?" she asked.

"Well, the diarrhea has subsided, but I am still having weird, hot flashy and anxious sensations."

"Willow, we got your test results back. I think I know why that may be happening. Your thyroid results are showing that you might have something called hyperthyroidism."

I stopped her, "What is that?"

"Willow, all that means is that you right now you might be producing too much thyroid, so your body reacts the way it does, like feeling anxious, or tingly, digestive issues, and reproductive issues, like lack of menstruation. I don't want you to get extra nervous before we jump to any full diagnosis. I want you to set up an appointment to meet with an endocrinologist I know very well - we actually went to college together. His name is Dr. Thompson. He's a great guy." I was sort of quiet, not sure what to say.

"Doc, should I be worried?"

"Willow, no, and even if it is hyperthyroidism, I can't begin to tell you how many women have these issues. It's just one of those diseases that can be misdiagnosed. If it is hyperthyroidism, what he will do is put you on a medication to help get your levels back in check. So, don't worry. It's usually hard to get an appointment with him because he's the best in the area, so when you call, tell them that Dr. Sloane called and said it is important that you meet with him in the next two weeks."

"Thanks, Doc. I'm driving right now - is there any way you can text me the number? I can't seem to find a pen."

"No problem, and Willow, we will resolve this. In the meantime,

I am going to recommend you try meditation for a while, or other relaxation techniques to help keep you calm."

"Okay, Doc, thank you."

We hung up and I immediately got that rush of anxiety, what was this thing and do I go home and look it up on the internet to check it out, or do I call Dad to check it out for me? He knows I can get carried away when I read those Web MD things and make myself extra neurotic.

I decided to call my father. He immediately went on the Internet and called me back about twenty minutes later.

"Willow, honey, not to worry I checked it out." He was able to reassure me that everything would be fine and to try and relax.

On the rest of my way home I tried not to get myself all worked up. I said a prayer to God to somehow let me know that I had nothing to worry about. A few minutes later, I turned the radio on and wouldn't you know, they were playing *"What a Wonderful World"* by Louis Armstrong! I filled up with joy, and immediately felt a little calmer and knew it was all going to be okay.

# Chapter 13

I KNEW I HAD BLOWN off Bernardo long enough and should call him. I also knew I was way overdue to contact Will. I figured I might as well contact both. Bernardo would be first, as he had left me two messages last night. I was a little worried he would be annoyed that I haven't called.

The phone rang and he picked up on second ring. "Willow, I was wondering when I would hear back from you."

"Bernardo, I am sorry, between work and still not feeling a hundred percent, I figured I would try you when I felt more like myself."

"Uh-oh, what is the matter? Did the doctor call you with any results?"

"Yeah, well they don't know for sure, but they think I may have some sort of thyroid issue. I'm meeting with an endocrinologist in a few days to help me figure out what's cooking."

"Oh, sorry to hear that. Is there anything I can do? More importantly, can I see you for a little? I miss you."

"I have missed you too," I replied.

"So, what do you say, you come over and we just chill and watch a movie tonight? Come snuggle with me."

"Come snuggle with you? Bernardo, do guys really still use that line?"

He laughed, "What, I am serious. I won't even try to kiss you. Okay, maybe a little kiss, but really, I just want to lie next to you. You don't even have to shower, come in your sweats."

"Bernardo, I am going to shower for sure, but will come over in my sweats. Let me have an early bite with Grandpa and I'll be over around eight-ish. Can I bring anything?" I asked.

"No, just your cute self," he replied. I will pick up the movie and some treats. What do you like?"

"Um-m, I love red licorice and popcorn."

"You got it. See you then."

We hung up, and I decided I might as well call Will. What was I going to say? I prayed I would get his voicemail so I could buy a little time until he called me back. The phone rang a few times, and his voicemail came on. YES! I heard the beep.

"Hi, Will, believe it or not, it's your mysterious friend Willow, from the airplane. We met a few weeks ago." Like he wouldn't remember.

"I'm sorry it has taken me a while to get in touch. My grandma did not make it, and I decided to stay in Florida to help my grandpa. I am okay, so no worries, but I hope you are doing well. I am sure your grandma has already told you she met me. She also informed me that you would be out here soon for a golf tournament. Give me a buzz and we can try to catch up. Hope you are well. Obviously, my phone number popped up on your phone, so now you have it. Okay, Mystery Plane Guy, talk to you soon."

My time chilling with Bernardo was good. We watched some cheesy 80's love flick and got a little busy. I had heard my phone go off at some point wondering if it was Will. I was obviously not going to check it until I left.

When I got in my car, I opened up my cell to see my missed call, and yes, it was Will. I hit 'play' on my voice mail, "Hello, Stranger from the Airplane, good to finally hear from you. There was no way I was going to wait another month to get in touch with you. Yes, my grandma told me she met you. I am jealous I was not there. I'm sorry to hear about your grandma. I hope you are doing well. Wow, you are a spontaneous girl, making the decision to stay in Florida. Anyway, I realize I am now going to have to wait a month to have that drink we talked about, but I would love a chance to talk to you beforehand.

Before you analyze this one, it's just a simple chat, so give me a call or at least text me to let me know if get to see you. Hope you are well."

I have to admit, it was kind of cute that he remembered that I was analyzing our little "just a drink" talk. I knew I would have to call him back at some point, although this time I was a little more curious than before. However, I wondered if I was being a little deceiving with Bernardo. I mean, we have not yet had the relationship talk. Regardless, on my drive home I had a moment of clarity. I realized that I had forgotten what romance was all about, and Bernardo was a good match to help me remember - whether this was going to be a fling or not.

# Chapter 14

I MADE IT TO THE endocrinologist a little early. It was only 8:32 in the morning, but when I looked up at the clock hanging in the waiting room, it said 1:11pm, which I thought was strange, but I made a wish anyway. I always did that when I was a little girl whether it was 11:11, 2:22, or 3:33.

After a few minutes of waiting, a nice looking older man with a friendly smile came out and said, "You must be Willow, come on back, let's check you out!"

He started feeling around my lower neck area. "Is this tender?"

"Maybe a little."

Then, he took my blood pressure. "Is your blood pressure always this low?"

"Um-m, not necessarily, but yes, over the last few months, I believe so."

"Well, Willow, how have you been feeling the last few days?"

"To tell you the truth Dr. Thompson, a little lethargic. I've been mostly feeling anxious, but the last few days, super tired."

"Okay, Willow. I'd like to take some more blood work and find out for sure what we are dealing with. We have a lab right next door. Can you go get it done now? If so, I can have your results back by tomorrow afternoon."

"Um, yeah, doesn't that usually take at least a week?" I asked.

"Yes, but I happen to be married to the woman who will be drawing your blood, and she knows how much I hate waiting for my patients' results."

"Wow, then yes, I can go now."

"Great, I'll call you tomorrow."

Instead of deciding to ask a hundred questions, I thought maybe I should try to be patient.

My phone rang around three o'clock the next day. "Hello, Willow, it's Dr. Thompson, how are you?"

"Good today, but anxious to hear."

"Okay. So, Willow, you have something called Hashimoto's thyroiditis, which is an autoimmune disease." Hashiwhatta? "According to your blood work, you have anti-bodies attacking your thyroid. How this happens is, at first, your body was producing too much thyroid hormone which was why your original blood work showed you might have been hyperthyroid, but your levels have now switched to the opposite, which means you may be, eventually, hypothyroid. This would also explain why you have felt lethargic over the last few days. Your body is tired from the thyroid's activity."

I fell silent because I was afraid, and unsure of what was he had just said. He must have sensed my silence and said, "Willow, Dr. Sloane mentioned you were a little bit of a nervous patient. I can reassure you that nothing bad is going to happen. I will call a prescription in and we will start you on a small amount of thyroid medicine to get your levels back in check."

"Doc, what if, for some reason, I decided not to take the medicine, will I be putting myself in danger? I mean, is there any chance this might sort itself out?"

"Danger, no, you are not in danger, but what may happen is that you will begin to feel more and more tired, worst case scenario. We can wait and see, if you like. Sometimes there is an imbalance, and this fixes itself. I have a feeling that is not what it is, but you can try. But, let's have you come back in three weeks and test you again."

"Okay, Doc. Thanks for calling me."

"No problem, but you will be okay one way or other, not to worry."

I immediately went to the computer and Googled this thyroid disease. I wasn't even sure how to spell it.

My grandpa came in and said, "So, was that the doctor? What did he say?"

"He says I have an autoimmune disease called Hashimoto's."

He raised his brow, "What? What is that?"

"Beats me, but I am checking it out right now as we speak."

My research pretty much validated what the doctor said, but the part of me that worried was where it said, "If left untreated, Hashimoto's could lead to major depression."

I read it all to Grandpa, and he said, "So, I know how anti-meds you are, but you are going to take the medication, right? Willow, I think you should really consider it."

I felt myself get hot and flushy. I knew he was right, but I was afraid.

"Um-m-m, well, the doc said I could play the wait and see game. I'm to go back in about a month for more testing."

"Okay, love, whatever you decide, but I hope you feel better soon. You know, if your grandma were alive, she would probably tell you to not be afraid to take it."

"I know," I replied, "but let me decide what I'm comfortable with."

"Of course, love, of course."

Over the next two weeks, I was sometimes feeling super anxious, and sometimes super tired. I read that this may happen. I opted to hold off on taking the medicine to see, if I tried an alternative approach, maybe I could make it go away. I researched like crazy to find out ways to overcome it, and I decided to cut out certain foods and tried to make small shifts. I did notice that I started to feel a little blue and in my head. I was also a little more obsessively thinking about my physical ailments, which we know only escalates it more. I did call out of work a few times, but I just didn't feel well enough to go in. Thank God Robert was understanding.

My muscles ached, and I didn't feel like doing anything, not even seeing Bernardo. We had hung out twice, but I was just not feeling sexy or particularly engaging with him, nor even had much of a sex drive, which I also read can happen. I know he sensed it, but didn't make me feel bad about it, which I appreciated. I began to wonder if I was falling into a psychosomatic mindset, or was I really just not myself? Maybe both. Whether it was emotion, or fear, or whatever, I started to begin to feel a shift in my overall well-being. Something inside of me felt like it was ending while something new might be emerging.

One thing for sure is that I felt more than ever like writing poetry. I decided that now might be a good time to start sharing it with Ed, or just sharing it in general. In the meantime, as bizarre as this may sound, I kept seeing the numbers 111 everywhere. Whether I happened to look at the clock at 1:11, or 11:11, or if I was driving, I would see it on license plates everywhere. Once again, I wondered if this might be sign of something else. It was happening too much to call it coincidence.

When I got to work, Ed was already there eating his eggs and rye toast. Today, he was wearing an interesting lime green hat, and of course, a green watch to match. I couldn't help but to go over to say hello. He looked like he was scribbling something.

"So are you scribbling deep thoughts or silly ones?"

He smiled, "Maybe a little of both." He looked up, "Oh, hey Willow, good to see you. I haven't seen much of you the last few weeks. How have you been?"

I put my hand on my hip and bit my lip, "Um-m-m, truth?"

"Willow, always the truth."

"Okay, not fabulous. Turns out I have this thyroid issue called Hashimoto's. If I take medicine they say it will help my symptoms.

If I opt not to, they could get worse, and I am starting to wonder if they are."

"Willow, would you be open to trying some alternative healing?" he asked.

"Ed, I would welcome anything before I take medicine."

"Okay, so I have a good friend, her name is Lotus."

I smiled, and he grinned. "Yes, Willow, just like the flower. It's not her real birth name, but it works well, especially considering the field she is in. I've known her for years. She does a form of Reiki and overall energy healing throughout the body. She is one of the best I know. I've sent lots of friends to her for different ailments, and they swear, after a couple of sessions, they felt better."

"Sounds great, can you give me her number ASAP?"

"I can do better than that. She happens to live a block away from me. I'll stop by on my way home to see if she has some time this week."

"Thanks, Ed, I appreciate it."

He took a sip of his coffee, "So, your thyroid - isn't that part of the throat chakra?"

I gave him a perplexed look, "Um-m, I think so, why?"

"Just wondering, Lotus knows all about this, so hopefully she can clear out any blockages!"

I lifted my brow, "Like what kind of blockages?"

"You know, the kind we keep locked up sometimes that can cause disease or other ailments in the body if we don't find a way to release them."

"Oh, well, do I need some release?" I asked.

"I don't know, Willow. Again, your thyroid is in your throat chakra, which is your expressive area. Have you had issues - not necessarily now, but at some point in your life - being able to express or voice your feelings?"

I went quiet. I never thought there might be a correlation, but I thought he might be on to something.

I said, "Um-m, yes, I suppose, especially in childhood, which we know can creep into adulthood."

"Well, Willow, maybe there's a connection somehow. Who knows? But, even so, don't be hard on yourself. Let's take it one step at a time and let Lotus check you out. She's more of an expert in this area than I am."

"Okay, thanks for getting me her number."

"No problem. So, speaking of expressing, have you written any poems you would like me to see yet? No pressure, just curious."

"Oh, yeah, a lot, but of course I forgot them. And I swear, I planned on showing them to you, actually today as a matter of fact. You know, I read that your thyroid can make you forget things, too."

"Really? Willow, you're not one of those WEB MD-aholics are you? You know, where you think because you have a few symptoms, you must be dying?"

I smiled - how did he know?

"Willow, you have to know better. It will drive you bonkers, stay offline."

"I know, I am trying, but right now, I'm really nervous. In the meantime, something else bizarre has been happening. I don't know, maybe I'm paranoid. Forget it, I'll let you get back to your breakfast."

"Willow, what?"

"Never mind. It's silly, and if my therapist were here right now, she would say I was searching for my signs. She says sometimes I look too much for them."

He sat up straighter in his chair and said, "I'm not your therapist; I'm your friend. So, tell me, you should know by now I am the kind of person you can say anything to, despite what others may have told you."

"Okay, so it's kind of strange, but for the last two weeks, I have been seeing a lot of the same numbers over and over, and it's too often to be a coincidence."

He smiled in a smirkish way - as if he knew what I might say. I nervously said, "What you are smirking at? Do you think I'm nuts?"

"Willow, please continue. I think I know where this going, but go ahead."

"Okay, so, it could be like three in the afternoon, or nine-something in the morning, but my clocks say 1:11, and license plates everywhere I drive have the same numbers - so I don't know, could it be some sort of sign or something or is my mind playing psychological games?"

He took a deep breath. "Willow, you believe there are no coincidences, right?" "Right?" He told me to sit down for a minute.

"Something tells me I was meant to share my story so that you won't be afraid, and hopefully you will feel more comforted."

I looked at him, perplexed. He took a gentle breath and said, "Do you believe in angels?"

"Angels, um-m yeah, I suppose, why?"

"Well, Willow, when I was about your age I had a similar experience. I had gone through a major depression, and I was feeling hopeless, and low and behold, I kept seeing the same numbers. I had a good friend who was a spiritual intuitive and worked with angels. She told me that sometimes when you are going through, or are about to go through, a hard transitional time in life, it's your guardian angel's way of trying to tell you that you are not alone, and you are indeed protected. It's sort of their way of assuring you that there is nothing to fear. But, it's important to try to stay positive through your changes. Your soul is ready to make some shifts for the better. It's sort of like a spiritual awakening." I felt a little nervous but very intrigued.

"Willow, it's nothing to be afraid of. Just know that whatever it is you are about to go through, your angels will help see you through. I must ask though, are you somewhat of an intuitive girl yourself? Your openness is what may be drawing these numbers, and your curiosity, to this. Also, you must me a light worker yourself."

"A light worker?"

"A light worker is someone who will someday have a message for the world. 'Ya know - being able to turn fear into unconditional love. Maybe this is part of your life's work?"

I replied, "As for the light worker part, perhaps, but the intuitive part – well, yes."

"Wow, thanks for your intriguing insight and for listening. As much as I could keep talking - and I could with you, Ed, for hours, I better get back to work."

"No problem. You know, Willow, sometime you should come with me to a group I go to called a Course in Miracles. Have you ever heard of it?" he asked.

"Um-m yeah, a few of my favorite authors have studied it. I always meant to look into it. It sounds interesting. Maybe I will do that."

"You should - I really think you would enjoy it. A lot of like-minded good people attend. We meet once a week."

"Okay. Sometime, yes - sounds great."

# Chapter 15

As ED PROMISED, I WAS able to get an appointment with Lotus at the end of the week. I looked at my watch - it was 10:20 a.m. My appointment wasn't for another ten minutes, but I wanted to check things out before, and make sure I wasn't late. I pulled up to this cute little house with a beautiful Japanese-type garden in front, with running water and beautiful statues of angels throughout the lawn. So far, so good. I liked that she worked from her home - it made it feel more inviting as I walked toward the front door. I rang the doorbell and this petite, adorable short-haired brunette, who must weigh no more than ninety pounds, answered. She was wearing yoga pants with a light pink leotard top. She smiled, and had this cute gap between her teeth.

"Welcome, you must be Willow. Ed has told me all about you."

"Yes, I am. Thank you so much for fitting me in. I hope you don't mind that I am a little early. I'm a little nervous because I've never done anything like this before. Massages, yes, but energy healing, no."

"Willow, you have nothing to worry about it. All you have to do is relax and let me take care of the rest. Would you like some water with lemon before we start?" she asked.

"Yes, thank you, that would be great!"

"Okay, follow me down the hall."

As we walked down the hall, I smelled incense coming from the room. I had a flashback of the stinky, Deadhead roommate I had in college who could not stop burning it all day as she smoked her weed.

I walked into the room and Lotus said, "Take off your shoes and lie down on this table."

As I looked around the room, I saw all these interesting crystals in boxes lying to my right. Part of me wondered *what did I just get myself into?* The other part was intrigued. Besides, I trusted Ed. I lay down on the table and noticed a beautiful photograph of a sunset above mountains, with one distinct bird caught in flight. To my left was a CD player with a clock on it. Chills went up my back, even though I knew it was 10:30 a.m., the clock said - you guessed it, 1:11p.m.

Lotus walked in and said, "Are you comfy?"

"Um, yeah, but truth be told, a little weirded out. You see, your clock, right now says it's 1:11p.m., but we both know it's around 10:30 a.m., right? Lotus, I know this may sound bizarre but I keep seeing these numbers everywhere."

She smiled and said, "I am not surprised to hear, sweet one. Please know it's nothing to fear. Your guardian angels are letting you know that you are meant to be here right now with me for some good healing."

I interrupted and said, "That's what Ed said."

She smiled and continued to speak, "Well, he's right, and I have worked with angels before. This is nothing to be frightened of, I promise. I knew as soon as I got your message that I was meant to work with you. So, no worries, I promise you are in good hands.

"Now, before we get started, Ed tells me you have Hashimoto's. I've worked with lots of women who have thyroid issues. Most of the work I do involves my rebalancing your chakras - you know your energy centers. I do this to help realign any negative emotions we might not realize are being stored in our physical bodies, and dependent on which chakra I am focusing on, I will use my hands as well as a few crystals to help.

So, in your case, Willow, I am talking about your throat chakra. If you don't mind my asking, would you say that you have or have had trouble in your past with self-expression?"

"You know, Ed asked me the same thing before. The answer is, I hate to admit it, but yes. I am sort of over the blame game with my family, but part of me always felt like I was not able to fully express myself. This has also led me into trouble with asserting my desires and needs in relationships. I'm sure you have heard this before, so I'll save you the drama, but to answer your question, one big YES."

She smiled. "Willow, you are a nervous one - I can feel your energy. No need to explain it, most of the women I have met with have shared similar stories. The reason I ask is because your thyroid is in your throat chakra, which is where we express ourselves. However, if there are years and years of unshared pain, or fears, or whatever, there can tend to be blockages. It could also be related to not speaking lovingly enough to yourself.

All you have to do is close your eyes, and listen to the beautiful music I'm playing. This session will be about forty-five minutes. I will be gently placing my hands, without touching you, around your throat and any other parts of your body that I feel may need work as well. Okay?"

I took a deep breath, closed my eyes, and said a prayer. "Okay, Lotus, I'm yours. Do whatever you need to do to start the healing."

After about ten minutes I became much more relaxed. In a weird way, I felt like she might have had some mystical healing powers. If nothing else, I felt my anxiety dissipate and my muscles relax a little more. At one point, she ran her hands over my left stomach area. For some reason, I felt a little tender pain and she wasn't even touching it. I jumped.

She stopped and said, "Are you okay?"

"Yeah, but I felt tenderness or something when your hand ran over that area. What is that?"

"Yes, Willow, I can feel it, try to relax. Your stomach has probably been tied up in knots from all of your nervousness. I am going to help you relax, and to improve your digestion a little better."

This woman was good. I took another deep breath and closed my eyes again. This time I fell asleep, and before I knew it, I felt an actual hand on top of mine gently tapping me.

"Okay, Willow. You're all done. I am glad you were able to fall asleep. That means I was able to relax you. How do you feel?"

I smiled, "I feel more relaxed already."

"Good, during the first session, not everyone is able to feel it. It may take at least two days to feel some of the effects. So, in the next week, I want you to notice if you feel any overall improvement in your physical and mental state. I'm going to recommend that we do at least three more sessions. Come to me once next week and we'll continue.

"Now, I can't promise that you might not still need medicine, but just trust that what I am doing can't hurt you, and will help to start assisting in your healing. You are going to be okay, Willow, one way or the other. I am an intuitive healer, and this much I know. It may take a little time, but you will feel better soon."

"Thank you so much, Lotus. Ed was right about you."

She giggled. "Ed is the best, right? Whenever I have dinner parties he is the life of them. Get a few drinks in him and he cleverly creates poetic stories."

I smiled. "He is wonderful. He is trying to encourage me to start sharing my poetry more."

She said, "How did I guess, a poet? Willow, he's right. The best thing you could do is keep writing and start sharing. Your thyroid is aching for you to express. Don't be afraid, dear one, to start using your voice."

"Thank you, Lotus. I will take that into consideration this week, for sure."

She walked me out and said, "Remember to drink lots of water all day. We did a lot of healing today, so drink up and let's clean the rest of the toxins out of your body."

I turned around and waved goodbye. "You got it. Lots of water, thanks again."

The next morning, my cell phone rang and woke me out of a dead sleep. I looked down – it was Aunt Ellen. I decided to pick up.

"Hello?"

"Hey, doll, did I wake you? Sorry. It's 8:30 so I thought you might be getting ready for work."

"I don't have to be in until 10:30 today. I'm second shift, but don't worry about it, I was going to get up soon anyway. What's up, El?"

"So, last night, Harold and I went to eat at Bernardo's joint."

I interrupted. "Wait, Aunt El, you mean you are back with Harold? I thought you had moved on."

"Well, I decided to give him another chance. When I came home from golfing the other day, he had a beautiful bouquet of flowers and a new necklace wrapped in a little blue box for me. You know what those little blue boxes are, right, doll?"

"Um-m-m, I don't know, El, Tiffany's?"

"How did you guess? Anyway, he went to Tiffany's and got me a gorgeous necklace, I mean gorgeous. So, I hate to pry, doll, but have you and Bernardo sort of, how do you kids say it, cooled off?"

I responded. "Um-m, why do you ask?"

"Well I got a sense when I asked him how you two were doing. He said that you were not feeling that great, and he had not seen you much. Honestly Willow, he seemed kind of sad, but I could tell that he didn't want to say too much because he knows, and I admit it, I can have a big mouth. I think he was holding back. So, Willow, is it true, are you done with this one?" she pried.

"Hold up, Aunt El, I never said anything about being done with him. You know I haven't felt great for the last few weeks on so many levels, so I have sort of kept to myself a little more. I will call him today. I know I've been a little more distant than usual, but I'll straighten it out."

"Okay, doll. Let's get together soon."

"Okay, Aunt El. Thanks for checking in."

"No problem," she said, "Talk to you soon."

We hung up and I started to feel that yucky sense of guilt creeping in. Part of me, though, didn't feel totally terrible. I mean, we never had that talk about being serious anyway. I was definitely not in the place physically, mentally, or emotionally to give him my all, not that he even asked. Either way, I'd better just call him. I looked at my watch and realized that he is definitely still sleeping. I'll wait until 10 o'clock..

The phone rang. "Hello?"

"Hey, Bernardo."

"Who's this?"

My stomach sank, he was mad. "Who's this, you mean you have already forgotten my voice? What – it's only been a few days."

"I'm kidding, Willow, but it's nice to see you react a little. I was beginning to think you might have forgotten about me. I am assuming your Aunt called to tell you she ran into me. This isn't a pity call is it?"

"Bernardo, please, give me a little credit. Sorry, I know I have been distant, just haven't quite been myself."

"Willow, why don't you come over tonight, let me make you one of my special meals, and we can just hang out and relax."

"Um-m, okay sure. Why not?" I wasn't feeling very engaging, but I knew seeing his sexy smile might perk me up.

"So, what time, handsome?"

"Six-thirtyish. Bring some red wine, will 'ya? That's it, just your cute self and the wine."

"You got it, see 'ya then."

We hung up, and I found myself smiling. Not even thirty seconds later, the phone rang again. Before I looked at the caller ID, I assumed it was Bernardo, so I just immediately picked it up and said, "So, what else did you want me to bring or forget to tell me?"

"Um-m-m, that I miss you. I'm guessing you expected someone else?"

My heart dropped to the floor, because it was not Bernardo's voice on the other line. I was speechless - it was Tom, my now ex-boyfriend.

"Oh, my God, Tom, sorry I thought you were - it doesn't matter. It's been a long time, I'm surprised to hear from you, how are you?"

"Good, Willow, how are you? What are you up to? The last we spoke you were flying out to see your grandma. How is she doing, by the way?"

Oh shit, I realized I didn't tell him, and knew he was going to probably be mad about the oversight.

"Um-m, well, unfortunately I am sad to say my grandmother didn't make it. She passed away a little over a month ago, and I decided to stay here in Florida with my grandpa for a while, until he is ready to move to Philly, near us."

"Willow, I am sorry, I know how close you two were. Why didn't you call me or tell me? I am surprised."

"Tom, I'm sorry. I was in a state of numbness and wasn't really ready to talk to you or have a mourning type of conversation with you just yet. But, you have me on the phone now, so I'm curious, what's up?"

"What's up? Well, I just got a new job in the IT field, and I start in two weeks. I just planned a trip to Italy by myself. I wanted to do something before I started my new job."

I felt a tinge of jealousy. One of my dreams, when we were together, was to travel to Italy with him and experience that incredible culture. He is of Italian descent, as well. We always said some day we would try to track down our ancestors' roots, of course while we ate our way through Italy. I wondered if he was trying to make me jealous.

"Wow, Italy, huh?"

"Yeah, I figured the odds of you ever going with me were slim to none at this point. Besides, weren't you the one who always said that traveling alone is the best way to reach your soul and learn about yourself?"

I smiled; he, at least, retained something good about me. I sarcastically and jokingly responded, "I did say that and still stand by it. So, did you call to rub it in my face or to make me jealous? 'Cause now I am."

"No, Willow, I called to tell you that I was thinking about you, I'm not trying to win you back. I just felt like since it's been months, it was okay to finally say hello to you. I do think of you often. So much reminds me of you. Anyway, do I dare ask if you are seeing someone else?"

I felt anxious. I didn't want to tell him the truth - that I still cared. Then again, God knows how many beautiful women he was about to meet and romance in Italy. If there was one thing Tom could do, it was his ability to turn the charm on!

"Tom, let's not go there. I'm not in the mindset to have a conversation like this."

"I know you so well, Willow, if you are responding this way then I know it's a yes. Listen, before you get all huffy and puffy with me, it's okay. I know now."

"You know what, Tom?"

"I know that it wasn't fair of me to ask someone to be with me when I said that I didn't believe in unconditional love, meaning not loving you, Willow, the way you deserved to be loved, and I'm sorry. Maybe that's why I'm calling you now - I want to say I am sorry. I was in such a bad place myself. I took a lot of crap out on you, which was not fair, and said a lot of things I did not mean at the time. I think I couldn't love you in that way, because at the time, I couldn't love myself in that way."

I sighed and said, "So, are you calling me to clear your conscience? I've forgiven you, Tom, so you can fly away to paradise now on a clean slate." He sensed my semi-sarcasm. We were always good at reading one another.

"Come on, Willow, whether or not you believe me, this is my way of apologizing."

I wanted to get off the phone now because I started to feel a little emotional. "Tom, as I said, in all seriousness, I do forgive you. I'm sorry we didn't have what it takes to make it work. But, in all fairness to you, I've started to learn something important - we can't look to our partners to fill our voids - that love has to also come from within. I think we both learned something here. So honestly, no hard feelings, I'm just sometimes sad because a lot reminds me of you, too."

He laughed, "Tell me about it, commercials, our little quirky sayings, it goes on. Willow, whoever he is, I hope he is, and will continue to, treat you well, you are an angel. You aren't mine anymore, but you are indeed an angel."

My eyes began to water, because I knew he meant that last statement. "Thanks, Tom. So, I hope you have a wonderful trip, eats lots of homemade pasta, drink lots of yummy wine, take lots of pictures, and bring your back-up sneakers, I know you'll need them."

"Thanks, Willow, you know me just as well, too. I'll be thinking of you! Send your family my best. It was so good to hear your voice today."

"You, too, Tom."

We hung up, and I realized that my heart still felt for him. I knew we could never go back to one another, but I knew that part of me was always going to love him.

I came out of the bedroom and saw my grandpa holding one of my grandmother's favorite sweaters to his nose as if he were smelling it. He must have heard me. He turned around and with a smile said, "Good morning, love. You caught me. I still love to smell her clothes, it reminds me of so much. Sorry, I can't help it, I know it may seem silly."

"Gramp, please don't ever apologize. They say your sense of smell is one of the strongest senses. It can bring back memories like no other and it brings me comfort, too. A lot of times, I will be in a store or restaurant and a woman will walk by wearing both Grandma Lu's and sometimes Grandma Dotty's perfume, and I always think of them. I think it's sweet!"

"Thanks, Willow, you always make me feel better. So, what is going on with you this morning, you seem a little out of sorts. Are you okay?"

"Um-m, well, you will never guess who I just got off the phone with."

Normally, this would have been a conversation I'd have been having with Carla or one of my girlfriends, but all were at work, so Grandpa had to be the fill-in sister/friend at the moment.

He poured a cup of coffee for both of us and sat down next to me. "Um-m-m, let me guess, the stranger from the airplane?"

"No, go back a little further."

"Whooh, Tom? What did he say?"

"Yep! It completely caught me off guard, but it actually was a half decent conversation. No fighting, just honest talk. He sort of apologized for being an angry jerk at times during our relationship, and was sorry that he was not able to 'love me the way he knew I deserved to be loved.' He got a new job and is going to Italy before he starts. That part kind of got to me - you know it was always one of my dreams to go there with him someday."

He smiled that Grandpa *it's going to be okay* smile and said, "So, you will have that dream with someone else, love, and it will be even better. I am glad you both got some closure, but I can see it in your eyes, you feel a little sad, huh?"

"Well, we did date for almost four years, destined to be together or not, he was still a huge part of my life" I replied.

"I know, love, but it's good that you have moved on. Who knows, there might be potential for a great love with this Bernardo, or Will - is that his name?"

"Yes, Grandpa. I don't know, it feels too soon even to think about words like love. I am thinking it's finally maybe time for me to learn to love *me* more, and then I can think about loving someone else more. Does that make any sense?"

"It does, Willow. Gosh, you are so much like your grandma, you know that?"

I nodded and said, "I know. So, what do you say we go for a bike ride this morning? I'd love some fresh air."

"Sounds great!" he said, "I got a new bike seat - you were so right, my ass was starting to get sore!"

I laughed and we walked outside. Once again, there it was - our beautiful cardinal. I said, "Look, Grandpa!"

He smiled and said, "Hey, look at that!"

He winked at me.

# Chapter 16

As I PULLED UP TO Bernardo's apartment, I wondered if I really felt like being there. In the meantime, I knew that Will was coming very soon, and was going to want to hang out. Bernardo and I still haven't had the conversation about dating or seeing other people. I know that part of me didn't want him to date other people, but the other part of me knew it was selfish of me. What if I did want to meet up with Will?

I walked up the stairs and it smelled like shrimp scampi? The aroma was garlic and butter. Yum-m! I knocked, and he opened the door with that amazing smile. He leaned in to kiss me. He had a towel thrown over his shoulder, and a little sauce on his right cheek.

I picked it off and said, "Here, let me get that."

He smiled, "Mama always said I made such a mess when I cooked."

"Me too, I am infamous for making a mess," I commiserated.

"Wait, you cook, Willow? I sort of had you for a take-out kind of girl."

"Well, I was, you know. I used to be a take-out girl because my mother never cooked growing up. She was a busy bee workaholic, so we always ordered out. I got my kitchen experience mostly from my grandma. I also dated a lot of Italian men. They all taught me well!"

He smirked. "So, come get comfy - tonight you are in for a treat. We are having shrimp scampi, Caesar salad, and garlic bread."

"I knew I smelled it! I *do* have a nose like no other. I forgot the breath mints though for all the garlic."

"Willow, who cares? We will have garlic breath together. Mama always said when two people both eat garlic, they cancel each other out."

I nodded back.

My cell phone text message went off. I looked down to see who it was. Wow, talk about power of the universe. It was Will. I opened it up. It read, *Hey, I was thinking about you and looking forward to hopefully getting together, when I come out. No chickening out, remember it's just going to be a drink!*

I smiled. Forgot to tell ya that instead of calling Will back a few weeks ago, I did text him that he should reach out to me about a week before he comes out, which he did. I knew I'd have to address this with Bernardo sooner or later. He must have caught me looking and said, "Must be somebody good - you are smiling."

I lied because he had caught me off guard, "Oh, it's one of my girlfriends from Philly. I miss them, you know."

He stirred the pasta, "I hear 'ya. You know, when I first moved out here it was just my cousin and me. I missed my family and buddies a lot."

"I know, I miss my sister especially right now. She has always been there for me when I am off kilter. This thyroid thing has been a little wacky. I was actually thinking of flying home to see her and my nephews in a few weeks. I miss them terribly."

"You should. They probably miss seeing the coolest aunt on the planet!"

I smiled. "You're good, and really cute, too, did I mention that?"

"A man never gets sick of hearing it! You're not so bad yourself." He walked over and kissed my forehead. I've always loved forehead kisses.

Dinner was delicious. I am not sure if it was the wine or what, but I was feeling extremely tired and definitely not in the mood for hooking up. I just wanted to chill out and relax, and was hoping Bernardo wouldn't try and put the moves on me tonight.

He came over and sat with me on the couch and put his hand on my knee. He leaned in to kiss me. I pushed his hand gently off of my knee. "Do you mind if we just chill out and watch some TV or something?"

"What is it my garlic breath? Is it too offensive?"

I smiled, "No, silly, not at all. I'm more in the mood to just lie with you than make out right now."

"Okay, sure, we can chill. Is everything okay?" he wondered.

"Yes, don't overanalyze. I promise, all is well, just want to hang."

For once, I wanted to NOT hook up. We both fell asleep on the couch. I decided I was too tired to drive home tonight. I had not yet technically stayed over Bernardo's, but I crawled into his bed anyway. I know I had told Grandpa that I would come home no matter what time of night it was. However, I called him to let him know I was just too tired tonight, so he wouldn't worry.

I fell asleep fairly quickly with Bernardo's hand wrapped around my belly.

I woke up at some point to go to the bathroom and noticed that Bernardo wasn't next to me. I thought *oh no, was I snoring and he had to go on the couch?* Just in case, I sneaked out quietly and found him in the living room on his computer. I immediately got a little curious wondering who he could be emailing this time of night - perhaps another girl? Could he be looking at porn? Instead of letting my mind run everywhere, I decided to come up gently from behind him.

It was definitely an email of some sort. He must have heard me, because he jumped and immediately shut the screen.

"Oh, shit, Willow, you scared me!"

"Sorry, I was wondering where you went."

"Sorry, did I wake you? I couldn't sleep and I usually end up writing old friends from back home. I am bad with keeping in touch, so when it's the middle of the night, I figure now is as good a time as ever."

I stepped back, "Any of these old friends happen to be lady friends?"

He smiled. "What, like ex-girlfriends?"

I smirked, "I don't know, yeah, maybe that is what I am asking." I now realized I was about to open a conversation.

"We've never really talked about that. You know, whether or not there are really other girls. Do you see anybody else?"

"Whoa, Willow! Did you have a bad dream or something? Where is this coming from at three a.m.?"

"Bernardo, we've been dating for a while. It's nothing to get defensive about, and I certainly think I have a right to ask. So, by you getting a little defensive, I'm even more curious."

He pushed his seat back and grabbed my hand, "Come, let's go back into bed. You are tired and cranky, I can tell. We can talk about this in the morning, okay?"

"Um-m I don't feel like talking about this in the morning. I'm up now and would rather talk now."

"Okay, Willow, so what would you like to ask me?"

"Um-m, Bernardo, I think it's pretty clear what I just asked you. What is the big hesitancy?"

"Okay, Willow, I am sorry. I want to be honest with you."

"Bernardo, please do," I implored.

"Okay, so I have not seen anybody but you, I swear on that. However, one of my old girlfriends - well, I wouldn't even call her that, we dated for about two months, is coming into town next week for business and asked me if I would have dinner with her. I told her I was seeing someone, and she said she completely understands and is not looking to rekindle anything, just wanted to have a friendly dinner.

"I told her I would think about it, which I did, and Willow, I was thinking it would be no big deal for I am completely over her."

I put my hand up, "So, are you asking me if I would care if you met up with her, or are you telling me that is what you want to do?"

"I guess both," he answered.

My immediate reaction was of sheer insecurity that he was not over this one. However, I remembered that Will was coming into town soon, and this would be a perfect opportunity to throw out my idea as well.

"Well then, to answer your question, I guess I'm not thrilled about the idea, but I don't see any harm in it." I decided to choose my words carefully.

I continued, "You know, I was thinking a little about this anyway. So, whether it came up at three in the morning or next week, I think it's important we address it. In fairness to you, I know that I have not been completely honest as well. I have a friend who's coming into town soon - yes, a male friend - and he wants to meet up with me, too."

He raised his brow and said, "An ex boyfriend as well?"

I smirked, "Well, not exactly. We met on an airplane on my way down here, and we never ended up getting together. I blew him off - well, I have been blowing him off. Anyway, it turns out his grandma lives where my Aunt Ellen lives, and he's coming back into town and wants to finally meet up with me. It's an innocent get-together as well."

He put his hand up and said, "Wait, what? You mean to tell me that you met some random guy on an airplane and haven't kept in touch at all? You must be attracted to him or else you wouldn't even consider seeing him. So, yes, I am a little jealous and not just because you want to get together with some stranger you met. It's actually how you met. It feels like a very romantic movie to me."

I rolled my eyes. "Bernardo, hold on. First of all, to address the first issue, NO, I have not kept in touch with him. I ran into his grandma one day at lunch, and she gave me a whole song and dance about how I never called her grandson, and blah, blah. He's coming into town - I felt bad. The least I could have done was call him. As far as being attracted to him, yeah, he's cute, but more importantly, he seems like a really nice guy."

He interrupted me, "Well, did you tell him you are dating someone, also?"

Oops, did not get that far. "Bernardo, I haven't even spoken to him on the phone yet, we left one another one voicemail each and that was it. So No, I haven't kept in touch all this time. But, in the bigger picture, truth is it's not that I want to date other people, it's that I just want to explore meeting new people in general, especially now. I have had a couple of hard months, as you know I came out of a four-year relationship, I lost my grandmother, I now have a thyroid disease I'm trying to get a grip on, and I'm trying to figure out what I want to do for the rest of my life. So, forgive me if for once I just want to let loose and feel free to do what I want. And Bernardo, I don't want to hold you back either, especially now since I'm going through all of this. I mean, is there any way we can keep this light for now?"

"Light? You mean you want me to date other women?"

"No, of course not," I answered, "but I know it would be selfish of me because I know where I am now. I'm sorry if this is not what you want to hear, but I think it's important to get it out on the table."

His whole body language changed, "Wow, this is a first for Bernardo."

I smiled, "What, a girl asking you to keep it light?"

"Sort of. You sure know how to squash a man's ego, Willow."

"Bernardo, I mean no harm on that ego. I adore you, believe me. I'm just trying to be realistic about everything, and tell you what I think would be best for now. I'm saying let's hang out and do our thing, and also allow one another to explore whatever it is we want to. I am not saying go crazy and sleep with a bunch of women, but you know what I mean. The only thing I ask is that we at least be honest with one another along the way, because trust is a biggie with me. So again, if you are dating whoever, just please be honest about it and I will be, too.

"So speaking of which, I'm confessing that it was Will who sent a harmless text to me before dinner, not my girlfriend - just letting me know he's coming into town. Sorry, but now that we have talked, I'd like to be honest, too.

He raised his hands and said, "Okay, I can't say I am thrilled about all of this, but I don't want to not see you anymore, either, so I guess we will try to keep it light, as you say, and yes, of course, be honest along the way."

I felt a little sense of relief. I grabbed his hand. "Can we get back into bed and snuggle for a little? That is what I would love to do."

He smiled, "Sure."

We walked into the bedroom. I knew there was no way I was going to fall back asleep, but I didn't want to leave in the middle of the night, either, that would have been a double hit on his ego. We lay there and I closed my eyes - part of me wished that I was home in my bed in Philly. I was missing my life there, but then I wondered was it home or was it my past? I was ready for change, but I was also not quite ready to leave the nest. The last time I looked at the clock it said 4:42 a.m.

At some point, I fell asleep but woke up at 6:30a.m. So, I must have slept an hour or so. I was absolutely exhausted and wanted to get home ASAP. I gently woke Bernardo to tell him I was going to go. He kissed me goodbye. As I got into my car something told me we would not be seeing one another much anymore. I was semi-sad, but also wanted to be free.

# Chapter 17

A WEEK HAD GONE BY and I felt a little badly about the conversation Bernardo and I had. I knew he was working tonight, and wanted to surprise him and stop by. Just because we were going to be casual didn't mean I still couldn't be spontaneous. I got myself dressed and finally put some makeup on. I drove to Tina's and felt a weird sinking feeling that maybe his ex was in town already. I hadn't asked him, and shouldn't assume, but what if she was there to see him play? I felt my gut beginning to rev up a little, but decided to ignore it, for what would the chances be?

I pulled up, put a little extra vanilla flavored gloss on to give him a kiss hello. I walked in and looked up at the stage right away, but realized he must be on a break because I saw an empty microphone and his stool.

I scanned the bar and saw the back of what appeared to be Bernardo's head. It looked like he was whispering something into an attractive blonde's ear. Her legs were crossed and I could see she had on very high black stilettos. My heart started racing as I realized it was, indeed, Bernardo and the woman must have been the ex. And, if this was not the ex, then it was clearly some girl he was interested in. Their body language was screaming sex.

I was feeling nauseated and wanted to get out quickly before he saw me. I would be so embarrassed if he saw me, knowing that I had seen them together. Who was she? Uchchhchch!

I gently turned around and walked toward the exit door, but didn't step out yet. I decided to test him a little. I texted him and watched to see if he would check his phone while he was with her. I knew that this was completely immature of me, and borderline stalker behavior, but I didn't care in that moment, and wanted to know. So I wrote, *Hey you, what are you up to tonight, do you maybe want to hang out?*

I peeked my head through the door. I saw him grab his phone, look down, read it, ignore it, and put it back into his pocket. I felt sick. I immediately got into my car and pulled out of the parking lot. I didn't trust him. Bullshit he didn't still have feelings for her! As I suspected, I heard nothing. Not the entire evening. I barely slept - I realized this insecurity couldn't be good for my well-being on any level. On the flip side, I knew we did talk about seeing other people, so why was I so annoyed? He was doing what I said it was okay to do. Maybe I was more upset at the fact that I felt rejected that he hadn't picked up my text. I tried to put myself in his shoes - what if I was on a date with Will or some other guy, what would I have done? Regardless, I did not like the way it felt.

I heard my cell phone text go off. I opened my eyes and looked at the clock. It was after eleven o'clock in the morning! I never slept this late. I guess I had needed it since I hadn't fallen asleep till 3 a.m. I was thinking that it must have been Bernardo. I looked down at my phone, and to my surprise, it wasn't Bernardo. It was Will, and it said, *Hey you, look forward to seeing you soon.*

Wow, how about that! I smiled, realizing more and more how the universe works in mysterious ways! I perked up right away. I looked up and said "Thanks, angels." I knew that this was a clear sign that something better was right around the corner. I also saw that at ten o'clock I had a missed call from Bernardo. Funny, I didn't remember hearing my phone. Could I have been in such a deep sleep? I hit play: 'Hey, beautiful, so sorry I didn't get your text until late last night. I was working and playing, by the time I got finished it was obviously too late to call you back, but so good to hear from you. What do you say I make dinner for you tonight?'

I felt sick to my stomach. Liar! But why would he have felt the need to lie? We said we would be honest when hanging out with others.

I did not call him back. Instead, I texted Will back, *Look forward to officially hanging out.* Something told me I didn't have to play games with this one.

I got out of bed and went into the kitchen. Grandpa was there and smiled at me. I half smiled back.

"Morning Willow, why the sad face this morning? You didn't hear from your ex again. Are you okay?"

"No, I didn't hear from Tom again. I didn't sleep that well last night. Um-m, without getting into the details, I think Bernardo and I are kaputz."

In Yiddish that means OVER!

"Oh, really? How come, love?"

"Well, I hate to say it, but I'm not sure I can trust him. I mean, I sort of caught him in a little lie. So, I am officially turned off."

"Willow, I won't pry, but just know that trust is an important value in relationships. Your grandma and I always told one another everything. Even if we were afraid it might hurt one or the other's feelings, we always told the truth. Your grandma, as you know, was big on that word, TRUTH."

"I know – that's why her middle name was Ruth." He smiled.

"See how clever your great-grandma was?"

"You always have a way of cheering me up - thanks, Grandpa."

"Willow, love, that is a grandpa's job.


Later, as I was walking out of work, I checked my voicemail. Bernardo had left me three messages and a few texts. I was clearly blowing him off and felt really turned off. At this point in my life, I was done playing games.

I walked out to my car and saw a rose sitting on my windshield with a note that read: *Whatever it is I have done, I am sorry. Please Willow, give me a chance to at least talk to you.* My stomach churned but I figured *let me just get my closure.* I decided to call him and get this over with. I got into my car, put my blue tooth on, and made the call. He picked up on the first ring.

"Hello?"

"Hi, it's Willow."

"Willow, so good to hear your voice. Did you get my note?"

"I did, and the rose. Thank you."

"So, Willow, what is it? Are you going to continue to blow me off, or are you going to tell me what it is."

"No, Bernardo, no more blowing you off. I am going to tell you exactly what it is. A few days ago, I decided to surprise you at your restaurant to say hello. I had felt a little off about how our conversation had gone the last time I was at your place. So, I wanted to talk to and surprise you. When I got to Tina's, I came in and looked up on stage. You weren't there, so obviously I assumed you were on a break. As I scanned the bar, there you were, whispering some sort of sweet nothings into some blonde chick's ear. I'm assuming it was your ex-girlfriend that you supposedly didn't have any more feelings for."

He tried to interrupt me, but I didn't let him and continued. "So, of course I remembered that you said at some point you were going to meet up with her, I just didn't think it was going to be the night I showed up to surprise you and say hello. So much for surprises. Not that it is your fault because you didn't know I was going to show up."

Again, he tried to interrupt me, "Willow, I am sorry."

"Bernardo, let me finish and then you can talk." So I continued with the story about him and the cell phone and how he silenced me into his pocket.

"Willow, can I speak now?" he asked.

"Go ahead."

"Okay, so yes, there is no way I can possibly talk myself out of this one. You witnessed me with my ex-girlfriend. I am not sure what you thought you saw at the bar, but maybe it was a flirtatious exchange between two old friends, not what you think."

"Bernardo, do you think I am some sort of clueless chick? One simple question, did you or did you not go home with her?"

He fell silent, and then said, "I did."

I said, "Okay, did you or did you not rekindle an old flame, even if it just was for the night?"

"I did, Willow, not that it is an excuse, but didn't you and I talk about us starting to hang out with other people? Wasn't it you who told me it was okay to see other people?"

"Oh, my Gosh, Bernardo, we did, but I didn't think we would be shady about it."

"Willow, I am sorry. I am truly sorry from the bottom of my heart. What I was going to try to tell you, that I realized the next morning, is that I wished it had been you lying next to me, not her."

I felt like I was going to puke, but I let him continue.

"Willow, I don't care if this scares the shit out of you when I say this - I think I am in love with you. Yes, I was with another woman, but all I could think about was you. I am sick to my stomach knowing that I probably just blew any chance of ever being with you again."

I sighed and said, "Listen Bernardo, I have been here before, and I have little energy at this point for these conversations. Let's just chalk it up to that you and I had our fun and this was probably not meant to be anything more than that."

I knew what I just said officially blew his ego, but I was pissed off.

"Willow, I know you are angry with me right now, which I deserve, but I don't believe it was just a fling with us. To be honest, I always wanted more, but I felt like you were the hesitant one."

"Bernardo, you seriously are not going to try to make this somehow to be my subconscious, underlying fault are you? 'Cause if so, you have a bigger set of balls than I originally thought."

"Willow, no, of course not. I take full responsibility for my actions.

What I am trying to say, if we are being honest, is that I always really did want more from you, but I was afraid that if I opened myself up to you more, that you might reject me. I, too, have been hurt, so I regrettably chose not to. But, Willow, something tells me it may not have mattered. I tried to get closer to you over the last few weeks, and you continued to push me away. I know you have been going through a lot with your thyroid - mentally, physically, emotionally, all around - but, whatever happened to you, I started to feel a distance between us."

"So, what Bernardo? You decided that sleeping with someone else might solve the issue?"

"Willow, again, no, no. I know it was bad judgment. I guess I just thought after our last conversation, well, I got the sense that you were already checking out from me, meaning it sort of felt like you might not want to see me as much anymore."

I had to admit, he was partly right, but a girl can change her mind, too, I was just a little too late.

"Bernardo, on some level, I can see your point of view. Yes, I am aware of my distant behavior over the last few weeks, but this is sort of just the way it is right now. I guess there is good news and not such good news. I suppose the good news is you realized that you are now over your ex-girlfriend. Your feelings for me may have been a little more than you originally anticipated, and you may now realize that by my reaction. I guess you can walk away from this also knowing my feelings for you were real, too. However, the bad news is that it's all a little too late, and the timing is not right."

He sighed and said, "Oh, Willow, please don't say that, please give me another chance. I know I screwed up, but why, dear Willow, would you want to walk away from something that could be beautiful? I know there is a hurt little girl inside who is so afraid to be loved. I am saying give me a chance to love you. Please, let's start over."

As tempting and sweet as the offer was, I felt numb, and wanted to get off the phone.

"Bernardo, listen, I am being genuinely honest right now when I say this to you, something went offline for us, I am not denying it. Whatever happened, I am going to say I am sad, but maybe it's for the best. So listen. I forgive you. You should be relieved that I am not going to continue to beat you up about this. I'm saying let's just walk away with another lesson. In the future, we will both try and not lie to our respective others, and we will not be afraid to open up more. Okay?"

He was silent, dead silent, as if he could not believe what I was saying.

"Willow, okay, what else can I say? As if I have a choice. I am just so sad right now. I wish there was a way I could have this with you, not the next girl. I want to be with you."

"I am sorry Bernardo, it's over! It's not going to be with me. I know you have a good heart underneath some of those insecurities, we all do."

"Gosh, Willow, sometimes when you say what you say, I don't know if it's a dig or genuine."

"Bernardo, unfortunately I think there was a lot you did not know about me, but I am okay with that. So listen, I am pulling up to my house and I can see my grandpa needs some help with groceries. I need to get off the phone."

"Willow, again, I am sorry. Is there any way I can still call you sometime, even if it is just to talk? I know dating me is out of the question, but just to talk?"

"Yes, but give me some time please, respect that."

"I will, Willow. Goodbye and take care of you!"

I hung up. My grandpa was not really standing there with groceries in his hands, but I felt an overwhelming need to get off that phone. I sat in the driveway for a few minutes and felt myself tear up.

I was sad - I did have genuine feelings for him, but something was off, and I knew no matter what that I needed to focus on myself and did not need the complication of him in my life right now. Besides, this gave me a perfect excuse to look forward to seeing Will, who was coming in soon.

I got out of my car and heard this interesting birdie call above my head. I looked up and for sure, it was my red cardinal! I took a deep breath, smiled, and went inside. I knew it was all going to be okay!

My reassurance unfortunately did not last that long for I couldn't sleep that night. I found myself just lying there, snowballing negative thought after negative thought. There was something about the vulnerability I felt after my conversation with Bernardo that began to stir the pot more and more. I was sort of angry with myself for being so guarded at times with men. I was also upset because I felt like an insecure teenage girl again from this incident, and how crappy I felt in my past when two of my ex-boyfriends cheated on me. I began questioning everything, and wondering what was wrong with me. I felt like my identity was off and I was doing a real number on myself, right down to fears about my lack of future plans. This blew itself up into a full anxiety attack. There was nothing I could do but just lie there and let it happen. I felt helpless and alone. It was a little after 2 a.m., and I knew I didn't want to call anyone this late. I started to cry and couldn't stop. Something told me that a major shift was happening for me, and as painful as this was, I needed to go through it to understand.

Next thing I knew, I found myself on bended knee by my bedside praying to God to help me start healing and to feel like myself again. I asked God to gently please show me the way and to please help me fall back asleep. I crawled back into bed. Somehow, I fell into a deep sleep. I had a dream that night that I walked into a beautiful lit room filled with six or seven people I had never seen before. Although, what was interesting was that they didn't feel like strangers, they felt like incarnated angels dressed like average people. I just remember they all had these beautiful smiles on their faces. It was the most welcoming room of people I had ever seen.

This beautiful woman walked up to me, took my hand, and said, "You must be Willow. We have been expecting you. My name is Faith and these are my friends. Welcome, my dear one, to the Course in Miracles. Your whole life and everything you thought you knew is going to change. Let the healing begin."

I remember not being frightened at all. I took her hand and sat next to them. I don't remember the extent of the conversations, but I remember that I felt safe and loved. It was a sign for sure. I couldn't wait to get to work to tell Ed my dream, and that I was going to go with him to his next group.

When I got to work, Ed was there. I ran right over to him and told him about the dream. He laughed a little and said, "So, what are you doing later today? My friend Gayla, who runs that group, called me last night and asked if we could all get together tonight around five o'clock, instead of this weekend. She has to go out of town. So Willow, what are the chances of that?"

I smiled, "I got it, Ed, and yes, I will come."

He scribbled on a pad and handed the sheet of paper to me, "Here is the address, and it's not far from Lotus and me."

I looked at the paper, and it said, 111 New St. I felt goose bumps go from the bottom of my toes up to my arms.

"Ed, is this a joke? Is this the real address?"

He laughed, "Willow, no, not a joke, and I knew you would fully appreciate it when it was time. It is time. Angels have a sense of humor too, you will learn that as well. Trust, Willow, trust."

I took a deep breath, "I'm nervous, but I trust you, Ed, so I'll see you there."

"I look forward to it."

After work, I went home, took a quick shower, and was trying to figure out what to wear. Then I realized that the group I am going to is all about love, they couldn't care less if I go in sweatpants or a dress. I decided on my favorite brown palazzo pants, blue flip-flops, and my new shirt that says 'love' on it. That fit. That said *me*.

I told Grandpa I was going to meet some friends at work for an early dinner - he doesn't need to know everything about my personal spiritual life. I kissed him on the forehead and headed out.

I got in my car and felt a little nervous. I looked at my watch and realized that it was almost five o'clock. Shoot, I didn't want to be late - not a good first impression. As I pulled out of the driveway, I looked up and I said a quick prayer. "God, angels, whoever is listening, I am new to this, and I am sorry to ask, but is there any way that this woman Gayla, who is running the group, might start a few minutes late? Can you work your magic? I hate to be the one who shows up late on the first day. Thank you."

I blew a kiss upward.

# Chapter 18

I PULLED UP TO THIS sweet, angelic-looking house. It was all white, with soft yellow shutters. I got out of my car and could immediately feel warm energy surrounding it. She had a beautiful garden, too. As I was walking up to her door, I noticed a big arrow pointing toward the front door, and above it was written, "Pathway to love straight ahead." I laughed and felt more relaxed.

I knocked on the door, and this tall woman with a pointy nose and a short bob hair cut opened it with a warm smile and said, "Hello, welcome." She bent over and gave me a hug. As I was leaning in, I said, "You must be Gayla. I am so sorry I'm a little late - my name is Willow."

She smiled, "No, I'm not Gayla, I am Mary, her good friend. Gayla called to tell me that she got held up at work and asked if I could get here a few minutes early to let everyone in. So, don't worry, you're not late."

I smiled and thought *oh, my God, miracle number one.* Be careful what you wish for! It was a harmless request, I know, but I was glad I wasn't late. I walked into a room and saw smiling faces all around. I immediately scanned the room for Ed and saw him chatting to a grey-haired woman. There were about six or seven women, all sitting on chairs in a circle, and a beautiful white Labrador retriever sitting on the side. Ed was the only male here. He made eye contact with me, got up, walked over, and introduced me to all of the women in the room. As I was walking around, something interesting struck me - all of their names began with the letter M - Mary, Marilyn, Meredith, Molly, Marybeth, and Maryanne.

Marybeth looked down at the dog, pointed and said, "Ed, don't forget our main supporter."

He laughed, "Oops, sorry, and this is Max, Gayla's dog. I don't care if you are a dog person or not, this is the most loving, coolest dog on earth." He waved him over, "Come here, Max, meet Willow."

Max jumped up and came over to lick my cheek. He was sweet, and I could feel his unconditional love. I said to Ed, "My nephew's name is Max, so I like this dog already."

For some reason, I then had a flashback of being a young child, maybe around three years old, and being bitten by my Aunt Ellen's dog. I was afraid of dogs for many years. That was until one day, when I was eight years old, Grandma Lu and I were on our way home from shopping at the drug store. I will never forget this day. I was eating a cherry lollipop she bought me as we checked out at the counter. We were walking back from the store, and out of nowhere, this large black dog in front of a green house started barking at us. I was petrified and starting screaming, crying, and wrapping my arms around Grandma's Lu's leg, hanging on for dear life. She tried to calm me down, but I wouldn't let go. Next thing I knew, in the sweetest, most gentle Grandma Lu voice, she bent down to me and said, "Willow, he's on a leash - you see, he's not attacking you. I know you are frightened, but Willow, you are a big girl now, and I don't want you to think that every dog is scary and will bite you. So, I am going to ask you to trust Grandma. Now, follow me slowly over to this dog and you will see he is really actually sweet. His name is Murphy. I know the owners of this house, Willow. He is a friendly dog."

"But Grandma, why is he barking so loud? It's scary."

"Willow, would you believe me if I told you as loud as that bark is, he is actually trying to say hello because he sees what a sweet girl you are, and he wants to be friends with you."

God bless Grandma for always knowing what to say to calm me down on the spur of the moment, and to make something frightening into a comforting scenario. Whatever she said seemed to have worked, for the next thing I knew, I was tiptoeing, still holding onto her leg, slowly toward Murphy. Grandma Lu slowly put her hand out, and said "Hey, Murph, it's Luciana, remember me? This is my beautiful granddaughter, Willow."

Murphy bent down and sniffed Grandma's hand, and started to lick it. She looked at me and said, "See, Willow? He is nice and friendly. Now, give me your hand, I promise he is not going to bite you, he just wants to smell your hand."

I looked at her and put my shaking hand towards him. He sniffed mine and started licking my hand, too. We both started to pet him slowly, and I remember that she made eye contact with me and said, "See, love, he doesn't want to hurt you. He wants to be your friend. Willow, honey, you are the top speller of your third grade class, am I right?"

I smiled and nodded, wondering what this had to do with Murphy, but I said, "Yes, Grandma. I win all the spelling bees - you know that."

"Good, sweetheart, then here's one for you. What does dog spell backwards?"

I was eight years old, but I knew right away what she was saying. "God, Grandma."

"That's right, honey, and do you know why that is?"

I shook my head, but even at eight years old, I had a strong sense of what she was trying to tell me.

"Willow, baby, there is a reason that dog is known as a man's best friend. Just like God, doggies will protect you and love you unconditionally, honey. You don't have to be afraid anymore, you understand?" I nodded and hugged her, and was never quite as scared of dogs.

After reminiscing, I came back into the room. Ed must have realized I tuned out a little. "Willow, you okay?"

"Oh, sorry Ed, I was just remembering a time with my grandma and dogs. In the meantime, how about all of the women in here whose names begin with the letter M?"

He laughed, "I know, we all joke about that. There is something about names that begin with M - these tend to be women with a loving maternal instinct, like Mother Mary."

I smiled, "Gotcha."

We sat down, and in walked Gayla. She looked like an angel. I swear, I could almost see a little halo over her head. She had soft, blondish white hair with rosy pink cheeks. She was wearing a white sweater with a pretty angel pin on her shoulder and cool retro eyeglasses.

She saw Ed, and walked right over to us and gave me the biggest hug ever, and said, "You must be Willow. I've heard lots of great things about you from Ed. I'm so glad you could join us."

My nervousness went away. "Gayla, so nice to meet you, too, and thank you for having me. I'm not sure what this is all about, but my gut told me I should be here."

She looked me right in the eyes with a gentle stare and said, "This course is going to help you become the person you never knew, but deep down you always were at core."

I wasn't completely sure what she meant, but I nodded politely, because it sounded like just what I needed to hear!

We all went around and re-introduced ourselves. Gayla was so nice. She knew it was my first time, so she tried to explain the course in a way that wouldn't make me feel like it was some preachy religious group.

"Willow, dear, we use terms a lot in this course - like the Holy or Divine Spirit - but not in a religious manner. In a spiritual nutshell, sweetie, this book gives you an opportunity to look at love from the eyes of Jesus. But, don't go running for the door because I said the word Jesus. This course is not here to preach about him. You see, many religious groups talk about salvation, sins, guilt, punishment

- etc. However, this course is the opposite. It is pretty much Jesus' way of saying, "Whatever they may have taught you in school about me, this course is my way of trying to teach you what I really meant."

According to the course, there is NO such thing as sin. God and Jesus want you to understand over and over that you are a worthy and loving being. Most importantly, you are already a part of them. You are not separate, honey. A lot of religions would have you think otherwise. So, this course challenges what religion denies you. God and Jesus want you to know that all of your amazing wisdom is already a part of you because they are a part of you.

You see, we have spent eons denying our true selves. The ego is our greatest challenge. It constantly wants to put us down or tell us why we are not good enough. It seems to always want to control. But when the course talks about the ego, although its related, is NOT talking about the kind you learned in psychology 101. Ego is really just another way of talking about the mind. There has been a joke amongst a few of us here in the group that the word ego actually stands for Easing God Out. However, this course is hoping to pull God back into your heart, for that is where He and the Divine Spirit truly live. So sort of like the ego or mind vs. God or your heart. It will also teach you how to love others and be less judgmental, and again, learn to love others and yourself with unconditional love. "

As she continued, I became fascinated by everything she was saying. I felt relief for the first time in my life that I might actually benefit from my fear of a punishing authority, and give my mind a new way to see things.

We read through a few paragraphs of this big blue book. Some stuff I was confused about, but some made miraculous sense! The next thing I knew she said to me, "Willow, if I could leave you with one important lesson today it is to ask yourself, in any difficult situation, do you want to choose love or fear? Which one feels better, because guess what? This course is always going to try to remind you which one to choose."

I always have a choice. Wow! For the first time I actually believed it - I *felt* her words - I can choose love. Just hearing the word love warmed my heart.

I smiled at her and said, "So, Gayla, for example if I find myself ruminating and obsessing about unpleasant negative thoughts, I should try to choose loving and compassionate ones not the other bullshhh…" I stopped, realizing I might offend someone with my word.

She laughed and said, "It's okay. Willow, you can say anything in here including 'bullshit'. So, yes dear, choose what God would want to choose for you - LOVE. And, according to one of my favorite lessons in this course, #11…" Before she could say anything I smiled - of course #11 - my number of all numbers!

She continued and said, "Willow, Lesson 11 is: 'My meaningless thoughts are showing me a meaningless world.' That's just what they are, honey. When you start obsessing about negative stuff, they are all illusions, not your real thoughts. The Divine Spirit talks a lot about this too, again - ego vs. God's mind. Which feels better? For when you are able to get in touch with God, your real thoughts come into place and you will feel at peace, at one, sweet child, with God." I smiled. I got it.

"Thank you, Gayla, for explaining, I got it!"

We closed out the group with a five-minute meditation, which helped to relax me even more. I was so relieved. I finally found something that may help me get over all of this negative bullshit I had been telling myself and that probably ended up making me sick. I was ready for a change.

When the meeting ended, Ed walked me to the front door, "So, Willow, what did you think?"

"Ed, I think you somehow knew this is exactly what I needed.

The universe really does work in mysterious ways. So, thank you. I will be back, for sure!"

He laughed, "Yes, Willow, I did somehow know, and I'm so glad you're open, because this is the first step toward trusting that true healing comes from knowing that you are nothing but love. You will learn this, Willow. It may take a little time, but you will see soon enough that this is what this journey is all about - to remember that you are love itself."

Agape popped into my head. I smiled, waved goodbye, and got into my car.

As I was on my way home, I was in sort of a daydream mindset. For once I didn't feel the need to turn on my radio for distraction, I was enjoying the peace of just silence, being able to be present with the moment. Something told me, as Ed said, this course is going to bring me true healing.

I looked in my rearview mirror and noticed an old white car coming toward me. As it passed, I couldn't believe my eyes, for the license plate said AGAPEIN. I knew that, once again, I was being shown that God's love is unconditional and that it will be the answer to my prayers. I smiled as gentle tears started to fill my eyes. I realized I had not seen Luke, who introduced me to the word, in a while. What were the chances I would see this word once again? I wanted to stop by and say hello.

# Chapter 19

I WALKED THROUGH THE FRONT doors of the assisted living facility hoping that Luke would be working. I went up and down the halls with no luck. I was about to lose hope, when in my left ear I heard a sweet humming coming from a corner room. I walked down the hall and knocked on the door. To my delight, there he was, bent over wiping something up.

"I'm cleaning up an accident. Excuse the accident and the view of my backside."

I giggled and said, "It's okay, it doesn't bother me – I'm full of Agape love!"

He realized it was my voice and turned around.

"Oh, Miss Willow, what a beautiful surprise again!" Oh, how I love that crooked tooth smile. "To what do I owe a lovely lady's presence?"

"Well, Luke, it's been a few weeks. I figured we were overdo for a little loving chat, you got a sec?"

"For you, Willow, I got a lifetime - just let me finish up. My break is in five minutes, why don't you meet me in the courtyard?"

"Sounds great, Luke, I'll meet you there."

I took a walk around the home and thought about whether or not I was able to stop by the room my grandmother had been in. I decided to courageously take a peek in and see who had taken her place. I gazed in and saw an older-looking man, resting. I looked at the door for the nametag - it said Samuel Calm. I smiled - what a cool last name! I don't think I have ever seen that for a last name. As I watched this man sleeping, I actually felt a feeling of calmness. Hm-m-m...

As I turned around to leave, I could hear over my shoulder, "Hey, you!" I must have awakened him. I pointed toward myself with a *who me?* face.

He coughed and said, "Yeah, you, with the long dark Pocahontas hair. Who are you?" Oops, perhaps I had read this Samuel wrong, for I sensed grouchiness in his tone.

"Oh, sorry. I didn't mean to disturb you, sir, I thought you were sleeping. This used to be my grandmother's room.

He hacked up this loud cough again, "Oh, did they move her down the hall?"

"No, she passed away a little while ago, this was her room."

"Sorry to hear that." He softened his voice.

"Thanks, she was a special lady."

He half smiled and said, "Well, sorry to take a dump on your reminiscing moment, but I ain't sweet, honey, and I ain't looking to be reminded of anything, either."

My eyeballs popped open, I was shocked and sad. How could a man at this stage in his life be so bitter? I decided I'd better let this go and find Luke, and be reminded about something pleasant.

I put my head down like a child who has just been scorned and said to Samuel, "Sorry to disturb you. Have a good day."

As I turned to walk out, I heard him say, "Oh, you don't have to go out sad, I'm sorry if I was harsh. I'm mourning the loss of my wife, too, sometimes this mean response comes out of me. I don't mean it. What's your name?"

I smiled, "It's okay, I understand. My name is Willow."

He scrunched his nose, "What did you say, Widow? Like the spider? Or someone like me, who just lost his loved one?"

I laughed, "No, sir, quite the opposite. It's Willow, like the tree, and you can let your mind decide whatever you want about that one."

"Well, I'll be darned. Willow was my wife's favorite tree. Of course I know what that means. She had me plant one right out front of our home."

I softened because he must have felt a sense of peace thinking about her.

I said, "Oh, how sweet."

He sniffed and coughed again, "Well, yeah, she was sweet, and I was the meanie. That's what she used to call me when she could tell I was in a grouchy mood, which was a little more than I am proud to say."

I laughed, "Got it! And by looking at your nametag on the door, I see you are Samuel. I like that name, and it's interesting that your last name is Calm."

He gave me the hand swish *done* look. Like, *don't bother asking*, but then he said, "Yeah, I know, my wife is convinced God gave me that last name to remind me to calm down whenever I find myself getting worked up. You believe that baloney, Willow?"

I laughed for I felt it in my heart - a sign for sure.

"Samuel, not only do I believe it, but I think that was your sweet wife's way of trying to remind you that underneath that hard shell of yours really lays a soft egg. So yes, I do believe that baloney, Mr. Calm." I Willow Winked him. He smiled. For the first time since her death, I really felt like my grandmother. This is something she would have said.

I looked at my watch and realized that Luke must be waiting. "Oops, sorry Samuel, gotta run."

He says back, "What, you got a hot date with one of the other old crooners here?"

"Not quite, I have a special friend waiting for me. Nice to meet you Samuel, maybe I will see 'ya around?"

He coughed again. "Yeah, maybe. You could come around again, I promise my bark is bigger than my bite."

He winked me back. I waved to him. I smiled, interesting

interaction. Something told me that this might be someone I should visit, a life lesson perhaps, not just for him, but me as well.

I saw Luke sitting on the bench drinking his Yoo-Hoo boxed drink, eating a ham sandwich on white bread, with an apple on his lap. How cute. I bet his wife made him lunch or dinner everyday dependent on his shift time.

He smiled and said, "I thought you bailed on me."

"Sorry, I am a little late. I ended up stopping by my grandmother's old room to see who had taken her place. It turns out the man who is there now is not quite as sweet as I thought, a Mr. Samuel Calm, do you know him?"

He laughed placed his sandwich down, and said, "Who? Mr. Calm? Ironic isn't it? The last name. Yeah, Willow, he is a mean old man on the outside, but I have broken him down a few times where he showed his softer side, which we know is in there."

I laughed, "Yeah, Luke, that is exactly what I said. He's harmless, I know it."

"Yeah, Willow, I think he is suffering from a broken heart and a bad cough. He has lung cancer, 'ya know?"

"I thought he had something related to that, wasn't sure."

"Yeah, he told me he was heavy smoker most of his life, and his wife always hated it and made him quit, but after she died, he was so distraught, he picked up smoking again, and landed himself in the hospital. It's a shame."

"I hear 'ya, Luke, loss can be tough!"

"It sure can, Willow, it sure can. So, enough about Mr. Calm - what brings you to see me?"

"Okay, well, I was on my way back from this beautiful group I just joined, it's called a "Course In Miracles." Have you ever heard of it?"

He smiled, "Yes, Willow, I am familiar with it. My old friend and neighbor, Kenny, used to be a student of it. I remember that we used to sit on our stoops and discuss religion, politics, love, all sorts of stuff. He was always telling me interesting lessons he learned. We were both raised in Christian families, but not always happy with words like sin and, you know, believing in punishment and all those things they taught us in school. Kenny used to challenge me sometimes with a quote here or there from The Course when he sensed I might be questioning myself."

"I know what you mean, Luke. So, as I mentioned, this group opened me up to feel at peace for the first time in a long time. You know, since this thyroid thing, I've been struggling with questioning everything about myself, and I don't have to get into the details about it, but everything, from my mind, to my past relationships, etc. You get it, I know, so they helped me to see the light."

He smiled and took another bite of his sandwich.

I continued "So, after I left, I was on my way home and there it was, out of nowhere Luke, another car with a license plate but this time it said AGAPEIN pulled up beside me. I couldn't believe it!"

He laughed. "Oh, Willow, the divine has a great sense of humor, doesn't it?"

"You're not kidding, Luke, but what I took from that, I guess, is the reminder that God is going to love me no matter what, and again I need to learn to love me, no matter what and this love can be found within myself!"

"Willow, you know you are pretty ...... what is that word?" as he snaps his fingers to try to remember it, "clairvognant, clairvoysomething?"

I smiled, "You mean clairvoyant?"

He grinned, and pointed at me, "Yeah, that's it, clairvoyant, 'ya know - very in touch with getting messages and knowing what they mean when you get them. My Aunt Anastasia was a lot like that, always letting me know when something was a sign. It is a nice gift,

Willow, but you have to be careful with that sometimes. 'Ya know, the whole sign thing?"

I raised my brow, "What do you mean?"

"Well, darling, sometimes we end up looking too much outside of ourselves for those signs to help us make decisions, and then it sort of defeats the purpose. One thing I remember pretty strongly that Kenny always talked about was the fact that the Holy Spirit is a part of us already, so again, when we keep looking outside to help fix or soothe, it becomes tricky. You know, the mind versus the God thing." He points to his heart which reminded me right away of Grandma Lu, and said, "Willow, the answers really lie in here, 'ya know? That's where your Agape God lives anyway. 'Ya know that, right?"

"I'm learning now, Luke, I am."

We continued to shoot the small talk, and he asked about my love life. I told him what happened with Bernardo, and about Will - how we met on the airplane. I told him about my prayer the night before my flight about if there was anyone important I was supposed to meet the next day, God should let me know.

He giggled, "Wow, Willow, really, that is cool. So, here is one little piece of advice - I am not sure why I feel compelled to say this to you, but let me say it. This Will, this Stranger from the Plane guy, something tells me that you take it slow with this one. He is going to have a tender heart, and you will learn something you need to learn from him. Not sure what it is yet, sweet lady, but something good."

I smiled, "Really? What makes you say that?"

"Willow, honey, I don't know. Maybe that is part of Luke's clairvoyant gift, sensing something loving coming your way." He winked at me.

"I like the sound of that, Luke, I really do. Thanks!" I Willow Winked him back.

# Chapter 20

I WENT INTO WORK, AND was so happy to see Ed. Today, he was wearing a turquoise blue hat with a fun pair of turquoise blue Converse sneakers and, of course, another cool blue watch. I walked right over to him. He smiled at me.

"Hey, you, I was hoping to see you."

"Morning, Ed, what's cooking?" I asked.

"Well, Willow, I have some good news."

"What's that?"

"It turns out my publisher is looking for me to put together a book of poems and short stories from people I have met throughout my life, who I believe to have real talent. I was thinking of you, and wondering if you might be interested in showing me what you feel is your best piece." I was stunned.

"What? Really?"

"Really, Willow. I think it's time you finally had the confidence to show me a few. I know your ego is going to try and talk you out of why you think they may not be good enough, but Willow, let me be the judge of that! I'm going out of town tomorrow for a few days. When I get back, I expect to see two of your best."

"Ed, I don't know what to say, but I am ecstatic, over the top, at the thought of one of my poems possibly being published!"

He giggled, "Not maybe, Willow, even if we have to play around with it, we will make it work."

I felt my heart almost burst with joy. "Thanks, Ed. I don't know what to say, but breakfast is on me today!"

"You don't have to say anything, Willow, I know you are grateful, and I know that you are meant to be a part of this book."

"Thank you again for giving me a shot!"

"You got it!"

After work, I pulled up to Grandpa's house and saw him planting something in the front yard. I have never in my life seen him plant anything! I was shocked. I got out of the car and gave him a funny look.

He pulled off a pair of gloves, which I was surprised he even knew to buy, stood up and said, "Before you continue to look at your grandpa all cock-eyed, let me explain."

"By all means, Gramps, what are you planting?"

"Well, Willow, yesterday morning I was reading an article in the *Times* about a husband who lost his wife to Alzheimer's, and he wanted to keep and honor her around their home. Apparently, oranges were his wife's favorite fruit - she ate them every day to keep her vitamin C intact. Anyway, her husband planted an orange tree in their front yard, not realizing what he was really doing, or if it would even work. Not only did it work, but what makes the story so special is that apparently, during the month of what would have been their anniversary, there was always the best batch of oranges - the sweetest, the brightest. He thought it was sort of her way of letting him know she was there. He also always shares them with his neighbors, who love him."

I stopped him and said, "Sweet, Gramp, but Grandma wasn't a big orange fan. If anything, she was an apple lover. She used to say, 'Willow, an apple a day keeps the doctor away.' Grandpa, I listened, because you know I still eat one every day." I Willow Winked him.

"Yes, love, I know. So, what your grandpa is going to try to do - you guessed it, plant a mini apple tree! Who knows, let's see, maybe your Grandma Lu, will give us a sign, too." He winked back at me. I melted at the thought of how much he loved my grandma.

"Sounds like a great idea."

I was so excited about the possibility of having a poem published!

I went through a bunch of them in my folder, and tried to pick the ones I thought might be representative of me. As I re-read each one, I was reminded of how much pain I had felt, and then of course, how enlightened I could be, with each verse. I thought maybe if I lay down and meditated for a while, I might be able to re-inspire myself to write something new. I closed my eyes and actually ended up falling asleep. Unfortunately, I woke up in terror from a bad dream again about my ex-boyfriend from my younger years, who was being really mean to me in the dream. He was trying to be intimate with me and I remember I didn't want to, like I sort of felt pressured, because I was afraid he wouldn't love me. I hated the way I felt and started crying in my sleep. When I woke up I felt so uneasy about the dream, and analyzing perhaps if I have somehow repressed emotional pain from my past.

I decided to call my therapist, Dr. Gatewin back in Philly, in anxious mode, asking her to call me back as soon as she could. I couldn't help the icky feeling from that dream. I waited patiently. I knew she checked her messages periodically. The phone rang about 30 minutes later. I explained the entire thing to her. She told me that it was time to start addressing some of this repressed emotional stuff. She told me that it would be hard for her to do this over the phone, but she actually knew someone whom she felt might be perfect to help me through this, and who only practiced about twenty minutes away from me. She was a spiritual psychologist who specialized in helping many with these types of issues.

Dr. Gatewin said she was proud of me for joining the Course in Miracles, and glad to hear I was getting on the right track with my thyroid, but said, "Willow, sometimes we need something a little stronger than basic therapy. I think we know the why's of it all, but it sounds like at this point in your life, you might need a little more faith in something bigger than we can see."

"Dr. Gatewin, I'm scared. Lately, I feel like the floor is being pulled out from underneath me, and I'm scared shitless - like I might die or something sometimes."

"Willow, honey, I promise you are not dying. What I think is actually happening dear, is that you are being reborn, as they say. Your soul is aching for you to re-awaken into who it is you really want to become."

I stopped crying for a little and thanked her for calling me. She recommended I take half an Ativan, reconsider taking thyroid medication, and to go write some poetry, because she knew it always made me feel better. I wasn't sure what I wanted to write, but I sat and allowed whatever to come, come. I also started to rethink taking a small amount of medicine.

I set up an appointment with the therapist for later in the week. I was not thrilled about the fact that on top of everything else I was doing, I had to go back into therapy. I was so freaking exhausted from trying to figure out how to fix everything. I just wanted it fixed already.

I got into my car, and while I was on my way to work, I started to get upset again thinking about how frustrated I felt lately. I felt the tears start falling and falling some more. I also had my period, which I knew was feeding into a hormonal frenzy. My tears turned into anger and I found myself praying out loud to God, saying *please God help me heal this anguish today, help me see something new.*

I ended up calling my father, like I normally do when I am upset and frustrated.

He picked up right away, "Willow, honey, what is it?"

The tears started pouring out more and more. "Dad, I'm scared and frustrated. I am so sick of going to doctors trying to figure out how to fix me. I just want to feel like myself again, is that too much to ask?"

Next thing I knew, a car pulled up next to me with a license plate that said 'MD 917'. I couldn't believe my eyes. My father sensed my silence.

"Willow, are you there? Are you there?"

"Dad, oh my God, you won't believe it!"

"Believe what, Willow, what?"

"Dad, a car just pulled up beside me with a license plate that says 'MD 917'. Dad, you know what MD stands for, right?"

He laughed, "Doctor, right?"

"Right, and what is 917?"

"Your birthday, Willow!"

"Dad, holy crapola - I get it. The message means *Willow look within to solve your stuff*, meaning I am my own best healer."

I immediately stopped crying. He giggled.

"There you go, sweetheart, you got your message. You are going to be okay, start trusting yourself more. I know you're frustrated by your anxiety at times, but as you get older, as I told your mother and your sister who also went through this, you, too, will get through it. I promise!"

"Thanks, Dad, I feel better already!"

We hung up. I fell silent. A few minutes later, I got a text from Carla that said, *Hey, you, I felt like you were having a bad day, hope you are well, miss 'ya lots, and whatever is cooking, I promise you will be fine.* I smiled. It's amazing how she always knows.

When I got to work, Brenda was there. She had been off for a few weeks away with her family. There she was, back in black, literally, with a sourpuss look on her face. You'd think being away would help her mood, but no can do. I tried to make small talk with her, but she wasn't interested. I decided to leave her alone. A few hours later at the core of lunch hour I noticed she was nowhere to be found. Her tables were waiting, so I asked Devon if she had left.

He said, "No, but I saw her go into the bathroom a few minutes ago. You might want to go check."

I refilled her tables with coffee and ran into the bathroom. I opened the door and could hear sniffling in one of the stalls, like someone was crying.

"Brenda, it's Willow, are you alright?"

"Yeah, I'll be out in minute. Just tell my tables to hold their asses." Isn't it horses?

"Okay, no problem, take your time. I'll cover you."

As I walked out, I realized I was right - she is not as tough as she appears. A few minutes later, she came out with black eyeliner smeared under her eyes. She must have been so upset that she forgot to check the mirror. She walked over to me, and for the first time ever, half-smiled at me and said, "Thanks for covering me."

"No problem, if you ever want to talk, I am a good listener. I mean, I know you aren't my biggest fan, but I'm here."

I saw her eyes start to well up again. I took her hand and said, "Everybody is covered right now, let's go step outside for two minutes and get some fresh air. I'll tell Devon to come get us if anyone needs something."

She surrendered and came outside. We sat on a bench. I took the initiative, "So what is it? Let it out."

"Well, I just found out my boyfriend of eight months cheated on me with some stupid slut for a one-night stand while I was away with my family. I knew I couldn't trust him."

I scrunched my face, "Oh Brenda, I am sorry. I know the feeling and it sucks, but I can tell you that his behavior isn't worth your sadness right now. I know you're a tough cookie, but you are beautiful girl underneath all of your dark makeup and clothes, with a good heart. When you start letting some of your tender side come out, I bet you will meet a new guy who will make you completely forget about what's-his-name"

She half-giggled and said, "Derek."

She took a deep breath and said to me, "Wow, you surprised me. I thought you were one of those prissy girls who only cares about herself."

"Brenda, really, do I have to pull out the whole *don't judge a book by its cover thing?* I just taught you a lesson, my friend."

She sighed and said, "You did, and I'm sorry if I was ever bitchy to you. You know, it's just my defense mechanism - I'm learning that right now in my Psych 101 class."

"Oh-h-h, a psych major, maybe? You don't say? I was one, too. You'll learn lots of interesting things about your behaviors and those of others around you, but don't necessarily believe everything you learn, either."

"I know. So, thanks for listening, you've already made me feel a little better."

"No problem - anytime."

As we walked back in, I thought about the Course in Miracles and how it stressed the importance of loving your brothers and sisters, and treating them the way the Divine Spirit would want. I felt that for the first time, hallelujah! I think I cracked Brenda's shell!

# Chapter 21

I PULLED UP TO THE therapist's office. I couldn't believe I was going to yet another doctor. How many doctors did I have to see? But, I knew that this was a spiritual doctor, and it was time to start clearing out some old emotional baggage. Besides, if that message on the license plate was true, perhaps this was just the right kind of doctor to help me start healing my issues.

I walked into the small, quaint waiting area. There was one of those sound machines playing white noise - I guess to block out all other sounds. I was starting to think that all therapists do this. On the wall there was a beautiful depiction of an angel holding the hand of a small child with all of this incredible light around them. Good sign.

The therapist opened the door with a gentle, warm smile and said, "You must be Willow. It's a pleasure to meet you. I'm Dr. Katie Mellow, but you can call me Katie."

She was a very pretty woman, with soft brown hair, pretty eyes with cool lavender eye shadow and lavender nails that matched.

I laughed and said, "Mellow, as in chill out?"

She giggled back, "Yeah, you think it was a sign I should be a therapist?"

"I would say so, I feel chiller already."

I followed her in. Of course, there was your standard couch and a comfy love seat. She told me to pick either, or. I opted for the couch.

She said, "Please, make yourself comfortable."

"Thanks."

"So, Willow, Dr. Gatewin gave me a little history, but I always like to sort of start where you are comfortable. So, if right here and now you have something you would like to address, I am open to hear it." I like her style already.

"Well, Katie, to make a very long history short, I lost my grandmother recently. Then I was diagnosed with a thyroid disease. I had no clue how much your thyroid can affect your well-being on all levels. I have felt a little more anxious and depressed than normal. I've had some unpleasant thoughts about my mental well-being at times, meaning that I've been trying to convince myself that I am not going nuts.

"To top it off, I had such an unpleasant dream about my first boyfriend, who I lost my virginity to, and it was a horrible feeling. I'm sad to say that I lost my virginity fairly young, and it was a bad experience."

For another fifteen more minutes I spoke a little more about my history as she listened patiently. At some point, I thought I should pause.

She smiled, and took the in and said, "So, Willow, I'm sorry to hear about your grandmother, but I'm sure she is in a better place and with you always. Your thyroid is a tricky part of the body, but it really can be helped with medication, are you on any?"

I squinted and said, "No, not yet. I'm sort of anti-meds, but I'm reconsidering."

"I'm not a big medication fan, either, she said, "However, I do feel that there are certain things that you should do. I think that medication is a good idea to consider. It would certainly help your levels a little more, which in turn, I think, would help you feel more stable emotionally and physically. You have a small frame, so I don't think you'll need a lot. You can take a small amount."

I nodded, she was right - I think it was time. She sighed and then said, "As for your unfortunate dream and experience as a young woman - I would like to try something with you that I call heart-assisted therapy. It helps to rebalance your emotional and stress response levels no matter what the subject matter entails. Have you ever heard of it?"

I shook my head, "No, but it sounds interesting. Tell me more."

"Okay. It has actually worked very well for some of my patients who have suffered some sort of trauma or something in their life that was upsetting, but not necessarily a trauma. It could be anything that causes anxiety. It involves a little muscle testing, and some deep breathing with your hands criss-crossed over your heart area. It's sort of like doing diaphragmatic breathing with your heart instead of your belly.

"The reason we use the heart area is to remind us that we are made of love. By taking these gentle breaths, we are able to come back to a peaceful place and clear out some of the pain you went through."

I smiled, "Well, it sounds like a good start for me."

"And Willow, you don't have to do anything but just breathe through it. If you want to cry, that's okay, and sometimes beneficial, too. Just trust that your inner wisdom, your heart wisdom, will guide you through your recovery. I can see, Willow, that it's time to start clearing a lot out. I'm sure I don't have to tell you about what the thyroid area represents, do I?"

I half-smiled, "No, Katie, I know. Maybe we will get into my fear of expression a little more next time."

She smiled, "Willow, you are a very intuitive woman, do you know that?'

I giggled, "I do now, sort of, which actually leads me to something I would also like to discuss a little which is my spirituality. I've been getting all sorts of interesting signs and things to help me through this time, have you heard of this before?"

She smiled. I realized what I had just asked and said, "Sorry, Katie, silly question. You are, indeed, a spiritual psychologist, so I'm sure you have."

"Willow, I have, and I'm comfortable sharing that I've had numerous experiences myself. I also work with angels, and do angel healing sessions, but we can wait on that."

"Wow, I *am* in the right place, I know that now."

"Yes, Willow, you are and we are going to help heal you." I took a deep breath, I felt calmer already. "So what are you doing in the meantime to help your anxiety or stress? Do you meditate at all?" she asked.

"I do, every day - well, at least try to every day, even if it's just for ten minutes to give my mind a break. I also write poetry. It's my way of expressing. I also try to do some sort of exercise each day, whether it's walking, running, boot camp workouts, whatever."

"That's good. Are you on any medication to help your anxiety?" she asked.

"Occasionally, just a little Ativan if I feel anxious."

"Okay, well, I'm glad to hear that you're meditating. It's important, same with the exercise. The poetry - what a great way to express yourself! Keep doing that through this process, it will help.

"But, before we close, I would like to address one thing that you said to me at the beginning of the session, your fear of losing your mind. Willow, I can assure you that is not going to happen. That is your anxiety talking, and your ego mind trying to be very convincing. It is not. I think what you are experiencing right now is a temporary state of hyper-vigilance that's making your sensitive body feel off kilter. Again, I would like to recommend that we at least get your thyroid in check, and we will go from there.

"You'll get through this, Willow. Here is the other big question: Can you *trust* that?" I paused and had to think about it. I lifted my shoulders like I was not sure what to say.

"Sometimes, Katie, sometimes, but I want to trust that more. When I do trust it, I feel at peace, even if it's only for a few minutes."

She smiled, "The reason I am asking is because in order for us to get through this, we might have to trust something a little greater than doctors' words, or our parents' or friends' reassurance, do you understand what I am saying?"

"Yes, Katie, I do. You are asking me if I believe that God is on my side, and I do. I should also mention that I'm a new student of A Course In Miracles. That has just begun to shift me into what I think is important for me to know and, yes, trust."

"Willow, I am happy to share that I, too, am a student and have been for the last few years. I am glad to hear you trust that God is on your side, which also includes your guardian angels, and anybody else you feel comfortable speaking or praying to. It doesn't matter who it is, you will always end up getting the same message which is that you are, indeed, made of pure love and peace."

She gave me one more comforting smile and said, "Now, how about if we close with those comforting thoughts and set up a time for next week?"

"Sounds great, Katie, thank you so much. I believe I'm in good and safe hands with you, and I trust that you are just the right therapist to help me through this."

"I am, Willow, and we will."

# Chapter 22

I GOT INTO MY CAR and immediately decided to call my endocrinologist to ask him to start me on a small amount of thyroid medication. I got his voicemail, but left a message to call it into my pharmacy. As I headed home, a white car pulled up next to me with a license plate that said, 'CALM' in capital letters on it. I laughed and knew right away it was a sign for me to begin to chill out, and of course, to stop by the assisted living facility to pay my friend Mr. Samuel Calm a visit.

I walked into the facility and noticed that his door was open and he was watching television. I knocked gently on the door. He looked up, made a huge cough with a yucky, phlegmy throat and waved me in.

"Hi, Mr. Calm, remember me?"

He smirked, "My wife's favorite tree, how could I forget?"

He hit mute on the TV and I sat down next to him in a big brown chair. Then he said sarcastically, "What brings you to this Old Folkin Paradise?"

I laughed, "Well, I was in the area, and you said not to be a stranger, so I'm here not being a stranger."

I decided to wait to tell him about the license plate. "Oh, really? You came to visit an old grumpy man like me just because, h-m-m-m, you sure you want to? They forgot my cherry Jell-O at lunch today, I am still not over it."

I smirked back and said, "Cherry Jell-O? I prefer vanilla pudding, it's sweeter."

He half-smiles, "You and my wife both."

He coughed again really loudly, trying to catch his breath, and gave me the *one second* index finger up.

"Sorry about this. It's the lungs - they are starting to go."

"It's okay about the coughing, I understand. So, let me ask you, Samuel, what kinds of things do you like to do, meaning music, sports, or any other activities you might have done in your day?"

"Well, that's easy. I was a big golfer. God, I miss it so. I also loved to play poker with my buddies, and smoke cigars. Gosh, what I would give to smoke one of those again. As for music, well I have my wife to thank for that. Friday nights were always poker with the guys, and Saturday nights were always for my wife. We would go dancing at this local club. She could really move, my wife. Her name was Angela, by the way."

I interrupted and said, "How perfect, an angel."

He smiled back and said, "Exactly! So, when we first starting dating, I had never danced before. I was always afraid that I would stink or step on my date's feet. I remember when I asked her what she wanted to do on our first date she said, 'Take me dancing, and win my heart.' You could imagine the pressure.

"Now, if it were any other woman, I would have said *forget it*. But, I knew this one was a keeper, so I begged my friend Lonnie to help me with some steps before our night. I knew I wouldn't be great, but I really wanted to try to impress her."

I smiled and said, "So, what happened?"

"Well, I picked her up in my brand new Caddy and took her to this fun place with great bands. We got inside, the music was blaring - and I mean blaring - folks everywhere were shaking their thing. All of a sudden, I started to sweat and I thought I was going to pass out. I got so nervous! I was worried I would forget the steps and everything.

"She must have sensed I was not feeling right, or I was really nervous, and said to me, 'Sam, I don't care if you have two left feet, I just want to have fun with you. I promise you, I won't judge you on your dancing.'

"I immediately felt calmer. She had that way, as I mentioned before, and I somehow got my ass on that dance floor. I had the time of my life! She showed me all sorts of steps. I couldn't remember the last time I'd had that much fun on date. As a matter of fact, it was the best date I ever went on. I knew by the end of the night she was the woman for me."

I could see his eyes well up a little. I put my hand on his and said, "I knew there was a sweet and softer man under there. I'm glad you met a woman who gave you an opportunity to open up like that, and make you smile, and of course, to make you feel calmer, Mr. Calm." I Willow Winked him.

He smiled back, "She sure did, Willow, she sure did."

"Well, truth be told Sam, there is a little more of a reason I came here today. What if I told you that I was driving to the grocery store and a white car pulled up next to me that said 'CALM' in capital letters on its license plate?"

He squinted his forehead, "Really?"

"Really, Sam, and I took it as a sign that maybe you could use a little company, and of course, that your wife and our guardian angels must have a funny sense of humor!"

He sat up in his bed. "Well, Willow, normally this would be the part where I would say it's just a coincidence, and make some sarcastic remark, and then my wife would come back at me with another possible explanation. However, maybe, just maybe, it could be true. Something weird happened to me last night, too. I had an interesting dream about my wife."

"Really, what happened?" I asked.

"Well, we were out sitting on our porch, rocking on chairs, and she told me that she didn't want me to be bitter for the rest of my time here, and she wanted me to find a way to reconcile with our son. I haven't spoken to him in years."

I couldn't help but interrupt, "But, why? Sorry, don't mean to pry."

He threw his hand up in the air, "It's okay. He's angry with me because in one of my drunken stupors I told him that his job as an artist was a joke."

"Why did you tell him that?" I wanted to know.

"Willow, I don't know, it was stupid. I took a dump on my son's dreams. I always wanted more for him. I ran my own construction business, which was originally my father's. At some point, I wanted my son to take over the business, you know, to make a good living. But he told me that even as a kid, all he ever wanted to do was be a painter. My wife always encouraged him to do it - she believed in him. Maybe that's it, Willow, she believed in him, and I, as his father, didn't make him feel like it was attainable.

"Other kids, while he was growing up, would be outside playing kickball, building ant farms, but not my son, he was inside drawing and painting really weird stuff. My wife, of course, always hung them up or framed them. The kid had talent, don't get me wrong, but I guess I wanted a different path for him."

I put my hand on his, "Well, if you don't mind my interrupting this for a moment, is he successful?"

"Yes, he is. He owns a gallery and he lives somewhere in Key West with his boyfriend, I think. His boyfriend runs some sort of a studio, what do you call that exercise? Yogee?"

"Yoga, Sam, it's called Yoga. I practice it, too. So, without getting too personal, could this falling out have anything to do with your son's sexual preference?'

"Willow, I had issues with it when I first found out, but I don't care anymore about that. The real reason we had a falling out was because, as I mentioned earlier, one stupid night I drank too much during our Thanksgiving dinner, and I told him I was disappointed in him for not taking over the family business - that he chose painting instead. He told me he'd had enough of my putting him down about the choices he made and just wanted a father to love him for who he was. He stormed out.

"My wife was so angry with me. She wouldn't speak to me, either. She made me sleep on the couch for days, not that I blame her. I know it was wrong, and I did try to apologize to him a few days later, but he told me it was too late.

"So, getting back to this dream I had, my wife told me it was time for me to tell our son, Joe, that's his name, that I am sorry for not accepting him for who he is, and to ask for his forgiveness. She thinks it would help me feel better."

I got chills up my arm as I remembered reading about how sometimes we get important messages from our deceased loved ones through our dreams. I think they are called visits.

"Well, Sam, I think your wife gave you an important message. It sounds like your conscience is knocking pretty loud as well. So, I am going to ask, does your son even know you're in the hospital now? When was the last time you saw or spoke to him?"

"I am sad to say, at my wife's funeral, which was about a year ago. He barely looked at me, but yeah, he knows I'm here. I guess he's still so angry."

"Samuel, may I recommend that you write him a letter? Sometimes, when we can't say things to a person face to face, writing them down is helpful. It's a safer way to express what you need to say without anyone directly attacking you. Sam, you have nothing to lose. Your time may be coming soon, and I would hate for you to have any regrets."

"Willow, I know you're right, and so is my wife, God bless her, so maybe I will write that letter."

"Do it, Sam, but do it from your heart, that is what my grandmother always said. Now is your chance. Let him know that you always loved him, and how deeply sorry you are for making him feel anything less."

"Wow, Willow, you remind me a little of my wife when she was about your age."

"H-m-m, Sam, interesting, don't you think, to meet someone who reminds you of her? I will take that compliment any day - she sounded like a special lady."

"She sure was, Willow."

"Well, Sam, I have to get going and pick up some stuff for my grandpa at the store."

"Ah-h, so soon, Willow?"

"Ah-ha! I'm growing on 'ya already, Sam, I can tell!' I Willow Winked him again.

"I'll come visit you sometime next week. In the meantime, write that letter!"

"I will, Willow, and thanks for keeping me company."

"You're welcome, Samuel. See 'ya next week."

"Bye, Willow."

As I walked out, I felt happy because I had made a connection with this man and softened him a little. I knew I couldn't leave without at least checking to see if Luke was around.

I walked up and down the halls and eventually found him sitting outside reading a book on the bench, drinking his Yoo-Hoo. He must have been on his break. I debated whether or not to interrupt his peace, but I knew he might want to see me. I opened the door and his eyes met mine. He smiled again with that crooked tooth smile I love so!

We sat for awhile and talked. I told him about the CALM licenses plate and how Sam started opening up to me. Luke giggled and we continued to trading stories about our synchronicities. At some point I looked at my watch and realized I had to get going home for grandpa.

We hugged goodbye and I told him that I would be back sometime next week. As I was leaving, I passed by Samuel's room and saw that he had fallen asleep. I decided to give him a little surprise gift. I went to the kitchen area and told one of the aids that my friend asked for some extra Jell-O and pudding - that they had forgotten to give it to him, and could they spare one or two? I walked over to Sam's room and quietly tiptoed in and placed one cherry Jell-O and one vanilla pudding next to his bed with a spoon. This way when he woke up, he would know a little birdie had stopped by to leave him a goodie.

I called Grandpa as I left and asked him if he would mind if I invited Aunt Ellen over for dinner, too. It had been a while, and I was hoping that maybe he would give in. He somehow agreed, so I called her ASAP to find out if she would come. She, too, somehow agreed. I told her to be at Grandpa's at seven o'clock. I decided to just pick up some burgers and hotdogs and make a barbeque.

When I got home, Grandpa was outside again where he had planted Grandma's tree, and was just staring at it.

"What are you doing, Gramp?"

"Um-m, just wondering if this thing is ever going to grow."

"Gramps, you think if you watch it, it will grow faster? It will grow, but it takes some time. It will be worth the wait, I promise."

"I hope you're right, love. So, what time is Big Mouth coming over?"

"Be nice - in about an hour. I bought your favorite, hot dogs with sauerkraut for dinner on your favorite potato buns."

"Oh my, Willow, you know me so well."

"I do, Gramp. Now, I don't have to remind you to be nice to Aunt El, do I?"

"Willow, I am too tired at this point in my life not to be nice to her. I will do my best."

"That's all I ask. That's all I ask."

Aunt Ellen came in with her waffling overbearing perfume and a bottle of red. Her dangly earring poked my cheek when she went to kiss me hello.

"Hi, doll. How is my Willow?"

"Okay, Aunt El, how are you?"

"I am good, honey. You look a little skinny, have you lost weight?"

"Yeah, well apparently it is thyroid-related. Although, I just started my thyroid medicine and I just started to get my appetite back, so I'm sure I will gain my weight back soon."

"Come sit down with me and let's catch up a little bit. Why don't you open the wine?"

"Sounds good," I agreed.

After we sat down, she asked "So Willow, I heard from a source that Will is coming into town – is that true?" She winked at me. I knew she couldn't help herself.

"Yes, Aunt El, that is true, and yes, I do plan on seeing him. That's all I know."

"I know he is looking forward to seeing you, his grandma told me. I saw her on the golf course yesterday. He sounds so nice."

"I'm sure he is. We'll see, I will keep you posted."

"Speaking of love life, I wasn't going to say anything, but guess who I saw last week at Tina's?" Like I didn't know.

"Um-m," I hedged. "I don't know - Bernardo?"

"Oh, Willow, I don't know what happened, not that it is my business, but Willow, he looked sad and uncomfortable to see me, like it reminded him of you. What happened?"

"Aunt El, I don't want to get into it, and I don't want to tarnish your image of him - he's a good guy, but he was not for me. Let's just leave it at that, okay?"

"Okay, Willow. I will leave it alone. I just hope you don't mind that my Harold and I still go to eat there. We really love the food and the music."

"Of course not, I wouldn't want you to stop going, just don't want you to talk too much to Bernardo about us. Out of respect for me, try to leave it alone."

"I hear you, Willow. I will honey."

"So, Aunt El, I guess you're back with Harold?"

"Well," she said, "I think I might have been wrong about him. It turns out the reason he was not there the way I needed him during your grandmother's death was because he told me that even at his age, he was emotionally shut down and he realized what a putz he was, by not being there for me more. He genuinely apologized for not being able to give me what it was I needed."

I nodded and said, "Well, Aunt El, sometimes it happens like this. It's ironic - you teaching him the important lesson that it's time to open up more emotionally."

"Willow, you're right, I didn't quite think of it like that, but you are so right. You know, you remind me so much of your grandmother sometimes, you're like a reincarnation of her."

"I know. Grandpa says the same thing - see you both have something in common." I Willow Winked her. Speaking of which, I heard him open the door and come out of the bathroom.

He smiled and said, "Hello, Ellen, how are you?"

"Good, Lex, how are you?"

He walked over and they gave each other a civil hug and kiss on the cheek. I was happy.

"You look good, Lex, have you lost weight?'

"I have, Ellen, I ride my bike now," he announced proudly.

"Willow mentioned that. Good for you, my sister would be proud of you." He smiled back.

I was relieved that this dinner turned out great. Believe it or not, there was not one jab at one another through the meal. We laughed and reminisced a lot about Grandma. I missed her so.

As I walked Aunt El out to her car, I thanked her for being good to Grandpa over dinner. She made me promise to call her with all of the details after I met with Will for our date. I nodded, but knew I would not be sharing too much.

When I came back inside Grandpa was sitting on the couch and asked me to come sit down for a minute.

"What's up, Gramp?"

"Willow, I just wanted to say thank you."

"Well, you're welcome, Grandpa. It was a good dinner, and thank you for being kind to Aunt Ellen."

"You're welcome, Willow, but I am not just saying thanks for dinner, I want to thank you for being here with your grandpa and taking such good care of me. I feel so lucky to have you in my life. You know, if it weren't for you being here, I am not sure what kind of depression I would have fallen into. You have already taught me a lot, and just by being here with me, you are a reminder of all the things your Grandma Lu did so beautifully. I almost feel like you being here with me is her gift to me."

I started to well up. I was touched and moved by his words.

"Gramp, as I mentioned before, there is nowhere else I could imagine being. I actually think this was a gift for both of us. Grandma Lu is making sure we keep one another loving the way she would want us to."

"You're right, Willow, she would.

# Chapter 23

I WOKE UP EARLY AND started going through some of my collection of poems. Ed was going to be in this morning, and as promised, I wanted to bring in two poems that I felt represented me. One was from my past, and the other I had written during the past few months.

I meditated for about ten minutes, and surprisingly, something inside of me felt quiet this morning, like there was an angelic voice inside my heart saying, 'You are going to be okay, Willow, you are at peace, so just breathe....' And, I also heard that my poetry was good enough - that it's my ego that makes me feel it isn't, and to believe in me.

When I got to the café, I immediately looked for Ed. You couldn't miss him, for today he was wearing an orange hat and an orange watch to match. I went to put my apron on, and saw Brenda on her cell phone. She had dyed her hair to a soft brown color. *Wow, much better*, I thought. I waved to her, and pointed to her hair, and gave her a thumbs up. She smiled back and mouthed *thanks* and pointed, saying *Ed is here and he has been waiting for you.* I said, "Thanks," and I was happy as I thought maybe she's naturally coming into herself.

I grabbed Ed's staple cup of coffee and walked over to him.

"Morning, Ed." He smiled and looked up from his paper.

"Well, well if it isn't the next published poet, Miss Willow. You can get her new beautiful book of poems called <u>Willow's Pocket Full of Wisdom</u>." I lit up!

"Ed, I like it, I like that title a lot. I may use that some day."

"I just made it up - it's catchy, huh?"

"It sure is. So, how was your trip?" I asked.

"Well, I was in Chicago. What can I say? It was windy, but exciting, and delicious - you know they have some of the best restaurants, but nobody has breakfast like Dotty's!"

"I hear 'ya. Okay, I did bring what you asked for. I was a little apprehensive about which to pick, so I brought the two and figured you could choose which one you liked the best. Let me put your order in, and grab my folder."

As I run into the back, I saw that Brenda was off the phone. I noticed that she was wearing less dark makeup, too.

"Wow, Brenda, your hair looks so great and your makeup, too! Did you get a makeover or something this week? Love the softer look on you. You look so pretty."

"Thanks. Yeah, I decided I wanted to sort of be my natural self again. That jerk- off boyfriend of mine always dug the whole gothic look, which I think was my way of trying to be something darker than I really was. I felt sort of alienated and angry all the time. I've realized over the last few weeks that I don't need to be so heavy with my looks to feel something, or try to make a statement."

"Brenda, I am so happy for you, where did you get your inspiration?"

"Well, for starters, your conversation with me was enlightening, so thanks, and also I had a good heart-to-heart with my mother. That was so overdo! I realized I was also angry for not getting the love from her I needed. I think I was acting out. My therapist, of course, helped with these revelations."

"Well, whatever it was, I'm happy I played a small role."

"Thanks, Willow."

"Anytime."

I grabbed my poems. There were only two other customers in the cafe, so I sat down across from Ed. "So, again, these poems were written at different times - especially during some of the harder times when I was sort of trying to figure out what was going on with me and if I would come out of my pain." I hesitated to hand them over to him.

"Willow, I have a better idea, I have always liked hearing poems read to me. I tend to feel them more. What do you say you read them out loud to me so I can get a better sense?" I felt a butterfly of nerves in my belly.

"What read it out loud? Um-m-m, I guess I could. I've never read them out loud to anyone besides myself, and maybe my dad."

"Well, Willow, now would be a good start. I can see you one day being on stage reading these to thousands of people. That is the best way a poet shows his true voice."

"Okay, I guess you're right. At some point, I have to be comfortable reading them aloud. Okay, here is the first one. It's called, 'My Unconditional Sea."

"My Unconditional Sea"

*If I close my eyes I see a beautiful horizon*
*I am on a boat alone and at sea*
*I am gently rocking back and forth but I am not afraid*
*I feel protected on this day*
*I am floating on a trust I have made with my divine masters*
*I am loved just as I am right here and right now*
*I am embracing this quiet ride and loving how present I am able to be in this moment*
*The clock is ticking by I don't hear it*
*My heart is beating but I don't feel it*
*In my stillness I am grateful for the body of water surrounding my little frame*
*My heart is still searching for its answer*
*However today it at least knows its capacity to give of its fullness*
*I am ready to share my boat with the world*
*Keep me smiling*
*Keep me present*
*Keep me dreaming*
*While I continue this journey on my unconditional sea*
*- Willow Mazer*

Ed smiled. "Willow, look at the hair on my arms standing up. That is always a good sign - it means I felt it. I love this. This is a great analogy for someone who trusts their boat, and knows deep down there is something greater that is holding her up and loving her unconditionally. Wow, I can't wait to hear the other one."

"Really? You like it, Ed?"

"Willow, I love it! Now, read the next one."

"Okay, Ed. I should tell you that this one is one of my favorites. I feel like it really represents me as a poet, it's called, "This Is Life.""

### "This is Life"

*The waves will continue to roll in*
*While the sailor makes it safely to shore*
*The chair will naturally rock*
*While the man drinks his beer and contemplates his life*
*The sky will show you light*
*While the clouds pass through as they do*
*The birds will flap their wings*
*While the old folks head south for the winter*
*The trees will blow gently in the wind*
*While the leaves fall to the grass*
*The eyes will close before bedtime*
*While someone somewhere outside your world is opening them right now*
*The heart will continue to beat*
*While God is hoping it becomes our second set of ears*
*- Willow Mazer*

I looked up at him again. He put his hand on top of mine.

"Willow, I can't believe you have been hiding this beautiful poet for so long. I love this, I got the message right away - it's in the last two lines - God wants me to listen with my heart. Willow, the world needs someone with these pure unconditional messages."

"Ed, I am speechless. I knew they had something profound within them, but I didn't know they were as good as you're making me feel they are."

"That's just it, Willow, they are good enough. I like both of them, and it will be tough to pick. Why don't you let me have these copies to take home and re-read a few times, and I'll see which one resonates the most with me, and then I'll decide. But, you can count on my choosing one to put in my book."

"Great, Ed, thanks! I'm ecstatic and grateful beyond words. I think you just lifted my confidence level to a new height."

"Well, Willow, I am being honest, which I have always been with anyone who has come to me for my opinion. You've got something here that needs to be seen."

"Thank you, Ed, for making my day. Breakfast will be on me again! As a matter of fact, let me go check on it now."

As I walked into the kitchen, I felt a burst of happiness like I had never felt before - well, maybe once. It happened when I was younger and won the spelling bee contest, or hit my first home run at a softball game. But, it was a sweet reminder of the little girl in me who knew once again that wonderful feeling that I could accomplish something. I brought Ed's food out, and I handed it to him, and said, "Thanks again."

"Willow, you're welcome, and thank you for allowing me to be a part of this journey."

"Part of this journey...." I was realizing more and more that I was being guided, and meeting more people to help me ease my mind. I thought about this as I stirred my spaghetti sauce around and around. I was making Grandpa dinner and waiting for him to get home so I could tell him all about my exciting news with Ed. I had already called my parents, Carla, and a few of my girlfriends. They were all so happy for me. I looked at my watch and saw that it is 6:45 p.m. H-m-m-m, where on earth could my grandpa be?

Next thing I knew, I heard the garage door open. He walked in, hung up his hat and coat, handed me a bouquet of flowers, and kissed me on the cheek.

"Hi, Gramps. To what do I owe these beautiful flowers? It's not my birthday."

"I know, Willow. Can't a grandpa buy his beautiful potential published poet some flowers?"

"You know! How did you know?"

"I spoke to your mom this afternoon. Sorry you didn't get to be the one to tell me, but she assumed I already knew" he replied.

"It's okay, Gramp. They are so beautiful - thank you. So, yes, I was waiting for you to get home, I was so excited. Ed, the guy I have told you about before, who is a published author, loved my poems and told me he is going to put one in for sure. So, of course, I am so happy!"

"That is my Willow, and if Grandma were here, she would be feeding you with her famous chocolate brownies to celebrate. Sorry, I can't bake those for you, but how about a sundae after dinner? By the way, what are you making? It smells so good."

"Well, I was in the mood for a delicious homemade meat sauce, and of course, some garlic rolls. So, Grandpa, where were you?" I wanted to know.

"I know you are going to laugh, but as you know, my apple tree for Grandma has not begun to blossom yet, so I ran back to the garden store and spoke to this guy, Ron, who apparently is an expert in planting fruit trees and knows all of the tricks of the trade. He explained tips on rooting, stalking, and pollination to help me."

I laughed, "Listen to you, Gramp, with all of your garden lingo!"

He laughed back, "Yeah, who would have thunk? Your Grandpa into gardening? Grandma would be proud of me, that I know."

"You got that right, Grandpa."

"How about, for old time's sake, we watch a little 'Jeopardy' over dinner? You know, it was Grandma's favorite game show."

"How could I forget, Grandpa? That and 'The Price Is Right.'"

"Yeah, your grandma liked the fun ones and the scholastic ones. I think it always made her feel smarter since she never went to college. Let me tell you though, she sure was a sharp cookie. Your grandmother knew answers I can't even imagine!"

"Well, you know me, too, - I was never quite good at this game. More of a 'Wheel of Fortune' gal. I like puzzles!"

"I know, honey. Okay, I'm going to put it on."

"Okay, dinner will be ready in five minutes."

As the game started, I heard Alex Trebeck introducing the contestants, and that *do, do, do, do, do, do* noise showing the categories. I could hear one was entertainment- related, another was something to do with transportation, and the last one was Greek talk.

"Hey, Gramp, can you turn it up? I can't really hear it."

"Sure, sorry."

Next thing I knew, I heard one of the contestants say, "I will take Greek for $500, Alex."

"Okay," Alex replied, "The question is: What word means spiritual love in Greek?" I felt the hairs on my arms stand up! I shouted out at the exact same time as the woman on the television, "What is Agape?" And Alex said, "You are correct!"

My grandpa smirked and said, "How on earth does my Willow know what that word means?"

"Oh, Grandpa, if you only knew. I had a close friend explain it to me - it really means unconditional love. Wow, what are the chances, Grandpa? I saw it on a license plate twice, and I think it's a continuing message for me."

"Gosh, really, honey? H-m-m-m, maybe your grandma brought you this message tonight." He winked at me

I walked over, sat down, and poured us each a small glass of red wine. I raised my glass and Grandpa said, "To my sweet granddaughter, who is going to inspire a lot of people one day with her beautiful words through her poetry and Agape heart."

I teared up a little, "Thanks, Grandpa, this means more to me than you know."

I couldn't wait to go see Luke tomorrow to tell him about the show, and of course, to see how Samuel Calm was doing, too.

# Chapter 24

I WOKE UP EARLY, AS usual, and decided to meditate a little. I found myself asking God what was it, I should know for today. I closed my eyes and the next thing I knew something very peaceful inside of me spoke, "You should know that you are a beautiful and a divine being of love. You are made of nothing but love, it is unconditional and I love you always, in all ways. You are light, you are love, you are an angel from up above, you are here on earth to remember your worth. You are worthy, my dear Willow, of love - as we all are. Now, breathe gently in and let it out slowly, and rid yourself of any negativity. You are peace and love."

I wasn't sure if this was God speaking to me, or what they call your higher self. Now, normally I would be freaked out, but this voice within in me was so gentle and calming that when I opened my eyes, I felt so much more relaxed than I had ever been. I was glad I was going to see my new therapist Katie again this week. I believe she might be able to help me understand this special inner wisdom I keep hearing about, and have now had a taste of. I got up, got dressed, and decided to go see Mr. Calm and Luke before I worked later in the morning.

I pulled up to the nursing home, went in, and walked down the halls searching for Luke. I wanted to tell him about the Agape answer on "Jeopardy." I decided to visit Sam first. I peeked into his room. He was up and watching what looked like a "Mash" re-run.

I knocked on the door and said, "Is anybody interested in a little company?"

He formed a smile and another hacking cough, which he couldn't control. He raised his hand and I said, "Do you want me to go get the nurse?"

He nodded and he tried to gasp for air. I ran to the desk, and the nurse came running in. She grabbed her oxygen mask and put it over Mr. Calm's nose. He tried to push her off, but her strength was obvious and she held him down and said, "There, there Mr. Calm. That's it, just breathe in and out nice and easy, you're going to be okay. Nice and slow."

He started to calm down and catch his breath. My heart had begun to beat pretty fast when I saw him in despair, but was starting to relax.

"Sam, I'm sorry I came at a bad time, I'll let you rest."

"No, no, Willow. It happens all of the time. Just give me a minute, will 'ya, don't go."

He waved me to come sit down. I walked over and plopped down. I sat down and we made some small talk about stuff. He asked me about my love life, I told him all about Tom, Bernardo, and my new potential love Will. I explained to him my tendency to be a little guarded at times. He understood but then said, "Willow dear, if I learned one thing in life, it's that walls don't serve us, whenever there is a potential for true love, you go for it, like I did with my wife."

"Okay, I hear 'ya. So, now, on to you?"

"Okay, me? Well, I wrote that letter to my son, which he got, and he called me. Thanks to your idea, he's coming next weekend for a visit."

I lit up the best smile and said, "Oh, Sam, I am so happy for you! You must be over the top!"

"Well dear, I never quite get over the top, but I am certainly glad he'll give me a chance to say my apologies in person. I even told him to bring his partner with him. I told him I would like to meet him."

"Sam, this is great, your wife would be very proud."

"Willow, honestly, something tells me my wife may have orchestrated this to happen, with, of course, your encouraging words."

"I'm happy to have done so."

"I like you, Willow. I don't like many people, but I like you," he announced.

I smiled and put my hand on top of his, "I like you, too, Mr. Samuel Calm."

We continued to talk for a little while longer, and I realized the time, "Oops, Sam, I hate to run, but I have to go to work. I'll come back again next week, promise. Good luck with your son's visit. Just remember to stay calm, Mr. Calm." I Willow Winked him as I walked toward the door.

"Sounds good, Willow. I promise to stay calm if you promise to leave your walls down on that date. By the way, thanks for the Jell-O. You got a good heart, Willow, now let it show." He winked back at me. I smiled and nodded and walked down the hall looking for Luke quickly before I had to go.

I found him talking to a nurse, laughing away. I love his laugh. I walked over. "Hey, Miss Willow, what are you doing here?"

"I just came by to see Sam and you, if you have five minutes. I actually have to go to work soon, but can I steal you away for a few? Pardon me for interrupting."

"Oh, no worries, this is my friend Sandra. She is the best nurse here. You don't mind Sandy, do you?"

"Not at all Luke. Nice to meet you, is it Willow? What a pretty name."

"Thank you, Sandra, nice to meet you, too."

Luke took my arm, "Come on this way, I have to go get a mop and clean up a mess down the hall, you don't mind walking and talking with me at the same time do you?"

"No, Luke, not at all. So, listen to this one, the other night I was watching 'Jeopardy' with my grandpa…"

I told him the whole story, and before I could finish he said, "Well I'll be darned, Agape."

"Luke, can you imagine? And when it came up, I said the answer right away and my grandpa looked at me and said, 'How on earth did you know what that word means?' Of course, I told him the story."

He said, "WOW! I'm almost thinking you should start a book or something about these experiences. Something is coming from this universe trying to reach you with this ongoing message of unconditional love. So, Willow, I guess the most important question left to ask you, pretty lady, is *are you getting it?*" I raised my eyebrow.

He continued, "Willow, I mean, are you actually starting to understand it's meaning for you? This word Agape, angel, remember it's about knowing God's love is with you in so many ways no matter what you do, or don't do," he explained.

"I'm starting to, Luke, I think so. I'm healing a lot of old wounds, so to speak, now. So, I'm in the process. But, yes, for sure I'm realizing that something greater is happening now.

"You know, Luke, I haven't told many people this, but I'm comfortable enough to share it with you. Ever since I was a little girl, I used to pray all the time to God, not even sure why, but I would pray every night before bed and tell God over and over that I loved Him. When I look back, I think I had a little OCD as a kid, do you know what that word means?"

He shook his head, "Obsessive something?"

I stopped him, "Yeah, Luke, it's called OCD which stands for obsessive-compulsive disorder. I don't like to use words like disorder, but I'm not ashamed to admit I have a little of that, we all do in some shape or another. Anyway, so I would do this ritual before bed every night, and I think I thought that if I did it enough, God would help protect me from anything bad happening. I prayed all the time, Luke, so maybe now, when I hit that low place in my life, God came back to me with this word to let me know that for all those years, it didn't matter what I did or didn't do, that He loved me all along."

230

"Willow, that is a very insightful thought, and yes, I would have to agree a hundred percent." He continued, "Okay, so here is what I think is really important to remember about this Agape love. This word is really important for you in order to understand that you are also worthy of this love, Willow. I am saying it again because I feel it's important to repeat - you are worthy of God's love, Willow, we all are. You don't have to obsessively pray for it, or beg for it, or even negotiate with God for it, it's yours to have, Willow, anytime.

"That Course in Miracles group, if I remember correctly, it teaches about remembering you are already one with God, not separate, so if you can try to see yourself and God as one, you'll know, or remember, that it has already been a part of you. Willow, it's time to start really learning to love yourself, to see your own light."

I felt the hairs on my arms stand up, and a lot of love. I remembered the meditation I had earlier where that message came through.

"Luke, has anyone ever told you that you really were and are an earth angel?"

He blushed at me. "My wife, when she's not mad at me," he admitted.

"What's interesting is that I just did a meditation this morning where I swore something gently spoke within in me, letting me know that I am worthy of this love. Seriously, Luke, your words almost sound as if God is speaking through you to me directly. So, I get it - well, I got it! It was almost if God was indeed talking to me to let me know this."

"It's funny you should say that, Willow. Sometimes, every once in a blue, I'll say something, and I am not sure where it came from, but I know it makes a lot of peaceful sense to the person I am talking to. Who knows, maybe Divine Spirit does that from time to time - 'ya know, speaks through others when there's the need to? Again, I think my next-door neighbor told me about that. I think it's called something like the holy instant?"

"The holy instant?" I asked.

"Yeah, it's sort of like when you become instantly clear about a message on something that has been bothering you which won't go away, so you surrender in prayer or ask for guidance, and then it happens - whether it's from someone's comforting words, a message, or a sign at just the right time. Something like that, I don't know the specifics, but it sure seems to be making more sense to me now. I knew there was a reason I kept listening to my friend go on and on sometimes. It fascinated me to know there might be another way of viewing things, other than the way I was raised."

"Wow, Luke, you know more than you think! Are you sure you haven't been to one of those groups before? Perhaps you would like to come with me to one of my groups. They are so nice there. You would be so welcomed."

"You know, Willow, that might not be such a bad idea. Yeah, why not? Someday I will go with you," he agreed.

"Sounds great! Well, thank you for your time, Luke. As always, it was enlightening."

"You got it, Willow, anytime for you. By the way, I think your visits with Mr. Calm have softened him a bit!"

"Yeah?"

"Yeah. The nurses said he is a little less snappy and a little more, shall we say, calmer. You should come around here a little more. Did you ever think you might be an earth angel yourself?" He smiled and winked at me.

"Maybe, Luke, just maybe." I Willow Winked him back.

# Chapter 25

I PULLED UP TO KATIE's office and was happy to see her, especially since tomorrow night was finally my first date with Will. But, I also wanted to talk to her about the meditation and another nightmare I had last night about being with my teenage boyfriend. I was trying not to analyze, because that's what I always tend to do, but I did wake up wondering *why is this popping up again?"*

I walked in, sat down, and took a long, deep breath as I plopped down on her couch.

"So, Willow, how have you been?"

"A little better. I started the thyroid meds. But, I would like to discuss something interesting that came up for me last night in another dream. So, I was a teenage girl again and was being sexual with my first boyfriend, and I remember in the dream that it was literally painful. I remember I wanted him to stop, because it hurt. I remember feeling so vulnerable in the dream, and afraid. I woke up thinking I don't want to be afraid to be physical anymore because of a stupid young choice. Then I got so in my head, wondering if there could be something wrong with me. Because, you know, I realized ever since that young foolish relationship that I have been afraid to get closer to men, 'ya know, really let myself go."

I decided to pause and she said, Okay, Willow. First, let me reassure you that it is normal to have dreams, pleasant or unpleasant, about former boyfriends, especially those from whom you suffered some discomfort. But, there is nothing wrong with you, you are just ready to let go of the young vulnerability you had and, yes, may have taken into your other relationships. You are ready to release that emotional burden.

"Also, you said you wanted him to stop, which again means you were young and vulnerable and now need to forgive yourself for doing it. You also mentioned that once you woke up, you wanted to be free, but often have felt like you can't."

"So, Willow, can you see where there is a part of you that wants to let yourself go fully with a man intimately without being afraid emotionally?" I nodded. She continued, "Let me again reassure you that this is normal. You've been through a lot over the last few months, and yes, you may be in a slight phase of identity stuff, meaning you are questioning everything about yourself. But, you're taking it to extremes - you're looking for reasons that something might be wrong with you, your mental state, now your body. This sounds a little like old habitual anxiety patterns, or the ego looking to find something to pick on.

"I think it might be time to change the story of Something Is Wrong with me, because it sounds to me like you are doing a number on yourself - from one thing to the next. Is this possible?"

I took a deep breath and said, "I suppose so. I do this all the time, Katie, I don't know why. It's like I am always looking for something to be wrong about me, and I question if I'll ever be able to fix it, blah, blah, you get my point. I sabotage, I admit it."

"So, Willow, it becomes a pretty uncomfortable convincing story right?"

"Yes, that is exactly what it becomes. I have an annoying habit - call it anxiety or whatever you want, but it's exhausting. Sorry, you must be exhausted already just listening to me."

"Willow, I am not exhausted at all, but I know that for you it must be exhausting doing this. Not feeling at peace is exhausting."

"It is."

Next thing I knew I burst into tears. "I am so tired, Katie, I am so tired. I don't understand this - I want to feel good! I just want to be free and at peace as you said, but I am exhausted. Every time one little thing pops up, assuming it has all of these underlying meanings. It's enough!"

"Okay, Willow, what do you say we try a little of this heart assisted breathing? Now would be a perfect time. Let's try to find a more compassionate story for you that doesn't entail your brokenness, but a story that involves your beautiful loving being."

I smiled and nodded. She continued, "So again, you don't need to understand this heart therapy, just follow my lead and you will be guided the way you need to be. Okay, now I want you to crisscross your hands, place them over your heart area, and repeat after me, 'Even though as a young teenage girl, I suffered painful intercourse, I forgive myself and know I am worthy of love.'"

I repeated it and took a deep breath. Then she asked me to repeat it three more times, as I reversed and criss-crossed my hands. I felt something within me say *I have gotten carried away with my thoughts and there is nothing wrong with me and I am love at core and made of peace.* As Katie was about to continue, I put my hand up for her to stop, and told her what just came to me, and also about what came to me in that earlier meditation.

She smiled and said, "Willow, welcome to your inner guidance, a gift from God to help heal you. So, let's repeat what just came and say, 'I love and accept myself, even though I get carried away with my thoughts, there is nothing wrong with me. I am love at my core and made of peace.'"

I, again, did just that, with repeating and switching my hands, and felt much lighter. Then, out of nowhere, I felt a little anxious again. Katie sensed my facial expression and asked if I was okay.

"Well, part of me is totally relaxed and happy. This sort of happened to me the other morning in a meditation, but the other part of me still feels a little antsy."

"Willow, this is normal because when we just start to open up spiritually, and are awakened, we can get a little scared. Our egos want to back away, or as someone once said in the Course in Miracles, the ego stands for "easing God out." We don't want that Willow - to ease God out - we want to embrace him. You need not be afraid now. This will take some time, but again, all you have to do is breathe through this. So, let's repeat what we just did."

I repeated and breathed slowly. Then the next thing I knew, something within me said *I now release my fear of intimacy and I am ready to trust my body with another man.* I told Katie, and she said, "Okay, good. Now let's say that aloud and take a few deep breaths and repeat it."

Again, I did, and I felt myself relax a little more. Will then popped into my head. I looked at Katie, smiled, and said, "Did I tell you that I have a date tomorrow night with that guy from the airplane? Wait! Did I *tell* you about the guy from the airplane?"

She smiled, as if she already knew, but to humor me said, "No, but tell me a little about him."

"Um-m, well a few months ago on my way down here, ..." I told her the whole story and all the weird coincidences between us.

"Wow, lots of coincidences, huh?" Katie responded.

"I know, so on some level, I was meant to meet this guy. The night before I met him I prayed to God and told Him that if there is anybody significant He thinks I should meet, I am paying attention." She smiled again.

"So, Willow, you are now ready to go on a date with this stranger from the airplane, who is not such a stranger on a soul level, perhaps?"

"Perhaps, Katie. Anyway, I'm a little nervous, but I'm telling myself that it's just a date."

"Yes, Willow, so keep it light, you don't have anything to be nervous about. Something tells me that he will feel like an old shoe, an old comforting soul." She winked again at me and said, "You see what I'm saying?"

I said, "We will see. Thanks for at least helping lighten up this session."

"Yes, Willow, we did a lot today. As I mentioned, we will take this slowly, just trust that we've healed some stuff already on lots of levels. Also if for some reason you feel a revving up again, you can take a few heart breaths and you will shift your nervous energy to a more calmer state."

"I will remember that, thank you, and I can see by the clock that our time is up."

"Willow, have fun tomorrow night, just be yourself."

"I will," I promised.

I pulled out of the parking lot feeling a little more at ease. As I was leaving, my cell phone rang It was Ed, so I picked it up right away.

"Hello?"

"Willow, it's Ed. How are you?"

"Lighter thanks, since I'm leaving my therapist as we speak." I was comfortable enough to tell Ed I see someone. Who hasn't, anyway?

"Well, Willow, this might just make your day a little lighter and brighter. I've decided to choose your poem 'This is Life.' It's my favorite one and represents you and a greater message for all to see. It was what my gut told me. The book will be out next month, so your name will out there soon enough."

"Oh, Ed, thank you so much! This means the world to me, I am so excited that you've given my work this chance to be seen."

"You're welcome, Willow. This is only the beginning - great things are to come soon."

"I am starting to believe it, thank you. I'm sure I'll see you this week."

"Hope so, Willow."

I called my grandpa, family, and friends on my way home. They were so excited. Of course, Carla was more excited about my date tomorrow night with Will, but happy for me.

I woke up the next morning and grandpa was anxious to take a bike ride with me. I agreed.

As Grandpa and I went around the complex, I wondered when Will would be calling or texting me about tonight. For a moment, I thought he probably would not do it before eleven o'clock, so he wouldn't seem too anxious. Then again, something told me he wasn't the type to play games. Next thing I knew, my text message went off. It startled me, and I almost fell off my bike. My gut knew it was Will.

I looked down and it said, *Looking forward to tonight, I am going to hit some golf balls with my grandfather. Will call you around 3 p.m. and will figure out plans.* I smiled and texted back, *Sounds great.*

My grandpa saw this and said, "How do you do that - ride your bike with one hand and text with the other? I hope you don't do that driving, Willow."

"Not all the time, Gramp. I know, sorry. It is dangerous."

"So?"

"So what?"

"Was it him? The Stranger from the Airplane?"

I blushed, "Yes, Gramp. Tonight is our first official date."

"Cool, as you say. What are you guys going to do?"

"I don't know - maybe dinner or drinks. He's going to call me later. Shoot, what am I going to wear?"

"Willow, whatever you wear, you will look beautiful."

"Thanks, Grandpa. You always know just what to say."

As we make our way back to the house, something inside me said, *you don't have to get all dolled up for this one.* It resonated for the rest of the afternoon, so I didn't worry about overly prepping or manicuring myself to look perfect. My phone, as promised, rang a little after three o'clock.

"Hello? Hey, you."

"Wow, Willow, is it really you?"

"It's really me, Will, how are you?"

"I'm great. I just had an awesome afternoon playing some golf with my grandfather, and now I'm looking forward to an awesome evening with you."

"Sweet."

"So, Willow, what would you like to do? I was going to go ahead and make reservations somewhere, but instead of taking the lead, I wanted to get an idea of what you might be in the mood to do." Good sign.

"Um-m, thanks. Well, I'm pretty easy, and we don't need to go anywhere fancy. I'm just as happy with a beer, a burger with fries and lots of ketchup, versus a glass of red wine and a filet mignon with a dainty dollop of sour cream on top of a baked potato."

He giggled. "A girl after my own heart, I like your style. Well then, if that's the case, let's downplay the evening and keep it casual. There's a great burger place I always love to go to here with my grandparents, it's called the Ale House. They have great food, pool tables, dart boards - it's a fun, casual place. How does that sound?"

"Will, that sounds perfect!"

"Great, would you like me to pick you up?"

"You're sweet, but I can just meet you there, no problem."

"Okay, how about seven o'clock? I'll text you the address," he offered.

"Perfect. See 'ya then."

"See 'ya then."

I smiled and thought *awesome, I am definitely wearing jeans!* I decided to settle for my favorite bell-bottoms, which give my tooshie a cute shape, and my favorite emerald green top with my favorite bra, of course.

I came out of the bedroom, and Grandpa looked up from his

paper, "Ah-h, look at my angel. Willow, you look perfect and just like you, not overly or under-done. Just my sweet Willow, as herself."

I walked over to him and kissed his cheek, "Thanks, Gramp, I was going for the whole, "just me" look. So, I'm off, wish me luck."

"You won't need it. Just go have fun."

"Thanks. See 'ya tomorrow, or early if it goes shitty."

"Willow, go have fun will 'ya?" he admonished.

I got into the car, and as I was driving and stopped at an intersection - what would the chances be that Fed Ex trucks would be to the left and the right of me? I was sandwiched with a smile! Hm-m-m-m...

# Chapter 26

I PULLED UP TO THE restaurant and wondered if he was at the bar yet. I walked in and didn't see him. I immediately went up to the bar and ordered myself a Miller Lite. In my cute fashion I decided to text him and I wrote, *She's wearing green*. Two minutes later in he walked with a great smile. I felt comfortable right away. He gave me a big bear hug and said, "Lady in Green, it's so good to see you again! By the way, green is one of my favorite colors."

"How did I know? Good to see you, too, Will. Let me buy you a drink?"

"No, No. I got it."

"Will, if there is one thing you should know about me off the bat, I don't always like to let the guys take care of everything, I'm lady of the millennium, it's all good. One beer, buddy, what will it be?"

He laughed, "Okay, I won't argue with that, I'll take a Miller Lite too."

I ordered him his beer, and he sat down. He was wearing a pair of jeans, too, and a casual grey shirt. He looked comfortable, and I liked that.

He grabbed his beer and tapped mine, "Cheers, to your finally taking a risk and having one drink with me. I'm sorry it took so long, but I am grateful."

"Cheers, Will, it's good to finally hang with you, too. So, talk to me, who is Will?"

He said, "Who is Willow?"

I grinned, "You first."

He puts his beer down and said, "No pressure, okay. Who is Will? Do you want to hear the short version, or the dragged out therapy session kind?"

"Um-m, I'll take the one that's brought you to the man you are today."

"Ah, I like that, Willow. Well, okay, I'll will give you the short version. I'm an easygoing guy. I have a great job with FedEx. I've worked with them over the last eight years. I also do part-time work for a construction company. I'm a hands-on kind of guy. I bought a house three years ago, I gutted it out, and did everything myself with a bunch of my buddies. I take pride in that."

I stopped him and tapped my beer to his and said, "I like that, and I'm the kind of girl who thinks it's kind of hot to see a man get dirty."

He blushed. "So, as I was saying, I'm that guy who likes to do things himself. I am not one who likes to ask much for help - the pride thing. As for schooling, I wasn't the best student growing up. I'm also trying to finish my college degree online now, in business."

I stopped him again, "Good for you, about the school part, sounds like you're a super busy guy. Do you ever stop and smell the roses, 'ya know, enjoy life?"

"Well, Willow, I actually enjoy working a lot. I've put a lot of time into my home and I like keeping busy, but yes, if you're asking if I like to have fun, I do."

"So, Will, what kind of things do you like to do?"

"Well, what I love more than anything is riding my motorcycle."

I lifted my eyebrow and was pleasantly surprised to hear that. Again, I am thinking *hot!*

"Yes, I have a bike, Willow, don't seem so surprised. It's my time for me, and I love the feeling of the freedom on the open road."

I said, "That's what I hear. I've never been on one, but I hear it's great."

"Well, maybe you'll have to take a ride with me sometime."

"Maybe, if you're lucky!" I Willow Winked him.

He laughed, "Oh, I'll get lucky! Kidding, Willow, so enough about me - I want to hear about you. How did you end up staying here?"

"Um-m-m, well, I'll try to give you the short version. I can't give you the whole shtick about what I do for a living, because I'm in a transition period. Besides, to tell the truth Will, I don't believe that what you do defines you. I believe it's who you are in your heart that does. My grandma always said that. It was tough to believe it growing up in a workaholic household. My parents weren't around much, but they did what they could to support me."

He said, "That makes sense, go on."

"So, I would rather tell you about my passions. There was a time when I thought that fashion was my passion, that was the original industry I was in. But soon enough, it became too superficial for me, and I wanted to get back to my heart, my roots, which was helping others and writing. I'm a poet and I'm hoping to write a book someday."

"Really, what's your book going to be about?"

"Um-m, kind of interesting stuff. I should also mention that I'm very spiritual. I believe there are no, or few, coincidences in life, and that everything happens for a reason. I believe in signs. My book would be about all of the interesting experiences and miraculous things that have happened to me on and off over the last few years. I'm not religious, let me say that. I was Bat Mitzvahed because my parents forced me to do it. All the while, they didn't realize I was cutting Hebrew school whenever I could. I was not interested in religion. I don't deny my heritage, I just believe in something greater. I was always more interested in a God who loves us all, no matter what. Yikes, am I over- sharing? I do that from time to time."

"No, Willow, you are not over-sharing. I find this very interesting. You should consider writing that book. How about the poetry?"

"Well, let me offer a toast now. I'm about to have my first poem published in a book! I work part-time at a breakfast place, and one of our regular customers and I have gotten pretty chatty. He's a published author and poet as well. So, this is a perfect example of no coincidence. He kept asking me to bring in my poems and to stop hiding them. Oh, yeah, I should mention that I have just started to come out of the closet with my writings. Anyway, I finally had the balls to show him. He told me that not only did he love them, but that he had a new book coming out with a bunch of poems that have inspired him, and he decided to choose one of mine."

He stopped me, "Willow, that is really great. I look forward to seeing your poem someday. I should be honest and tell you I failed English a few times throughout my school years, so my understanding of the language behind it's not so great."

"No worries, Will, my poetry's not hard to understand. My poetry is mostly inspirational and always written from the heart. That tends to be my theme these days, learning about the heart on a metaphoric level, if you know what I mean."

"Um-m-m, you mean about love?" he asked.

"Yes, I'm learning more on the truth behind love, and not just lessons from my grandma, but the people I have met since I have arrived here in Florida."

"So, what is the truth?"

"Um-m, I believe that it comes from within. It's unconditional, and you can't really fully love someone unless you learn to love yourself. That much I know, but again, I'm still learning."

He said, "I can see that. So, may I ask you, Willow, if it's not too soon, how many times have you been in love?"

I smirked, "Will, you can ask me anything, anytime. To answer your question, do you mean lust or real love? There's a difference, my friend. The problem is, many can't differentiate between the two, so more times than not, they end up putting all of their energies into a lust-filled, doomed relationship. The potential for real love might just be staring them in the face, but they are too cowardly to embrace it."

He sat back jokingly, "Yikes! Tell me how you really feel, Willow!"

"Sorry, I went off on one of my tangents again. Okay, so to answer your question, lust a few times, but in love? I would say three times, maybe four, and you?"

"Wow, you are way ahead of me, only once, and honestly, I was in my young twenties. I'm not going to bullshit you, I haven't had much luck in the relationship department. I know, that's not the sort of thing you should tell someone on the first date, but it's my truth, Willow. I've definitely dated a few nice women, and gave them my heart, but I got hurt a few more times than I would have wished."

"I know what you mean, Will. You don't have to be ashamed to tell me that, I like honesty in a man. Besides, maybe the women you chose were cowardly and couldn't see the grace standing in front of them." I smiled and he blushed.

"I never quite thought about it like that, Willow, or heard it said in such a poetic way, but you could be on to something."

I continued, "Or maybe, just maybe, it wasn't the right time. Maybe you were waiting for a cute stranger on an airplane to show you the true meaning of love?" I Willow Winked him. "I'm kidding, Will, relax - unless, of course, I'm not. Oh, yeah, did I also mention that I think things also happen when you least expect them - like meeting random strangers in certain places, which may end up not being so random?"

He laughed and said, "I know what you mean, and yeah, it's true. It was kind of random that I met you."

"Yeah, Will, I was not even supposed to be on that flight, but who knows? Maybe I was meant to be on it."

He smiled, "Maybe. So, lucky you, Willow, in love, what did you say? Maybe three times? Let me guess, you were probably one of those girls that always had a boyfriend, perhaps the girl in high school I always had a crush on, but who would never give me the time of day?"

"Um-m, yes somewhat, to answer your question about the boyfriend. Most of my relationships were pretty long term, but being the spiritual cat I am, I honestly believe that the people we end up in relationships with sometimes end up being our teachers. We learn a lot about who we are and who we are not. As far as the girl in high school question, if I blew you off, it wasn't because I was snotty, not my style. My girlfriends might have been a little bit, but if anything, I was more distracted by the bad boy I was dating."

"Really? Willow, you don't cross me as the bad boy loving type."

"Well, not anymore, but I dated a few. Unfortunately, that lesson took me a few more years to learn. But, now that I look back, even the ones that seemed to be heart breakers I now know were just scared kittens under their lion facades, and were afraid to love themselves."

"Willow, you sure you're not still in school to become a psychologist? You seem to really have an understanding about all of this."

I smiled, "Well, maybe someday I'll go back and get my Masters in counseling, but I have always been a student, so to speak, on the desires and behaviors of human nature. I'm fascinated by what it is that touches human's hearts, and what makes them really feel. That is what I really believe, that humans want to feel and be touched by life. I don't know, I'm going on and on. Let's take a little break from this philosophy class, shall we? I'll tell you more, I promise, but let's lighten things up a bit. I am getting hungry, and would love to kick your ass in a game of pool. You down with that?"

I pointed to the table across the room. "I see they have a pool table. Why don't we go sit at one of the round tables, order some burgers, and play a game or two while we wait for our food?"

I saw his face turn a little red. "What Will, you're not nervous to shoot some stick with me, are 'ya?"

"No, no. I just didn't picture you to be a shooting pool kind of a girl. I am pleasantly surprised. I should warn you, I suck. I haven't played since my early twenties."

"Will, come on, it's a just a game, not ESPN's Billiards Tournament!" I Willow Winked him.

We ordered some burgers with fries. While we waited for the food to arrive, I kicked his butt in pool a few times, and drank another beer. I started to feel a little buzzed from having an empty belly.

Will looked at me after we finished the game and said, "Okay, I've had enough butt-kicking for one night. Let's take a break, shall we?"

"Sure."

I pulled out my hand sanitizer and grabbed his hand and said, "Here, you need some of this, you don't know where these pool sticks have been."

He smiled, "Thanks. A little germophobic, are we?"

I laughed and said, "Yeah, certifiable, won't bullshit you about that one!"

He tapped my hand and said, "It's okay, I have my phobias, too. You should see me at work wiping down the office computer keyboard and the phones. Somebody is always coughing or hacking on them. It's gross."

I laughed, "I can top that one. When I go on an airplane, I usually wear a hooded sweatshirt, you know why?"

He smiled and nodded, so I said, "Yeah, because who knows how many heads have touched the seat, ew-w."

"Wow, Willow, you are a little neurotic, huh? But wait, I don't remember you wearing a hoodie on the plane when I met you. Were you wearing one?"

"Yeah, of course, but I probably didn't think about it - I was distracted by a cute stranger on the airplane who made me forget about germs." I Willow Winked him again.

"You're a fun flirt, Willow, you know that?"

"I've been told."

Our food arrived and I opened the ketchup bottle and poured it all over my burger. I don't know if it was a shitty rocking table, or my natural clumsiness, or the last beer I had drunk, but next thing I knew, as I went to cut my burger in half the plate fell in my lap! I was mortified. The waitress saw what happened, ran over, and said, "Oh, my God! What can I get for you?"

"Um-m-m, how about a hundred napkins, some club soda, and a few more beers to get rid of my embarrassment?"

Will was so sweet - to not make me feel embarrassed he said, "I've done it, too, not on a first date, but I've done it. It's all good. I'm kidding, Willow, you do not need to be embarrassed. In fact, I think it's kind of cute. I am pretty sure I saw an extra t- shirt laying in the backseat of my grandfather's car I'm borrowing. Do you want me to check, so you can change out of that ketchup-filled mess?"

"Um-m, that would be great, if you don't mind. In the meantime, let me run to the bathroom and try and get some of it off of these jeans."

No problem, let's get you another burger, too, you can share mine 'till it comes."

"Okay, thanks."

As he walked out, I decided that I had to call Carla quick and tell her about my mishap. She's going to laugh because she knows I'm such a klutz, and it is a classic Willow move. I ran into the bathroom and dialed.

She picked up on the second ring, "Oh, my God, that is so weird

- you are calling! I was just thinking about you and wondering how the date is going?" Must be that intuitive sister thing.

"Oh, my God, Carla, I am in the freaking bathroom. We just ordered hamburgers and fries and lots of ketchup - because you know I drown everything in ketchup - and when I went to cut my burger in half, the whole thing, with ketchup, fell on my lap and splattered me everywhere. I wanted to crawl under the table and hide."

She started cracking up. "Classic Willow, oh no, first date! I know you well enough to know you are calling me to reassure you that you don't need to be mortified. Willow, you think he has never spilled anything on himself in front of girl before? Where are you guys anyway?"

"I know what you mean. Besides he's sweet. He just ran out to his car to grab me an extra t-shirt. We're at some fun bar with pool tables and dart boards, casual, my style."

"Willow, good. See? That's a good sign. He thinks quickly on his feet by going to grab you that shirt. Besides, knowing my sister, you have already kicked his ass in a game of pool, and he's the embarrassed one for being beaten by a girl."

"Actually, three games, but thanks for making me feel better."

She continued, "So, aside from your ketchup spill, how is the overall date going?"

"Um-m-m, okay. I'm not going to lie, it's good. I'm not feeling over the top sparks, but we are having fun. He seems like a really easygoing guy."

"Willow, I didn't have over the top sparks with Marcus on our first date."

"You didn't?"

"No, we had fun, but it wasn't like fireworks central or anything. Willow, can you take a little advice from your older sister right now, without getting defensive?"

"Go ahead, Carla, I'm all ears."

"Okay, Willow, so listen. As you get older, you begin to realize that there are different kinds of loves on different levels, and sometimes, as you know from past boyfriends, sometimes what seems so hot at first, can sizzle pretty quickly when there aren't other important factors there. So, all I am saying is, just have fun, appreciate this guy for who he is, remember it's just a drink, and start to open up more."

"You're right, Sis, thanks for the chat. I'd better get back. I'll call you first thing tomorrow when I wake up."

"Promise?"

"Promise."

I tried to wash off the ketchup, and now I had yucky, sticky, wet jeans. Oh, who cares at this point? I came out of the bathroom to get the tee shirt. He handed it to me and I ran back into the bathroom to change. I obviously don't look as cute because it's an extra large, but I know he doesn't care.

I came back to the table, and as I sat down I said, "Thanks, Will. Sorry, not quite as cute as my other shirt, but this will work."

"You look fine, and you're welcome. So here, let's share this burger to start. I took the liberty and cut this burger in half, just in case." He winked at me.

"You're not going to let me live this one down are you?"

"After you just buried me on the pool table, hell no."

I smiled. He's got a cute sense of humor.

I changed the subject. "So, talk to me a little about music. Who do you like? I'm very passionate about it. I'm curious - who rocks your world?"

He put down his burger and said, "Wow, music, that is one of my passions, too. I am a big classic rock guy."

I smiled, "Me, too. Nice, so who do you like?"

"Well, I'm a big Zeppelin fan. I love the Stones, Hendrix, and Clapton. I also like The Dave Matthews Band. I could go on."

My face lit up. This date was about to go a lot better. I stopped him, "Wow, you must be my musical soul mate. They're some of my favorites, too. Nice taste, Will. I'm pleasantly surprised."

"So, how about you, Willow?"

"Well, definitely, as I mentioned, a classic rock girl. Nobody plays guitar like Jimmy Page, Clapton, and Hendrix, except Carlos Santana."

He smiled, "Wow, you're right about him."

"Will, I don't know what it is, but there's something magical about that guitar and his passion when he plays. I feel it in every ounce of my being. I also love Lenny Kravitz. He's the hottest musician ever. Dave Matthews I love, too. I mostly appreciate him for the lyrics to his music. As far as I am concerned, he sings to every woman on the planet. He is able to say, through his music, what men don't have the balls to say in general."

"Gee Willow, again, tell me what you really think!"

"Sorry, I have strong opinions about my men and my music. I also love a little old fashioned, soul-filled blues, like Billie Holiday. She sings from her soul, and I love Sinatra. Who doesn't love Sinatra?"

He responded, "You could hang with my grandpa. He's obsessed with Sinatra. He has every album he ever made. He and my grandmother have been to God knows how many concerts."

I smiled, "I'm jealous! I'd have loved to have seen him play just once, my Grandpa Lex and Grandma Lu also loved to see him perform. My sister likes him too, so speaking of, tell me about your family, any sib-lings?"

"I have one - I have an older sister who has adorable twins. They're five years old."

"Twins," he said, "That's awesome. What are their names?"

"Mandy and Jack."

I got goose bumps. I knew right away it was a sign.

"Will, one of my nephew's names is Jack, too."

"Really? Cool."

"It's one of my favorite names for a guy. Everybody likes a Jack."

"You're right about that," he agreed. "So, that's it. I have one older sister, Becky, and you? Tell me a little about your family."

"As I mentioned, I have an older sister, Carla, and two nephews who I love more than life itself. My grandma was the light in my life. She taught me so much about the importance of love, especially between family members. I miss her a lot, but I carry her wisdom with me every day.

"My grandpa and I are very close. I try to take good care of him, not as good as Grandma did, but I do my best."

He stopped me, "Willow, I think it's amazing that you offered to stay and help take care of him. That says a lot about you right off the bat."

I smiled, "Thanks, Will."

"So, do you think you're going to stay here in Florida and settle down?"

"Um-m, no. I think my grandpa and I will move back to the Philadelphia area in a couple of months or so, when he feels ready. We have a great place lined up for him in Philly, 'ya know, one of those assisted living-type places, but he is nowhere ready right now for that, or to leave Florida."

"I hear you. So, change of subject - what are the big Willow dreams?"

"You mean, like what I want to do for a living or to be a wife and have a family kind of thing?"

"Well, yeah, I guess all of the above."

I thought *wow first date putting it right out there, this is a first*, but I took a deep breath and said, "Well, as far as a job, my dream is to become a published author/poet. I would also like to design cool cards with my own poetry and quotes on them, or pictures with quotes and drawings on them somewhere. As far as marriage and a family, 'ya know, to tell you the truth, Will, when I was younger I was convinced that I would get married and have kids. But, over the last ten years, I'm not sure if it's because of the men I dated who were completely anti-marriage, or my rethinking what it is I want in life, but I'm still kind of up in the air."

"As for the children, I'm still growing up myself a little, so I also believe you have to feel confident about who you are in this world before you bring a child into it. I'm a late bloomer, so I'm pretty sure I want at least one, or maybe adopt one someday. I don't know, but if for some reason I choose not to, I don't want to be judged."

He got sort of silent.

"Oh, no. I haven't scared you off with my responses, have I?"

"Not at all."

"So, what about you, Will? What are your big dreams?"

"Well, Willow, I would love some day to own my own business, perhaps something technology-related. I'm a really good at using computers and at electrical work." This guy is seriously gaining points.

He continued, "As far as the marriage and family thing, yes, I know one hundred percent, for sure, I do want it. I would like to provide for my family someday. It's an important value of mine."

I nodded. Part of me felt a little nervous for this was also a first - meeting a guy who knows for sure he wants the marriage and family thing. There was an anxious feeling within me, but also a happy feeling to be with someone who wasn't afraid to say what he wants.

"Good for you, Will, to know what you want."

He smiled. We continued to talk a little more about life, just basic stuff. I looked at my watch, and it was getting late. I felt kind of tired. I don't know if it was the extra beer or two I drank, or my thyroid, but part of me felt like I was ready to call it a night.

He noticed me looking at my watch and said, "What, got a hot date you've got to get to?"

I giggled, "Yeah, actually Will, you are date one, I have a late night booty call waiting for me at midnight."

He smiled - a little nervous that I might be serious. "Will, come on now, you know I'm kidding. Seriously, though, I'm a little tired."

"Oh, no, Willow. I haven't bored you already, have I?"

"No, not at all, I just feel like I've had enough to drink, and I'm not sure if it's thyroid-related or what, I just think I want to go home and lie down. Don't think I'm bailing on you, or this date sucked or anything."

He squinched his nose, "Thyroid thing?"

I figured no need to tell him about my medical issues on the first date, but since I brought it up... "Um-m, yeah. I was diagnosed recently with a thyroid disease that's now finally being managed by medication, but every once in a while, I get exhausted. I'm okay, just tired. So, how long are you in town?"

"Um-m-m, 'till Tuesday morning. You think, Willow, there is any chance I might get to see you one more time?"

"Maybe, I have to work at my café the next few days, but I'm sure we might be able to work something out."

He looked kind of disappointed that I wasn't more enthusiastic, but I did have to work, and didn't want to commit to anything.

"I know, Willow, you told me before that you're a spontaneous girl, so if I call you and catch you, maybe you will join me?"

I laughed. He got me on some level and called me on it, too.

"Um-m-m, yeah, more than likely we'll have that second date. Why don't you call me sometime Monday and perhaps we'll catch up in the evening."

"That would be great."

We started to walk out to our cars. I had hoped in the back on my mind that he wouldn't try to lay a kiss on me, for I didn't feel ready. Not that I didn't think he was attractive, I just wasn't feeling in the mindset to do it on the first date this time. As we continued walking, he wrapped his hand around my waist and I leaned into him. There was something very natural about that simple embrace. I felt like I had done it a hundred times before.

As we approached the car, he said, "I really had fun with you tonight."

"Me, too," I answered.

I think he could sense I wasn't going to make out with him, so he leaned in for a hug, which was also nice. I kissed his cheek and said, "So, will I see you maybe on Monday night?"

"Maybe," he said, and winked at me.

I got in my car, and he shut the door. I put my window down. I turned the radio on low, and it was that Van Halen song, "Hot for Teacher."

I laughed and turned it up, "I love this tune."

He smiled back, "Me, too. Oh, yeah, forgot to mention that I'm a big Van Halen fan."

"Me, too. So I have to ask really quickly before I go, David Lee Roth or Sammy Hagar?"

"With the exception of this song, gotta go with Sammy," he responded.

"I knew I liked you, Will."

He sneaked a quick peck on my lips, and I put the window up and waved goodbye as I pulled out. It was a good first date, not a fire-cracking, over the top, sparkly one, but it was a comfortable first date.

When I got home, Grandpa was still up in front of the television. "You're still up Grandpa. You weren't waiting up for me, were you?"

"No, love, couldn't sleep."

"Are you okay?"

"Yeah, just miss your grandma tonight a little more than usual."

"Sorry, Gramps, anything I can do?"

"Well, how's about you tell me about your first date with Will. That might cheer me up. Did you have fun?"

"Yeah, it was good; we had fun. Nothing over the top, but it was good."

"I know, my Willow, so why do you seem disappointed?"

"I'm not disappointed. I guess I thought I would be more, I don't know, overly excited?"

"Willow, my love, you can't always judge a potential love story by the first date. Those love at first sight moments are rare, I believe, and I think your grandma would agree with me. She was the one with more words, but she would agree that the best love stories are ones that take time to grow into something beautiful. The ones that start off too soon usually fizzle pretty quickly."

"Grandpa, you are so right, you always know what to say! Carla said the same thing about Marcus, too."

He nodded his head at me and said, "I rest my case. So, the most important question is, is he a good guy?"

I nodded, "Really nice. There's something naturally comfortable about him. I can't fully explain it, but when he walked me out to my car, I felt there was something like home to me about him - if that makes any sense."

He smiled wide.

"What, Gramp? Why are you grinning at me?"

"Because your grandma said the same thing to me, later on, after our first date. So, will you see him again before he heads back home?"

"I think so. Wait - Grandma said the same thing about you?"

"Yeah, after a few dates she told me there was something that felt like home about me, and she said that was the best kind." I smiled.

"That is so sweet, Grandpa, Grandma Lu always knew, right?"

"She sure did. So I am asking again, will you see him before he leaves?"

"Probably."

"Willow, honey, just hang out with him if you want to, don't play games anymore."

"Play games, Grandpa? Who said anything about playing games? I don't play games."

"Okay, maybe 'games' is the wrong word. I was trying to use your generation's language, but what I mean is, life is short, honey, and this guy is only in town for a few days. Have fun and give something a chance if there is potential."

"There is potential, I think. We will see. I will let you know." Grandpa responded, "fair enough."

The next morning as promised I called Carla. After she drilled me for details and settled on me telling her there would be a second date, I said, "Carla, change of subject, so how are my delicious boys?

I miss them so. I was thinking of flying up in the next few weeks to see you guys. I miss you all."

She responded, "That would be fantastic! Jack asks me from time to time where his Aunt Wiwwow is, and when you two can draw together, or catch butterfwies."

He couldn't pronounce his L's yet, so it sounds that cute. "Ahh, I miss him. I might just have to visit."

"I would love that, and so would the boys!" I promised her to consider it and of course call her after date two.

# Chapter 27

IT WAS NOW MONDAY, AND date two. I got a text later in the day telling me to meet him at Sunset Park at around six o'clock and to dress comfortably. I liked the sound of it, h-m-m, what to wear? I decided on Capri jeans, a cute tee, flip flops, and my favorite zip up sweatshirt in case I get chilly.

I walked out into the living room and Grandpa looked up from his paper and said, "Well, where is my angel off to this evening?"

"Date two, Gramp, remember?"

He winked at me, "Of course I remember. So, where are you two going tonight?"

"He told me to meet him at some park - I think it's called Sunset Park?"

"Oh, how romantic! I was there a few times with your grandma. Willow, they have a beautiful lake, and yes, one of the most magnificent sunsets I have ever seen. He has good taste."

"Cool, I love lakes. This should be nice. Okay, I gotta run - how do I look?"

He smiled, "Like yourself, comfortable, and cute, and down to earth."

"Good answer, thanks. Okay, gotta run! Will see 'ya in the morning, unless…"

He interrupted me, "I know, Willow, unless the date stinks and you are home early, but my big round gut tells me I will see you in the morning. Goodnight, sweetheart."

I kissed his forehead, "Goodnight, Gramp."

I pulled up to the park and popped a piece of my favorite bubblegum in my mouth. I got out of the car and saw him sitting looking out at over the lake, with a big soft yellow blanket and what looked like a picnic basket. I liked this already.

I had chills from how beautiful the lake was. To my left, I heard some young children running, giggling, and playing chase with one another. To my right, I saw a herd of runners exhaling as they jogged by. As I walked toward him, he must have felt my presence because he turned around. He looked more handsome than I remembered on the last date. He was wearing a collared red shirt and a pair of comfy cargo shorts.

He smiled, and said, "Surprise."

"Wow, Will, I sure am. This is beautiful! How did you know I love lakes?"

"Well, I figured being a poet, you must have a love of nature and would appreciate this."

"It's perfect, I've written many poems sitting by water. Actually, I hope one day to build my dream home overlooking a lake or some body of water."

He laughed, "Well, how did you know that was part of my dream, too?"

"Really?"

"Really - I've always been drawn to them, too. There's something calming for me, being near water. I admit I'm not the deepest guy, and I know I tend to work very long hours. However, there's something comforting to me about the thought of coming home from a long day, and sitting on my back porch overlooking a lake. It would be a great way to come down from my day. Does that make any sense?"

I fell silent with that fuzzy feeling when he said this. "Will, for someone who says he's not deep, I felt some depth in those words."

"Well, coming from you, Willow, I'll take that as a compliment."

He waved and patted his hand on the blanket for me to sit down.

I kicked my flip-flops off and plopped down. I leaned over and kissed his cheek. He blushed.

"That was sweet."

I smiled and said, "*Just because.*"

He blushed, "*Just because*, I like that."

"I am a *just because* kind of a girl. You know, I love those moments when, for no reason at all, you remind someone of their sweetness or your affection for them, so *just because.*" I winked at him, hoping he would remember those words.

"I gotcha, Willow, so *just because*, would you like a beer or a glass of wine? I wasn't sure what kind of mood you would be in tonight."

"Um-m-m, how about a glass of wine, what kind did you bring?"

"White, pinot grigio, I hope that's cool."

"Will, it's perfect. It's actually the only kind of white I like."

He pulled out a bottle of *Santa Margherita*. My eyes lit up and opened up wide. He saw and said, "What, did I do okay?"

"Will, it is my favorite kind! My girlfriends and I have done some damage on these bottles together."

He giggled, "Well, I wish I could take credit for the wine, but the truth is that my grandmother gave it to me. I hope I don't lose points for that, 'ya know, asking Grandma for her opinion on what wine to bring. She told me if I want to do it right, I have to bring this bottle."

"Well, you can thank her personally for me."

He popped open the wine and poured me a glass. He then poured himself one and raised his glass and said, "To what I hope will be one of many beautiful sunsets to watch with you."

"Perfect toast." I toasted him and said, "So, where did you get the picnic basket? I know you didn't bring this from Philly and place it above your head on the flight."

He laughed, "What do you mean? I always travel with picnic baskets as my carry- on luggage. Okay, in all seriousness, my grandma had it. I told her I felt a little dorky carrying it, but she told me to get over my fear of looking anything but romantic."

"I'm starting to like this Grandma, she's right."

"So, are you hungry, because I brought some snacks?"

"What kind of snacks?" I asked.

"Um-m, let's see what I have in here."

He reached in his basket and pulled out a bag of cashews, some carrots and dip, and some little mozzarella and tomato sandwiches on mini rolls.

"Will, this is super cute. Let me guess, Grandma also helped make this little basket of goodies?"

"Okay, you've caught me once again. But wait, this one was my idea," he pulled out a bag of red licorice.

I laughed, "Nice! I love red licorice, how did you know that?"

"I didn't, I was sort of hoping, because I should tell you, Willow, I am a kid at heart when it comes to candy. I love it even with wine. I have a sweet tooth like no other."

"Will, it's all good. I'm a candy freak, too. Sometimes I wonder, because my dad refused to let me have sweet cereals or candy as a kid, why I overindulge now."

"Willow, I love cereal, too. It's one of my favorite things to eat."

"What's your favorite?"

"I gotta go with Corn Pops."

I smiled, and said, "Nice, I love Cinnamon Toast Crunch, or Frosted Mini Wheats, the vanilla ones. Have you tried those yet?"

He laughed back and said, "Hell yeah, and have you tried the strawberry ones? They're yummy, too."

I nodded. "Well, Will if nothing else, at least we have cereal and candy in common." I Willow Winked him.

He said, "Wait, what about music? Oh, here's an idea - how about, on our third date, we rock out to some Zeppelin over a bowl of Pops?"

I laughed, "I like your style. Now you're talking, but in the meantime, I'll try one of those delicious sandwiches." I took a bite. "Yum, this is good! Tell Grandma she makes a great sandwich."

He giggled. "Hey, I helped, too."

We sat and chatted for a while about simple stuff. The sun was setting, and I felt really comfortable and at this point, a little buzzed. I felt our bodies begin to move a little closer. He put his hand on my knee, and I put my hand on top of his. For whatever reason, I felt like I wanted to lean in and hug him. I did. He surrendered and just held me close. We didn't say anything and just held one another. I placed my head on his shoulder and could feel his breath close to my neck. I felt like I could stay in this spot forever. He felt so good and comfortable.

I sat back up and said jokingly, "Eh-h, *just because.*"

He leaned in and kissed my cheek and said, "Eh-h, *just because,* I can play, too, right?"

Then it felt like the right moment, and I leaned in and pecked him on the lips. "*Just because.*"

He fell silent and grabbed my face with his hand and kissed me tenderly. It was one of the sweetest and best kisses I had ever had. I was pleasantly surprised, and as I was kissing him, I thought to myself, *this kiss is good.* This made up for whatever sparks weren't there on our last date.

I found myself getting nervous, so I stopped and smiled at him.

"Wow, Will, who taught you how to kiss so well?"

He laughed, "I was just thinking the same thing! So, can we do it again? You know, *just because.*"

I laughed and kissed him again. This was fun! We kissed and chatted a few more times, but realized it was getting dark and a little chilly.

"So, Will, what time is your flight tomorrow?"

"At 7 a.m."

"7 a.m.? Oh, no, I didn't know it was so early! You have to probably get up at, what, like 4:30?"

"Um-m, five o'clock will be enough. I'll roll out of bed, take a five second shower, and make it to the airport by six."

"Okay, well, I don't want to keep you out too late."

"Willow, are you kidding me? If I don't sleep the whole night, this time with you would be worth it."

I smiled, "You're sweet. Okay. Well, let's see, it's almost 9:00, is there anything else you want to do? I wish I could say let's go back to my place and watch a movie, but my grandpa is still up."

He laughed, "Yeah, me too. How about some ice cream? I wanted to bring it, but obviously, it would have melted. What do you say we go get some ice cream?"

I smiled, "Yeah that sounds like a great idea."

We packed our goodies into the basket and I hopped into his car. I turned on the radio, and what do you know, Zeppelin is playing. I turned it up.

"Awesome, the DJs must have known we'd be together."

He put his hand on top of mine. As I looked over at him driving, I looked at his eyes. He sure was sexy to me right now. I smiled to myself because this was the first time I saw him that way. I liked it and felt compelled to kiss the side of his right eye. *"Just because* you look cute."

We stopped at a stoplight. He pulled me in close and started making out with me. We were like two teenagers in the car. We heard a big honk behind us.

"Oops," he said. "Stop distracting me, Willow, at least until the next stop light."

I smiled as we pulled up to the ice cream parlor. As we got out, he grabbed my hand, which felt so natural - I loved it.

We walked in and he said, "What kind are you going to get?"

"Now, normally Will, I would probably get a fat free something, but I want to let my hair down tonight. I'm thinking mint chocolate chip with chocolate jimmies. And you?"

"I'm a cookie dough freak, but I like mint chocolate chip, too."

"Awesome, you get one, and I'll get the other. But, can you at least get colored jimmies on yours? They're my favorite."

He smiled, "You got it, Willow."

We sat down in a hot red-colored booth across from one another and ate our ice cream. I was happy, and literally felt like a kid in an ice cream parlor. I looked at him and said, "Are you ready to try mine?"

He said, "Yeah, are you ready to try mine?"

We both took scoops out of our cups and fed one another a taste. Our eyes lit up.

"Yummy, can I get some more of that?" I begged.

He gave me another big scoop. He placed his spoon back into the ice cream and said, "So, when do I get to have ice cream with you again?"

I had a feeling he would ask. I decided I was going to go home in a few weeks to see the kids, and now, of course, to see him.

"Well, Will, it just so happens that in about two weeks I'm flying home to see my nephews. Perhaps we could meet for some ice cream then?"

His face lit up. "Really? Two weeks? Great! So, do I get to see you again? Can you squeeze me in for a visit or two?"

"I think I can manage that."

"Good, because I would hate to wait another month to come back out to see you."

"A month?"

"Yeah. I'm flying back out in four weeks to play in another golf tournament with my grandpa, but I am happy to get a chance to see you before."

"Yes, you will."

In the meantime, I was thinking *I better book my flights ASAP before the airfare goes up ridiculously!*

We finished our ice cream, got into the car, and drove back to get mine. As we pulled up, I leaned in to kiss him.

"Thanks, Will, I had such a great time tonight."

"Me too, Willow. I am a little smitten. I have to admit."

I sat up, "Just a little bit?"

"Okay, a lot, but don't want you to get too ego-filled on me. You are something, and I would like to know more."

He kissed me again, passionately, and said, "I will definitely want more of these great kisses, too."

"I can arrange that. Thank you for an awesome night."

"You're welcome, and thank you."

I kissed him one more time and got out of the car. As I got ready to pull out of the parking lot, I saw him pulling behind me. For whatever reason, I stopped my car and got out, and walked over to his car and said, "I forgot to tell you something."

I leaned in and kissed him one more time and said, *"Just because."* His face lit up - the best smile I had ever seen. As I walked back to my car, I thought to myself, *yeah that'll leave him a reminder until the next time.*

I texted Carla on the car ride home to ask if she was still awake. She immediately called me back.

"So?"

I smiled, "It was so much better than the first date, really romantic. I met him at a park that overlooks a lake, and we watched the sunset, and he set up a little picnic. Then we went for ice cream. It was fun."

She giggled, "So, did you kiss this time?"

"Yeah, and Carla, he is a good kisser.

"Wow, Willow, sounds like an awesome date! So, will you see

him again when you come to see the boys and I? You did book your flight right?"

"I'll book it when I get home. Yes, for sure I'm coming and I'm happy now that I have two things to look forward to."

"Sounds great, Sis, I have a good feeling about this one."

"Me, too, but don't want to jinx it."

"Oh, Willow, no jinxing. Stop with your superstitious mindset and just be open to loving. H-m-m, now there's a great idea!"

"I know, Carla, for once, I will try."

"Good, so the boys and I are so psyched that you're coming home!"

"Me, too."

We hung up and I walked into the house, Grandpa was asleep. I tiptoed in, changed my clothes, and got down on one knee before bed and said, "God, thank you for a wonderful evening, and I am not sure why yet, but I'm going to try to trust why you have brought this wonderful man to me. So, thanks again, and I love you."

I woke up to a text from Will that read, *Miss 'ya already.* I smiled, and texted back, *Me, too.* I got myself dressed and, as usual, Grandpa was waiting for me at the kitchen table with his coffee and *New York Times*.

"Morning, sunshine. So, how was it?"

"It was really great, Grandpa, so romantic and sweet. What a beautiful place. I can now see why Grandma loved it so much. Those sunsets are enough to make anyone fall in love, or fall into heaven's palm, or something exquisite."

"Willow, gosh, I have never heard you quite as poetic as that! It must have been a really good date. So, is that what happened? You already fell in love?"

"No, Grandpa, don't be silly, but I definitely fell into more of a liking. He's an easy guy to be around and he has a genuine heart, that much I can tell."

"Great, honey. So, when do you get to see him again?"

"Well, I decided that I'm flying home in two weeks to see the boys, so I'll see him then. You know, Grandpa that reminds me, I was thinking, how would you like to come with me for a long weekend?"

I already knew the answer, but I figured I would try to at least put it out there.

"Willow, honey, I love 'ya for thinking of me, but I will be fine, and I don't quite feel like going anywhere right now. You know, I am not just an up and go kind of a guy. I am an old fart who doesn't move so fast anymore."

"Okay, Gramp, just thought I would try."

"I know, love, and again, I love you for it, but I will be fine!"

"Alright, well I better get in the shower, I have to be at work in a half an hour."

"Okay, love, glad it went well."

"Me, too."

# Chapter 28

I WAS HOPING TO SEE Ed at the café, but then I remembered he told me he was meeting with his editor. I smiled knowing somewhere, someone soon, was going to be reading one of my poems. As I went to make some coffee, I heard the door open and I looked to see who it was. My stomach dropped - it was Bernardo. I thought *holy shit, of all times to pop in, what on earth is he doing here?* We made eye contact and he started walking toward me.

"Bernardo, what brings you here?"

"Well, I have some news, Willow."

"Okay, what's up?"

"I am moving back to Barcelona next week."

"Really? So fast?"

"Yes, it turns out, my uncle has a friend who is looking to open up a new club and needs a partner. It is in one of the most happening parts of town."

"Wow, Bernardo that sounds great. Congratulations on the opportunity."

"Yes, Willow, thank you. So, I knew I could have called you, but I wanted one last chance to apologize and see you in person before I went. I was afraid if I called and asked to see you, you would have said no. So, sorry to just pop in here on you."

"It's okay, Bernardo, I'm genuinely happy for you, and I wish you the best of luck. I think you will do well, but my one wish for you is to never stop playing your music."

He smiled. "Well, that I can promise you, no doubt. So, I also wanted to say thank you." I raised my brow.

"For what?" I asked.

"Well, Willow, for teaching me that there is more to life and to love than what we sometimes think."

"What do you mean?"

"It is hard for me to put into words, but you softened me somehow, and moving forward, I think I am going to look at women a little more gently, with more respect and honesty. More importantly, I am grateful to have had the pleasure of such a beautiful woman's company, and I am not talking just about your physical features."

I smirked and thought to myself once again *this guy is good*, but part of me believed his sincerity, too.

"Thanks, Bernardo, I am happy to have met you, too. I just learned something from you, as well." He looked surprised.

"You did?"

"Yes, just now. I learned that forgiveness is a gift, and I learned that I have the ability to help open up other's perceptions."

He smiled, "I like that. So, can I have a hug goodbye?"

I leaned in and gave him a great big hug. He still smelled so good, but right away Will popped into my head, and I thought *no comparison on kisses*, and was grateful to have already met him.

"Okay, I better get back to work, but good luck."

"Thanks, Willow. You, too. I have a feeling I will see your poems someday."

"You will indeed." I Willow Winked him one last time.

As I watched him leave, Trisha came over to me, and said, "God, he is a looker!"

I laughed and said, "He sure is, and you should hear him play that guitar!"

"Why can't I ever meet someone like that?"

I looked at Robert, who was sitting at a table paying bills. "Well Trish, sometimes I think God may have someone else in mind for us that would better suit our hearts." She looked at me with curious eyes.

"What made you look over at Robert when you said that?"

"I don't know, just a feeling," I replied.

"Really, Willow? Cause, can I tell you something a little strange?"

"Sure, Trisha, you can tell me anything. Believe me, nobody does strange better than me."

"Okay, thanks. Well, last week I went to my psychic, Bezzy, and she said someone I work closely with has a major crush on me, but is afraid to tell me." I laughed, for her psychic was right.

"Wow, really?"

"Yeah, honey. I can't help but think if it could be Robert. I mean, I never really thought about him like that. You know, I'm usually attracted to the tattooed Harley driven men who drink too much."

"Well, Trisha, perhaps you're ready to think about dating another type, one who will treat you well and embrace your sweet heart."

"Willow, I always knew I liked you for a reason. Thank you, honey. Anyway, stay tuned, because lately I've done a little more flirting than usual with him, 'ya know, to see if it could really be him. He's been flirtatious back. I don't know, we will see. Leave it to me for it to take a psychic to tell me I have a potential for love with someone I work with."

"Trisha, you know what I believe?" I asked.

"What's that, honey?"

"I believe psychic, or no psychic, sometimes we need to hear something new to help awaken us to other possibilities, and for the potential to be really happy. There's more to life and love then what we originally thought. Does that make any sense?"

"It does, honey."

I immediately thought of Luke as my pseudo psychic. I wanted to go see him and Sam again, and tell them both about my second date.

On my way home from work, I stopped by the assisted living home hoping both Sam and Lucas would be there. I walked in and decided to look for Lucas first. I went up and down the halls as usual, and couldn't seem to find him. I asked one of the nurses where he might be. She told me he was off for the day, so I made my way to Sam's room. I noticed as I got closer, I could hear some voices coming from inside. It sounded like two men talking, followed by an ongoing, non-stop, hacking cough from Sam.

"Dad, are you okay, are you okay?"

I smiled for it was clear that his son was with him. I didn't think it would happen so soon. I debated whether or not to knock on the door. I didn't want to interrupt their time, but part of me wanted to meet him and his partner. I decide to knock. Immediately, both men looked over, and Samuel saw me and smiled.

"Sorry to interrupt you guys. Samuel, I was passing through and wanted to say hello."

"Willow, what a nice surprise, come on in." I walked in. "Willow, I would like you to meet my son, Joe, and his partner, Noel."

I put out my hand. "It's nice to meet you guys, I have heard a lot about you, Joe." He smiled.

"And Willow, I have heard nice things about you, too. I heard you've kept nice company with my father, and actually may have had some influence on this visit right now."

I felt a little awkward, but smiled anyway, "Oh-h-h, that's sweet. Thanks, but your meeting with your dad was all his doing."

"Either way, Willow, thanks and it's nice to meet you, and I am glad we made the visit now. Dad just told us the sad news." I scrunched my brows and looked perplexed.

"What do you mean?" He looked over at Sam.

"You didn't tell her?"

"Tell me what?"

Joe put his hand on his father's and said, "Sorry, Dad, I just figured she knew."

My heart sank, and I knew what they meant.

Samuel sat up and said, "It's okay, son, I just found out a few days ago. Willow, my cancer has spread quite pervasively, and I don't have much time."

I put my hand on top of his other open hand and said, "I am so sorry, Sam. What can I do?"

"Willow, you have already done enough by encouraging this gift sitting right next to me."

He looked over at his son, and winked at me. My heart filled with joy, knowing I did have an influence on this reunion.

"Oh, Sam, I knew there was a sweet old man in there." I Willow Winked him back. "Well, your time is precious now, so I don't want to take it away from you guys. I will come back to see you soon. Spend some overdo time with your son and his partner."

"Okay, Willow, thanks for stopping by. By the way, how was that date? Did you ever go out with that guy?"

I smiled, "Yes, and I will tell you all about it next time I see you, okay?"

"Fair enough," he agreed.

"Joe and Noel, it was so nice to meet you both."

"You too, Willow, thanks again."

"You got it."

As I walked out the door, I smiled again, feeling like an earth angel doing my stuff. Lucas would have loved this story. I hoped he'd be here when I came back.

I pulled up to Aunt Ellen's place then walked into the café and scanned the room for her. She wasn't hard to miss with her fluorescent pink lipstick and matching fingernails. I saw her wave and I walked over. I leaned down and she gave me one of those kisses that left me gagging from her strong perfume.

"Hi, Aunt El, how are you?"

"Great, doll, how is my niece doing?"

"A little better since you saw me last."

"Well, I'm curious. Could it perhaps be from a new gentleman named Will?"

"Perhaps. Date two was so much better then date one."

"I heard." I lifted my brow.

"What do you mean you heard?"

"Well, honey, you know how grandmas are. I ran into Salma the other day and she told me that she helped prepare a sweet picnic dinner for the two of you to have at Sunset Park. Very lovely place, I know, I have been there myself for a few dates. It's very romantic." I rolled my eyes.

"Oy. Yes, Aunt El, it was very romantic and lovely! I like him. He's a solid guy with a genuine heart." She smiled.

"I just want my Willow to be happy, so I am happy. When will you see him again?"

"Well, I'm flying home next weekend to see the boys, so we'll meet then."

"Sounds good to me. You know, I think he is really smitten with you, honey. I also got the sense from his grandmother, in a subtle way, well you know me nothing is subtle with me, but in her subtle way she hopes you are into him, too, and that you're not a heartbreaker."

I felt my face get flush, "'A heartbreaker'? What on earth would give her that impression?"

"Willow, calm down doll, she wasn't insinuating that you were, she was saying to me that he has been hurt in the past, and that she knows how much he likes you and hopes that you feel the same way too, that's all honey, that's all." I let out a sigh.

"Okay, Aunt El, but easy, you know we just started dating, and I want to take it slow, and I..."

She put her hand up and interrupted me and said, "I know, I know what you are going to say next, I know my niece better than she thinks sometimes. You were going to say that you don't want to jinx it." I smiled at her. "Well, Willow, so am I right?"

I nodded, "Okay, you're right. Besides, we live in two different states right now, so it's not like we can get that close so soon anyway."

She squeezed a lemon into her iced tea and said, "Willow, that is why I think it's good timing. I mean, did it ever occur to you that this would give you a perfect excuse to take your time with this one and get to know love at a slower pace? I know you are probably thinking what do I know about love? We both know my history, Willow. I am not completely blind to myself, but I do know whether you marry someone or not, that there are ways to know love and grow with someone."

I smiled and said, "Thanks Aunt El for your thoughts, they make sense. So speakin of love, How have you and Harold been?

"Much better, honey. I told him I am too old for this shit, 'ya know, playing games or insensitive behaviors, so I think I finally straightened out his droopy ass to try a little harder. But, I told him I am still not sure I ever want to get married."

"Aunt El, what are you so afraid of, really?"

"Willow, everyone always thinks it's because I am so afraid of commitment. The truth is, I was always more of a free spirit. I never felt as if I needed to have a ceremony or a ring on my finger to prove my love for my significant other. I know, again, everyone has their judgments about me and my behaviors, but just because I never married these men, doesn't mean that I loved them any less, or didn't treat them as a husband would want to be treated."

I was silent, as I just learned something new about my aunt that made sense.

"Aunt El, it makes total sense, I can kind of relate and I respect your answer."

"Thank you, Willow. Your spirituality has opened you up, and I like that, now if I could just get all of the other yentas here to stop their whispers."

I smiled, "Oh, you don't really care what they think, do 'ya?"

"Honey, for the most part no. But, sometimes, yes, doll. Sometimes, even at this age, that little insecure thirteen year old still gets a little bothered by what the other girls think. Some things are hard to grow out of, if you know what I mean."

I nodded. We ordered some burgers and fries. As we were waiting, I told her about Bernardo stopping by my work. When I was done with my story, she sat up and said, "I am a little sad, who is going to play music now for my dancing nights out with Harold? But, I am happy for him, I know it is part of his dream. So, how do you feel?"

"Well, I feel over it. He apologized again for what happened."

As I said those words, I realized I had never given her the full story, but it didn't really matter at this point.

She stopped me and said, "I don't really know what ever happened, but it doesn't matter, Willow, I knew he was not the right one for you. I just wanted my niece to get back in the game and have some fun, 'ya know', to live a little."

I smiled, "And I did, Aunt El, so thanks. We said goodbye on good terms and I wished him well."

"Good, honey. That's the way it should be."

I nodded. We finished lunch and took a little walk. She told me she would take me to the airport when I went to Philly, since she gets up early anyway.

# Chapter 29

I woke up early to prep for my flight. As soon as I brushed my teeth, I got down on one knee and prayed to God, asking that He get me home safely and said that, once again, I was paying attention if there was someone significant that I should be looking out for at the airport. For this trip home, I asked Carla to pick me up at the airport, with the boys, if possible. I decided that since it was such a short visit, I wanted to stay with her and my nephews for the two and half days I was there. I was so excited to see them I could hardly wait. I had told Will that Saturday night would be better because I was going to see my family for Friday night, and Sunday I had hoped to see my two best girlfriends, Melody and Krystal, for lunch.

As I packed a few things and shoved them in my wheelie, I realized that the last time I was on a plane was on my way here, and when I met Will. Oh boy, who was going to help me lift this heavy bag this time? I had to admit, I was also looking forward to seeing him, too! I walked out into the living room and saw that Grandpa was already up. I was shocked. He never got up this early.

"Grandpa, what on earth are you doing up this early?"

"Well, I know my Willow is going away for a few days, and I wanted to see her pretty face for a few more minutes. I even made you some of your half and half coffee. Besides, I am happy to tell you that my tree has officially been growing some beautiful apples. I even packed you one for the flight."

"Grandpa, you are the best. Are you sure you're going to be okay?"

"Willow, my love, I am going to be better than okay. I promise you, don't worry about me so much."

"I can't help it!"

I looked at the clock and realized that I had better get dressed. I kissed Grandpa on the cheek as he told me that he was going to go back to sleep. I went into my closet - what to wear, what to wear? I decided on my favorite turquoise sweat suit and a navy blue top. I was in the mood to wear blue. I heard Aunt Ellen's car pull up.

She dropped me off at the airport, and I thanked her and kissed her cheek. As I got out of the car, she said, "I can't wait to hear about your third date with Will! Call me on Sunday morning, so I know what time to pick you up." I smiled and nodded.

As I walked toward my gate, I wondered who on earth would be sitting next to me this time. I had a few minutes to kill, and decided I needed some reading material. I went to the bookstore next to my gate and was looking for a mindless magazine. But, as I was making my way over I passed the new age section, and no joke, this book fell off the shelf and onto my sneaker. As I bent down to pick it up, I couldn't believe my eyes - this was the book Ed had told me about that he thought I should read. It was called, _A Return to Love_ by Marianne Williamson. I knew right away that this was a sign to give it a read. Ed said that I would relate to the woman who wrote the book, and that she had learned a lot from the Course in Miracles, which inspired her writing.

As I walked onto the plane with my heavy wheel-on, I saw a late fifty-something looking woman sitting in the center seat next to the aisle seat I would be in. I opened up the luggage compartment and right away she asked if I needed help. Surprisingly, I was able to manage to get my own bag in this time.

"Thank you, I think I have it, but thanks for asking."

I sat down and noticed that she was also wearing a turquoise sweatshirt.

"Nice sweatshirt."

She realized we were wearing the same color and said, "Thanks, my favorite color."

"Me, too."

She then proceeded to say, "Yeah, it's mine as well. It's the color of your soul."

I sat up, "So I hear. My friend, Ed, told me that, too."

She laughed, "Did you ever notice that most people love the color blue? No matter what your taste is, we can all agree on liking some shade of blue. I love the color so much I actually named by Labrador retriever Blue."

I nodded and thought to myself *who is the woman?* She put out her hand and said, "Hi, I'm Marisol."

"Hi, I'm Willow."

"Wow, Willow! What a pretty name - you must have a nature lover in the family."

"Yes, I do, my father. How could you tell?"

"Oh, let's just say I have a sense for this kind of thing."

I knew I was sitting next to the right person. I also recognized another name with the letter M, h-m-m-m.

"Doesn't your name mean the sea?" She smiled.

"Yes, it does. That's probably why I have always been drawn to it, too. How did you know that?"

"Well, I've met a few Mar's let alone M's in my life."

She smiled, "Interesting. So, Willow, are you headed home to Philly?"

"Yes, well, I'm living here temporarily now, but I am headed home to see my nephews, Jack and Max. I haven't seen them in months, and I miss their sweet faces. I can't wait to squeeze them and laugh with them. They really lighten me up, 'ya know?"

She smiled, "I do know, I have two of my own and they lighten me up, too. It's a labor of love, but I love them so. Willow, do you have any children?"

I sat up straighter, "Oh no, not yet."

"Do you have a special someone?" she asked.

"Well, we have just begun, but to answer your question, yes. I think I have met a special someone. As a matter of fact, would you believe me if I told you I met him a few months ago on an airplane? We were both flying here to visit our grandma's although I never left. I stayed to take care of my grandpa after my grandmother passed away."

She put her bottom lip down. "Oh, Willow, I am sorry to hear about your grandmother, but she watches over you, you know that, right?"

"I do. How do you know that?"

"I just do. It's part of what I've been researching all my life, the power of something greater than science can prove. I'm a retired psychology professor and therapist. Well, I am more of a spiritual psychologist then a scientific one. I always had a hard time teaching my students about this disorder and that disorder, when the truth is, I don't know how much I really even believe in disorders. I mean aren't we all really made of love? When you hear the word disorder, you immediately think something is wrong with you." She reminded me a little of what my therapist Katie said to me and my Course in Miracles group.

I smiled, "I know what you mean, I am trying to start believing I'm more than my anxiety disorder. 'Ya know, you sound a lot like one of the ladies in a new group I have joined, who speaks that way. I like it. "

She perked up curiously and said, "Oh yeah, what group is that?"

"Um-m-m, the Course in Miracles. Have you ever heard of it? Its spiritual psychology, should be right up your alley, yes?"

She laughed, "Oh, Willow, you want to talk about miracles? What if I told you that I run my own group in Philadelphia?"

I smiled, "I would say I believe you. Marisol, when I tell you the amount of non-coincidental things that have happened to me over the last few months, down to the people I have met, and the signs from the universe. It is, yes, miraculous!"

"Well then, Willow, I am happy to be a part of your journey, even if it's only for a two hour plane ride."

I smiled, and reached into my bag. I pulled out the book I had just bought.

"A good friend recommended that I read this. Have you read it?"

She giggled, "Have I read it? It's part of what started my journey many years ago. I've also seen Marianne speak a few times, and she's a beacon of light. She speaks of the Course in a way that makes beautiful sense. Oh, Willow, you are going to love it!"

"Great, I look forward to reading it. So, I have to ask Marisol, of all the lessons in the Course, do you have a favorite one you like to teach and review, or that especially resonates for you?"

"That's a tough one to answer. They have all brought me so much peace in their own way, but I would probably have to say my favorite is Lesson 97, which is, "I am spirit." Its basis is on reminding you that we are in fact a spirit, not a body. The ego always wants to associate you with a body, and the spirit reminds you that you are one with God, so anything else is an illusion. When you remember this, a lot more healing and openness can come to your being.

"You know, Willow, most people associate way too much with their bodies. They become fixated on their looks, or physical ailments, when the truth is we are spirits having physical experiences, not the other way around like the ego wants you to believe."

I took a deep breath and said, "I like that lesson. This lesson would certainly come in handy for someone like me who has always been sort of fixated on my physical body and a hypochondriac by nature. Also, this is really a perfect time because I was recently diagnosed with a thyroid disease and it rocked my world, so to speak,

280

but not in a good way. Let's just say I have had a hard time physically, mentally, and emotionally."

I realized that I was once again about to go off on one of my tangents and said, "Sorry, I will shut up now. I tend to do this sometimes, you get me started on a topic and I take off."

"Willow, first of all you do not need to apologize for sharing. Forgive me for getting all analytical on you, but people who feel the need to apologize for sharing are beings who learned somewhere that it was not okay to fully express themselves. We do not have to have a therapy session on it, but sweet Willow, isn't it interesting that even in the same sentence where you talked about your disease, you felt like you couldn't?

Some of that lack of expression, Willow, could be more of your creative energy anxious to flow out also."

I smiled and said, "I know what you are saying - that's why I'm writing more poetry now than ever."

She smiled, "That's great, Willow. And, as I was saying before, the Course in Miracles is a beautiful tool to help us all learn more of our true essence. So, lesson 97, 'I Am Spirit,' would be a great one for you to practice and breathe on. You know something tells me you probably learned a lot of goodness from your grandmother."

"You are right about that one, Marisol. Again, how did you know that?"

"Well, let's just say the more you learn to practice the Course, the more your spirituality opens up, and the stronger your intuition becomes. I can tell that you are an intuitive woman, too - you see this is what happens, Willow.

"When you surrender to the universe, you will begin meeting more and more like-minded people who appreciate the beauty of what God has in store for all of us. That is why, my dear, over the last few months, you have been connecting with all sorts of people who will help guide you and support you along your path."

"Wow, Marisol. Thank you. That makes perfect sense, down to the perfection of meeting you and your wise words to help reinforce me."

"Exactly. So, tell me, you really have me curious, who is this soul mate you met on the airplane a few months ago?"

"Soul mate?" I echoed.

"Yes, Willow, when I say 'soul mate' I don't necessarily mean your one and only. I believe we have many soul mates throughout our lifetimes. Something tells me you were clearly meant to meet him for a reason. What reason, I'm not sure yet, but I don't have to tell you, it's no coincidence that you met him on your way down here."

I nodded, "No you don't. It's still a very new, but I have a feeling I have probably met a man who is not going to be afraid to love. In a sense, it's not about what I look like anymore. He's somebody who has more of an unconditional loving nature. He seems like one of those guys."

She put her hand up for me to pause and said, "As opposed to most of the men you have dated?"

"Yes, exactly. Gosh you are really good at this!"

"I've had many years of practice, Willow, but the beauty of all of this is I now realize, after I am already retired, that I never actually needed my PhD to know this stuff. 'Ya see, Willow, if there's one thing I can tell you for sure, no matter who comes into our lives on a romantic level, if we can't believe we are worthy of being loved, then we will have a hard time letting that love in and reciprocating. Everyone is worthy of love, but somehow, whether it was during our childhood years, or a boyfriend or girlfriend during our teenage years, our ego minds became corrupted. We forgot about this notion of love, but, Willow, I mean the real notion of love, the kind of love that never left you, the one God instilled in your heart but, again, somehow got misplaced in our noisy world."

I smiled wide and said, "You mean like Agape kind of love?"

She laughed, "Yes, that's exactly what I mean! How do you know about that word?"

"Well, let's just say it has been coming to me miraculously on license plates, "Jeopardy," 'ya name it!'"

She giggled again, "Well, Willow, then I hope you are paying attention now to its meaning."

"I am, I really am starting to."

"So, Willow, moving forward, I hope whether it's this guy, or the next, that you are able to learn to love them for who they are, and most importantly, love you for you. God loves you for yourself. Now, believe it in your heart. Once you can find a way to believe that you were never separate from God, that He loves you unconditionally and He would never forsake you, or that He really is truly a part of you, then the whole world will light up in a way you never realized, and love becomes a much more beautiful thing. Willow, my dear, I have a feeling you are going to be a voice echoing this notion. I'm not sure why, just a hunch, but you are going to teach God's words to many."

I felt her words. "Thanks, Marisol! I believe you in a strange, but comforting way. You really seem to have this whole Course in Miracles verbiage down pat."

She smiled again and said, "It has taken many years of practice, but I do believe in its message."

We ended up talking through the whole flight. She shared stories about her teaching days, and her kids, and we shared wonderful stories about our little angelic signs and non-coincidental stories throughout our lives. I was so elated to have met one more person who was giving me advice that felt good. I was beginning to feel more trust now that God and life were really on my side. We exchanged emails and phone numbers and promised to try to keep in touch. She also told me that if I ever decided to move back to the Philadelphia area, I should join her Course in Miracles group. As I walked off the plane, I felt so much excitement about seeing my nephews for the first time in months.

I waited out in front of the airport and decided to text message Will, to let him know I landed, as I promised. He texted me back that he was psyched to see me tomorrow night. I liked the idea of being home with my family and seeing Will.

Carla had pulled up in her minivan, and I saw Jack smiling wide and waving his hands at me. She rolled his window down so I could see his cute little face.

"Hi, Aunt Wiwwow, look what I made you." He held up this paper mache butterfly on a stick.

"Ahh, thank you, sweetness. You always know how much I love butterflies."

"That's why I made it for you."

"I love it, Jack! I'm going to hang it up in my home."

As I looked to the left of Jack, I saw my other cute nephew Max.

"Oh, my goodness, Max - look how big you've gotten! And where did you get those blonde curls?"

Carla looked at me and sarcastically said, "The mailman. I don't know, Marcus and I have been trying to figure out where they came from. Neither one of us ever had curls, let alone blonde hair like this, but who cares? It's gorgeous, isn't it?"

"So gorgeous he might even pass for a girl."

"So, how was your flight?"

"Flight was good and quick. I sat next to an interesting woman who I had a lot in common with. We chatted about all sorts of spiritual and loving stuff. She's a retired therapist and very intuitive, and thinks I have the gift of intuition, too."

"Sounds cool. You do meet some interesting people, Willow, in some interesting places. So, speaking of, when are you going to see Will and do we get to meet him?"

"Carla, really, we've been on two dates, not yet."

She gasps, "Why not? Doesn't the fact that you live in Florida, for now, give you a free pass for things like meeting family?"

"I don't know, we'll see."

Out of the backseat I heard my nephew say, "Whose Wiw, Wiwwow?"

Then I heard Carla, say, "Jack can you say Willllllllllllllllllllll and Willllllllllllllow?" He repeated it back. She's a speech therapist, and it drives her nuts that he is still having a hard time pronouncing his L's.

"Carla, he's three years old. He will, eventually, get the hang of it. Besides, he sounds so cute when he says 'wiwoww'."

"I know, but I want him to start to get the hang of it," she whined.

I responded, "Jack, Will is a new friend of mine."

He smiled with his purple juiced-stained lip and said, "Can he be my friend, too, and come over and play trucks with me?"

My heart melted with every word this boy said. Carla looked at me and said, "See, even Jack wants to meet him, how could you say no to that?"

"Again, we will see. Maybe I'll have him come over and pick me up tomorrow night a little earlier so you can meet him." I heard "Yippee" out of the back.

"Carla, does he hear everything these days?"

"Yeah, tell me about it. So, how is Grandpa doing? He told me he bought a bike and a computer. I am shocked."

"Did he also tell you he planted an apple tree, too? The apples are actually delish. I had one on the plane. Anyway, he seems to be doing a little bit better, not as depressed, and trying to keep himself busy."

"That's good. When do you guys think you will make a move back up here?"

"I don't know, maybe in a few months. I feel like a part of me already wants to come back home. It's hard to explain, but I sort of feel a pull toward..."

She stopped me and said, "...toward being closer with the ones you love."

"Yeah, exactly. And also, just maybe, ready to grow a little more into my own, surrounded by those that I love. You know I can't believe I am going to say this, but I think my being in Florida has been a way to give me space to find out more about myself than perhaps I might have been able to do here."

"Are you saying that you couldn't quite be yourself here in Philly?"

"Maybe Carla, with all due respect to my family and friends, I hate to rehash the past, but I sometimes wonder if part of my struggle with my thyroid is somehow directly linked to my childhood fears, and not just relating to parental issues, but also about the school we went to. Even though I had a ton of friends, I remember feeling constantly judged, or pressured to be something more than I really ever felt like being or doing. Does that make any sense?"

"Um-m, yeah. I can relate on some levels. I remember I went through some of this in my later twenties, right before I met Marcus, and yes, bounced around with different issues, but therapy and medication is what helped me through it. I know how anti-meds you are, but I can tell you that it saved me from spiraling into God knows what."

"I know, and I forgot to tell you, I did decide to start a small amount of Zoloft about three weeks ago. I think it's just starting to kick in. Dr. Gatewin prescribed a little for me."

"Ah-h, sis, I am so glad to hear that - you'll see it really does work. You won't have to be on it forever. Just allow it to rebalance your brain chemicals back to where they should be."

"I know. I admit it Carla, there is a time and place for medication in life, and I know that my thyroid condition was a big lesson in this.

"So, speaking of family and such," I said, "How are Marcus and Mom and Dad?"

"They are all doing fine. Dad is amazing with the boys. He's like a little kid himself with them, dressing up in superhero outfits. And Mom is really good with Jack, except when she feeds him things I specifically tell her not to. You know she likes to play by her own rules."

I rolled my eyes, "Don't I know it. 'Ya know, Carla, speaking of which, I had a revelation a few weeks ago about her food pushing. 'Ya know how it always has driven us crazy? Well, I think it's her way of showing love. I hate to admit it, but she probably learned it from Grandma Lu - it's an Italian/Jewish thing, to push food."

"I hear you, Willow. It makes sense, but I don't want the boys to eat a ton of crap, either."

"Carla, knowing you, they are probably a few of the only organic eating toddlers around. So, speaking of, what time are Mom and Dad coming over?"

"In a few hours, Marcus is going to make a barbeque."

"Sounds great."

I played with my nephews for a few hours. I was in heaven! I hadn't thought about anything negative since I had been there. They were a great distraction from my wandering mind. I heard the doorbell ring, and it was my parents.

I opened the door, "Willow, so good to have you home honey, how are you?"

I leaned in to kiss my mother and hug my dad. It felt great. They smelled good, too, a comforting reminder taking me back to childhood.

My mom said, "You look good, Willow, did you gain a little weight?"

"Um-m-m, yes Mom, I did actually, now that I have my thyroid running back on track, I have gained my weight back."

"Good, you looked like you were getting much too thin."

I looked over at Carla and rolled my eyes. I saw Jack and Max come running toward the door, "Look who's here, it's Grandma and Grandpa with a big box of chocolate chip cookies!"

I heard Jack scream, "I want one, I want one!"

I smiled at Carla without saying a word. We have the sister nod for when we get what the other one is thinking without having to say it.

My mom said, "Carla, can I give him one?"

She sighed, "Mom, after dinner."

I heard Jack whining, "But, I want one now."

"Jack, for dessert. You know the rules."

Marcus came down the stairs, "Jack, you heard Mommy - after dinner. Why don't you come help Daddy with the dinner? You can help me prep the hotdogs and hamburgers."

Marcus is tall; I mean 6'3" tall. My sister looked like a cute little button standing next to him because she and I are only 5'3". My dad chimed in, "That sounds like a good idea, Jack! Why don't you, me, Max, and Daddy, help prep dinner and let the ladies catch up?"

Somehow, my father had a way with words, for Jack seemed to listen to everything he said and did it.

My mom grabbed my hand and said, "Why don't you make your mother one of those great martinis you used to make, and fill me in."

I made my mother a martini and poured myself a glass of wine. We sat in the living room.

"So, how is Willow doing?"

"I'm a little better these days. I finally started taking some medication and I have found a wonderful therapist. She has been a tremendous help in teaching me some new techniques on breathing and learning to be more nurturing to myself."

She took a sip of her of martini, "Sounds good. And how is my father?"

"He's doing much better. He's picked up some new hobbies - biking, gardening a little, 'ya know."

"I'm glad, and I am glad you are there with him." I nodded.

I knew she was going to ask soon after, "So, what is going on with you and this Will guy? Getting serious?"

"Mom, we went on two dates."

"So, your father and I got serious after our first date, it does happen."

"Um-m-m, I will tell you this, he is a great guy, and so far I like what I see in him. Real down-to-earth guy."

Next question, "What does he do?"

"He works for Fed Ex and does some side work with computers and construction."

"Sounds nice."

"He is, and we have a date tomorrow night. So, we will see."

She sensed that I was done with that part of the conversation. A lot of times in the past, when relationship conversations have come up with my mom, I tended to get defensive because I felt like she was meddling, so now I keep our conversations a little lighter.

As I looked over at my mom, sipping her martini with her enormous rock on her finger, I realized as much as I do love her, we are not quite the same in some ways. For some reason the Course in Miracles then popped in my head, and it would say, "So what if she likes nice jewelry? You still love her for her." Then Max came waddling over with his blonde curls and distracted her. I went into the kitchen and helped with the rest of dinner. Again, it was good to be home!

We decided, since it was such a beautiful evening, that we would have dinner outside on the porch. Jack announced that he wanted to play the "guess what animal I am talking about game."

So, he started off with, "I am thinking of an animal that is tall and has wong wegs."

Marcus said, "You mean long legs?"

Jack nodded. "Uh-huh."

My dad said, "Is it a giraffe?"

And Jack smiled, "Yep! Okay, Grandpa, your turn."

So, we all took turns except for Mommy, and Jack said, "Mommy you haven't gone yet."

Carla started off and said, "I'm thinking..." and then, out of nowhere, she said, "I am thinking of a beautiful red bird, look behind you!"

And there it was in its radiance, a lush red cardinal had landed on the chair behind me. Goose bumps! She smiled at me for we both knew.

Jack blurted out, "A cardinal, a cardinal!"

I actually felt myself tear up a little. I knew in my heart that it was the angels letting me know that this was Grandma's way of showing us she was right there, and how perfect for we were playing a guessing game about animals, of all things.

After hotdogs and burgers my mother couldn't wait to pull out the cookies. Jack came running over, trying to grab at least three or four in one hand. My sister grabbed his hand on top and said, "Just one."

"But, Mommy, I ate my dinner and you said I could have three of them!" I looked at her and Willow Winked her - he was a manipulative little thing at times.

Carla tilted her head and said, "Jack, I don't ever recall saying you could have three. One is enough."

My mother chimed in and said, "How about two? We can compromise."

I saw my sister fuming and saying, "How about what *I* say?"

My mom responded, "Take it easy, Carla, it's just a cookie."

As she turned around I saw my sister getting more pissy, and I shook my head at her like *let it go*.

About a half an hour later, Jack decided to let me read him books before bed instead of Grandpa. My father is usually the one who reads to him, but Jack decided to let me do it tonight. As I piggy - backed him up the steps, I felt his sweet little hands squeeze my shoulders tight. I plopped him into his Spiderman-themed bed and read him a few stories. I saw him start to get sleepy, so I kissed his forehead and said goodnight. As he turned on his side, and grabbed his little stuffed giraffe he liked to call Raffee, I was melting as I watched his cute little nose breathe in and out. I felt so much love toward him I almost could have cried. I remembered hearing a meditation once about learning to love yourself the way you love your own child. I understood for the first time the power of the words. Perhaps it was time to practice more of that!

I woke up looked at the clock, 8:12 a.m. Yes! I slept through the night for the first time in a while. I went to look at my cell phone, I could have sworn that I heard my text message alert go off sometime around midnight, but I was too tired to check it. I opened it up and it said, *look forward to tomorrow night.*

He told me he was taking me out to go see one of his buddies who plays in a band, all classic rock cover music. I was psyched; I hadn't gone to see live music in a while. I came down the stairs and saw my nephews all cuddled up in Carla's lap, both sleeping on each side. She gave me the sh-h-h-h finger when she saw me.

I whispered, "What? They fell back asleep?"

"Willow, I am so exhausted. Jack came into my room at 4:15 this morning. Jack must have woken Max up. I told them it was too early, but they refused to go back to sleep. So, I brought them down here to play and read them stories. They fell back to sleep about twenty minutes ago. I'm afraid to move - I don't want to wake them up."

God bless my sister and her patience. She is such a good mommy.

"Ah-h, Carla, do you want me to get you some coffee?"

"Um-m-m, yeah, and could you inject it into my arm please?

Actually, can you gently help me to put the boys in the other guest room bed until they wake up?"

"Of course."

I gently picked up Jack while she held Max, and we carried them and laid them down onto the bed. Carla slowly shut the door behind her. She wiped her index finger across her head, "Whooh, okay, now maybe I can enjoy a hot cup of coffee."

"Carla, why don't you try to go back to bed for a little? I'm up and here, take advantage. If the boys wake up, I'll take care of them."

She tilted her head, "Now, Willow, you know by now that once I am up, I am up - there's no going back to bed, but thanks for the offer. Besides, I have a surprise for you about what we're going to do today," she announced.

"You do, what?"

"Well, I know it's been a while since you had some treatments. Besides, since you've got a hot date tonight, I'm taking you to the salon, and we are getting you a good mani and pedi."

I smiled and said, "Really? To what do I owe this goodie?"

As she made the coffee she said, "No reason. Can't a sister just do something nice for her sister? Besides, I saw your feet yesterday and you are not going on a date wearing your opened toed sandals without cleaning those babies up." She winked at me.

"Awesome! Thanks, Carla."

As I sat under the dryer to let my feet and nails dry, I noticed that the woman next to me was doing a crossword puzzle. I was always fascinated by how quickly people could do them. I saw her get up and watched her leave her puzzle on the seat. I noticed that there was one word missing. As she left the salon, out of curiosity, I looked at the puzzle. As I was scrolling to see the clue, I was thinking *yeah right, I am going to be able to figure this out.* But, as I searched I saw it was a five letter word - *a Greek word for unconditional love or a mouth wide open as in astonished*, which I now was! The hairs on my arms stood up. I shouted out AGAPE, forgetting where I was in my excitement. Everyone, including Carla, looked up at me like *huh?*

I crouched my head down and said, "Oops, sorry, just got a word to finish my puzzle."

Carla came to sit next to me and I told her all of my Agape stories.

She said, "So, are you getting this, Willow? This concept of unconditional love? Because it seems that the universe it shouting it right at you!"

I saved the crossword puzzle to show Lucas when I go back to Florida.

# Chapter 30

SOMEHOW, I GOT TALKED INTO letting Will pick me up from my sister's so she could oh, so subtly meet him. The doorbell rang at 7 p.m., and Jack went running to the door. I came downstairs to try to open it, but Jack beat me to it. The door opened and my sister came from behind, too. I saw Will's face turn red from nerves. He had a big embarrassed smile on his face.

Jack looked up at him and said, "Who are you?"

Carla answered, "This is Willow's friend, Will."

Will looked down and said, "Hey, buddy."

Jack looked up and asked, "You want to see my train and truck cowwection?"

Will made eye contact with me and I winked at him. He smiled and looked back at Jack and answered, "Sure, buddy."

Jack started to pull Will's hand into his playroom. My sister said, "Hold on, Jack. Sorry, my son's not shy at all. I'm Willow's sister, Carla. It's so nice to meet you."

"You too, Carla - it's all good. Besides, I have a set of twins, so I know about kids wanting attention ASAP."

As Jack pulled him in, "Come on Wiw, come wif me."

"I'm coming, Jack."

I kissed him hello on the cheek, "I'll be right in."

"Take your time, I got it covered, I love trains. I had a bunch of sets as a kid."

"Cool, thanks, do you want a beer before we go out?" I asked.

"Sure."

Carla followed me into the kitchen and gave me a huge smile.

"Good sign, he's great with Jack and he's really cute."

I smiled and nodded, "I know."

I grabbed two beers out of the fridge and headed in to watch the two of them play. For a couple of hot minutes I thought to myself *if this man were my husband he would be great with kids.* A few minutes later, Marcus came down the steps and came in to meet Will. As they shook hands, Marcus said, "Hi, nice to meet you. Sorry it took me a few minutes to come down. My computer's acting up again, and I was trying to fix it."

Will said, "No problem, did you figure it out?"

"Ah-h, sort of. I think there is something up with my hard drive, but whatever, I will figure it out."

Right away, Will said, "Do you want me to take a look at it? This is what I do on the side, fix computer issues."

Marcus looked pleasantly surprised and said, "That would be great, as long as I'm not holding you and Willow back from your date. I really appreciate it."

Will stood up, "Sure, no problem, as long as I don't get the certified computer nerd award when I leave." We all half giggled.

About ten minutes later they came down, and Marcus said, "Willow, he's a keeper. I've been at this computer for the last hour, and Will figured it out in less than five minutes."

I smiled, "Nice, thanks Will. I suppose I will keep him around for a little."

I Willow Winked him again, then looked at my watch and thought, *Um-m-m, maybe I should keep first meeting to a minimum, not overdo it.*

"Okay, so I'm getting hungry. You ready to go get some grub?"

"Sure," he said, "I hope you're down for some wings. They have awesome wings where my buddy's playing tonight."

"Sounds perfect."

Will shook hands one more time with Marcus and Carla, and gave Jack a high five. As we walked out the front door, I turned around and saw them both giving me the thumbs up. I already knew they were going to like him, for he is a likeable guy.

As we got into the car I said, "I hope that wasn't too painful. Jack liked you right away, which in Carla's book is a good sign."

He smiled, "Are you kidding? They're so nice. They remind me a lot of my family. I'm sorry I didn't get a chance to meet Max."

"Yeah, he was already sleeping - maybe next time." As we drove away I felt happy and more of myself.

We watched his friend play a couple of music sets, which were awesome. I felt a little tired but was not quite ready to go back to my sister's, so we decided to go to a local park and sit and listen to music and chill for a little. Once we parked again, we were like two teenage kids, making out like there was no tomorrow.

He put his hand on mine and said, "Are you sure you have to leave so soon?"

I found myself right away saying, "I know, but you could always come back and visit me in Florida. Aren't you headed back to play golf with your grandpa soon anyway?"

"Yes, in about two weeks. It just seems so long, but I will wait patiently."

I smiled and said, "It will be worth the wait."

We continued to kiss. I was now officially curious what the other bases might look like, and hoped we could have some privacy soon. I was all for a good make-out session, but I was not about to take my clothes off in a dark park. After about twenty minutes, he drove me home, and walked me to the door. Normally, I would have invited him in, but I felt completely awkward with my nephews being upstairs.

I gave Will one last long kiss, and said, "Till we meet again."

He kissed my forehead and said, "Yes, 'till me meet again."

I woke up the next morning to my nephew Jack poking his little index finger on my nose, and then jumping on my bed, "Wake up, Wiwwow, wake up! It's time for waffos and bacon!"

I stretched and grabbed and tickled him until I could hear his belly giggles, which were among my favorite sounds.

"Okay, okay, little man. Let Aunt Willow go brush her stinky breath and I'll be right out."

I walked into the kitchen, and Carla and Marcus were making breakfast. Carla slid a cup of coffee to me across the island in the kitchen.

"So, Willow, how was your night?"

"Really fun! His friend's band is so great! Marcus you would have liked the music."

He flipped the bacon and said, "Cool. I really liked Will. I think he seems like a great guy."

Carla nodded as well and said, "Yeah, just really easygoing and nice to be around. I am happy for you."

"Thanks guys, me, too. We'll see where it goes."

"Are you hungry? Marcus and I just made a ton of waffles and bacon."

"Thanks, maybe a little waffle. I'm meeting my girls for a late brunch / early lunch in about an hour or so. But, I'll sit with the boys."

"Sounds good. So, what time is your flight tonight?"

"Um-m-m, I think around seven o'clock. Can you drive me?"

"Of course, unless Will is free?"

"He asked if I needed a ride last night, but I told him, you'd take me."

"How come you didn't want him to take you?"

"I don't know, maybe I wanted a few extra minutes with my sister and nephews. Is that cool with you?"

Jack touched my hands with syrupy fingers and said, "Wiwwow can I go with you on the airplane?"

I smile at Carla, "How could I say no to that?"

"Sorry, buddy, you can't go on the airplane with me tonight, but I would love it if you could ride with mommy and me to the airport. You can at least see lots of the airplanes there."

Carla wiped his face and said, "Yeah, you can come with us in the car."

"Yippeee! Can Max come, too?"

"No, honey. Daddy will have to put him to bed, but maybe next time."

# Chapter 31

I WAS SO HAPPY TO finally see my girlfriends. We had spoken casually maybe a few more times, but hadn't had any real girl time. I walked into the diner, and they were already there, sipping their coffee and laughing. My second favorite sound - my girlfriends' laughter. I really felt at home now. They jumped up and we gave each other big hugs.

I said, "Girls, you look great!"

"You too, Willow, you too."

Krystal jokingly smacked my arm and said, "So, do tell, Melody filled me on most of it, but please tell us more about this Will guy. You know, the more I think about it, I already love the story of how you two met. Willow, you and I always said we would meet good men when we least expected it, and not all dolled up."

I laughed, "So, obviously, yes, I decided to finally reach out to him. But, let me back up for a second. Bernardo turned out to not be so trustworthy, but by that point, I was finally ready to meet Will. So, yes, it's true I was in my sweatpants when we met, with barely any makeup on. Yes, it's random, but of course, not so random how we met. But, I like him. We went out to see his friend's band last night. Krystal, I totally thought of you and Davis."

As I mentioned before, Davis is her boyfriend who also plays in a band, and is an incredible drummer!

"You guys should see his friend's band. They are really good. The drummer especially, not as good as Davis, but good."

Krystal nodded, "Sounds good. So, are you bummed that you already have to go back?"

"Yeah, but at the same time, you know what, ladies? I was thinking it's better that I take my time with this one. I mean, if I was home here in Philly, maybe we would have rushed into things, and I want to move slower with him. This feels like more of a grown up type of relationship that I want to take my time with."

Melody said, "Sounds healthy, Willow. So when will you get to see him again?"

"In a few weeks. So, until then, I am happy with things as they are now."

Melody and Krystal both smiled at me at the same time and said, "Well great, you seem really happy."

"Thanks. I'm better than I was, that's for sure. Ladies, that thyroid thing threw me for a loop."

Oh, yeah, I forgot to say that one of things that my soul sisters and I have had in common is our physical ailments. Not necessarily at the same times, but I swear, at one point or another throughout our lives, we've had similar issues. Krystal had a thyroid issue in her mid-twenties which was rocky, but now under control. Melody had a hormonal something or other, which is now under control.

Krystal said, "Well, you don't have to tell me, nobody knows better than me what a freaking nightmare that was to deal with."

Melody added, "I haven't told you yet, but about three weeks ago I was starting to get more lethargic than ever. Knowing what happened to the two of you, I was curious myself, so I asked the doctor to check my thyroid. Low and behold, it was off, meaning I am low and not producing enough."

I chimed in, "So, are you on something now?"

"Yes, a small amount, and as I mentioned to you before, Willow, there's a reason they make medications, as anti-meds as we all are. There is a time and place for them."

I nodded, "I know, I know. So, on a different note, how are things with Wayne?"

"Well-l-l, you know we've been together on and off for almost nine years. I'm at a place where I'm thinking to myself *something's gotta give.* I mean, I don't have to cover up for the two of you. Obviously, it's convenient having a relationship with someone who lives in another state that I cannot see every day. However, I wonder why I haven't made that next step with him, I mean even living with him. Is it because I don't want to give up "me" time, or is it because I think there's someone better out there for me?"

I answered, "Maybe both? But, Mel, at this point, maybe the real question you should be asking yourself, is *what am I so afraid of?* Whether it's having the courage to walk away from this relationship, or the courage to take the next step? Maybe you need to really meditate on that one. "

She sighed, "Oh, Willow, what would I do without your insights?"

"You know I'm right."

"I do," she agreed.

Krystal said, "Yeah, Mel, what are you so afraid of?"

Mel sighed again, "Ladies, I have got to figure this out on my own time."

Krystal and I look at one another and know she is right, and nod. Then this revelation about relationships popped into my head: no matter how much we think we know who is right or not right for someone, it's not our place to project our opinions. Everybody is here doing the best they can to learn their own truths about love in their own way. I smiled as I also realized that I've been having a lot more light bulb moments these days.

"So, Krystal, what's going on with you?"

"Well," she said, "I have a little surprise for you ladies, and sorry, Mel, I know my timing is not great coming on the heels of this conversation, but I can't hold it in any longer."

She put her finger up twisted a ring around, and showed us a beautiful engagement ring. Melody and I looked at each other with our mouths open wide, and at the exact same time and said, "Shut up! When? Why didn't you tell us?"

She beamed a smile and said, "Because I wanted to tell you in person. He did it last weekend when we celebrated our five-year anniversary."

"Ah, Krystal, congratulations! I am so happy for you!"

Melody said, "Me, too."

I took a bite of my eggs and said, "So, when do you think it will happen?"

"Um-m, maybe sometime next fall. But you guys know me, it will be a very small affair. I don't like overly flashy or too big."

I said, "I know, of course whatever you want. Just so happy for you!"

Krystal responded, "Thanks, ladies, and who knows, Willow, maybe you'll bring Will to my wedding." She winked at me.

I said, "Slow down, we've been on, like, four dates - but maybe, we will see."

Then she said, "I don't know, Willow, there's something about him. I have a feeling, but I will stay chilled for now. I know how much you hate to jinx things."

We sat for about an hour more and caught up, and gossiped, and laughed about our future /careers. I was so grateful for my girlfriends/ soul sisters.

I waved goodbye to Carla and Jack as they pulled away. My heart melted as I thought about the next time I was going to see them, which made me think about when it might be time to move back to Philly. I wondered if I might be able to have a conversation with Grandpa about it when I got back, sort of a time frame for when he might be ready.

My flight home was smooth sailing and we arrived on time. As I waited in front of the airport for Aunt Ellen to pick me up, I noticed an older woman sitting on a bench waiting for her ride as well. She looked a lot like my grandmother, Dotty. She made eye contact with me with a warm smile. I naturally smiled back. Her purse fell off her lap and as she bent down to pick it up, her gigantic suitcase tumbled over. I quickly went over to help her retrieve it. As I lifted it up, I couldn't believe my eyes. I noticed the nametag. Her first name was Dorothy. Goose bumps!

She said, "Thank you so much."

I responded, "No problem." Aunt Ellen then pulled up and I said, "Have a good night!"

She answered, "You, too, darling." Interesting, h-m-m-m.

# Chapter 32

So, BACK IN FLORIDA I was. Thank God I was off today, I wanted to do some laundry, go food shopping, and visit Luke and Samuel. I woke up early and had breakfast with Grandpa and told him all about the visit. I decided to wait a few days to bring up the moving part. I got myself dressed, and told Grandpa I was going out to run errands and to visit with some friends.

I walked into the facility and started to walk toward Samuel's room. As I got closer, an overwhelming feeling of loss came over me. I wasn't sure if it was related to being surrounded by people on their way out of this world, or if it was the feeling I had when my grandmother passed, but it was there, and felt heavy. I walked up to Samuel's door and I knew right away why I felt sad, he was gone. At first I thought *oh, maybe they moved his room*, but then my gut told me he was gone. My eyes began to fill up as I searched for a nurse on the floor to tell me what happened. To my dismay no one was around, so I went looking for Luke, perhaps he knew, because he knew everybody on the floor. I went up and down the halls in tears, huffing and puffing that I didn't get a chance to say goodbye to Sam. I started to sweat, worried I would not be able to find Luke.

Then, around the corner, there he was. His eyes met mine right away, and he saw my tears and said, "Oh no, Miss Willow, I am sorry. Samuel passed yesterday morning. I was going to call you, but I knew you were with your family, and I did not want to make you sad. Forgive me, angel."

I walked right up to him and gave him a huge hug. "It's okay, Luke, it's okay. I understand. What happened?"

"Well, about two days ago, his breathing got harder and harder for him. He was having those coughing fits he couldn't stop. I had a feeling that it was time. I knew his son would not be able to make it back in time to say goodbye, so I sat with him so he wouldn't be alone."

I grabbed his hand and said, "You are an angel, Luke, a saint, a heaven-sent loving man."

"Oh, Willow, you sure know how to make a grown man blush, but honestly, how could I not be there? I couldn't just watch him die. We talked for a while the day he passed. He told me about his lovely wife, and Willow, he also said something so sweet about you."

My eyes lit up, "He did? What did he say?"

"Willow he told me that he felt so grateful to have met you and that if it wasn't for you and your encouragement that he reach out to his son, he would not have had a chance to make amends. He also told me to give you a message, and I told him I had a bad memory, so I would write it down. I have kept it locked safely in my wallet, until I could see you."

As he reached into his pocket, I was surprised, yet nervous with anticipation as to what Samuel, a man of not many words, would have to say to a gal like me.

Luke said, "Come with me, Willow, where we can have a little privacy."

We walked outside to the courtyard and sat on our bench. He opened up the letter and said, "My handwriting is worse than a doctor's so of course, I would have you read it, but I am afraid you won't understand my writing, so let me read it to you if that is okay."

I nodded, "Of course, Luke, go ahead."

"Okay, so here it is:

**Dear Willow, well what can I say, except for that it is time. But I am not sad, Willow, please don't be sad, either. I finally get to be reunited with the love of my life - my beautiful wife. She promised me she would be there when it was my time, and it is. As you know, I was never much of a spiritual man, but this time I am going on**

faith that what my wife said is true, and I will be surrounded by her love and all of the people in my life I swore didn't care about me. They, too, will finally be there to tell me they loved me all along. Who knew during my final days, I would have this type of clarity? More importantly, Willow, thank you so much for encouraging me to take the chance to reach out to my son. I got to spend the time with him that I needed to so I could apologize for not being the father he deserved growing up. And Willow, I told him I loved him for who he was, and didn't care that he made different choices than I did. His face lit up, and I finally, for once, felt like the kind of father I always wanted to feel like. So, if that is not the greatest gift in the world, I am not sure what is. So, thank you again. If I could leave you with one more thing, I would tell you, Willow, that you are a good person and I hope you have the courage to be who you are always. Don't be afraid to love, either. You have such a good heart and a gentle way of breaking down the walls of others, including mine. I hadn't met anyone who had that power since my wife. Any man will be lucky to have an angel like you, just keep wearing that pretty heart of yours on your sleeve, and everything will work out just fine. So, farewell for now, pretty Willow, and I will make sure the angels up in heaven continue to do their job of watching over their angel down here on earth. Love always, Sam."

My eyes filled up again, and I said to Luke, "Thank you so much for writing it down and taking the time to do that not just for me, but for being there with him."

"Willow, like I said, I wouldn't have it any other way. He thanked me, too, and told me he appreciated my being so nice to him during his stay here, even though he could be a grinch. One of the last things he said to me was, 'I don't know what it is about this place, but it ended up bringing out the best in me. For once Luke, I felt more happy and at peace.'" Luke continued, "Willow, I felt good about being there with him, like it was a calling of some sort."

"I know, Luke, you felt it because like me, you might just be what they are calling earth angels. Something in our hearts tells us when it's time to comfort someone."

He put his hand on top of mine and said, "You may just be right about that, Miss Willow. Changing subjects, how was your trip?"

I told him all about my trip, including the lady on the airplane, the other's luggage tag, and of course, the Agape crossword puzzle. He giggled with that sweet crooked tooth smile and reminded me how incredible God's love is for me.

I was looking forward to going to work to see Ed and find out how his book tour was going. I remember he told me he would be home for a few days in between cities. I walked in, and there he was, glowing in an orange hat this time and yes, of course, a sherbet-colored watch to match. We immediately made eye contact, and he smiled. I walked right over and said, "So, how is the book signing going?"

He lit up, "Willow, I am happy to share that you're an inspiration to up-and- coming poets. I had two young women tell me that your poem helped to remind them of the importance of listening to their hearts. I also had a young professor, who came with his class, tell me that he loved the use of metaphors throughout your poem."

I was elated beyond words. "Ed, what can I say? I am overjoyed with gratefulness that you've given me an opportunity to be seen."

"Willow, it's my sincere pleasure, and I'm grateful that I have gotten to meet an up and coming inspirational author."

"Once again, Ed, I love the sound of that. I hope you're right, and if and when I'm published on my own, I promise your name will be on my thank-you page in capital letters." I Willow Winked him and he smiled back.

"So, Willow, didn't you just get back from Philly? How was your trip?"

"My trip was great, short but sweet. I got to see my nephews, who I love more than life itself, and I got to spend a little more time with Will."

He smiled and said, "So, what date are we on? Four, perhaps?"

I laughed, "Something like that. We had fun. I have to admit, he is growing on me a little."

"Willow, that is the way it should be, too much passion right off the bat fizzles quickly - I know you know that."

"I do. I also think it's good that we don't live in the same town right now, so I can gradually get to know him better slowly."

He sat up, "I agree, just don't be afraid to show your loving. I know the poet in you naturally is a good partner. But perhaps, from past hurtful relationships, maybe you built a little bit of a wall around yourself?"

"Ed, Um-m-m, yeah, I know you're right on some level, and I feel it's time now to break down the walls and yes, love naturally, the way I want to love. It's funny, I'm so good at helping others let down their walls, yet when it comes to my own, I still need a little work."

He lifted his coffee cup in the air pretending to toast me and said, "Amen to that! But don't be too hard on yourself, you'll get there. Just try to remind yourself of that every time you think you shouldn't be affectionate or loving the way you want to, or tell him how you really feel. You get my point."

"Ed, if I may ask, where is this little lesson on loving coming from?"

He responded, "I was just at one of my Course in Miracles sessions. Every time I go, I always find myself overly reminding others to be their true loving selves in any situation. Speaking of which, it has been a while for you. Do you want to go with me tomorrow morning before I leave for my trip? I try to get as many groups in as I can in between trips. I feel that it's good for my soul to take my lessons with me, especially with all of the strangers I meet on the road. It helps me to not pre-judge them, and remember that they aren't really strangers after all."

"You're right, Ed, sure sounds great. I'm off tomorrow anyway. Is it at Gaylee's house?" I asked.

"Yes, 10 a.m."

"I'm there for sure. You know, Ed, I have a sweet friend named Luke whom I've been telling about this group. Do you think I could invite him to come along?"

"Absolutely, Willow - the more the merrier."

"Thanks, Ed. I'm not sure if he has to work, but I'd like to invite him if he's free."

"Definitely, Willow - do it."

"Alright, Ed. I'd better get back to work. We're starting to fill up."

"No problem. Speaking of filling up..." He lifted up his coffee cup and pointed.

"Yes, I will refill ASAP."

# Chapter 33

I CALLED LUKE, AND I guess it was no coincidence that a co-worker asked him to switch shifts so he was off today and able to come with me to the group. I told him I would pick him up and met him at the assisted living facility. He looked handsome in a button down and khakis - I was so used to seeing him in uniform.

He got into my car and I said, "Look at you! You clean up nice, Mr. Brown." He blushed.

"Well, thank you, Willow. It's not often that I get to be without my uniform. Besides, my mamma always told me the importance of looking presentable when meeting new people, and how first impressions really do stick."

I smiled and said, "You're nice, Luke, but the best part of this group we're meeting with is that they could care less about your appearance. They care more about your heart." I Willow Winked him.

He buckled his seat belt and said, "I like the sound of it already."

I gave him a heads up about everyone in the group, including Gaylee and Ed, and how open, warm, and loving the group was.

When we pulled up, he said, "Wow, what a beautiful setting. My wife would love that garden."

I said, "Tell me about it. Who knows maybe you could bring her some day."

He tilted his head, "Maybe."

We knocked on the door and heard, "Come on in."

I opened the door and everyone was seated in a circle with their big blue books on their laps, and great big smiles on their faces. Gaylee got out of her chair, and she and Ed came over to greet us with a big hug. I introduced her to Luke, who seemed a little bashful at first, but very gracious as she introduced him to everyone around the room, especially all the ladies whose names began with M.

Ed came over and said, "I'm so glad you made it and that your friend could come, too."

"Me, too, Ed. He's sort of new to this, but something tells me that he'll fit in just fine. He told me he had a neighbor who was student and used to talk about it, which always intrigued him. He told me he'd be happy to come with me sometime to see what it was all about. He is such a sweet man."

"He seems like it."

"He is, and has sort of been like an earth angel to me over the last few months. Isn't it strange, Ed, the people we meet along the way with messages for us?"

"Willow, you know my answer to that - yes, but lovingly strange."

I nodded, and smiled, and waved to Lucas to come sit next to me.

Gaylee spoke and said, "Okay, everyone — let's do a brief meditation before we start. Close your eyes, take a slow, deep breath in and out, and set an intention for the day. May we each embrace a peaceful feeling and a loving truth from our group today."

We sat in silence for two minutes, then she rang the bell and said, "Okay, so I thought today we would discuss Lesson 83. It's a review of Lessons 64 and 65, which are "My only function is the one God gave me," and "My happiness and function are one." She pointed to Marilyn and said, "Why don't you start reading?"

Marilyn read the lessons, and Gaylee said, "So, basically, these lessons are a reminder that the reason we are here is to be unconditionally loving and healing lights to ourselves and to others, including forgiveness for those we may feel have wronged us on some level. And, by doing this, we're able to remember our true function, which will naturally bring us peace and happiness. But, as you all know and have experienced, the ego can be a tricky thing. It's always tempting us to see our purpose in material terms and things that have nothing to do with our real journey here, which is really about spreading God's love and believing in it, and of course, trusting it is already a part of us. The light is in us. It never leaves; it's never separate. The ego always wants to separate, and the course is saying, *end the separation and we will remind you of your light.*" I looked over at Luke who was smiling at me like a little light bulb had gone off in his cute long-shaped head.

Gaylee asked, "Any comments or questions?"

Luke raised his hand and said, "So, what you are saying is that God just wants us to all be loving individuals to ourselves and to others, and whatever else we decide to do, he doesn't care as long as we do it with love."

Gaylee nodded and smiled, and said, "Yes, Luke that's exactly what I am trying to say."

He nodded again and said, "Well thank you. You see, I don't tell many people this, but I am comfortable enough with you all to say that for many years, sometimes I felt a little ashamed of what I did for a living. I'm a janitor at an assisted living facility, and I was afraid that people would judge me for what I did, or think something less of me. But, I always tried to take pride in my work, and I have had moments throughout my lifetime where I swear it was like God came through me in prayer telling me that he was so proud of all the loving I have given to patients at the place. It was the love that I gave, not the mop in my hand that was really doing God's work."

My eyes watered. Without even realizing it, once again Luke had given all of us a gift with his loving- clarity filled wisdom.

Gaylee said, "Yes, Luke, this is what the Course is trying to say - your ego makes you think you're not good enough, but your work at the assisted living facility is so beautiful because you do it with so much love. No one there sees you as the janitor. I bet they see you as the angel you are already."

I raised my hand and said, "I can vouch for that! He is an angel, alright, and has transformed many of the lives there with his loving heart."

He blushed again, placed his hand over mine, and said, "Thank you."

We continued to talk for a while as a group. At the end of the meeting, we all said a thankful group prayer and hugged goodbye. As we walked out, I wished Ed good luck on his next stop, and heard Luke thanking Gaylee for welcoming him saying how much he had enjoyed it. She encouraged him to come back again. I heard in the background, "Oh, I will Miss Gaylee, for sure."

As we got into the car, he said, "Willow, thank you for introducing me to that room full of nice folks, and reminding me of my true function here. You were right about the power of this course. I would like to come again sometime if my schedule will allow me."

"Oh, I have a feeling it will. Speaking of which, don't you find it funny how you happened to be off the day I asked you to come? I believe you were meant to come with me, Luke. God set this up for us to happen perfectly."

He laughed, "Oh, my goodness, you're right Willow he did! Our Agape father sure did."

As I drove down the street, I turned on the radio, and there it was just perfectly starting, "Don't go changing, to try and please me, you never let me down before, mmhhhhmm. I couldn't love you, any better, I love you just the way are." We both let out a loving gasp and I said, "Yes, Luke, just like you said, 'Our Agape father loves us just the way we are.'"

# Chapter 34

A FEW DAYS HAD PASSED and I felt it was okay to ask Grandpa about when he thought might be a good time to make the move. I asked him to go on a bike ride with me.

"So, Gramps, I was thinking."

He interrupted and said, "Uh-oh."

I sighed, "No, Gramp, nothing bad. I was just thinking, since the last time I went home, how wonderful it was to be close to the family."

Again he interrupted me and said, "And your new boyfriend."

"He is not my boyfriend. Anyway, yes, it was good to see Will, too, but that is not why I'm bringing this up. I was wondering what it might be like to be in Philly again, and if there was any chance you might be ready to do that soon?"

He stopped riding, looked at me and said, "Really? Already?"

Not the response I was hoping to get, so I said, "Not like tomorrow, Gramps, but perhaps in the next couple of months. I don't know, I was just thinking it might be nicer to be closer to Mom and Dad, Carla, and the kids."

He started peddling, "I know, Willow, you are right. I wasn't sure when this topic would come up, but I know in the back of mind that it is time."

Just as he said it, don't 'ya know, a beautiful dragonfly flew past us. I laughed, "Grandma Lu agrees - she just sent us a sign."

He gasped back, "Oh, Willow, such an imagination on you! But, okay if it makes you feel better."

"Gramps, alright, so what do you think? Like two months - is that enough time?"

"I guess. You know the beautiful apple tree I planted for your

314

grandmother not too long ago? Well, I wonder who's going to take care of it when we go?"

"Gramps, I promise, whoever decides to move in here, we'll make sure it's taken care of, and please don't let a tree be an excuse not to leave. We take all good memories of Grandma with us no matter where we go."

"I hope you're right, Willow."

"I am right. Trust your granddaughter on this, will you?"

"I will, for my Willow." He smiled, "You like that - your grandpa has a little creative poet in him, too."

"You do?"

"Sure I do! Well, I'm not Robert Frost or anything, but I have written a couple of roses are reds and violets are - what color are they again? To your Grandma." He winked at me.

"Ha-ha, Grandpa! Alright, I'm going to call Dad later and let him know you've at least given me the okay about making a possible move."

"Okay, Willow. The truth is, it's not so much leaving here that I am apprehensive about. It's more about moving into a place with strangers."

"Grandpa, you are not going to be sharing an apartment with anyone. Of course, you're going to have your own room, and you'll like it. It's sort of like a resort for grandparents."

"But, Willow, you know I am not the most social man."

"I know, but maybe you will become a little more social."

"I doubt it, Willow."

"Alright, grumpy old man, that's enough negativity. Let's go back and I'll whip you up one of my omelets."

He spun around, "Now, that sounds like a plan."

I immediately thought about Will and felt excited to tell him that we might be moving home sooner rather than later. I felt my ego mind say, *don't tell him right away. He might think he's playing a part in it.* Then I thought of Ed saying, "No more games Willow, just love the way you want to, don't hold back." I settled for sending him a cute text message saying, *come see me soon, I miss you.*

And so he did as planned, two weeks later. It was close enough to his birthday, and I wanted to do something fun and different. I had heard of a local Zeppelin cover band playing in the West Palm area. So, I figured that this time, I really wanted to have a sleep-over night with him. Staying at either one of our grandparents' didn't seem comfortable or feasible. I knew he was going to be playing golf with his grandpa early Saturday morning, but I decided to book a hotel room for that night in West Palm Beach, and to take him to dinner and a Zeppelin show. I told him to tell his grandparents that he would be with them Friday night, but that on Saturday night, he would be sleeping out. I would take him to the airport on Sunday morning, and of course, where we were going was a surprise. I told my grandpa not to worry - that I am a grown woman and was with a safe man. He nodded an okay, but I know was partly biting his lip still thinking I was a little girl.

I picked up Will and he looked a little nervous. He grabbed my hand and said, "So where are you taking me?"

I smiled, "Come on, you should know, right off the bat, that I'm the kind of gal who likes to give surprises, and likes a guy who likes surprises, so can't you just be surprised? Besides, it's not that big a deal, just wanted to do something different with you."

He kissed my hand, "I'm pleased either way. I'm just happy to see you again."

I kissed his hand back and said, "Good answer."

I took him out for an awesome dinner, and made sure the waitress put a little pre- birthday candle in it for him since I wouldn't see him blow out the candles on his actual day.

He reached across the table and gave me a kiss on my cheek, "This is so nice, and I'm not used to all of this."

I leaned back, "Used to all of what - being taken out for dinner and a piece of chocolate cake? What, none of your other lady friends have treated you to some good eats?" I Willow Winked him.

He wiped chocolate off of the corner of his mouth and said, "Honestly, Willow. Not really. I mean, now that I think about it, no. Besides, I've never really made a big fuss over birthdays, nor did my parents. So, thanks for making me feel special."

"You got it. So, are you ready for part two of your surprise?" I asked.

"I am. Are we going bungee jumping?" I tilted my head, and then he said, "Okay, are we going disco dancing?"

I said, "No, but that's not a bad idea. Sometime, okay? I will tell you we are going to watch a Zeppelin cover band, that truth be told, I have never seen, but read some online reviews that said that they were great. You in?"

He lit up and said, "Hell, yeah! I am psyched. Chocolate cake and Zeppelin - what could be better?"

I paid the check and we headed toward the bar. We sat for a couple of sets. They were awesome, but it was so noisy. I think I seriously might have done some damage to part of my ears. We had a couple of drinks, so I didn't care that much - that was until we left and I had that weird echoing noise coming in and out of my ears. As we were walking to my car, he grabbed me and kissed me on the street. I loved that, a spontaneous man who will just pick me up and kiss me and not give a hoot who's standing around. I grabbed his hand and pulled him to the car, "Come on, let's go have some fun for surprise part three."

I won't lie, in the back of mind, all day I was wondering if tonight would be the night. I decided I was not going to plan it this time, if it felt right, I would go for it. If I felt like I wasn't ready, then we would at least be able to make it past second base. I wondered, if we hit a home run, did he bring protection? I did not this time. Either way, I didn't want to overanalyze this decision.

We pulled into the garage and I could tell he seemed a little nervous. I looked over at him and said, "Don't get too excited, it's not like I got the penthouse or anything, or hired you a stripper with tasseled nipples to sing you Happy Birthday." I Willow Winked him again.

He started cracking up laughing. I checked into the room, and as soon as we got into the elevator we started making out. Again, like two young, teenage kids. We walked into the room, and as I was going toward the mini bar to ask if he wanted a beer, he grabbed me again and picked me up this time, and put me right onto the bed.

I stopped him and said, "Boy, you don't waste any time, do you? Now, don't be getting cocky on me. Just because I got this hotel room, doesn't mean we're having sex."

He grabbed me again, and kissed me, and said, "Willow, I don't need to have sex with you at all. I could be happy with just kissing and holding you all night."

Whether it was a good line or not, I bought it, and on some level actually believed him. Next thing you know, one by one, our clothing came off. We were lying naked, next to one another in bed. He was in close quarters, if you know what I mean. I felt like I really wanted to, and I felt safe, which was a new feeling for me.

He looked me in the eyes and said, "Do you want to?"

I paused, "I do. Did you bring anything? 'Cause I didn't." He nodded a yes. "Okay."

He went into his overnight bag, got a condom, and crawled back into bed. I asked him to be very gentle and slow, which he was. After it was over, he held me close. It felt amazing lying in his arms. I was happy, but scared and had moments on and off throughout the night wondering, *holy shit, could this be my one or one of my ones?* I tried to tell myself not to sabotage any of it, because I really wanted to enjoy myself and feel happy for once.

I had been up since around 4 a.m., staring at the walls, not being able to sleep, wondering when would be an okay time to wake him up. I looked at the clock, and it was 7:12, is it too early to get up yet? I knew his flight was leaving at around 11 o'clock, which meant I had to get him there sometime at around 10. I was antsy, hung over, starving for some pancakes and bacon, and wanted to shower, which I decided to do.

I got out of the shower, dried off, and wondered if he was awake. I opened the door. He was sitting up watching television. I made eye contact with him and he smiled.

I said, "Sorry if I woke you, I just wanted to shower so badly."

He replied, "No problem, you should have woken me and I could have joined you."

"I don't shower with anyone on the fourth date." I Willow Winked him.

I was wrapped in my towel, about to put some clothes on when he said, "Come here."

He pulled me into bed and hugged me. I then felt a little poke here and there, if you know what I mean, but I was more hungry than horny, and wanted to get up and get some grub before I had to drop him off at the airport. I sat up and took the initiative.

"So, Stranger from the Airplane, what do you say we get up, go downstairs, have some greasy something, and I take you to the airport?"

"You trying to get rid of me already?" he asked.

"I'm hungry, and I should mention that I can get kind of grumpy if I don't get to eat."

He sat up and said, "Well then, by all means, let me take a quick shower, and get you some food. I hope they have pancakes, actually blueberry pancakes - that's what I'm craving."

I smiled, "That's what I was thinking! I want pancakes, too, with bacon, of course!"

As he walked into the bathroom, he said, "With extra syrup."

After breakfast, as we drove toward the airport, he said, "So, when will I get to see you again? This long distance thing can be complicated." Complicated?

"Will, it only gets complicated if we make it complicated. I'm not looking to make it complicated, are you?"

He responded, "Of course not, I just want to see you again sooner rather than later."

I took a deep breath and said, "I know. We'll figure something out, besides absence makes the heart grow fonder, right?"

"I hope so, Willow, or you know what else they say - out of sight out of mind."

I scrunched my nose, "Will, I like the sound of mine better, don't you?"

"I do. I'm sorry, I know this is my insecurity speaking. In the meantime, I wouldn't want you to be swept off your feet by some other stranger perhaps you might meet in a coffee shop, or a bookstore."

I figured this was his not so subtle way of asking me about seeing other people, so I decided to come right out and asked,

"So, is this your way of putting out there that you would not like to see other people?"

He just lifted my hand, kissed it, and shook his head *no* as he did it.

"No, Willow. I know it may seem early for me to ask this of you, but no. If I had my wish, it would be for you to not want to be with anyone else. Am I ballsy or crazy for asking? Please help me out here - I'm sort of new to this right and wrong of what to do. I know I don't want to scare you off, either."

Now, in the past this approach would have had me running for the border, but instead, I found myself saying, "In the past maybe, but not now, Will. It's okay. Don't worry - I'm not really interested in kissing any strangers, I'm only interested in kissing you."

His face lit up, "Really?"

"Really. And, as a matter of fact, I wasn't sure if I was going to say anything this time, but there's a chance my grandpa and I may be making a move back to Philly sooner than I originally thought."

His face lit up again, "Really?"

"Really. But, don't get too excited yet - Grandpa may take a little more convincing than I anticipate. We briefly talked about it the other week, and he sort of gave me the okay, but I know him, and this may take a little more coercing."

He responded, "Okay, I understand, but I would be so happy to know I might have a shot at getting to see you more."

I kissed his hand, "Me, too."

We pulled up to the airport. I got out of the car walked around to the other side. He grabbed my face like they do in the movies, kissed me passionately and said, "I had such a great weekend with you. Thank you for everything."

"You're welcome. I had a great time, too."

"I will miss you."

"You, too."

As I got in the car and drove away, I saw him through my rearview mirror staring at me pulling away. I thought *I am falling in love.* As I contemplated this thought, I found myself saying out loud, "Dear God, please do not let me find a way to ruin or sabotage this one, or get scared and find a reason to run. I really like this one, so thanks for hooking me up, and I hope we can make it work."

I turned on the radio and heard once again, "Don't go changing to try and please me, you never let me down before....." What is it with this song? Perhaps God's reminding me, through Billy Joel, that this could finally be a relationship where we learn to love on another just the way we are. H-m-m-m...

# Chapter 35

Two weeks went by, and I thought about him every day. We spoke once a day and had a few text messages here and there. I wanted to try and have a talk with Grandpa again about moving back home to Philly. Not that I wasn't content, but part of me felt a tug, or a push of some sort, to want to be closer to my family. I decided to make Grandpa some delicious spaghetti and meatballs to cushion any anxiety, and poured us each a glass of red wine to relax any negative vibes that might come out.

"So, Grandpa, let's make a toast." He lifted his glass. I continued, "Let's make a toast to having the courage for new beginnings, and trusting that this move to Philly will be just fine."

He toasted me, took a sip, and said, "So, you really want to go, huh?"

I nodded my head and said, "Well, Gramp, I'm not sure there's any reason for us to stick around here anymore. I mean, I miss seeing everybody, and no I won't B.S. you, I wouldn't mind spending some more time with Will."

He smiled and said, "You really like this one, huh?"

"I do, Gramps, but it's not about him. It's about feeling an aching to just be closer to my hometown, and also, I think it might be time for me to take into serious consideration what I'm going to do with my life."

He nodded and said, "Well, my love, I knew this day would come. So, if you are looking for me to give you the final okay, I am saying okay. I know you are right, and I don't want to hold my angel back from moving on with her life. If you would be happier in Philly, than I say we should go to Philly. Your Grandma Lu would say the same thing."

I leaned over and kissed his forehead, "We can do this, Gramps, together. It will not be as uncomfortable as you think. Nobody knows more than I do how shaky change can be, but it could also be a wonderful and refreshing opening to something better."

As he twirled his spaghetti around his fork, he said, "When did you get so smart and poetic?" He winked at me. I Willow Winked him back.

"So, can I call Dad?"

"Yes, but can I enjoy the rest of this delicious home cooked meal before you do?"

"Of course, Gramps, and I promise to make you at least one big home cooked meal a week, so you have plenty of leftovers to eat."

He giggled, "That sounds great! I know that where I am going they won't be able to make a meatball like you or Grandma Lu." I smiled back.

After dinner, I waited for Grandpa to go into his room to call Carla and my parents. They were all thrilled at the idea that grandpa gave the final okay! Carla knowing me so well, told me I could stay with her as long as I needed to until I found a place of my own, which I was happy about. Also my dad said he would make arrangements sooner than later for us to return. When we hung up the phone I felt a little surge of excitement yet anxiety too.

I had a hard time sleeping throughout the night. One moment, I was okay with the decision and the next, I was playing, the "what if" game, which never serves me well. I decided to call Katie in the morning to see if she could squeeze me in a therapy appointment either today or tomorrow. I was hoping she would have some insight on how I would make this transition back. As far as telling Will, I wanted to wait until after I had therapy, when I felt calmer all around.

Luckily, she called me back within half an hour and told me she had a divine cancellation for me to come in the afternoon. She calls them divine because she knows when some of her clients need sessions more than others, it usually always works out that one cancels at just the right time when another needs one. Well, by the time I pulled up there, I needed it. Somehow more of my excitement turned into fear, and I was hoping we could heart breathe through some of it.

I walked into Katie's office and sat down.

"Take a deep sigh…." Katie said. "So, Willow, what's going on?"

"Well, I was doing great yesterday when I thought, well, at least I thought, I was excited about the idea of moving back to Philly to be with my family - and yes, I will admit, being closer to Will. So, I sat down with my grandfather and asked if he would be willing to make the move soon, and he said yes, which I was pleasantly surprised about. Everything felt great, than all of a sudden I started over-thinking, which you know I do, and I felt scared shitless of going back home. I mean what am I going to do? Which led to where am I going to live? Which then led to maybe I am not ready for a relationship and am I really into this guy? By the way, I slept with him a few weeks ago, which of course led to should I have had sex with him so soon? Which then led into I am a hopeless, anxiety-ridden gal that Will is eventually going to see and not want, which led to…….., you see where I am going with this snowball effect, that got bigger and bigger."

Katie put her hand up to stop me and said, "Yes, Willow, I know very well how this routine goes. I see it all the time. But, part of my job as the therapist I have become, is to help you begin to break out of old habitual patterns. What I am starting to sense from you, Willow, is that you have a little bit of what I call a "limit – worthiness" thing going on. Let's try and clear it out with some heart breathing, shall we?"

I gave her a perplexed look and said, "What do you mean by a limit-worthiness thing?"

"Well, Willow, it sounds to me as though a lot of times, when you get to a place of finally allowing yourself to feel good or excited about something, you then find a reason to sabotage it. It's as if you hit your limit and question all of the reasons you might not be able to do something or feel good. You deserve to feel joy."

"Willow, I know most people don't believe this, but happiness and love are our real reasons for being here. It's not something that has to be earned. As you open up spiritually you will have moments like these, where your intuition is telling you that it's okay to go home and be happy, while your ego mind will tell you all the reasons why it's not okay. You know, it's the head versus the heart thing. Learning to trust your guidance is a beautiful thing that God wished we would do more. Wasn't it you, in your beautiful poem that you read to me about life, where God said he wished that our heart would become our second set of ears?"

I immediately started to feel a little less anxious by her natural understanding of how my mind can throw me for a loop.

I said, "Yes, you're right, but Katie, this is new for me and I'm afraid that moving home, I'll be forced to figure out everything too soon, and Will, as sweet as he is, and as much as I love being with him, does not seem like the kind of guy who I will have a lot in common with, especially poetic-wise. He has also told me he hasn't dated many women. I'm thinking that he will probably want to be with someone who's not so emotional at times."

She stopped me and said, "Okay, so what you are trying to tell me is now you think that you aren't going to be good enough for Will, and are now ready to sabotage this or look for a reason he might not be a good match. Willow, did it ever occur to you that God perhaps has now set you up with someone who is going to want to be with you in spite of all your imperfections? Don't kid yourself; he's not perfect, either. We all have history and baggage that we take with us into relationships, but Willow, this may take time. Perhaps the two of you came here to learn something greater about love than all of the fairytales we heard about growing up. Let's just take this relationship one day at a time with Will. You're still in the beginning phases, allow yourself to enjoy one another's company.

"Let me ask you something else - when you decided to have intercourse with him, at the moment, did it feel right? And I don't mean because you were horny or a little buzzed. I mean now, sitting here with me, when you think back to being with him, did it feel right?'

I paused and said, "Yes. To tell you the truth, Katie, I felt really safe with him. I can't explain it, it was just a feeling."

She smiled and said, "Bingo! Once again, an example of your intuition saying it's okay to allow myself to be with this man - even your body was telling you it was okay. Now, Willow, you are now seeing how our minds love to say, *but this, but that*. Try to stop *butting*. What I am here to remind you of is that our intuition and the wisdom of our bodies, especially in intimate moments like you had with Will, is a beautiful opening up and a new beginning.

"We can continue to work on this, and talk, but let's take a few heart breaths right now in relation to this decision to move and your relationship to Will."

I nodded my head as in *yes*.

"Okay, Willow, place your hands on your heart, and repeat after me, 'I love and accept myself and am at peace knowing I am going to be moving back to my hometown where I may be physically closer to the ones I love and care about.'

I repeated it three times and switched my palms, while I took a deep breath slowly in between. I told her something within me was speaking gently and she told me to repeat what was coming.

I said, "There is no decision about my future that has to be made either, to just be loving and kind to myself and to remain present."

Katie said, "Okay, let's go with that. Now, repeat after me, 'I deeply love and honor myself for the being of light that I am, with no decision having to be made about my future, and I cherish being in my present moments.'"

I once again repeated it three times, and started to feel more at peace.

Katie asked me, "So, how do you feel now?"

"I am feeling a little more at ease, and also something in relation to Will is now telling me I am, indeed, safe to let myself go with him."

I lifted my shoulders to her as if to say *I am not sure where this is coming from, but I am grateful.*

She smiled and said, "Okay repeat after me, 'I love and accept myself. Although I have been hurt by my relationships in the past, it is now safe for me to trust and let myself love again in my current partnership with Will.'"

I again repeated if three times with crisscrossed hands and gentle breaths.

She then said, "I just want to add one more important statement to this session before we stop. Repeat this, 'I am worthy of feeling happy and loved.'"

I repeated it with each breath, in and out. I then opened my eyes, and she asked me again, "So, now how do you feel?"

"Much better, and more trusting of whatever it is we are calling this."

She half giggled and said, "This beautiful internal guidance."

"I guess so."

She continued, "Willow, what is interesting about this session is that it went a little differently then I have done in the past with other clients. What I mean is that your intuition ended up taking over this session more than usual, and we were both being guided together to help you have a better understanding and trust. This is a wonderful tool. Can you now see the simplicity of placing your hands over your heart and allowing this guidance to come in and calm you down? If you find yourself getting frazzled again, just know, even without me present, that you have this gift now to do it for yourself. Usually, it takes my clients a while to trust this and pick it up, but yours has come beautifully and divinely quickly."

I smiled. "Really?" She nodded.

"So, Katie, this guidance system is like angels? God? My higher self?"

She laughed and said. "How about all of the above. It's LOVE, Willow, speaking to you, reminding you of your true essence. Call it what you want, but it is a beautiful part of who you are, reminding you that you are never alone, and it's already a part of you! Doesn't the Course in Miracles talk about ending that separation, reminding us we are already a part of this great guidance?"

I nodded and thought about the last Course in Miracles group. "I got it Katie, more than you know. So, you think I'm going to be okay?"

She smiled again and said, "Absolutely! Yes, trusting this wisdom may take a little more time, but Willow, I can promise you that the more you do it, the more it will help ease and change those habits, and actually help to shift some of the worn out neural pathways in your mind."

"Really?" I asked.

"Really," she said.

I left her office calmer than I anticipated. I turned on the radio, and as I pulled out of her parking lot, the song was playing, "Keep it coming love, keep it coming love, don't stop it now don't stop it now," by KC and the Sunshine Band. Something inside of me said, *listen carefully to the lyrics.* I giggled.

After therapy, I decided, since I was in a more relaxed state of mind, that I would call Will and tell him. I got his voicemail, so I left him a message saying that I had some good news, and to call me when he could.

In the meantime, I was already thinking about how much notice I should give my work, and getting Grandpa all packed up. How many boxes would I need? Oy! Two minutes later, my cell phone rang. I looked down and it was Will.

"Hello?"

"Hi, sorry. I was on the phone with a customer, what's the good news? Are you coming home this weekend to surprise me?"

"Sorry, not that news, but guess when I will be coming home?"

He hummed, "Um-m-m, I don't know - the weekend after?"

"No, in about four weeks or so."

He blurted out, "Four weeks! You mean I have to wait over a month to see you again? No can do. I will have to fly out again in between."

I laughed, "Will, slow down! What I'm trying to tell you is that in a month I'll be home in Philly for good."

"No way! You spoke to your grandpa and I guess he said yes. Oh, I'm so happy, but still bummed I have to wait to see you."

"Will, when I come home for good, you can see me whenever you like."

He laughed, "I know, that *is* great news. So, have you thought about where you are going to stay?" Easy, boy.

"Um-m, yeah. I think I'm going to stay with my sister and the kids until I find a place to rent."

"Sounds good. Well, you know, you could always stay with me, if you need to. And don't get all freaked out by my saying that, either."

"I know, I know. Thank you for the offer, but I should be okay. But, I will finally look forward to seeing your place."

He then said, "I better start cleaning now, my place is a pig sty! It might take me a month to really clean it up well. Oh, yeah, I never told you that growing up my mother was so overly obsessive-compulsive with keeping a clean house, that I think I leave mine dirty these days just to spite her."

"Nice, Will. Well, you don't have to make it spotless for me, just the bathroom has to be clean."

He laughed, "It's all good. So, this is good news, how are you feeling about it?"

"Well, I'm happy to be closer to my family, and of course, you, but part of me is nervous - you know trying to figure out the rest of my life and what to do next." I confided.

"I hear you, Willow, but just take it one day at a time, and you'll figure it out."

"I know – thanks. Alright. Well, I better call my yenta aunt and tell her the news. I know she's going to want to see me a lot. So, have a good day and talk to you soon."

"Alright. Let me know if you need help with anything."

"Thanks. We should be good."

We hung up; I felt better. Maybe this was all going to be okay.

I called my Aunt Ellen. "Hi, doll, what is going on?"

"Um-m, so I can't believe it, but Grandpa and I are heading back north in a little over a month."

"You don't say! I think it's a good idea. He will be happier closer to your parents."

"Yeah, I just hope he can leave his house - I think it will be very emotional for him to say goodbye. You know how many memories he and Grandma Lu had there."

"I know, honey, but it's time. As much as I bitch about your grandpa, I want him to be happy, and of course my sister would want the same, which is to be with all of you."

"Thanks, El, for your words. So, I was thinking, we will definitely get together a few times before I go."

"Of course, darling! And if you need any help with movers, let me know. I know a lot of people."

"Thanks, El. So, I will call you soon about getting together."

"Sounds good, doll. Alright, I am off to meet my man for an early cocktail. Adios."

"Bye."

# Chapter 36

I SPENT THE LAST FOUR weeks working more shifts to make some extra money, going to therapy, and I had one more healing session with Lotus. I went to a couple of Course in Miracles groups, and I visited with Luke when I could. Time went fast. I told my work I wanted the last week off to get my stuff together and help pack up my grandfather. Robert, my boss, was very understanding and told me to promise he would let them throw me a small goodbye party before I left. I also promised Luke that I would allow his lovely wife to cook me dinner one night, too. He told me she wanted to meet me and thank me for introducing her and Luke to the Course in Miracles. Luke told me that once he went home from our first meeting together, he had felt a sense of peace and shared everything with his wife. He also said they bought the book and had been practicing it together at home. I was so happy to have introduced them to the course. They don't call it a miracle for nothing.

I wanted to buy Luke's wife some pretty flowers on my way to dinner. He told me she loved flowers, all kinds, even studied them, and that I should bring a mixed bouquet of something. I pulled up to his house. It was a modest and sweet ranch style home with a beautiful garden and immaculate lawn. I could picture the two of them on Saturday afternoons, working outside, taking real pride in their lawn. As I walked up to the front door, I could smell something fried and something sweet. Whatever it was, it smelled like heaven. I rang the doorbell and Luke answered and gave me a great big hug.

"So glad you could make it, Miss Willow! Ah, and you brought flowers. They are beautiful; my wife will love them. Come on in. Can I get you something to drink? My wife just made some delicious homemade lemonade. She'll be down in a minute - she is just fixing her hair. Let me go put those pretty flowers in some water - I will be right back. Go sit on the couch."

"Sounds great, Luke, thanks."

I walked into the living room and saw a ton of pictures everywhere of grandkids and lots of little knicky knacks and statues of horses. I wondered if his wife was raised on a farm or liked to ride. It was a lovely living room, and I could tell it held a lot of history, full of love. I envisioned their grandkids playing board games on their living room floor. I could hear a little squeaking coming down the stairs. As I looked up, I saw this loving and warm smile come toward me in a beautiful vibrant blue jacket, and pretty pink nails waving at me. Lorraine was eccentrically beautiful. She's half Native American and half African American. Her skin looked healthy and ageless, like she took good care of it.

"Well, well, you must be Willow, and you sure are prettier than Luke described. Come over here, child, and give me a hug."

I immediately felt at home, got up off the couch, and gave her a warm hug. Her perfume reminded me of my Grandma Dotty's.

"Thank you so much, Lorraine. It was so kind of you to invite me into your home and for dinner."

Lucas came out with the bouquet of flowers in a pretty vase and said, "See what she bought us!"

"Ah, Miss Willow, you shouldn't have, but they are beautiful. Thank you, honey."

"No problem, I know your husband said you love flowers, I can see by the passion you've put into your beautiful garden out front."

She lit up, "Ah-h, thanks, Willow. So, come sit next to me. Dinner will be ready in a little bit. It's in the oven. I hope you like catfish, macaroni and cheese, string beans and biscuits. Although I can tell by looking at you that you probably don't eat a lot of this stuff."

I smiled, "Oh no, Lorraine, I sure do eat, and I can't wait to taste your delicious food. Your husband has raved about it for months now." She looked over at him and winked.

"So, Willow, Lucas tells me you are headed back to Philadelphia. I think it was so wonderful of you to have moved here in the first place to stay with your grandpa. You have a good heart, I can tell."

"Ah, thanks. Yes, I didn't want to leave him alone. He and my grandmother were very close, a true love story. So, it took some convincing, but I think he's ready to be closer to my folks and my sister and her kids now. But, it all worked out for the best - my being here, anyway. I've met some wonderful people - your husband being on the top of my list."

I Willow Winked him, and said, "I've learned a lot about myself in the meantime."

She paused. "Yes, yes, Luke has told me a little bit. Willow, you are a strong young lady who is coming to her own. I can tell. My love for God has taught me a lot, and has opened me to lots of things and to an overall better understanding of people in general. Do you know what I mean?"

I responded, "I do, especially now more than ever. My spirituality has also taught me a lot over the last few months, especially in relation to God - excuse me, our Agape God." I Willow Winked Luke again.

Lorraine laughed and said, "Yes, yes, Luke told me your stories. Isn't it amazing how we are reminded of God's nature? The universe is speaking to us all of the time, the question is whether or not we are really listening."

I nodded, "You're right, you're right. So, I can thank the two of you for educating me on Agape, and I am sure there is more to come."

She said, "Oh, honey, it would have found you anyway, but we should be thanking you for introducing us to this wonderful book."

She pulled out the big blue <u>Course in Miracles</u> book and said, "I have traded this baby for my <u>Bible</u> these days, if you know what I mean. It's a lot nicer."

I smiled, "I'm glad it has brought you both some more peace."

She smiled and said, "It really has, especially in helping us to remind one another of our love for each other and our family. It has actually lightened me up, and given me a better perspective on forgiving my sister Dory for some of her behaviors that I have judged throughout her life."

I said, "I'm glad, Lorraine. I am new to it, too, but it seems to work, or make sense to many in ways that are not threatening, and certainly not preachy, like religion can be."

She said, "Mm-m-hm-m. And Luke is going to try and take me to one of those meetings you went to. He said Gaylee was such a lovely woman."

I responded, "She is. They are a very comforting and accepting group of people." She nods her head.

"Sounds good. Okay, angel, let me just finish up fixing dinner."

"Can I help you in any way?" I asked.

"Oh, no, honey. Thank you for asking, but I am fine. I've got my hubby to help me. You just relax."

As she walked into the kitchen I said to Luke, "You're a lucky man."

He smiled, "Don't I know it."

I asked Luke about the horses. Lorraine must have overheard me from the kitchen and yelled, "Oh, I can tell you about that. It started way back with my great- great-great granddaddy. He led a tribe. My great grandfather and my grandfather also ran a farm, where, as I child I got to ride a lot of the time. I love riding them, it's so freeing. My ancestors were very spiritual, and always believed that a horse represented wisdom, courage and freedom. As a child I always felt drawn to them and safe in their presence."

I replied, "Wow, what a beautiful thought. Do you ride anymore?"

She laughed, "Oh, child, I wish, but with these old hips. I am lucky if I can climb into Luke's truck these days. No, this collection of horse statues that I keep around the house will have to do. It's okay though, at least they help remind me of peaceful feelings whenever I am stressed."

I smiled and said, "Well, that definitely makes sense, and I agree, animals can be very comforting and intuitive. I remember one time in my twenties, I was in my bedroom with the door almost shut, lying in my bed, hysterically crying about a boyfriend at the time and over God knows what. Next thing I knew, I heard my dog, Eddie, come running down the hall. He pushed the door open and came over and started nuzzling me and licking my face. It was like he knew somehow that I was sad and was trying to help comfort me. He also always laid next to my sister during her first pregnancy, and never left her side."

Lorraine laughed and said, "Oh, yes, Willow. Animals know, they really do. They speak the same language of God's love when in our company."

I said, "I know, especially dogs. When I was a little girl, I was frightened of dogs, but my Grandma Lu helped me get over my fear, and reminded me that there is a reason that dog spelled backwards is God."

She giggled and said, "Yes, Willow, your grandma was a smart woman, and a sweet one, from what Lucas tells me."

I smiled, "Yes, she was. Thank you for acknowledging her."

We sat down to dinner, and it was probably one of the best meals I had ever had. "Lorraine, this is one of the best meals I have ever had, no joke."

She laughed, "I am not modest, I believe you, that's why my

grandkids can't stay away. I would cook all day and night if it made them happy."

I smiled and said, "And I believe you! I can tell by your pictures and Luke's stories that you have a wonderful family. You know, you two make a perfect couple. I feel in my heart you were probably made for one another - down to the fact that your names sound so smooth together, Luke and Lorraine, a perfect combo. You know my grandparents are, I mean were, well, before my grandmother passed, Lex and Luciana. You know, you two remind me of them a little bit."

"Ah-h, Willow that might be one of the nicest compliments we have gotten. Yeah, we do have a lot in common when it comes to matters of the heart, but truth, honey? It took us a while to get through everything we did. You know, no relationship is perfect. We do work on it every day and try to accept one another for who we are, that is the key to staying together. Agape loving, honey, that is what it's about. Learning to love your partner no matter what, for that is what we all want isn't?"

I nodded and said, "Yes, it is, to be loved for who we are."

She then said, "So, Willow, you have anyone special in your life? I don't want to be too nosey, but curious a beautiful sweet lady like yourself should have an angel to hold hands with, too."

I smiled, "Well, yes, I do. It's still sort of new, but I think I may have found a keeper, we will see. His name is Will."

She laughed and said, "How about that, Willow and Will! Talk about a match made in heaven." She winked at me.

I laughed, "I know, I know. I thought about that the first day I met him. Not sure what the future holds, but I know I have at least met someone who believes in unconditional love. When I move back to Philly we will see how it goes. I'll keep you and Luke posted."

"Oh, dear, I hope you do. Just know the key is also to remember to not be afraid to love. Too often we hold back out of fear of getting hurt, but everyone wants to be loved, so that is part of our secret, too, keep the love flowing."

"That's sounds like good advice, Lorraine, thanks."

She continued and said, "So, speaking of, I was going to wait until after dinner, but I think now would be a good time, seeing what we are talking about. Lucas and I have a little something for you."

I was shocked. "You do? Dinner was enough, you guys didn't have to get me anything. Just being in your presence is a gift in itself."

Luke stood up and said, "Oh, Willow, we want you to have this as a comfort for the rest of your life, hold on I will go get it - you will love it."

He came back to the table with a big blue box wrapped in a red bow. I couldn't imagine what it was. I opened the box and it was a beautiful navy and baby blue blanket.

I said, "Wow, this is so beautiful! Thank you."

Lorraine says, "Hold on, child, open it up, and read what I knitted on it."

As I opened it up, in soft blue letters it read, AGAPE. My eyes teared up. "Thank you so much. This is one of the most beautiful presents I have ever received. I am speechless. You made this for me?" They both nodded.

Lorraine said, "Yes, honey, this is your special blanket to wrap around you and cuddle with, remembering that God's unconditional love is always wrapped around you like a blanket. And some day, Willow, if you choose to have children, you can wrap it around them, too."

I smiled and got up from the table and went over and hugged them both and said, "Thank you so much. I will cherish this gift forever. Wherever I live for the rest of my life, this will go with me."

They both lit up and said, "That's all we want."

Lorraine said, "Alright now, I hope you saved some room for my apple pie."

I replied, "Only if you have vanilla ice cream to go with it."

She opened up the freezer, "Well, of course, what else would I have?"

I hugged them both goodbye and thanked them over and over. I pulled out of their driveway and felt so happy and grateful to have met this couple. Part of me wishes I could pack them up into my suitcase and take them home with me. It's nice to meet genuine people to remind you of what life is about. I started to feel a little more at ease too, about going home to Philly!

# Chapter 37

ROBERT TOLD ME TO COME into work around 4:00pm, since we would close at around 3:30pm for my little goodbye party. I wanted to look half decent since I was always in uniform and an apron, so opted for a cute yellow sundress. I wasn't sure who was going to be there. I had called Ed earlier in the morning to let him know about my little get together. I hoped that he would stop by so I could at least see him before he left for another business trip, since he would not be back before I left. When I arrived at Dotty's, I walked in and saw Trisha counting her day's worth of tips and Devon combing his hair.

Robert made eye contact with me and said, "Look who's here! Wow look at you - you clean up nice."

"Thanks, Robert."

Devon walked over and gave me a hug, "I always knew you were a fine looking thing."

I laughed and said, "You, too, Devon. So, who else is here?"

"Aaron, is in the back, Brenda is on her way, and a few others."

"Ah-h-h, thanks guys. Robert, I called Ed this morning and invited him. Hope that is cool?"

"Willow, I would hope he'd stop by. He's pretty much a part of this family since he's here all the time. So, how about a beer before the rest arrive?"

"Beer, is that cool, boss? Serving without a liquor license?" I Willow Winked him.

He responded, "See that sign in the front window that says CLOSED? We are now at liberty to play. In the meantime, hang out with everyone until the rest arrive. I have to finish making my famous wings with dip and homemade pizzas."

"Sounds good, thanks Robert. I am salivating already."

I walked over to sit next to Trisha, "So, how have you been?"

"Well, Willow, I am so over this getting treated like crap by loser men. My mamma always said, no matter how hard you try in life, you can't shine shit."

I put my hand on her shoulder and said, "So, stop trying to shine it and allow yourself to be treated the way you deserve to be treated. There are a lot of good men out there, and even the bad ones are not so bad, they have just forgotten how to love and have treated women poorly because that's how they treat themselves."

She leaned her head on my shoulder and said, "Oh, Willow, I don't know if that guy really exists. I'm starting to lose hope."

I then said, "Trisha, you haven't lost hope, you just haven't fully opened your eyes." I nodded my head as if to point toward Robert in the back, and continued to say, "Trish, I have seen the way he looks at you when you don't even realize it."

She responded, "Who, Robert? Please! He's too good for me. He's a mamma's boy who has no business with a girl like me."

I said, "So, Trish is that the story you've been telling yourself your whole life? That you don't deserve a guy like him? It's time to change this story. What do you have to lose? Start believing that guys like Robert want to remind you of your beauty and your worthiness."

She kissed my forehead and said, "Willow, I am sure going to miss your words of wisdom around here. I know that whatever it is you decide to become, a psychologist or whatever else, you will help many. Alright, let me go powder my nose, I'll be back in flash." I smiled at her.

"Thanks, Trish."

Next thing I knew, Brenda walked in. I was pleasantly surprised as we weren't the best of friends while I was here, but I was happy to see her. She walked over to me and said, "So, you skipping town, huh?"

"Well, I figured it was time to have a little more courage in making some positive changes for my life, besides, I miss my family."

She then said, "Well, I wish I could relate on the missing family part, but I don't get along with them. But at least, I can relate on the having courage for making positive changes part. I just signed myself up to take some art classes at the local college."

"Ah-h, Brenda, that is great! I knew there was an artist in you dying to come out."

She replied, "Yeah, thanks, I feel good about it. I will let you know how it goes."

I smiled and said, "I hope you will."

I heard the door open, and it was Ed with flowers and a gift of some sort wrapped up. He looked great, as always, we almost matched. He was in a fun yellow hat, with a watch to go with.

He walked toward me and I said, "Did you know I would be in yellow today, too?"

He hugged me and handed me the flowers and said, "Great minds think alike."

I said, "I am so happy you came! Thank you for these beautiful flowers - you shouldn't have, and what is this?" I asked, as I pointed to the box.

He said, "You're welcome for the flowers, and this gift, don't open it up until you get home later."

"Okay, I'll wait, but I'm curious," I said as I shook the box.

He then said, "You will love it, but let it be for your eyes. Not everyone here has to see it - as you know some poets like a little privacy before they share." He winked at me. I knew right away that it was something poetic and said, "Gotcha," and Willow Winked him back.

Robert came out from the back and said, "Okay, I would like

to make a toast. Everyone raise your beers or your fruity wine things. So, as I was saying, I would like to make a toast to one of the sweetest servers we have had here. It's been a pleasure working with you, and you are sure going to be missed around here, by both the staff and your patrons."

Ed lifted his glass and said, "I second that."

We all toasted.

Then, I said, "Well, I would just like to thank you all for making me feel at home here, and for treating me well. I am sure going to miss you all, too. I would like you all to give me your contact info before I leave tonight so we can stay in touch. Besides, I promise to send you all a copy of the first book I have published."

Trisha said, "Sounds good. You should write a book on love - you seem to know more about it than most."

I said, "Well, maybe, I am still learning, but maybe." We all toasted.

Robert then said, "Alright, everyone, let's eat some goodies, huh?"

Devon said, "Amen to that, boss, I hope you bought some extra hot sauce and blue cheese for me?"

Robert replied, "Devon, please! Like I don't know how you like your wings after all of these years? Just be happy I was giving you a break from having to cook tonight!'

Devon nodded his head and said, "Fair enough, boss."

We had so much fun. It was nice to see a looser side to everyone outside of their uniforms. Ed was the first to leave, which I knew he would be.

He walked over to me and jokingly said, "Sorry, don't weep for me Willow, but I have to get up very early tomorrow to catch a flight, so I should get going."

I leaned in to hug him and said, "Ah, this Willow tree, got it. Ed, what can I say? If it wasn't for you, I may have not have had the guts to even consider going home or pursue my writing. Thank you for everything, I mean everything - from publishing my poem to introducing me to a Course in Miracles, and for helping me to feel more courageous in showing the world who I am."

He responded, "You're welcome to all of the above, but, I like the last part of what you said the best. If I did nothing else but help you feel more comfortable in your skin, and to write your heart out, then I have done my job, and God is proud of me."

I said, "He sure is, and I am grateful He brought you to me. You are, for sure, a part of my journey, so thanks again."

He nodded and hugged me one more time and said, "You're welcome, Willow, and keep believing in your-self, and what is in that box is a part of you."

I felt overjoyed and sad at the same time. How many Ed's am I going to get to meet in my lifetime? How many mentors do we get to show us the way?"

After a while, I had drunk, and certainly eaten enough and was ready to go home. I hugged everyone and thanked Robert again and again. He walked me toward the door and gave me a hug.

I said, as I pointed toward, Trish, "Go for it, it will take her some time to warm up to being treated well for once in her life, but you're perfect for her. Her head doesn't know it yet, but her heart will be reminded soon enough, trust me."

I Willow Winked him and he said, "How did you know?"

I replied, "I can read people's hearts. I see these things sometimes before they even manifest on a physical level, and of course, I can tell by the way you watch her." I smiled at him.

He then said, "Thanks, Willow I will consider your thoughts, and thank you for putting a lot more smiling faces onto our staff and customers. I know whatever it is you are going to do, you will do well, and I want that first copy signed."

"You got it. Thanks for everything, Robert."

As anxious as I was with excitement to open up Ed's gift, I waited until I got home. As soon as I walked in the door, I saw Grandpa at the kitchen table eating his coffee cake with his black coffee.

"Hi, Gramps. Having a little night snack?"

"Hi, love. Yeah, a little treat. So, how was your farewell party? Wow, nice flowers!"

"Yes, I know. It was really nice, I am sure going to miss those people - especially Ed. He's one of our best customers. You know, the one that got me published. He bought me these beautiful flowers and this gift, which I was told not to open until I got home. I have a feeling it's a poem of some sort."

Grandpa said, "Well, what are you waiting for? Open it up, let's see!"

I opened the box, and in it was a beautiful poem in a soft pastel pink and green frame. I put my hand over my mouth, "Oh, my God, this is beautiful! I am speechless."

"Willow, are you going to share it with your Gramps, or is it too personal?"

I said, "No, of course not, Grandpa. It's a beautiful and metaphoric poem about me, to remind... well, let me read it to you."

*Sweet Willow Tree*

*I see you sweet Willow tree*
*Your branches swaying back and forth as they go*
*The wind shifting you around*
*Like a heart playing tug of war with the ego*

*I hear you sweet Willow tree*
*As you whisper wisdom and light*
*It's saying "no need to weep no more"*
*"It's okay to surrender the fight"*

*I feel you sweet Willow tree*
*As your leaves tickle my cheeks*
*You remind me once more*
*Strength comes when you have the courage to seek*

*I touch you sweet Willow tree*
*As you wrap your branches around me*
*I then hug you back and feel you say,*
*"Your precious heart knows the way"*

*I smell you sweet Willow tree*
*As I place my nose to your bark*
*I feel a magical healing and smile*
*As I am no longer afraid of the dark*
*- Ed Thomas*

I teared up a little and Grandpa said, "Wow, this guy is good. No wonder he is published."

I nodded and said, "Isn't that awesome? He even remembered how I told him Dad came up with my name by the lake. I'm going to call him tomorrow and thank him. I'm psyched that this will be my first piece of art that I put into my apartment - wherever that may be."

Grandpa said, "Yeah, have you decided what you are doing?"

"Well, Carla told me I could stay with her, and as soon as I find an apartment for a decent price, I will lease it."

"Sounds good. Well, you know if you ever need help financially love, you can count on Grandpa."

I kissed his forehead and said, "I know, Gramps, thanks. I am the luckiest granddaughter on earth. I'll be okay. Alright, I am beat. We have a long day tomorrow - I plan on packing up a lot of boxes 'cause the movers are coming in two days."

He sat up erect and said, "Don't remind me."

"Aw-w, Gramps. Are you sure you're okay with this?'

"Yes, love. I just can't believe it is here already. Time has gone so fast. I sure am going to miss it, 'ya know. Lots of memories with your grandma."

I said, "I know, but it will be okay, I promise."

He then said, "In a way, I think you are right. I didn't tell you this morning, but last night, as weird as this may sound, I had a dream that I was outside standing by the apple tree that I planted for your Grandma Lu, and she showed up in her favorite red sweater and comfy khaki pants. All I can remember her saying to me was, 'Lex, you are going to be fine. It's okay to go now. I go with you wherever you go, whether it's in Florida or Philly. I am with you, and thanks for planting me this beauty,' as she pointed to the tree. And then she said, 'I love 'ya so, Lex.' And I said, 'I love 'ya, too, Lu.' And then she left."

He lifted his shoulders and said, "I woke up and felt at peace, like she was really there."

I got goose bumps and smiled and said, "Gramps, she was there. I know you don't believe much, but I believe that is what we enlightened ones call a visit from the other side."

He laughed. "Well, not sure but I will admit it was the first time in a long time that I felt her presence by me. It seemed so real, like she was really there and she was even wearing her perfume that I loved so."

I nodded, "I know what you mean, Grandpa. To me, it was a gift for you from Grandma to reassure you we are doing the right thing. P.S. you know what they say about our sense of smell."

He nodded back and said, "I know love. Alright, go get some shut-eye."

"I love you, Grandpa."

"You too, love."

# Chapter 38

I WOKE UP EARLY IN the morning and wanted to run over to the supermarket to get some extra empty boxes to pack up stuff in the house. I decided to stop for a cup of coffee at my favorite Dunkin' Donuts, and a blueberry muffin to accompany it. I sat down and noticed a homeless man pacing back and forth in front of the shop. He was wearing a torn gray sweatshirt, with a matching head of dirty grey hair and worn out jeans. He looked like he might be talking to himself, mumbling something. For some reason, I couldn't take my eyes off of him. I felt this overwhelming feeling of compassion, and wondered if he might be hungry. Part of my ego mind said, "Leave him alone," but the heart said, "Offer him something." As I continued to eat my muffin, I wondered when the last time he might have eaten was, which then became small potatoes compared to wondering when the last time he had felt love in his life. I got myself up, and as I walked out the door, I stopped his rapid walking and said, "Hi, how are you? Are you hungry?"

He looked surprised that I even stopped to talk to him, and he said, "No, thank you. Thank you for the offer, but I am okay."

I responded, "Okay, I hope you have a nice day. What's your name?"

I put out my hand. He hesitated, assuming I wouldn't want to shake his dirty hand and said, "You don't want to shake my hand."

I put my germaphobeness aside and said, "Sure I do. Hi, I'm Willow."

He smiled, "Willow, like the tree?"

I smiled back and said, "Yes, Willow like the tree, but not the weeping kind," as I Willow winked him. Ed lovingly popped into my head.

348

He then felt a little more comfortable, and shook my hand and said, "Hi, I am Jerry."

I said, "Like the lead singer of the Grateful Dead? Or like the little mouse that likes to taunt Tom the cat?"

He laughed, and I wondered *when was the last time this guy laughed?* He jokingly said, "How would you know my dream of becoming a professional Dead Head would lead me here? These old clothes that I'm wearing might still be from the last Dead show I attended."

I responded, "I like your sense of humor, Jerry."

He said, "What? Homeless guys can't still have a sense of humor?"

I said, "No, I would never say that, I'm just happy to see you smile. For some reason, more and more these days, I'm moved by the simplicity and magnitude of a smile between humans."

He said, "Wow, are you like a poet or something? You speak like one."

"Actually, Jerry, I am. Well, I hope to do more in my future. So, what do you say - would you like a cup of coffee or a bagel or something? My treat. They have delicious muffins, too."

He hesitated and then said, "That would be great. I haven't had a hot cup of coffee with cream and sugar in God knows how long, and I sure would love a warm toasted bagel with butter to go with it."

I said, "You got it. I'll be right back."

I ran back into Dunkin D's ordered his food, and decided to order an extra muffin, and got him two bottles of water, as it was going to be a hot one later today. My intentions were to not get too personal with this man, but to keep it simple. However, with my track record, this doesn't always happen.

I walked back out and handed him his coffee and food and said, "I got you a few extra things cause it's gonna be a hot one."

He responded, "Wow, you are really kind, Willow. Thank you for stopping to talk to me. Most people don't even acknowledge me.

Sometimes I want to stop them and say, just because I'm homeless, doesn't mean that I'm heartless. Anyway, thanks for making me feel like a human being. As an aside, just know as good as I know this bagel and coffee is going to taste, they will never compare with how your beautiful smile made me feel." He winked at me.

I got goose bumps and found myself responding, "God bless your heart, and thank you for making my day. It was so nice to meet you, Jerry. I gotta get going - my Grandpa and I are about to move back to Philly."

He says, "No shit, you from where Rocky Balboa is from?"

I laughed and said, "Yeah, I'm from where the Italian Stallion was filmed."

He said, "Cool, but I'm kind of sad. I was hoping I would get a chance to see you again."

I smiled back and said, "I'm sorry, but something tells me another angel will make her way towards you soon."

He laughed and said, "I knew it, you're one of those earth angel types my wife used to talk about. She loves angels. I bet you are one of those that help random people with an open heart."

I responded, "Perhaps, Jerry, either way, just remember no matter where you are, what you are doing, or not doing in your life, God's love for you will never change, I can promise you that. He loves you no matter what."

He got really silent and said, "Really? I mean you could understand why a guy like me might have lost a little faith in something bigger looking out for me."

I nodded, "I do, but God's love is pure and unconditional. On some greater level we are not always aware of, sometimes situations that occur in our lives are great lessons to us, and they end up teaching us more about life, especially an appreciation for things."

He said, "You got that right, my wife kicked me out a year ago. I can't say I blame her, my drinking got out of hand, and yes, I am a classic story. I lost it all, my decent job, my beautiful wife, and..." He started to get a little teary and said, "Even my beautiful daughter, Jenna. She's only three years old. I have such shame. It breaks my heart thinking that my little angel will not grow up with a father. All I want is to be given another chance. I haven't drunk in over six months, but my wife doesn't believe me yet, and won't give me a shot."

I realized that we had gotten into it more than I had anticipated, but I knew this man, right here and now, just needed a sounding board.

I put my hand on his shoulder and said, "Jerry, my friend, and I do consider you my friend, I promise you, and I don't know how I know this, but I promise you sometime soon, when the time is right, you will get your shot. Out of fairness to your family, these things take time, but the key is to never give up and never lose your faith in God. You can talk to him. He will listen to your prayers, and at some point when He feels it is the right time, you will get to be reunited with them and your beautiful little girl won't even know you were gone because you are going to have so much love to give her. So, when you get your chance again to hold her in your arms, and you will, she will remember instantly why you feel like home naturally, for you are her daddy. I have faith in you, Jerry. The question is, do you have faith in yourself?"

I wasn't even sure where this was coming from, but part of me felt like what the Course in Miracles calls a holy instant moment, like Luke's neighbor mentioned or where spirit somehow speaks through you in a loving gentle way because he then said, "I do now, have faith, thanks for reminding me. You really must be one of those Earth angels. Thank you so much, Willow."

"You're welcome, Jerry, and who knows? Maybe our paths will cross again someday. God works in mysterious ways, that much I know."

He smiled and said, "He sure does, and if nothing else, I can at least promise you that the next time I see a Willow tree, I will always think of you."

I said, "You are sweet, although I am not sure how many willow trees are in Florida, I think they are outnumbered by all of the palm trees."

He then said, "Yeah, maybe, but no palm tree could every compare to your sweetness." I laughed and teared up a little because I thought again of the poem Ed wrote to me last night, called "Sweet Willow Tree." What are the chances? I then thought who is the angel now, Jerry or me? I realized it didn't matter, for this is the beauty of life, that loving circle God talks about. It always comes back around somehow. I didn't care that Jerry stunk, or hadn't showered forever, I leaned in and gave him a hug and said, "You are going to be fine, I believe in you."

He said, "Thanks again for treating me like a human being and restoring my faith. Something tells me with a heart like yours you are going to be just fine, too."

As I walked away, I turned around one more time to see if he was still standing there and he was, watching me walk away. He lifted his hand and waved goodbye. I waved back.

As soon as I got into my car I called Ed to thank him for the incredible poem and, of course, to share the story of what just happened. He laughed and said, the Course in Miracles had taught me well. I was overcome with joy and thanked God for allowing me to bring some loving to this man. For the first time in a while, I felt like I had really grown overall as a person.

I spent the majority of the afternoon packing up box after box. I felt a bit of sadness as I watched my grandpa pack up some of the rest of my grandmother's things. He decided to send the remainder of her clothing to the Salvation Army, because he knew that she would want them to go to a good place. I walked into the kitchen and saw my grandfather sitting at the table with an open shoebox, full of cards. I saw him wiping tears from his eyes as he read them one after one.

"You okay, Gramps? What are you doing?"

"Oh, hi, my love. I am just reading your Grandma Lu's anniversary cards to me. I saved them all, all fifty-seven of them. Your grandma was really something. When I read these cards, I am reminded of how lucky I was to have her all of those years. I responded, "Aww that is so sweet." He nodded his head and I could tell he wasn't in the mood to say much more.

Alright, change of subjects – so, since tomorrow night is our last night here, I was thinking in honor of your grandmother that we should go to her favorite restaurant. It's the one we went to for our anniversary each year once we moved here to Florida. It is called Beana's Botanical Garden. They have delicious meals and yes, it overlooks a beautiful garden."

In the back of my mind, I thought, oh shit, I was going to invite Aunt Ellen over tomorrow night to say goodbye, so I nodded and said, "Sure, Gramps, it sounds great, whatever you want to do. Maybe I will just call Aunt El to meet tonight instead. Sorry, I guess I should have thought about asking you first if she could join us for dinner on our last night. I just didn't want to leave without saying goodbye."

I was happily surprised to hear the next words out of his mouth when he said, "You want to invite her to come along?"

"Wow really, Gramps, are you sure?"

He said, "Yeah, what the heck. I know it's officially time to bury the hatchet. Besides it's what your grandmother would want, to have three of her favorite people together."

I kissed him again, "You're the best, Grandpa. I will invite her to come, thank you."

As I walked out the room he said, "Just tell her she is not allowed to wear her perfume, or you have to bring my doctor's mask."

I sarcastically respond, "Ha, ha, Gramps, you are hysterical."

I could barely sleep that night, knowing the next day was our last. I gave up the fight at about 5:30 a.m. and decided to take one last walk around Grandpa's complex. I put my iPod on, and as I started walking I felt like I wanted to talk to my grandmother. I always wondered why people felt embarrassed to admit talking to our deceased ones. If you give it a chance, in your own way specific to your loved one who has passed, you will get your sign that you were heard. It may not be right at that moment, but your heart will know it when it happens. And so, I began walking around pretending like I was singing on my iPod, so no one would think I was talking to myself.

I said, "Good morning, Grandma Lu, can you hear me? Calling on Grandma Lu! Angels, bring her to me, please! Hi, Grandma, and so here we are, our last day in Florida. I think we're making the right decision. I would ask you what you think, but I already know the answer. Thanks for showing up in Grandpa's dream the other night.

"So, to tell you the truth, Grandma, I am a little nervous about this transition, 'ya know I always get a little iffy with change, but I am hoping you will be there to help both Grandpa and me with it. I'm not sure what I am going to do with my life, Grandma, but honestly, I just want to be happy and feel connected to people. I mean, who really gives a crap what it is that I do, as long as I put my heart into it. I just want to be a good loving person like you taught me and share my love with world. I remember when I was a little girl you always used to say to me, 'That smile is going to change the world.' I hope you're right, Grandma. Well, my heart knows you're right, though my mind always likes to second guess me. But really, Grandma, I just want that simplicity, 'ya know like the kind of exchange I had with Jerry the homeless guy yesterday. I made someone feel like a person again. I brought my loving energy right from my heart into his. That is what I want to do, Grandma. I don't care about making a lot of money or having the nicest house. I just want to feel comfortable, and loving, and happy, and I hope God will be proud of me."

Next thing I knew a dragonfly came flying up next to me. My eyes filled up, I knew right away and said, "Thanks, Grandma, I would have been happy with the cardinal, but the dragonfly? You are the best."

The movers came at around three o'clock. Two big Italian guys jumped out of the truck. One was wearing a tee shirt that read, "I am not as tough as I look." The other guy had on a Philadelphia Eagles jersey. I smiled right away and said, "See, Gramps, it's a sign. He is wearing an Eagles jersey. Where we're headed, it's all good." I Willow Winked him. He smiled at me, but I knew he was clearly distracted. The men walked over toward my grandfather and put out their hands to shake his, "Hi, how ya's doing? Are you Mr. Lex Ovsenthal? And you must be his granddaughter, Willow."

We shook their hands and I said, "Hello, yes we are Willow and Lex, and you two are?"

"Hi, we're Vinny and Chad. Nice to meet you."

I said, "Nice to meet you, too." I looked at Chad and said, "Did you wear that Eagles jersey in our honor?"

He laughed and replied, "Yeah, I guess I did wear it in your honor. I am a big Eagles fan."

I smiled back and said, "Thanks, it's a good sign for us. So, let me show you guys into the house where you can get started." Grandpa told me he was going to take a bike ride while they move everything. He said it was too hard for him to watch, but he promised me he would be back within enough time for them to take his bike, which was going into the moving truck, too. As I watched the movers put one thing at a time into the truck, I began to feel a little uneasy again. I decided to step inside and take a few heart breaths like Katie taught me. I continued telling myself *it is safe to go.*

After I calmed down, I went back outside and saw that they were almost finished. Then I saw my grandfather coming down the street. As he pulled into the driveway, I said, "You okay?"

"Yeah, love, just wanted a little time alone. Are they finished yet?"

"Just about. I'm going to run inside and get them some bottles of water and snacks for the road, they have quite a long trip ahead of them."

He said, "You're just like your Grandma Lu. Oh, that reminds me, I will be right back and meet you outside here."

I saw him walking toward the backyard. I ran inside to grab the guys' goodies, and as I walked back out to the driveway, I saw my grandpa handing them each two apples and saying, "These will be the sweetest apples you ever had, I promise you that."

As I walk toward them, I said, "I can vouch for that. They are pretty damn good, and here, I know this is not part of your contract, but I packed you some water and snacks - you have a long trip. I wish I could have packed you a Philly cheese steak for the road, but you will just have to enjoy one when you get there."

Both Vinny's and Chad's eyes lit up.

Vinny said, "Boy, you's sure are nice. We wish all of our customers treated us so good. Thank you so much."

I replied, "You're welcome. My grandmother taught me well. So, have a safe trip and, as I mentioned, my father or mother should be there upon your arrival at my grandfather's facility. Any problems, just call me, or my dad's or Mom's cell numbers, which I gave to you."

They hopped back into the truck, and as they pulled away, my grandfather took my hand to hold it and gave it a squeeze. We didn't say a word - I just squeezed it back to let him know I understood and it was going to be okay.

# Chapter 39

My father set us up to stay in a hotel attached to the airport that night, since all of our furniture had been taken. Before we went out to dinner, my grandfather asked me to go wait in the car and let him do one more walk through the house to make sure everything was in place. I knew he was really going to say goodbye to it.

"Of course, Gramps, take your time. Whenever you are ready, come out."

I walked around back and grabbed some apples off of Grandma's tree to take on the airplane. Then I quickly went to knock on the neighbor's door to give her some, and to say thank you for making sure Grandma's tree was okay. She promised my grandpa she would take care of it.

An older redhead answered and said, "Hello?"

I said, "Hi, I'm Willow, Lex's granddaughter."

She said, "Oh, yes, of course. I've seen you walking around here a bunch of times. I'm Eve Reiner. I knew your grandmother fairly well. She used to come to our group meetings for just the ladies, what a lovely woman. I am sorry for your loss."

I said, "Thank you, and yes, she was lovely. I am a lucky girl. I apologize that I am now just introducing myself. You know, we're leaving tomorrow - well, tonight – we're staying at the airport. So, I won't keep you, but I just wanted to say thank you so much for keeping an eye on my grandfather's masterpiece in honor of my grandmother. I know at some point, someone will move in. You can tell them the story, and of course, please help yourself to as many delicious apples as you would like."

As I said this, I realized the irony that her name was Eve. Then

I wondered if she even believed in that preachy biblical story written millions of years ago, trying to separate us from God.

She responded, "Absolutely, I will watch that beauty out there and do my best to keep it alive, and yes, in honor of your beautiful grandmother. I must say, Willow, I am glad you kept your grandfather company all this time. I think you brought him out of his shell a little. I had never seen him outside of the house so much, between his biking and planting, and anyway, you are a sweet girl. I hope someday my granddaughters will do the same."

I said, "Thank you, Eve, and I'm sure they will. It was so nice to meet you."

She responded, "Yes it sure was. I wish you and your grandfather a safe trip and happiness in Philadelphia."

"Thank you again."

I walked toward the car at the same time Grandpa was walking to it.

He asked, "What were you doing at Eve's house?"

I answered, "Oh, just making sure she watches over Grandma's apple tree, and I told her to help herself to as many apples as she liked, and then I promised her that she would not be punished. How ironic though, right?"

He then said, "How what ironic?"

I replied, "You know, asking Eve to watch over your apple tree." I Willow Winked him.

He laughed as he realized what I just said and responded, "Did I mention her former husband's name was Adam?"

I exclaimed, "No way!"

He winked back at me and said, "No, it was Ronald, but that would have made a hell of a story!"

Aunt Ellen met us at dinner. She was so happy to hear that my grandfather was the one to have invited her. We sat outside at a table overlooking an assortment of stunning flowers and ordered a bottle of wine to celebrate our big leave. When we opened the wine, Aunt Ellen said she would like to make a toast.

As we raised our glasses she said, "I would like to toast in honor of my beautiful sister, Luciana, who I miss every day. I would also like to toast to a new beginning for my lovely niece, Willow, and to my brother- in-law, Lex. I will miss you, but I am happy and grateful that, Willow, we got to spend the time we did together, and to you, Lex, I am glad we have been able to put our differences aside."

Grandpa said, "Thank you for the toast, and I will drink to that."

I knew it wouldn't take long for her to ask me about Will.

"So, Willow, tell me how you feel about moving home closer to Will. You know I ran into his grandmother yesterday, and she said that he is very excited about you moving home. She asked me where you would be settling down. I told her at your sister Carla's for a while, and then your own place. She jokingly said that maybe one day they will live together."

"Aunt Ellen, that is, like, way down the road, so you can tell Will's grandmother next time you see her, that I like to take things slowly. I know she probably wants her grandson married with kids already, but I'm in no rush."

She said, "Willow, darling, calm down. I only brought it up to let you know how happy Will is to be closer to you."

I said, "Okay, sorry for snapping. I'm just a little anxious about the move and want to take everything one step at a time."

My grandfather interjected and lifted his glass to mine and said, "I will toast that again."

For the rest of dinner, we continued to exchange stories about Grandma Lu, and Aunt El told me a few stories about herself and Harold, as my grandpa kicked my foot a few times under the table. That was much better than what he used to do - blurt out some sarcastic remark to her. After dinner, we walked around the garden for a few minutes and Grandpa took us to see Grandma's favorite part - a bed full of lush roses and marigolds, some of her favorite flowers. As we walked through, he told us the reason Grandma had loved these flowers so much was because they represented more than just flowers.

He said, "Your grandmother told me that, as we all know, the rose represents love and the marigold represents a courageous heart."

Aunt Ellen and I both smiled.

Aunt Ellen's cell phone rang and she said, "Excuse me, for a minute, it's Harold. I am going to meet him from here."

As she walked away, I was thinking how nice it would be to put one of these flowers on Grandma's grave, especially since it was from her favorite spot. I knew it was against the rules to pick someone else's flowers, but I figured one yellow marigold wouldn't hurt. I wanted it as a piece of memory for Grandma.

My grandpa saw me take it and I said, "Oops, you caught me."

He said, "It's okay, love, I was thinking the same thing. I was just too nervous to do it myself."

I said, "It's okay, it's for Grandma. At first, I was thinking I wanted to keep one as a memory. But now, I am thinking maybe we would stop by her grave site before we head to the hotel since it's still a little light out. We could maybe place it where she's buried. What do you think?"

He said, "Sounds good, as long as we are at it. I am going to subtly pick one of those pretty pink roses your grandma loved so. This way we can both have something to place." He picked one off the vine and next thing I heard was, "Shit."

"What, Gramp, what is it?"

"I just pricked my finger with the thorn, and it's bleeding. It figures."

I said, "Alright, calm down, I have a Band-Aid in my pocketbook.

Let's put it on now and when we get to the hotel, I'll clean it up." I temporarily put some hand sanitizer on his finger and blew on it so it would ease the burn. Then I covered it up with the Band-Aid.

He said, "Did I ever mention how much you are just like your grandma? I used to always make fun of her for carrying Band-Aids in her purse. I used to say, 'Lu, what are the chances you are going to need a Band-Aid?' and she would say, 'Lex, hush up, 'ya never know.' And look where we are now! This must be her way of saying, 'Ha-ha, Lex, I told 'ya so.'"

We both laughed and waved Aunt El toward the parking lot. We gave her hugs and said goodbye.

Once we got in the car, I said to Grandpa, "Thanks for an amazing dinner and for being so nice to Aunt El. Grandma would have been proud of you."

He nodded and said, "I know, and you're welcome. Okay, let's go drop these flowers off."

We pulled up to the gravesite, and I saw Grandpa getting teary already.

I asked, "You okay to go over there?"

"Yeah," he responded, "But you know, Willow, I think I might want a little time alone, you go first, take a few minutes, and then I will go after you."

"No problem, Gramps," I reassured him.

I walked over to the stone and felt my eyes welling up. I gently placed the marigold over her spot. I took a few minutes and then said, "So, I couldn't help but pick this beauty for you, a courageous heart, huh? I can see that. That is what you've taught me, Grams, boy am I lucky. I know we had our moment this morning on my walk, but I can't express enough to you how much I love you, and what a big part of my life you have been. Please make sure Grandpa and I get to Philly safe and sound tomorrow. You know how much he hates flying, but I will do my best to keep him calm. Okay I'll talk to you soon."

I walked back to the car, got in, and said to Grandpa, "Okay, it's your turn."

He got out and I watched him slowly walk over. Then I saw him break down and cry. I debated whether or not to get out and go console him, but I knew he needed to do this alone, so I decided to wait for him patiently. After a few minutes, I saw him pull his hanky out of his pocket and wipe his eyes. He kissed the rose and placed it down.

He walked over to me, and as soon as he got into the car I asked, "You okay?"

He responded, "Yes, love, it was just hard to be standing right above her, you know, but I actually feel a little weight has been lifted. I am glad we came and did this. I needed that cry, and I am not ashamed to admit it."

I leaned over and gave him a hug and said, "Of course you don't need to be ashamed, never ashamed, real men aren't afraid to cry, anyway."

He smiled and said, "Alright, Willow, let's get going. We have a big day tomorrow."

We both took a deep breath, and as we were pulling out of the parking lot to the cemetery, across a beautiful sunset sky, I saw a star shoot right across it.

I blurted out, "Oh, my God, Grandpa, did you see that? What are the chances?"

He smiled at me and said, "I sure did."

I said, "It was Grandma! I know it, letting us know she heard us."

He didn't answer me, but again grabbed my hand and squeezed it. I let it be, and just looked up above me and silently mouthed the words, "Thank you."

# Chapter 40

THE FLIGHT WAS SMOOTH SAILING. My dad picked us up and we headed toward the retirement community to see my mom and make sure that Grandpa's stuff arrived okay. If you haven't figured it out by now, my grandfather is quite particular about where he likes his things placed, so we promised him we would stop by.

When we pulled in I saw a big sign that said, "Welcome to The Hills, a unique living experience."

My father said, "Dad, isn't it beautiful here? It's like we're in the country. It's so peaceful and quiet. Do you see the horses over there?"

My grandpa tried to crack a smile to seem enthused, but I knew he was not feeling so thrilled at the moment.

I placed my hand on his shoulder and said, "I told you it's going to be okay, I promise, you know that."

He said, "Yes, honey, I do know."

My dad said, "You're going to like it here, Dad. We made sure you had a corner room on the quietest hall."

Grandpa said, "Thanks, I am so lucky to have you all."

We walked in the main entrance, and to the left I saw a beautiful library full of tons of books, and to my right, I saw a game room where two men were playing a game of chess.

I said, "Oo-h-h, look Gramp, they have a chess room. You love chess!" He smiled at me. We walked down a long hall or two to get to Grandpa's room. When we arrived, my mother was there, unpacking some boxes.

We walked in, "Hi, guys! Dad your furniture just arrived. So, I know the place looks full of stuff right now, but we will fix it up for you in no time."

He nodded and didn't say anything. He kissed my mom hello, and started to walk around. He walked into the bathroom and then walked out saying, "I don't like the shower curtain. It's too dark, I like plain white." No surprise. I looked at my mom and roll my eyes.

She said, "Okay, Dad, we will get you plain white. Go check out your closet. It is really nice."

I was thinking he could give a crap about the closet, but he walked in to appease her, anyway.

I pulled my mom aside and said, "You know, this is going to take a little time."

"Yes, Willow, I know my father better than you think. I am just trying to lighten him up a little."

I said, "Of course, I know you know Grandpa. It's just that you haven't been with him over the last two days. He's nervous."

He came out and nodded his head again. I knew he was not saying much because he was trying to take it all in with a reality check.

He said, "Yes, the closet space is great. I am not sure if I have enough of my Hanes T shirts and tightie-whities to fill it up, but I will make it work." He winked at me.

We all spent about an hour unpacking, and decided we were hungry for lunch. My mom said, "Hey, Dad, let's go try the café they have here, I heard they have a great corn beef special. I know it's the only sandwich you will eat besides turkey, and yes, they have that, too."

He said, "Is the turkey fresh? 'Cause you know I hate that wet processed stuff." My mom rolled her eyes and said, "Ah, yeah, Dad. I think the turkey is fresh, not that wet and rubbery kind you hate." He agreed and we went off to have lunch.

The staff was very friendly. The food was pretty decent, and the turkey, thank God, was roasted and not processed. After lunch, we thought my grandpa had had enough for one day, between the flight and taking in his new living arrangements, so we took him home to my parents' house. I decided to go home with them, to get my car and some extra clothes that I had left there, before I headed over to my sister's. I couldn't wait to see my nephews again. I kissed my grandpa goodbye, and told him that I would be back tomorrow to take him back to the Hills to help him finish unpacking and setting up.

As soon as I got in my car, I called Will. He picked up on second ring.

"Hi, how was your trip?"

"My flight was okay, but I'm exhausted. It has been a long day so far. I am so psyched to get to my sister's, take a shower, see my nephews, and just chill."

He said, "I hear 'ya. So, not even a chance I could stop by and see your pretty face tonight?"

I said, "Ah-h-h, forgive me. I am so wiped out! Can I rain check you tomorrow? As a matter of fact, I have a better idea. How about I come see your place tomorrow night, since I have never been?"

He jokingly said, "Sounds great. I'll start cleaning now, and how about I make you dinner?"

I answered, "Okay, nothing fancy."

He said, "How about some burgers?"

"Sounds good - send the directions to my email."

"You got it, and Willow, I'm glad you're home. God, I like the sound of that, to be able to now say, 'you are home.'"

I laughed, "Me, too Will, me, too."

I got to my sister's, and as soon as I walked in I heard, "Wiwwow, Wiwwow, is that you?"

Jack came running toward me, grabbed my hand, and said, "Come, Wiwwow, come see what I made you this time."

He pulled me into the playroom and he showed me a picture he drew of what I thought was a caterpillar on one side, and a butterfly on another. There was a sun with three rays sticking out with a smiley face in the middle, which I had taught him to make. I told him that the sun always smiles.

I said, "Aw-w-w, Jack. Thank you for this beautiful picture! Is this what I think it is? A caterpillar and a butterfly?"

He said, "Uh-huh, and you know why I made it?"

I guessed, "Um-m-m, because you know how much Aunt Willow loves butterflies?"

He said, "Yep, and I learned in school that caterpiwars turn into butterfwies.' Still having a hard time pronouncing his l's.

I said, "How did you get so smart?"

He lifted his shoulders and said, "I don't know, but you know what else I think?'

I asked, "What's that?"

He answered, "That you are now a butterfwy."

My heart melted onto his coloring station. I had no idea that a three year old could use terminology that a metaphoric mind like mine could conceive, but there is a reason that kids say the funniest and sometimes profound things at times.

So, I responded, "Thanks, lovey, you are the best! Yes, I was a caterpillar who just turned into a butterfly."

I heard my sister come down the stairs holding Max on her hip, "Hey, Willow's here! Did Jack show you what he made you?"

I smiled, "He sure did, your bright and poetic son. I think he might be more genetically like me than you."

She handed Max to me, to whom I gave a squeeze and a kiss. She laughed and said, "Yes. Jack's very creative and sensitively sweet like his Aunt Willow. Come on. I'll show you to your room. I completely cleaned out the closet, so you'll have plenty of space for your stuff."

"Thanks so much, Carla, I can't thank you enough. I hope I'm not putting you and Marcus out."

She said, "Of course not. What are sisters for? As I mentioned before, you can stay as long as you like. Don't worry, there will plenty of times we'll need you to baby sit, as a thank you."

I said, "Of course, and I will - anytime."

# Chapter 41

THE NEXT DAY, I WOKE up and headed right over to meet my grandpa and Mom at the Hills to continue setting up his apartment. The community is so large. I got a little lost when I got there. I asked a woman with bells hanging on her walker which way to Section C, and she happily pointed the way. Every which way I walked, everyone had a smile on their face, and I could hear laughter behind me, too. Grandma Lu would have liked it here. This place felt right, and I was glad that we had chosen it. We spent the majority of the afternoon finishing up Grandpa's apartment. I told my parents and Grandpa that I wanted to get home to shower in enough time to prep for Will's.

My mom said, "When are we going to get to meet this guy?"

I replied, "When I feel ready. Okay, gotta run. Love 'ya. Bye."

I rushed home, got myself showered, and grabbed a bottle of wine from Carla's stash so I didn't have to stop along the way. I decided to wear my comfy sweat suit.

As I was walking out, Carla said, "So, should I expect you to come home, or will tonight be a sleep-over?"

I laughed and said, "Good question. Um-m-m, how about I text you later and let you know so you don't worry? But, if I think I'm comfortable enough to stay, I probably will."

She said, "Sounds good. And yes, you should stay if it feels right."

I nodded, and I was on my way. The directions he gave me were so-so and I got lost a little, but somehow figured out my way. I pulled up to his house, and was happy to see that it was a modest ranch-style house. I could tell it was older and that he had fixed it up a lot.

I popped my bubblegum into my mouth, and knocked on his door. He opened it, picked me up, and gave me a great big hug.

He said, "What, did you get lost?"

I said, "Um-m-m, yeah. Your directions sucked."

He laughed, "What? I am the king of giving perfect directions! I have never gotten anybody lost before - not that I have had much company."

I jokingly said, "Well, you got this queen lost on the way to the castle, and what a cute castle it is."

He said, "I know the walls are bare, and it's not that fancy, but it's just me and it works for me."

I said, "Will, it's perfect, and it looks like you've done an incredible job. I am fully impressed."

"Thanks, it took many late nights of working on it with a few of my buddies, but I am proud to say, I did most of it myself."

I nodded, "Very nice work."

He pulled me close and said, "Come here, you. I have missed you."

We started making out right away. He pulled me onto his couch, and before I knew it, clothing was already coming off. Not what I expected within the first five minutes, but hey, I figured if it felt right, just go for it. And I did.

When we were all finished, he said, "God, I have missed you."

I responded, "You, too."

He said, "Are you hungry?"

I answered, "I am now."

He got up, put his cute cargo shorts on, and said, "Why don't you open up that bottle of wine? I'm going to start the grill. Hey, while you're at it, go pick out some music. I have a ton of CDs - put something in."

I asked, "What are you in the mood to hear?"

"Surprise me."

I popped open the bottle of wine, and went back into his living room. As my eyes roamed across his collection of CDs, I smiled, now knowing we had a ton in common with music. I saw Van Morrison. Perfect. I popped in the CD, and played one of my favorite songs, "Tupelo Honey." I turned it up so he could hear it on the patio. I walked outside and handed him his glass of wine.

I toasted him and said, "Here's to good company and new beginnings with great music."

He paused and said, "Ah-h-h, good choice. I have a confession to make. I played this song the other day on my iPod and it reminded me of you."

I blushed and said, "Aw-w, you're sweet."

And he said, "Not as sweet as tupelo honey - like you."

I got up from the chair and kissed him. As I sat and watched him simply flip burgers, I thought to myself how comfortable I was, and realized how much I was falling for this guy. I hoped to have many BBQs with him in the future.

After dinner, we lay on the coach and I snuggled up to him. He said, "I know it's like your second night back and all, but do you want to just stay over? I mean, you had some wine and should probably stay anyway."

I smiled and said, "Aw-w-w, you don't have to throw the whole wine part into the mix to convince me to stay. I will stay because I want to stay."

I texted my plan to Carla. Then, we got into bed, and he held me tight. I never wanted him to let go.

I got up early and was ready to get going and shower, for sure, since I didn't bring a change of clothes. Will saw me get out of bed and put my clothes back on.

He said, "Where do you think you're going so soon? Come back to bed."

I was so used to bailing and running away in my past relationships, or trying to play tough to make the boys wonder, that I was not used to hanging around so much.

I responded, "I feel yucky and want to get home and shower. And I promised my grandpa I would be there to spend his official first day at his facility."

He said, "What's ten more minutes going to do? Besides, I am sure Grandpa would understand. Come on, come back and lie with me."

I surrendered and crawled back in. Our snuggling led to a touch and embrace here and there, and before I knew it, we were getting busy. I felt really connected to him - more so than ever this time.

No sooner had I gotten comfortable than I heard my cell phone ringing. I looked up at the clock and realized that it's probably Carla wondering about my evening, or my grandfather calling to find out when I planned on coming over.

I said, "As much as I could lie here with you all day, and I could, I better get going - my grandpa needs me."

He said, "I understand, of course. Can I see you again this week?"

I kissed him and said, "Definitely."

We got dressed, and he walked me to my car and gave me another passionate kiss. As he looked into my eyes, I almost felt like he wanted to say "I love you," which I know would be much too soon. But what a cool feeling, I thought, that I could feel his love for me already. As I pulled away, I wondered if part of me felt like I was in love with him already, too.

I spent the rest of the week helping Grandpa to settle in, and looking for apartments. I decided that I wanted to rent an apartment not too far from my grandfather, so if he needed anything, I would be right around the corner. I ended up finding one that I loved with a lease that started in a few weeks. My dad said he would come with me to check it out, and help by co-signing it since he was going to help me pay for part of each month's rent, anyway. This was, at least, until I started working.

Speaking of working, I knew that I had to make some sort of decision about what I wanted to do sooner rather than later. I had a habit of doing a number on myself when I was not working. So I actually decided just for now till I figure things out I would ask for my job back as a part-time waitress at the breakfast joint I worked at before I left for Florida. Fortunately, when I called my old boss Ben, he happily agreed to give me a few shifts.

# Chapter 42

So I SPENT THE NEXT few weeks working at the restaurant, and hanging with Grandpa, Will, and my nephews. My parents asked if they could meet him, which I thought I was ready to do. My sister decided to have brunch at her house and invite everyone over. Will told me he was a little nervous about meeting them, but I reassured him that they were easy to get along with. I told my mom to dress very casually, and to try not to drill him with too many questions. Tough request for a mom, but she promised.

The doorbell rang and it was Will. I kissed him hello and said, "Are you ready?"

Jack came running out, "Wiw, Wiw, come with me and meet everybody," and again grabbed Will's hand. He pulled Will into the living room where everyone was sitting. My mom stood up first and said, "Well, well it's about time we met you, and it is a pleasure. I am Willow's mom, Janice, and this is my husband, Stephen."

I walked him over to my grandpa and said, "This is one of my favorite people, Grandpa Lex."

He shook hands with everyone. I could see his face was a little red.

My grandpa said, "It is great to finally meet you. Willow has told me so much about you. It's nice to finally put a face with you."

Will says, "It's nice to meet you all, too, and Willow has told me so much about you all as well. I almost feel like I know you already." Good line.

We all sat down to our spread of bagels and lox. My dad was thrilled to talk with Will about construction and building. My mom asked a couple of questions about his family. It was easier than I anticipated. When Will excused himself to go to the bathroom, everyone gave me the thumbs up.

After brunch, Will and I decided to catch an afternoon movie. As we got into the car, I said, "So, what do you think?"

He said, "They're great, very down to earth. You're like both of them. I see a little more of your father in you, but definitely your mom, too."

I said, "Yeah, I am sort of a mix. So, when do I get to meet your family?"

He got quiet and said, "Well, maybe soon, my mom is a little on the quirky side and Dad….."

I stopped him and said, "I like quirky. I don't care, I want to meet them soon."

He nodded and kissed my cheek. I got a text message from my mom when I got out of the movie theater saying, they really liked him. I was happy.

I spent all day Saturday moving into my new apartment. Will had to do a side job in the morning, but came over to help me throughout the afternoon. He helped me hang pictures and unpack boxes. I set up my bed, and he came in to lay down with me. He told me he had to run to his car for a second because he forgot something. He came back two minutes later and handed me a card. I slowly opened it up with anticipation. It had a beautiful picture of a sunset and when you opened it up, it had Louis Armstrong singing "What a Wonderful World". He wrote inside, *Just Because I know you love this song and thought it would put a smile on your face. Good luck with the new apartment.*

I actually teared up and said, "This is one of the best cards I ever got."

Right then and there I knew I was falling for this man. I said, "Thank you so much for this, I love it. You are amazing."

He kissed me and said, "I love you."

I felt it in every ounce of my body, it was the first time he said it. I froze and wished I could have said it back, but instead, kissed him passionately and we ended up making love. I was trying not to overanalyze why I didn't say it back, and hoping he wasn't either. It wasn't that I didn't love him, I just wasn't used to saying it.

He stayed over with me that night, and we hung around Sunday morning. As soon as he left, I called Carla.

She picked up right away, "So, how was your first night at your place?"

I said, "Great, Carla. Will stayed with me and he told me he loved me for the first time."

She said, "And, did you say it back?"

I replied, "No. Shit I wish I did, but I froze. You know me, I just …"

She interrupted me and said, "Willow, you're just what? Stop holding back and start trusting that you can love. He's crazy about you, and I can tell you are crazy about him. Stop being nervous and just say it! He's not going to leave."

I asked, "How do you know?"

She said, "Just a hunch, besides, we've talked about this. At some point in your life, Willow, you have to take a leap of faith. I feel like you were meant to meet him for a reason. So, how did he react when you didn't say it back?"

"He didn't say anything, we started getting busy, so I just let him know in that way."

Then she said, "Yes, Willow, I know, but at some point you can say 'I love you' and have sex, and not be afraid that he is going to use you. You're not a teenage girl anymore."

I said, "I know, I know. Okay, next time I feel right in the moment, I will say it."

I couldn't sleep much that evening. I wondered why I had difficulty saying the words *I love you*. I began twisting, and turning, and thinking, and doing some more thinking about everything in my life that felt great. But, soon enough, I started to find a way to sabotage it in my head. I remembered my conversation about that worthiness thing with Katie, my therapist. I tried to tell myself *no more*. Then I started to wonder and question if I really loved Will. I found myself nitpicking things about him, and I wondered if he could or could not be right for me. Then my mind went to why I hadn't shared a lot of my angel stories, or Agape stories. I wondered if was I worried about what he would think about all of my spirituality, and could I really tell him all about my love for God and what I have learned? H-m-m-m..

I decided once again to think really hard about all the reasons why I was crazy about this man. I took a deep breath, and at four a.m., tried to meditate. As Katie recommended, I asked my higher self what was going on, and what would it like me to know. What came to me in my meditation was that I needed to stop being such a sabotager, and to try to not project my fears or high expectations onto Will, and to just love him. All I kept hearing in my head, almost like a mantra, was *You are safe to love this man, You are safe to love this man, You are safe to love this man..........*" Somehow, ten minutes later, I was able to lie back down and fall asleep.

# Chapter 43

MY NEXT FEW WEEKS OF work at the restaurant were great. I had a lot of locals tell me that I seemed much happier and relaxed. I was getting much better tips than I used too. I also noticed that my connection with the customers in general was more agape-ish and less judgmental. I was growing more as a person.

Something miraculous happened to me on my way home from work. I could not believe my eyes when another car with a plate that read AGAPE77 pulled in front of me! I was all smiles and goose bumps and said, "Holy shit, how do you do that?" For a second, I wondered *what are the numbers for*? And then I realized, oh, my God - 77 is one of my favorite lessons in the Course in Miracles. The lesson was "You are entitled to miracles." And this was a miracle. In fact, another miracle. I was so excited that I decided to call Will right away to tell him my Agape stories. If he thought I was nuts, so be it, but even a non-believer had to admit there was something to this.

He picked up on the second ring and I told him the stories. He didn't respond much but said, "Hey, that's pretty wild. I don't know, guess a weird coincidence."

I said, "There's no such thing."

He said, "Maybe you're right, wait, that is weird!'

I asked, "What's weird?'

"A car just pulled in front of me whose license plate says, 'KNOWGOD'

I said, "You're pulling my leg. Are you serious? Because that is what Agape is all about."

He assured me, "Yes, I am serious. Wow, that's pretty cool."

I said, "See? No coincidence. I'm always reminded, in some mystical ways, of what life is all about."

He said again, "I guess. Cool, so you want to meet me for dinner tonight?"

I said, "Sure, I'm kind of in the mood for sushi. Are you down with that?'

He replied, "Sounds good. I know an awesome place in between us. I'll text you the address soon."

As we hung up part of me was a little disappointed that he wasn't more excited about my Agape experience, but then my heart thought *how cool is this*. Maybe it was a little boost from God to share a moment with Will about His message. I also knew he wasn't a student, like Lucas or Ed, of Agape's meaning, and that I shouldn't hold it against him.

Speaking of, I decided to call Luke on my way to dinner to tell him the incredible story. I got his voicemail, but left a detailed message and told him that I missed him and to tell Lorraine that I said hello and to call me soon. I knew he would get a kick out of this story. I also decided it might be time to call that lovely woman, Marisol, whom I met on the airplane. I remembered that she runs a local Course in Miracles group. This way, I would have more like-minded people to share my stories with.

As I was on my way to work I was thinking about how much I missed my best friend from college, Amelia. She and I became like sisters, and have remained close over the years. I just wished we lived closer so we could see one another more. She now lives in Danbury, Connecticut. We have a lot in common with fears and anxieties. Since our freshman year of college, we always found a way to reassure one another when we felt nervous about something especially related to our bodies. I can't begin to tell you how many times we talked one another out of not having cancer, brain tumors, potential heart attacks, etcetera. We're both two neurotic nellies, with hearts of gold and creative minds. We learned, over the years, that when we felt anxious or obsessive about something unpleasant, we should put our energies into our creative juices.

Amelia is a part-time schoolteacher for children with special reading needs. Her passion, aside from helping children, was to have her own line of cards one day. She must have felt my energy, for the next thing I knew my cell phone rang, and it was she.

I answered, "Oh, my God, Amelia! I was literally just thinking about you, and was going to call you but wasn't sure if you were already at work." We hadn't talked in a while, so I was super excited to hear from her.

She said, "Hey, you. Yes, normally I would be working, but Ryan's got a cold right now, and a high fever, so I'm taking him to the doctor. He's going to be fine right?"

I said, "Yes, Amelia, I promise he's going to be fine. It's just a cold and a fever, my nephews get them all the time. So, I promise, it's not anything else scary you've concocted in your mind. Remember what I said when your little muffin was born? I said to try not to project your own fears onto him with every ailment he has! But, don't beat yourself up. It's the nature of the anxiety beast, and this is a habit we can break, it's just going to take some time for us to grow out of it."

She laughed and said, "I know, I know. You know me so well. Alright, so I swear I did not call just to get your reassurance. Willow, guess what?"

"What?"

"So, I decided to take your advice and make that line of cards I've been talking and talking about forever. Over the last two months, Ryan has started to smile non-stop, so I came up with a nickname for him 'SmyRy.' I don't know where it came from but one Saturday afternoon, when I put him down for a nap, I couldn't stop making cards, and thinking about his smile. I came up with the name for my line of cards, SmyRy, and Willow, the best part? I took a chance and went to some of the local gift stores here in Danbury, asking if they would be interested in trying to sell a few, and they're beginning to sell like hot cakes now."

I stopped her and said, "Oh, my God, Amelia, that is awesome! I'm so happy for you. I love the name by the way, it's cute and catchy. I knew this would happen, and the best part is that it was your son's inspirational smile that helped make it so."

She said, "Thanks, Willow, you were right. You always said that there's nothing like my son's love to bring out my creative energy. So, I designed an amazing line of cards with sweet pictures of flowers, butterflies, nature stuff, and fun silly faces for boys and girls."

"Aw-w-w, Amelia, it sounds so great. I'm a little jealous - you know my dream is to have my poetry framed and selling in stores, too."

She replied, "I do know, so Willow, what are you waiting for? Why don't you do it, start putting your poems on beautiful paper, and frame them, and see if they'll sell at local stores. You never know. What do you always say to me, Miss Queen of Quotes? 'Faith is taking the first step, even when you don't see the whole staircase.' I love that Martin Luther King quote! I have it hanging up in my classroom. Seriously, Willow, try it."

As she said it, a car pulled next to me whose license plate said CREATE. I laughed so hard.

She said, "What's so funny?'

I chuckled, "Well, you know how I've told you before about my signs with license plates? One just pulled up beside me that says, CREATE.

She laughed back, "See, Willow, it's a sign. Go create it. I have a better idea, why don't you send me one of your masterpieces, and next time I go to one of the card stores, I'll tell them that I have a close friend who's interested in starting her own line of framed poetry and see if they're interested. You have nothing to lose."

I lit up at the thought, "Thanks, Amelia! Maybe I will do that."

She said, "You definitely should. So, change of subject, how are things going with Will?"

I said, "Good. He told me he loves me, but I haven't said it back yet."

She asked, "Well, do you love him?"

I said, "I think I do."

She said, "Then why are you so afraid of telling him? Willow, we talked about this. You know about not holding back anymore, not playing games, especially with this one, he sounds great."

I agreed, "I know, I know. Carla said the same thing. I'm trying, Amelia. It's hard for me - I mean, you know my history with heartbreak."

She said, "Yes, I do. But, I also know you well enough to know that at some point you have to believe you deserve to be loved by a good man, and trust that you won't get hurt."

I took a deep breath and said, "I know you're right. You always know what to say to make me feel better."

She said, "Likewise. Okay, I just pulled up to the doctor's office. So good to catch up, and next time we talk, I expect to be calling you to thank you for sending me your amazing poem, and for me to be telling you how proud I am of you for telling Will that you love him, too."

I laughed, "You got it, and in an hour when you come out of the doctor's, I expect you to send me a text message letting me know that Ryan is fine, and just has a little cold."

She laughed, too, "Ha-ha! Okay, talk to you soon. Love 'ya lots."

I said, "Love 'ya lots, too."

We hung up, and I found my mental wheels starting to roll in my mind about her poem idea. I begin to daydream about a heartbroken woman walking into a card store seeing my poem and tearing up because it brought inspiration to her heart.

# Chapter 44

I FELT, NOW MORE THAN ever, that I wanted to write. As I was on my way home from work, I thought that I could really use some fresh air. I decided to bring my journal and take a walk at a local park not too far from my apartment. I had kept meaning to stop by - so I did.

As I pulled up to the park, I noticed a long and beautiful trail that led down a hill to something I could not see yet. As I got out of my car, I was curious to notice three beautiful birds above me singing an unfamiliar song. I took a deep breath, it was now the beginning of fall, and I was happy to be home where the season was changing.

Autumn is my favorite season. It always felt like the new beginning of something for me. I continued to walk the trail with anticipation as to how far it went, and what was down that hill. With each step, I was reminded how much I loved being in nature and how it fed my soul. As I got to the top of the hill, I looked below me, and to my heart's delight there it was - sitting by itself. Its branches were swaying in the wind like a dancer moving her arms free from any fears. It was perhaps the most beautiful and innocent willow tree I had ever seen. I was so drawn to its beauty that I couldn't get down that hill fast enough to get up close and personal with it, no pun intended.

As I stood face to face with this tree, all of a sudden, something inside of me said, *have a seat sweet one.* I gently sat under this willow tree, and closed my eyes for a few minutes, and began to meditate. As I took deep breaths slowly in and out, something else inside me said, *This is now your spot to do as you may, let your inspiration come through your heart.* I began to fill up with joy as to how much love I was feeling, and then Ed's poem popped into my head, specifically the line that says, "I hear you sweet Willow tree, as you whisper wisdom and light." Then I sat for a few more minutes and just breathed and felt at peace. I continued to think about the changes I had begun to finally make in my life. I felt at home with this tree, and decided it would be my new spot, a wonderful escape from the loudness of the outside world. I thanked God for bringing me to it, and promised myself to come back again soon.

On my way home, I decided to call Marisol and tell her I was back in town. She answered on the second ring, "Hello?"

"Hi, Marisol, it's Willow from the airplane, remember me?"

"Oh, of course I remember you! How are you doing?"

"I'm okay, thank you. Just trying to get a little more adjusted to my new life now that I'm back in the Philly area."

"Oh, you've decided to move back here, huh?"

"Well, it felt like the right time, so I've been here for a little while and think it might be time to join a new Course in Miracles group. Are you still running one?"

"Well, yes, as a matter of fact I have a group this Sunday at one o'clock. Would you be available to come? We would love to have you."

"Oh, Marisol, yes. That would be great. Can you email the address? You still have my email, yes?"

"I do. I'll send it to you later today, and Willow, I am so delighted to have you in town. Our group could use a soul like yours."

I laughed, "Thanks, Marisol, I look forward to seeing you soon, and by the way, you were right about the Marianne Williamson book, it was amazing. In fact, so great I want to learn more about this course."

She responded, "See, I told you so, well I think you have come to the right person to continue your journey. Look forward to seeing you, too."

It was late afternoon on Saturday, and I knew that I was supposed to head over to Will's for the night, but just didn't feel like it. I was having an off day. I was about to get my period, and was grumpy and wanting to be alone. I decided to call him and tell him I was not feeling so good, and let's do it tomorrow night instead.

His phone rang and he picked up and said, "Hey, I was just about to call you. What time are you coming over?"

I responded, "Hi, well, do you think we could rain check until tomorrow? I am just not feeling so good today, and think I would rather just chill alone."

He was silent and said, "Oh, is everything okay? You sound a little distant."

I replied, "Yeah, I am just having one of those off days, and my company would not be so fabulous tonight, so let's again do it tomorrow night."

He said, "Okay, if that's what you want, but I'd like to say one thing."

I responded, "Okay, what's that?"

He said, "Well, I just want you to know, Willow that you don't have to hide from me when you are not feeling great all the time. Sometimes, I feel like when you get in these moods, and this is not the first time, that you end up pushing me away."

I interrupted him, "Hold on, Will. When have I been like this before?"

He answered, "Last week, and it doesn't matter, specifically. My point is, I don't want you to be afraid to show me your vulnerable side. I know nobody is perfect. I am the first to admit it. So, you can talk to me. I want you to know I'm here for you."

My heart was a little relieved to hear him say that, but my mind, which was defensive by nature, automatically said, "I appreciate what you are saying, but let's not overanalyze this. Sometimes, I do just get in these moods, and I'm sorry. Sometimes, I just want to be left alone. I am not going to lie, Will, sometimes I can be a little complicated. So please don't take this personally."

He took a deep sigh, "Okay, I hear what you are saying. It's just that I care about you so much, and maybe it's my own insecurity, but it's hard for me not to take it personally."

I said, "I'm sorry if you are taking personally, but again, sometimes, when I get like this, I just need to chill. I'll feel more like myself again tomorrow, so let's just talk tomorrow."

He sighed again, "Okay, if that's what you want. If you change your mind, or want to talk, call me."

"I will, have a good night. I'll call you tomorrow afternoon after my group."

He asked, "What group?"

I felt a little nervous to say because I was afraid he would judge me, but then I thought this is who I am, so I better let it show now.

I said, "It's called a Course in Miracles. I joined a group when I was living in Florida, and it really helped heal me from a lot of negative stuff. It's not a religious group or anything. It's a group for people like myself who like to look at life from an alternative perspective, so actually, the more I think about it, the better the timing is, they always get me out of a funky mind set. It reminds you of God's love for yourself and for others." I paused and he didn't say anything. "Will, are you there?"

He said, "Yeah, I'm here, just listening to what you were saying. Sounds cool. Okay, well, I hope it helps you feel better, and call me afterwards. Goodnight."

We hung up and right away I was analyzing whether or not he thought I might be not so perfect, or kooky. I took a deep breath, and again decided that if I was going to have a future relationship with this guy, then he does, indeed, need to know all of who I am, and this course is most certainly a big part of who I am.

I crawled into bed, and tried to fall asleep, but once again my mind started to go into overdrive about my future.

After twisting and turning until the wee hours of the night, I finally gave up, got down on one knee again, and said, "Dear God, please let me live a life of feeling worthy of having good things, and please do not let me continue to push others away or sabotage things just when they are beginning to feel right. I see myself starting to do this with Will and I don't want to do this. Tomorrow when I go to this new Course in Miracles group, could you possibly help to address this issue and bring me some peace of mind? I love you, goodnight. P.S. Could you please send my angels to help me fall asleep now? Thank you. Goodnight."

I got back into bed placed my hands over my heart like Katie had taught me. I took a deep breath in and out and something inside of me gently said, *You are indeed worthy my dear Willow. You are a beautiful light to this world. Now close your eyes and breathe a calming peace into your heart.* Next thing I knew, I was able to fall asleep.

When I woke up, I felt a little badly about my conversation with Will last night. I decided to text him and wrote *sorry about last night. I feel a little better this morning. Look forward to seeing you.* Five minutes later, he texted me back and wrote, *Glad to hear it. Have a good day. Call me later.*

I got to Marisol's on time. I knocked on the door and a large man with the most beautiful blue eyes answered the door and said, "Hello, I'm Richard, but you can call me Big Rich. You must be new."

I replied, "Yes, I am new. Hello, I'm Willow, nice to meet you Big Rich." I said the "Big Rich" part in a hesitant way.

He jokingly said, "Aw-w-w, don't let my pleasantly plump figure scare 'ya. I'm fully comfortable with who I am," as he rubbed his belly like a big Buddha statue.

I half giggled and said, "Well then, Big Rich, I must be in the right place. I hear this is the place where miracles happen, which involves learning to love yourself for who you are and feel comfortable in your skin. Yes?"

He smiled and said, "Yes, Willow, you have come to the right place. Now, follow me."

I followed him into a quaint living room with about seven rocking chairs set up in a circle. Four of them were filled with friendly faces, one being Marisol. As soon as she made eye contact with me, she lit up and got up to hug me.

"Willow, how are you? I am so glad you could make it!"

"Yes, thank you, Marisol. Me, too."

She grabbed my hand and introduced me to an older African American couple who reminded me a little of Luke and Lorraine.

She said, "This is Irving and his lovely wife, Ilene."

I smiled and said, "Lovely to meet you," and shook their hands. Then I saw a tall lanky-looking woman with a bright pink headband on, and mint green and polka dot pink socks, stand up with an innocent smile.

Marisol said, "And this is Bethenny."

I said, "Nice to meet you, too, Bethenny."

Marisol then pointed to Richard and said, "You have obviously met Big Rich. He is the jokester of the group."

I smiled, "Yes, I did."

She continued, "Well, we are still waiting for a few others, but they may not make it, so let's get started and if they show, they show."

As I eased into my rocking chair I felt at home already.

Marisol said, "Well, welcome everybody, and glad you could make it. Let's give a brief introduction as to how we got to the Course, and then we will get started."

I listened carefully as each person told his story. I was amazed at no matter how much pain we as humans go through, we all want the same thing, which is to be shown another way. I was particularly fascinated by Big Rich's story. He said that he grew up in a very religious house and attended a strict Catholic school where he was constantly frightened of a fear of punishment by God. This somehow led him to develop addictive behaviors such as alcohol and eating as a way to soothe all of his confusion. He made the joke at one point, saying that he is now a "recovering Catholic," and knows that he will not go to hell anymore for his behaviors or whatever he chooses to say or do.

When it came to my turn for answering, I said, "Hello, I'm Willow. I came to the Course a few months ago when I was living in Florida. I, too, was going through a hard time physically, mentally, emotionally, you name it, and was looking for another way to find peace, for everything else I was doing was not quite working the way I had hoped. So, a friend recommended that I come, and I did, and was fascinated and relieved after my first group. So, now I am back in Philly. I was pleasantly surprised to have met Marisol on an airplane. No coincidence that I did, but I'm so happy about that. And now here I am in my life, starting a new job, and I'm in a relationship with a nice man. I'm trying to get to a place where I can just rest into it all, and feel good and positive about my life. I want to stop looking for reasons to sabotage myself, you know, sort of feel more worthy for the things I have, if that makes sense."

Marisol placed her hand on top of mine and said, "It sure does, and I think today's lesson will make more sense to you in relation to what you just shared."

I nodded back with a smile.

Marisol told us to open our books to Lesson 44. She then said, "Okay, so today we will be reviewing Lesson 44 which states, 'God is the light in which I see.' This lesson is an invitation to allow God to reach you, to turn on the switch in your heart, and lessen the darkness in your mind. The lesson reminds us that you cannot see in darkness on God's will, which is to see the loving beings we are. Too often, I think we forget that God resides within us. For the Course says, and I will quote it, 'In order to see, you must realize that the light is within, not without.'"

She paused and said, "So, Willow, this is to remind you that you are already made of light and God's pure love. If you could try to become an observer of your thoughts, let them pass by when you feel them heading toward negative or dark. And, in your moments of reflection, know that God goes with you wherever you go. This may allow your ego mind to settle down more. The Course always stresses that God knows your real thoughts. You see, Willow, truth is the light in which you see. Your heart knows the truth."

I smiled and said, "Thank you, Marisol, for explaining it so well. Especially the last thing you just said - my grandmother always told me that my heart knows the truth."

She smiled and said, "Well, your grandmother was right, and remember, that is where God resides. So, in conclusion, the most important thing to also know is that because you are made of God's light, you are automatically entitled to know you are worthy of love on all levels. The key, once you remember, is to then also apply it with all of those you encounter." Again I nodded, as I understood.

We continued to talk for a while, discussing the lesson. I decided that I really liked this group a lot, and wanted to come back again. When it was over, everybody hugged. Marisol told me there was another group next week, and asked if I would like to come back. I nodded *for sure,* and thanked her again.

As I walked out of her house I noticed a quote hanging up in a frame along her wall that said, *"My real PhD is in LOVE."* I laughed, remembering the story she shared with me on the airplane about realizing she didn't need her actual PhD, after all of her years of hard work learning how to understand love. As I got into my car and pulled away, I knew I was in the right place. What was interesting was that there were, easily, at least five cars that pulled in front of me all with the number 44 somehow written on their plates. Then it was a big yellow school bus, #44. Then, it became even stranger when I went to stop at the local deli on the way home to pick up my sandwich. My order number was #44. Coincidence? Not even close. I realized that Lesson 44 was to be remembered.

# Chapter 45

ON THE WAY TO MY car, I realized I had forgotten to check my mail that morning. I walked over to my box, and as I opened it, a large pink card that barely fit in it, stood out, and a little package. As I pulled it out, I read on the front, "Miss Willow Mazer and Guest." Wedding invitation? But, from whom? As I went to open the back of the envelope, I saw that the return address was Florida. I opened it up and couldn't believe my eyes! It said, "Please join Trisha and Robert in exchanging of vows." Oh, my God, Trish and Robert were getting married! Holy shit! I couldn't wait to get the scoop.

I then opened the other package, and it was a book from Luke. The title of the book was <u>Spiritual Liberation</u> written by the man who started the Agape center. He added a little note saying, "Hope you are well. Thought you would enjoy this book. It will keep you on your Agape toes. I miss you, Willow! Love, Lucas."

On the way to Will's, I decided to call Lucas first to thank him. I got his voicemail again, but left a message thanking him, and telling him how much I was looking forward to reading the book. I then called Trisha. She picked up. "Hello?"

"Trish, it's Willow. Congratulations!"

"Oh, my gosh, Willow! So good to hear from you, thank you."

"Trisha, please do tell, how did it happen?"

"Well, honey, you were right, he is the one, we at least one of my ones. To make a long story short, one day after work I was supposed to get picked up by Tony - this guy I thought was so hot that I met outside of my hair place. Anyway, he told me he was going to pick me up for a date and he never showed up. I was so embarrassed and humiliated. The only person left was Robert, who saw me crying. So, he took my hand sat me down and said, 'Trisha, it's enough with these guys. You deserve so much more than you know.' Willow, he went on and on, saying all of these beautiful things about me as a person. My heart began to melt. He was so sweet and sincere. I finally stopped crying. He put his hand on mine, and pulled me over, and said, 'Come here, you!'

"He sat me on his lap and just held me tight in his arms. I can't explain it, Willow, but once he held me, I felt like I never wanted to let go, there was an 'at home' feeling with him I never had with any other man. It felt incredible. I have hugged Robert here and there throughout my years at the cafe, but never like this. Anyway, next thing I knew, I was looking him in the eyes and we kissed. He then confessed how much he has always loved me. Willow, right then and there, again I can't explain it, but I realized how much I really loved this man, too. I was maybe just afraid all of these years of letting someone like him love me. And, he told me, Willow, that right before you left, you mentioned to him to someday have the courage to tell me how he felt, and he finally did it."

I stopped her. "Oh, Trish, I'm so happy for you both! I always knew you would be a good match! So, how did the proposal come so soon? I mean it's only been a few months right?"

"Well, honey, after that day we were inseparable. I mean, aside from working alongside one another every day, I ended up staying at his place every night. He told me after two weeks, he wanted me to move in. I know it seems fast, but Robert and I have known one another for years, so it kind of seemed right.

"So anyway, getting to the proposal part, one day after work, Robert asked me to come take a walk on the beach and have an early picnic. It was simple, yet romantic. He brought some champagne and strawberries and some snacks. We were lying on my blanket and he said, 'Trisha, if I may speak honestly, I never thought I would ever be able to love another woman again after my first wife died. And then, there you were, you came along and made me think otherwise.

My only regret is that I have waited too long and wasted too many years not telling you how I really felt. If I knew then what I know now, meaning how much love there really is between us, I would have opened up sooner.'

"At this point, his voice started to get a little shaky, but he continued and said, 'Trisha, my point is, I don't want to waste any more time. I have never met anyone who makes me feel more alive than you. Each day I want to give you my unconditional love more and more. I know it may seem quick, but I know in my heart that I want to spend the rest of my life with you. Will you marry me?' And he pulled this beautiful round diamond out of his pocket and placed it on my finger. I cried and cried tears of joy, but I said yes. I figured what the heck, why wait? So, we are getting married. It will be small but simple. We decided to close up Dotty's for the day and do it there since that is where we met and all. His first wedding was in a hall somewhere, but he thought it would be special to do it at Dotty's, because it was his family's restaurant, as you know."

I said, "Aw-w, Trish, again I am so happy for you both. This is amazing. How did Eliza take it?"

"She said she was happy, and that she also knew all along that her daddy had a crush on me. Besides, you know, Willow, she has always sort of been like a daughter to me anyway! I love her like she is my own. So, Willow, how are you? Are you still dating that guy from the airplane?"

"Yes, I am. He's good guy."

She said, "That's great, Willow, good to hear, you deserve a good guy, too. So what do you think, honey? Do you think you could make it out here for our special day? I mean, part of the reason we're together is because you encouraged Robert to open up to me, and you helped me see that I really do deserve a man like him. So, what do you say? How about you and that nice fellow of yours come to our wedding? It's in about two months. Airfare should still be decent."

I answered, "Trish, I wouldn't miss it for the world. Let me see what Will's schedule is like, and hopefully we can do it. I know I will be there, no matter what, I will make it happen. I would love to see the two of you get married."

She gasped and said, "Oh, Willow that is great! You just made my day. I know Robert will be happy to hear it, too. We really miss you around here. It's not quite the same without you."

"Aw-w, thanks Trish. How is everybody? Do you see Ed at all?"

She laughed, "Everyone is well. Devin and Aaron are fine. Brenda is much nicer than she used to be. And Ed, honey? Well, of course I see him in his staple matching hats and watches. I think he misses you, too, for he doesn't quite connect with me and the other servers like he did with you. I think he missed the poetic talk you two had, but he is still friendly, and always tips me well. We actually invited him to the wedding, too. He and Robert are pretty close friends now."

I said, "Yes, I know he's a good tipper. I owe him a phone call, for sure. And that would be great if he comes. In the meantime, will you tell Robert and everyone else I said hello?"

"Of course I will, and see what you can do about coming. Get that boyfriend of yours to come, too. I would love to meet him."

"Will do, Trish, I'll call you soon."

As we hung up, I was so happy to know that the two of them had finally given it a chance. I then switched my thinking to wondering how Will would feel about flying out to go to this wedding with me. I hoped he would want to. I decided I was definitely going to ask him.

I tried to call Ed on the way to Will's, but got his voicemail. I missed him, and hoped he was doing well. I left him a message. I pulled up to Will's and knocked on the door. He opened it up, and gave me a big hug and a kiss.

"Hi, how are you? How was your group?"

"It was good, thank you. So, listen to this. You know the place I was working at in Florida. The breakfast place?"

He said, "Yeah, what about it?"

"Well, it turns out that the owner, Robert, and one of the servers, Trisha, are getting married. Robert had a crush on her for, like, ten years or so and finally took my recommendation to tell her how he feels. She was always into dating deadbeats who treated her like garbage, and finally she decided to try it with the man who always loved her for herself. Anyway, I just got the invitation in the mail and called her right away. I was so happy for them. She told me she insists that I come *and* with you. It's in about two months, what do you think?"

He smiled and said, "I think we could do it. Maybe we could stay with my grandparents when we go?" Not my first thought, but I am sure I can make it work.

"Um-m-m, yeah, maybe we could. I was thinking you could take either Friday or Monday off and we could make it a long weekend."

"Sounds good, let me just check my work schedule."

"Okay."

He tapped the couch cushion and told me to sit down. I sat down and he then said, "So, how are you feeling since yesterday?"

"I'm okay. I just get in those moods sometimes. I hope in the future that you will try not to take them too personally."

He nodded and said, "I will try, just want to remind you that I'm here for you."

"Thanks, I know you are."

"So, what do you say we grab some Chinese food? I'm craving wonton soup."

"Sounds great."

When we finished our sodium-filled chicken and broccoli dish, the waitress came over with our fortune cookies. I said to Will, "Oh, my favorite part. You have to pick the one that is pointing to you, and I'll take the one pointing toward me."

I couldn't believe my eyes as we slowly opened the cookies up, mine said, 'Our first and last love is ....self–love.' Will saw my eyes and said, "Well, what does it say?"

I read it to him and said, "This is so amazing considering everything that has gone on in my life over the last year. Just another reminder, wow! So, what does yours say?"

He said, "Someone you love is sitting across from you."

I blushed and said, "Really?"

He winked at me and said, "No, but I like the sound of it."

I said, "Me, too. So what does it really say?"

"Okay, it says, 'Darkness cannot drive out darkness, only light can do that.'"

I lifted my brow and said, "Wow, I guess that one is kind of deep for you, huh?"

I then realized that I thought both of these fortunes were meant for my eyes. For the Course in Miracles Lesson 44 popped right into my head again.

He said, "Well, maybe a little bit, but I still like my fortune better."

I don't know what compelled me to do it, but I got up from my side of the booth, walked over, and sat down next to him so that we were on the same side. I then whispered into his ear, "I love you." I felt sweet tingles up my arm when I said it, like a release, and happy freedom to be saying it for the first time.

He looked at me and said, "God, I'm happy to hear you say that. I love you, too." Next thing I knew, we started to make out and he said, "Okay, let's get out of here."

We went home to his place and made love.

# Chapter 46

I SPENT THE NEXT SEVERAL weeks or so in the same type of routine. Work, visit with Grandpa, hang with Will, go to Course in Miracles groups, and see my nephews. I was having moments of feeling good, and then of course, looking for reasons to not feel so good. Will and I were getting ready to take that trip to Florida next week. I was on my way home from work and once again, I began to ponder why, like my therapist Katie mentioned, did I have a worthiness limit? Couldn't I just, for once, really start to enjoy my life and feel good about my relationship with Will, and not worry if he would stop loving me, and not look for reasons to sabotage everything? I mean, really? Enough already. In the meantime, I knew I was right around the corner from my special willow tree spot that I had not been to in a few weeks. I decided that now more than ever would be a perfect time to sit there and meditate and try to relax, and try to figure out why this was showing up again.

I somehow got myself to the spot. I grabbed my journal and headed down the hill to my tree. I took a seat under it and began to cry. I ended up asking God and my higher self to please help me ease out of always looking for a reason to sabotage things, and to help me feel more loving toward myself. I closed my eyes and meditated on it for a while. I took some heart breaths and finally started to relax. And then something miraculous happened, for something inside of me gently said, *Go ahead and start writing.* I wasn't sure what it was, but I wrote down exactly what was said:

*You are worthy, my dear child, you are worthy of knowing and having this love. To look outside of yourself or to another to fulfill this love is not necessary, for I gave you everything you needed the moment you came into this world. I want you to believe that you are enough for this world, and for others, to share your love with. Your search outside yourself for the love I have already given you enough of, is like trying to tell a stranger you know how the rest of his life is supposed to be. What I mean is that you are blind to my truth – my real truth. My real truth is for you all to remember why you really came here, which was to re-member yourselves as love, and to circulate its meaning around and around again until you feel it in your hearts. Willow, I believe in you and your dreams. I want you to let your walls down now, and just trust my Agapeness in everything you do or don't decide to do in this lifetime. Willow, oh, dear Willow, just let it down, angel, just let down that wall of yours now and really trust, that I want what's best for you and that beautiful heart of yours. It's time now, Willow, to know yourself, as this love, and to give it out to this world, for isn't there a great song that says, "What the world needs now is love sweet love, it's the only thing that there's just too little of....?" So, Willow, my darling beam of light, go out there now, and sell this story of a heart-filled journey about a young woman who had once forgotten why she is here, but God somehow miraculously rocked her back into place and replaced her negative delusional thought system, and allowed her heart to speak the rest. Yes, dear one, your heart is a good place to rest. Now go out into the world and continue to share and hold the hands of millions who are looking to be reminded. I have a good idea – let's sit for a few more minutes under this Sweet Willow Tree and write a poem that might touch the hearts of these millions of people and let them know what God is really trying to say. How about we call it' Love: Your Unconditional Key'?* And the next thing I knew, I started writing this poem, which I believe was coming right from God's mouth onto my paper. This is what I wrote:

*"Love: Your Unconditional Key"*

*There is a deeper love here*
*The one that lives in your heart*
*The one that will never leave you*
*The one that stemmed from your start*
*It is what you are made of*
*It is in the air that you breathe*
*It is a part of life*
*Wishing you to be, all you can be*

*This love already knows your worth*
*This love you are all safe to share*
*This love wants you to remember*
*Trusting it has always been there*

*It's time dear ones*
*To let down your walls*
*To learn to love one another as is*
*For it is your true nature's call*

*Let your fears about love go*
*Wear your hearts a little more on your sleeves*
*Let your eyes meet others a little more*
*Connect the way God wishes you to see*

*Love is who you are*
*Love is who you will to continue be*
*Love is the answer*
*Love is your unconditional key*
*- Willow Mazer*

I read it and then re-read it a few times. I felt like I was in heaven. I had never felt such peace or clarity after I had written a poem. Something inside told me that this was the one. This was the one to send to Amelia, and hopefully, touch the hearts of others. I believed that letter, and that this poem was a message from God to share with all the real truth about love. It was an amazing moment for me. I felt so connected to life and to God finally! I took a deep breath, and said to God, "Thank you, for I finally think I've got it!" Then something inside of me said, *You've got it, or you've God it! Same thing, angel!* I laughed because I understood, and remembered reading in Neale Donald Walsch's book that God has a great sense of humor!

The wind blew and one of the branches brushed and tickled my cheek, just like it did to my father's over thirty years ago, and just like Ed wrote about in the poem. It all felt so miraculous. I laughed. I got into my car and headed home with a glow in my eyes.

The next thing I knew, a car pulled up next to me, and all the license plate said was LOVE LO. My heart was pounding. I started to tear up because I could not believe my eyes, LO are my grandmother's initials. In astonishment, I said out loud, "Oh, my God, really?" And again, another car pulled up on the other side of me whose license plate said UNCANNY. I blurted out "Holy shit." With tears of joy coming down my face, I looked up above and blew a kiss and said, "Thank you, Grandma Lu, for letting me know you are still with me, and reminding me of the truth."

I decided not to waste any time. I went right home and typed up this poem on my computer. I printed it out. I had a beautiful frame my Grandmother Lu had given me years ago that I thought would be perfect to place it in. I gently wrapped it up and decided first thing in the morning, I would go to the post office to send it to Amelia.

I also made another copy of my poem to give to my grandpa. I wanted to stop by after I went to the post office and drop it off. I pulled up to the Hills and walked through the café to pick us up some coffee. I had to admit they had great coffee. As I walked down to his apartment, I saw a lovely older woman in a walker with a blue ribbon tied to it. She stopped me and said, "Are you Lex's granddaughter?" How did she know?

"Um-m, yes, I am. How did you know?"

"Well, I have seen you here a few times with him at the café. Hi, I'm, Dolores Stein. Nice to meet you."

"Nice to meet you, too, Dolores."

She then said, "Your grandpa - he is not the most social guy, is he?" Um-m, a little blunt!

But, I half giggled and said, "Well, he is a little shy."

She then said, "I can tell. 'Ya know, my girlfriends and I have invited him to join us for dinner a few times, and he always turns us down." How awkward was this?

So, I said, "Well, please don't take it personally. I think ever since my grandmother passed, he really just keeps to himself. But, he is a great guy."

She leaned in to me and jokingly whispered, "I know. The single ladies here are dying to get to know him. He is good looking, too."

I smiled, "Yeah, he's still got his looks. My grandmother always said he was the most handsome man she knew."

She said, "Aw-w, your grandmother sounds like she was a special lady."

I said, "The best," and Willow Winked her. "Well, it was nice meeting you, Dolores. I better bring this coffee down to Grandpa. He gets grumpy when it gets cold."

She said, "Very nice to meet you, too, and tell your grandpa to not be afraid to be friendly. We don't bite around here."

I smiled, "I will."

As I continued down the hall, I giggled to myself - how about it, the ladies here having the hots for my grandpa.

I knocked on the door and heard, "Door's open, come in."

"Hi, Gramps."

"Hello, my love, how are you?"

I say, "Okay. So, guess who I just met?"

He said, "I don't know - some yenta in a walker or a wheelchair?"

I said, "Wow, you're pretty good - a walker, how did you know?"

He replied, "Willow, they are everywhere."

"Grandpa, I met Ms. Dolores Stein. She's a nice lady. She told me she has invited you to join her and her friends at the café a few times, and she says you always turn her down."

He said, "Oy, Dolores, does she ever shut up? Willow, you know me well enough to know that the last place you will find your grandfather is having lunch or dinner with a bunch of ladies."

I handed him his coffee and said, "Grandpa, I think she and a few of the other ladies have the hots for you!"

He perked up and sarcastically said, "Get out of here, for me? Not possible. It must be my bald head. Most of the women fall for Dr. Leonard. He is the retired doctor. He is the looker here."

I smiled, "Yeah, but so are you, and you are the one with the good sense of humor. Grandpa, you know women, no matter what age we are, we love a good sense of humor."

"Yeah, yeah honey, I know, that is what your grandmother always told me she fell for me first. So, what brings you here today and what's in the bag?"

"Wait, Grandpa, I'll let the topic go, but just wanted to say, it would not kill you to be a little social here and there. These women, and I quote Dolores, won't bite you. They are just looking to be social. And, so what even if some of them are lonely and are looking for a little male companionship? It's just a sandwich or a cup of coffee, nothing to run away from. Didn't you say the same thing to me when I first met Will? Actually, he said it to me, too - that it's just a drink."

He said, "Okay, my Willow, I hear you and appreciate what you are saying, but let me just say this once so you know. There will only ever be one woman for me in my life. I am not even the slightest bit interested in Dolores or anybody else. Your Grandma Lu was it for me. I think I would feel uncomfortable, and not know what to say if one of these ladies tried to, what is it you all call it these days, hit on me?"

I laughed, "Alright, Gramps, I heard you, ha-ha. So, let me tell you why I am here." I pulled out the framed poem. "Grandpa, I think I have finally found my inspirational spot to do my writing and meditation. One day, when I was on my way home from work, I found this park and this beautiful willow tree. I felt compelled to go sit under it and write. And yesterday, I was feeling a little anxious, so I stopped by and I think I wrote one of my best pieces. In a weird way, I almost felt like it wrote itself. Anyway, I was so excited about it. I made a copy and sent it to Amelia - you know, the friend I told you about who now sells her greeting cards. Well, she told me to start sending some of my poems that would inspire others. This is the first one I felt really good about sending."

I read it out loud to him. He put his hand on mine and said, "I love it, honey. It reminds me of something your Grandma Lu would say."

I put my hand on top of his and said, "As I always say, when you relate me to Grandma, that might be the best compliment ever. So, thank you."

I then shared the license plate story about Grandma's initials. Grandpa first got quiet, but then said, "I don't know, Willow, you're starting to make me a believer. Maybe, just maybe, it's your grandma's way of letting you know she's here."

He then said, "So, speaking of love, how is Will?"

"He's good. We're actually flying together to Florida. I was invited to go to my old boss's wedding to one of the waitresses I worked with. I gave in and told him we could stay with his grandparents.

"Also, I finally told Will that I love him."

He lit up. "And how did it feel saying it? He is still there. He hasn't run away yet? Am I right?" He winked at me.

"You know me better than I thought, Grandpa. No, he has not run away. Actually, he was the one to say it first to me, and I was the one who held back, and yes, Grandpa, out of a little fear. But, now I'm not as afraid. So, I'm learning, but also, like this poem says, remembering we are already made of love and should share it. That's what I believe God wants."

He smiled and said, "Willow, my love, yes. The key is to share it and remind others as you have so beautifully done in this poem. Boy, I hope Will knows just how lucky he is to have you."

"Thanks, Grandpa, I think he does." I then said, "So, what do you say we go for a little walk?"

"Sounds good! Let me go grab my sunglasses and stop at the potty before we go."

As I waited for Grandpa, I looked around his apartment and saw so many pictures of him and Grandma Lu around. Each picture really said how much they loved one another. He came out, and saw me looking.

He said, "She was so beautiful, wasn't she?"

I replied, "Inside and out, Grandpa, all the way! Come on, let's go get some air."

A few days went by, and I got a call from Amelia to tell me she had received my poem, and that she loved it and was on her way to drop it off at the local gift store where she sold her cards. I was nervous, yet excited at the thought of someone being touched by my poem, and hopefully wanting to buy it. However, I definitely did not write the poem for the money, I wrote it for the message. I remember Ed once told me that most who are in the writing/poetry industry are usually not in it for the money - they are in for the heart. He was right. I realized this more and more as I felt increasingly passionate about my work.

I couldn't believe how quickly the weeks went. Will and I were packed and ready to go to the wedding. I called Luke and Ed a few weeks ago to let them know I would be in town, and wanted to see them both, and of course, for them to finally meet Will. Luke told me he had to work, but to stop by with Will at the assisted living center no matter what to see him. I also told Luke how much I loved the book he gave me, and that it was another inspirational one to add to my shelf. When I got a hold of Ed, he told me at first he wasn't sure that he was going to the wedding because he didn't know a lot of people, but once he heard I was coming, he said he would make a special appearance. I also decided to take a framed copy of my new poem for Luke and Ed. I knew they would both appreciate it.

# Chapter 47

THE MORNING WE LEFT, I said a prayer to God asking Him to get us there safely and thanking him for where I was in my life at the moment. I continued telling God that I didn't think at this point, there was anyone else important I needed to meet. But, of course, I was paying attention if that was His will, and that I was now open to meet anybody else who might enhance my spiritual path. Amen.

We arrived at the airport a little early. As we sat and waited for the plane, I watched Will reading his paper, drinking his coffee, and eating his donut. He looked cute and caught me smiling at him. I kissed his cheek. Next thing I knew the text message went off on my phone. I looked down and saw that it was Amelia. I opened it up and read: *The gift shop owner loves your poem and asked if you could send her a dozen more to sell and if you had any others you wanted to share. She said she thinks it will be a big seller. See Willow? I told you, you had a gift!*

I was ecstatic - over the top. I jumped up and Will said, "What? Who was it?"

"It was Amelia. Will, the gift shop owner loves my poem and wants to sell it and asked me to send more."

He hugged me and said, "Congrats, this is great. What a wonderful way to start a weekend!"

"You're telling me."

I called Amelia immediately thanking her for doing it, and giving me this opportunity. She reiterated how much she believes in my poetry and asked me to send a few more. I was so happy, and couldn't wait to share the news with Ed, in person, when I saw him. He would be so proud of me.

As we continued to wait for the flight, I noticed a lot of other people around. To my left was a young teenage girl who was picking black nail polish from her fingernails. She was listening to dark music on her iPod so loudly I could hear the venom of lyrics shooting through her headphones right into my left eardrum. Ouch! Then I noticed that in front of me was a very handsome African American man with cool dreadlocks, talking on his cell phone, and wearing a navy blue suit. This man had a striking and confident, yet peaceful, presence about him. As I continued to look at him, I realized that he looked sort of familiar. He looked a little like the guy on the cover of the book Luke sent me and a little like a teacher I had in middle school. I wondered if he might be in the entertainment industry. I nudged Will's arm and said, "Do you see that guy in front of us with the navy suit? Does he look familiar to you at all?"

He looked up and said "No, but he is a good-looking man, I will admit that." H-m-m, I thought as I continued to stare at him. After a few more minutes of contemplation, he caught me staring. He looked right at me, and I froze out of embarrassment. Then he smiled right at me. This might have been one of the best smiles I had ever seen. It felt like the kind of smile from a stranger at just the right moment, to let you know everything was going to be all right in life. So, what else could I do, but smile back? My gaze was then interrupted by the speaker system. "Good morning ladies and gentlemen. We are now ready to board those passengers flying to West Palm Beach. We would now like to start the process of pre-boarding for those who might need special assistance."

Will said to me, "I forgot to ask, which row are we sitting in?"

I replied, "Row 11, of course - my lucky number. I got you an aisle seat so you can stretch your legs, and I don't have to bother a stranger to get up a dozen times if I have to pee. I'm sitting in the middle, but if we are lucky there won't be anyone sitting by the window, so we'll have the whole row to ourselves. So, sit tight. We still have a few more minutes - they always board the back of the plane first."

As they continued to call zones and rows, I noticed Handsome

Navy Suit Man was still on his phone, not boarding. For a second, I wondered if he might be sitting near us, which I wouldn't mind. *How on earth do I know this man?*

Finally, they called our zone. As Will grabbed my hand to walk onto the plane, he smiled and said, "Who would have thunk?" I leaned in to kiss him. As he opened up the overhead area, I jokingly said, "Excuse me, sir, could you help me lift this bag?"

He giggled back, "Why, yes, I'd be happy to."

We sat down and buckled ourselves up. I wrapped my arm around his and snuggled into him. As the rest of the people continued to board, I realized this flight was fuller then I anticipated. I still had not seen Handsome Guy get on. I bent down to my pocketbook to get some gum and asked Will, "Do you want some?"

"Yes, please."

I popped my bubble gum into my mouth, and as I came back up, I felt Will nudge my arm and say, "Looks like you might get your chance to know who this guy is."

"What?"

As I looked up, Handsome blue suit man was standing right in front of our row. He then said, "Good morning, pardon me, I have the window."

My heart elevated a little - I had an immediate feeling that this man was meant to sit in my row, even though I still wasn't sure from where I knew him. He sat down next to me, but I didn't want to ask right away who he was, so I was trying to think of a conversation starter. It was easier than I thought it would be. As soon as he sat down, he opened up the side window shade.

I said, "Thank you, I meant to open that, it was a little dark in here. I could always use a little light."

He responded, "Me, too. I'm in favor of light on more levels than one, if you know what I mean."

I said, "I do. You know, you look so familiar to me. I'm not sure how. Is it possible I've seen you somewhere before?" I put out my hand, and said, "Anyway, good morning, my name is Willow."

He smiled again and put out his hand, and covered mine. "It's a pleasure to meet you. My name is Michael. And to answer your question, you may have seen me before, perhaps on television, or read one of my books, or heard me speak somewhere."

I then said, "Really. Without getting too personal or nosey, what do you speak about?"

He answered, "Have you ever heard of the Agape International Spiritual Center? Well, I started that in the mid-eighties. I speak about God's unconditional love. Are you familiar?"

I was speechless. My mouth dropped, my eyes opened wide. I felt triple goose bumps, and my eyes tear up.

I then said, "Michael, saying it is an honor meeting you right now, would be an understatement. Of course I know who you are! God has an incredible sense of humor and love in everything he does. Michael, I would love to tell you my story about how it is I came to learn what the word Agape means over the last year. But you, my new friend, wow - you really are the icing on the cake."

His face lit up and said, "Yes, Willow, indeed I would love to hear your story, as long as it ends with knowing you found out the **real truth about love**. The one that reminds you God lives in your heart unconditionally."

He winked at me, and I said, "Oh yes, this story indeed has a happy ending now! The real truth about love, I *GODDDD* it!" I Willow Winked him back. This was the best day of my life.

# The end.

# Acknowledgments

I WOULD LIKE TO FIRST thank God and my angels for helping to guide me along my spiritual journey. This book was a healing gift to write at a tumultuous time for me. I would also like to thank my incredible family and my friends for all of their amazing support throughout the writing of this book and also to those who helped inspire some of its material. A special loving thanks to BD, my "true nectar". Thank you to my teachers at the Woodlynde School for encouraging me to believe in myself.

I would like to also give a special thanks to two people who have helped teach me about the power of divine love: Thank you, Kathy Milano and Rick Dorociak. Also, thank you to my wonderful editor, Carol Post. I am hoping that this is the first book of many that we will work on together. You have all played such a pivotal role in my life. Amen to that!

And last but not least, thank you to all of my inspirational pioneers who have given me courage to come out of my spiritual shell, Neale Donald Walsch, Michael Bernard Beckwith, Louise Hay, Marianne Williamson, Joan Borysenko, Wayne Dyer, Deepak Chopra, Byron Katie, Helen Schucman, Morrie Schwartz, and Oprah Winfrey.

# Song Credits

"Earth Angel" written by Jesse Belvin, Gaynel Hodge, and Curtis Williams, recorded by The Penguins

"The Way We Were" written by Marvin Hamlisch, Alan Bergman, and Marilyn Bergman, recorded by Barbra Streisand

"Three Little Birds" written and recorded by Bob Marley

"What a Wonderful World" written by Bob Thiele (as George Douglas) and George David Weiss, recorded by Louis Armstrong

"Just the Way You Are" written and performed by Billy Joel

"Hot for Teacher" written and performed by the Van Halen Band

"Tupelo Honey" written and performed by Van Morrison

"Keep It Comin' Love" written by Harry Wayne Casey and Richard Finch, recorded by KC and the Sunshine Band

"Samba Pa Ti" written and recorded by Carlos Santana

"Unforgettable" written by Irving Gordon and performed by Nat King Cole (1951, arr. Nelson Riddle)

"Willow Weep for Me" written by Ann Ronell and performed by Billie Holliday

"You Are My Sunshine" written by Jimmie Davis and Charles Mitchell, recorded by Jimmie Davis

"Do Your Ears Hang Low" children's song

"Miss You" written by Mick Jagger and Keith Richards and performed by Rolling Stones

"What the World Needs Now" – written by Hal David and composed by Burt Bacharach and recorded by Jackie DeShannon.

N.B.

Recording credits of the songs listed above are for the purposes of this novel only. Other artists have recorded versions as well.

# Book Credits

I would like to acknowledge Helen Schucman and her book, *A Course In Miracles*. Her work helped inspire some of the text in *The Real Truth About Love*. Thank You.

CPSIA information can be obtained at www.ICGtesting.com
Printed in the USA
BVOW04s1608250314

348707BV00001B/2/P